INVITATION TO MAGIC

Stile stared down at the amulet. Belief in magic! Yet the fellow seemed sensible in other respects. Maybe it was a joke, an initiation rite to see what foolishness newcomers could be talked into.

He shook his head. "All right, I'll play the game—once. Amulet, I invoke you." And he put the chain over his head.

Suddenly, he was strangling. The chain was constricting, cutting off his wind and blood. The amulet seemed to be expanding, its demon figure holding the ends of the chain in miniature hands, grinning evilly. Stile ducked his chin down against his neck and tightened his muscles. He grabbed the grinning demon by its two little arms to haul them apart.

But still the demon grew, and its strength increased in proportion. It drew its arms together, constricting the loop about Stile's neck.

The demon had become a living creature, swelling horrendously as it fought. Now it was half the size of Stile and fiendishly strong. Stile felt his consciousness going. And the demon was still growing . . .

By Piers Anthony
Published by Ballantine Books:

Split
Infinity

Piers Anthony

A Del Rey Book

BALLANTINE BOOKS • NEW YORK

A Del Rey Book
Published by Ballantine Books

Copyright © 1980 by Piers Anthony

Library of Congress Catalog Card Number: 79-20282

ISBN 0-345-30761-5

Manufactured in the United States of America

First Edition: April 1980

Paperback format:
First Edition: January 1981
Seventh Printing: August 1983

Cover illustration by Rowena Morrill

Map by Chris Barbieri

TABLE OF CONTENTS

CHAPTER 1

Slide

He walked with the assurance of stature, and most others deferred to him subtly. When he moved in a given direction, the way before him conveniently opened, by seeming coincidence; when he made eye contact, the other head nodded in a token bow. He was a serf, like all of them, naked and with no physical badge of status; indeed, it would have been the depth of bad taste to accord him any overt recognition. Yet he was a giant, here. His name was Stile.

Stile stood one point five meters tall and weighed fifty kilograms. In prior parlance he would have stood four feet, eleven inches tall and weighed a scant hundredweight or eight stone; or stood a scant fifteen hands and weighed a hundred and ten pounds. His male associates towered above him by up to half a meter and outweighed him by twenty-five kilos.

He was fit, but not extraordinarily muscled. Personable without being handsome. He did not hail his friends heartily, for there were few he called friend, and he was diffident about approaches. Yet there was enormous drive in him that manifested in lieu of personal warmth.

He walked about the Grid-hall of the Game-annex, his favorite place; beyond this region he reverted to the nonentity that others perceived. He sought competition of his own level, but at this hour there was none. Pairs of people stood in the cubicles that formed the convoluted perimeter of the hall, and a throng milled in the center, making contacts. A cool, gentle, mildly flower-scented draft wafted down from the vents in the ceiling, and the image of the sun cast its light on the floor, making its own game of shadows.

1

Stile paused at the fringe of the crowd, disliking this forced mixing. It was better when someone challenged him.

A young woman rose from one of the seats. She was nude, of course, but worthy of a second glance because of the perfection of her body. Stile averted his gaze, affecting not to be aware of her; he was especially shy with girls.

A tall youth intercepted the woman. "Game, lass?" How easy he made it seem!

She dismissed him with a curt downward flip of one hand and continued on toward Stile. A child signaled her: "Game, miss?" The woman smiled, but again negated, more gently. Stile smiled too, privately; evidently she did not recognize the child, but he did: Pollum, Rung Two on the Nines ladder. Not in Stile's own class, yet, but nevertheless a formidable player. Had the woman accepted the challenge, she would probably have been tromped.

There was no doubt she recognized Stile, though. His eyes continued to review the crowd, but his attention was on the woman. She was of average height—several centimeters taller than he—but of more than average proportions. Her breasts were full and perfect, unsagging, shifting eloquently with her easy motion, and her legs were long and smooth. In other realms men assumed that the ideal woman was a naked one, but often this was not the case; too many women suffered in the absence of mechanical supports for portions of their anatomy. This one, approaching him, was the type who really could survive the absence of clothing without loss of form.

She arrived at last. "Stile," she murmured.

He turned as if surprised, nodding. Her face was so lovely it startled him. Her eyes were large and green, her hair light brown and light-bleached in strands that expanded about her neck. There was a lot of art in the supposedly natural falling of women's hair. Her features were even and possessed the particular properties and proportions that appealed to him, though he could not define precisely what these were. His shyness

2

loomed up inside him, so that he did not trust himself to speak.

"I am Sheen," she said. "I would like to challenge you to a Game."

She could not be a top player. Stile knew every ranking player on every age-ladder by sight and style, and she was on no ladder. Therefore she was a dilettante, an occasional participant, possibly of some skill in selected modes but in no way a serious competitor. Her body was too lush for most physical sports; the top females in track, ball games and swimming were small-breasted, lean-fleshed, and lanky, and this in no way described Sheen. Therefore he would have no physical competition here.

Yet she was beautiful, and he was unable to speak. So he nodded acquiescence. She took his arm in an easy gesture of familiarity that startled him. Stile had known women, of course; they came to him seeking the notoriety of his company, and the known fact of his hesitancy lent them compensating courage. But this one was so pretty she hardly needed to seek male company; it would seek her. She was making it look as if he had sought and won her. Perhaps he had, unknowingly: his prowess in the Game could have impressed her enough from afar to bring her to him. Yet this was not the type of conquest he preferred; such women were equally avid for Game-skilled teeners and grayheads.

They found an unoccupied cubicle. It had a column in the center, inset with panels on opposite sides. Stile went to one side, Sheen on the other, and as their weights came on the marked ovals to the floor before each panel, the panels lighted. The column was low, so Stile could see Sheen's face across from him; she was smiling at him.

Embarrassed by this open show of camaraderie, Stile looked down at his panel. He hardly needed to; he knew exactly what it showed. Across the top were four categories: PHYSICAL—MENTAL—CHANCE—ART, and down the left side were four more: NAKED—TOOL—MACHINE—ANIMAL. For shorthand convenience they were also lettered and numbered: 1—2—3—4 across

3

the top, A—B—C—D down the side. The numbers were highlighted: the Grid had given him that set of choices, randomly.

THE GAME: PRIMARY GRID

	1. PHYSICAL	2. MENTAL	3. CHANCE	4. ART
A. NAKED				
B. TOOL				
C. MACHINE				
D. ANIMAL				

Stile studied Sheen's face. Now that she was in the Game, his opponent, his diffidence diminished. He felt the mild tightening of his skin, elevation of heartbeat, clarity of mind and mild distress of bowel that presaged the tension and effort of competition. For some people such effects became so strong it ruined them as competitors, but for him it was a great feeling, that drew him back compulsively. He lived for the Game!

Even when his opponent was a pretty girl whose pert breasts peeked at him just above the column. What was passing through her mind? Did she really think she could beat him, or was she just out for the experience? Had she approached him on a dare, or was she a groupie merely out for a date? If she were trying to win, she would want to choose ART, possibly MENTAL, and would certainly avoid PHYSICAL. If she were on a dare she would go for CHANCE, as that would require little performance on her part. If she wanted experience, anything would do. If she were a groupie, she would want PHYSICAL.

Of course she could not choose among these; *he* had the choice. But his choice would be governed in part by his judgment of her intent and ability. He had to think, as it were, with her mind, so that he could select what she least desired and obtain the advantage.

4

Now he considered her likely choice, in the series she did control. A true competitor would go for NAKED, for there was the essence of it: unassisted personal prowess. One wanting experience could go for anything, again depending on the type of experience desired. A dare would probably go for NAKED also; that choice would be part of the dare. A groupie would certainly go for NAKED. So that was her most likely choice.

Well, he would call her bluff. He touched PHYSICAL, sliding his hand across the panel so she couldn't tell his choice by the motion of his arm.

Her choice had already been made, as anticipated. They were in 1A, PHYSICAL/NAKED.

The second grid appeared. Now the categories across the top were 1. SEPARATE—2. INTERACTIVE—3. COMBAT—4. COOPERATIVE, and down the side were A. FLAT SURFACE—B. VARIABLE SURFACE—C. DISCONTINUITY—D. LIQUID. The letters were highlighted; he had to choose from the down column this time. He didn't feel like swimming or swinging from bars with her, though there could be intriguing aspects to each, so the last two were out. He was an excellent long-distance runner, but doubted Sheen would go for that sort of thing, which eliminated the flat surface. So he selected B, the variable surface.

She chose 1. SEPARATE: no groupie after all! So they would be in a race of some sort, not physically touching or directly interacting, though there were limited exceptions. Good enough. He would find out what she was made of.

Now the panel displayed a listing of variable surfaces. Stile glanced again at Sheen. She shrugged, so he picked the first: MAZE PATH. As he touched it, the description appeared in the first box of a nine-square grid.

She chose the second: GLASS MOUNTAIN. It appeared in the second square.

He placed DUST SLIDE in the third square. Then they continued with CROSS COUNTRY, TIGHTROPE, SAND DUNES, GREASED HILLS, SNOW BANK, and LIMESTONE CLIFF. The tertiary grid was complete.

Now he had to choose one of the vertical columns, and she had the horizontal rows. He selected the third, she the first, and their game was there: DUST SLIDE.

"Do you concede?" he asked her, pressing the appropriate query button so that the machine would know. She had fifteen seconds to negate, or forfeit the game.

Her negation was prompt. "I do not."

"Draw?"

"No."

He had hardly expected her to do either. Concession occurred when one party had such an obvious advantage that there was no point in playing, as when the game was chess and one player was a grandmaster while the other hadn't yet learned the moves. Or when it was weight lifting, with one party a child and the other a muscle builder. The dust slide was a harmless entertainment, fun to do even without the competitive element; no one would concede it except perhaps one who had a phobia about falling—and such a person would never have gotten into this category of game.

And so her reaction was odd. She should have laughed at his facetious offers. Instead she had taken them seriously. That suggested she was more nervous about this encounter than she seemed.

Yet this was no Tourney match! If she were a complete duffer she could have accepted the forfeit and been free. Or she could have agreed to the draw, and been able to tell her girlish friends how she had tied with the notorious Stile. So it seemed she was out neither for notoriety nor a dare, and he had already determined she was not a groupie. She really did want to compete—yet it was too much to hope that she had any real proficiency as a player.

They vacated the booth after picking up the game-tags extruded from slots. No one was admitted solo to any subgame; all had to play the grid first, and report in pairs to the site of decision. That prevented uncommitted people from cluttering the premises or interfering with legitimate contests. Of course children could and did entertain themselves by indulging in mock contests,

6

just for the pleasure of the facilities; to a child, the Game-annex was a huge amusement park. But in so doing, they tended to get hooked on the Game itself, increasingly as they aged, until at last they were thoroughgoing addicts. That had been the way with Stile himself.

The Dust Slide was in another dome, so they took the tube transport. The vehicle door irised open at their approach, admitting them to its cosy interior. Several other serfs were already in it: three middle-aged men who eyed Sheen with open appreciation, and a child whose eye lit with recognition. "You're the jockey!"

Stile nodded. He had no trouble relating to children. He was hardly larger than the boy.

"You won all the races!" the lad continued.

"I had good horses," Stile explained.

"Yeah," the child agreed, satisfied.

Now the three other passengers turned their attention to Stile, beginning to surmise that he might be as interesting as the girl. But the vehicle stopped, its door opened, and they all stepped out into the new dome. In moments Stile and Sheen had lost the other travelers and were homing in on the Dust Slide, their tickets ready.

The Slide's desk-secretary flashed Stile a smile as she validated the tickets. He smiled back, though he knew this was foolish; she was a robot. Her face, arms and upper torso were perfectly humanoid, with shape, color and texture no ordinary person could have told from a living woman, but her perfectly humanoid body terminated at the edge of her desk. She *was* the desk, possessing no legs at all. It was as if some celestial artisan had been carving her from a block of metal, causing her to animate as he progressed—then left the job unfinished at the halfway point. Stile felt a certain obscure sympathy for her; did she have true consciousness, in that upper half? Did she long for a completely humanoid body—or for a complete desk body? How did it feel to be a half-thing?

She handed back his ticket, validated. Stile closed his fingers about her delicate hand. "When do you get off work, cutie?" he inquired with the lift of an eyebrow. He was not shy around machines, of course.

7

She had been programmed for this. "Ssh. My boyfriend's watching." She used her free hand to indicate the robot next to her: a desk with a set of male legs protruding, terminating at the inverted waist. They demonstrated the manner the protective shorts should be worn for the Slide. They were extremely robust legs, and the crotch region was powerfully masculine.

Stile glanced down at himself, chagrined. "Oh, I can't compete with him. My legs are barely long enough to reach the ground." A bygone Earth author, Mark Twain, had set up that remark, and Stile found it useful on occasion. He accepted Sheen's arm again and they continued on to the Slide.

He thought Sheen might remark on the way he seemed to get along with machines, but she seemed oblivious. Ah, well.

The Slide was a convoluted mountain of channels looping and diverging and merging. Dust flowed in them—sanitary, nonirritating, noncarcinogenic, neutral particles of translucent plastic, becoming virtually liquid in the aggregate, and quite slippery. The whole was dramatic, suggesting frothing torrents of water in sluices, or rivulets of snow in an avalanche.

They donned the skin-shorts and filter masks required for protection on the Slide. The dust was harmless, but it tended to work its way into any available crevices, and the human body had a number. This was one thing Stile did not like about this particular subgame: the clothing. Only Citizens wore clothing, in the normal course, and it was uncouth for any serf to wear anything not strictly functional. More than uncouth: it could be grounds for summary termination of tenure at Planet Proton. Such Slide-shorts were functional, in these dusty environs; still, he felt uncomfortable. Their constriction and location tended to stir him sexually, and that was awkward in the company of a creature like Sheen.

Sheen seemed to feel no such concern. Perhaps she was aware that the partial concealment of the shorts attracted attention to those parts they concealed, enhancing her sex appeal. Stile, like many serfs, found a certain illicit lure in clothing, especially clothing on the distaff sex; it represented so much that serfs could only dream of. He had to keep his eyes averted, lest he embarrass himself.

They took the lift to the Slide apex. Here at the top they were near the curving dome that held in air and heat; through its shimmer Stile could see the bleak landscape of Proton, ungraced by any vegetation. The hostile atmosphere was obscured in the distance by clouds of smog.

The Slide itself was a considerable contrast. From this height six channels coursed out and down, each half filled with flowing dust. Colored lights shone up through it all, for the channels too were translucent. They turned now red, now blue-gray and now yellow as the beams moved. The tangle of paths formed a flower-like pattern, supremely beautiful. If Stile found the clothing physically and emotionally awkward, he was compensated by the view from this vantage, and always stood for a moment in minor awe.

For any given channel the colors seemed random, but for the arrangement as a whole they shaped in shifting contours roses, lilies, tulips, violets and gardenias. Air jets emitted corresponding perfumes when applicable. An artist had designed this layout, and Stile admired the handiwork. He had been here many times before, yet the novelty had not worn off.

Sheen did not seem to notice. "On your mark," she said, setting the random starter. The device could pop instantly or take two minutes. This time it split the difference. The channel barriers dropped low, and Sheen leaped for the chute nearest her.

Stile, surprised by her facility, leaped after her. They accelerated, shooting down feet first around a broad bright curve of green, then into the first white vertical loop. Up and over, slowing dizzily at the top, upside down, then regaining velocity in the downshoot.

Sheen was moving well. Her body had a natural rondure that shaped itself well to the contour of the chute. The dust piled up behind her, shoving her forward. Stile, following in the same channel, tried to intercept

9

enough dust to cut off her supply and ground her, but she had too big a lead and was making too good use of her resources.

Well, there were other ways. This channel passed through a partial-gravity rise that was slow. Another channel crossed, going into a corkscrew. Stile took this detour, zipped through the screw, and shot out ahead of the girl.

She took another connection and got in behind him, cutting off *his* dust. This was the aspect of the Slide that was interactive: the competition for dust. Stile was grounded, his posterior scraping against the suddenly bare plastic of the chute. No dust, no progress!

He put his hand to the side, heaved, and flipped his body into the adjoining channel. This was a tricky maneuver, legitimate but not for amateurs. Here he had dust again, and resumed speed—but he had lost the momentum he had before. Sheen continued on in her channel, riding the piled dust, moving ahead of him—and now they were halfway down.

Stile realized that he had a real race on his hands. This girl was good!

He vaulted back into her channel, cutting off her dust again—but even as he did, she vaulted into his just-vacated channel, maintaining her lead. Apt move! Obviously she had raced here many times before, and knew the tricks, and had more agility under that sweet curvature of body than he had suspected. But now he had the better channel, and he was unmatchable in straight dust-riding; he moved ahead. She jumped across to cut him off, but he was already jumping into a third chute. Before she could follow him, the two diverged and he was safe.

They completed the race on separate channels. She had found a good one, and was gaining on him despite his careful management of dust. He finished barely ahead. They shot into the collection bin, one-two, to the applause of the other players who were watching. It had been a fine race, the kind that happened only once or twice on a given day.

Sheen got up and shook off the dust with a fascinating shimmy of her torso. "Can't win them all," she remarked, unperturbed.

She had made an excellent try, though! She had come closer than anyone in years. Stile watched her as she stripped off mask and shorts. She was stunningly beautiful—more so than before, because now he realized that her body was functional as well as shapely.

"You interest me," he told her. In this aftermath of a good game he was flushed with positive feeling, his shyness at a minimum.

Sheen smiled. "I hoped to."

"You almost beat me."

"I had to get your attention somehow."

Another player laughed. Stile had to laugh too. Sheen had proved herself, and now he wanted to know why. The mutual experience had broken the ice; the discovery of a new challenge completed his transition from diffidence to normal masculine imperative.

He didn't even have to invite her to come home with him. She was already on her way.

CHAPTER 2

Sheen

Sheen moved into his apartment as if it were her own. She punched the buttons of his console to order a complete light lunch of fruit salad, protein bread and blue wine.

"You evidently know about me," Stile said as they ate. "But I know nothing of you. Why did you—want to get my attention?"

"I am a fan of the Game. I could be good at it. But I have so little time—only three years tenure remaining —I need instruction. From the best. From you. So I can be good enough—"

"To enter the Tourney," Stile finished. "I have the same time remaining. But there are others you could have checked. I am only tenth on my ladder—"

"Because you don't want to have to enter the Tourney this year," she said. "You won't enter it until your last year of tenure, because all tenure ends when a serf enters the Tourney. But you could advance to Rung One on the Age-35 ladder any time you wished, and the top five places of each adult ladder are automatically entered in the—"

"Thank you for the information," Stile said with gentle irony.

She overlooked it. "So you keep yourself in the second five, from year to year, low enough to be safe in case several of the top rungers break or try to vacate, high enough to be able to make your move any time you want to. You are in fact the most proficient Gamesman of our generation—"

"This is an exaggeration. I'm a jockey, not a—"

"—and I want to learn from you. I offer—"

12

"I can see what you offer," Stile said, running his eyes over her body. He could do this now without embarrassment, because he had come to know her; his initial shyness was swinging to a complementary boldness. They had, after all, Gamed together. "Yet there is no way I could inculcate the breadth of skills required for serious competition, even if we had a century instead of a mere three years. Talent is inherent, and it has to be buttressed by constant application. I might be able to guide you to the fifth rung of your ladder—which one would that be?"

"Age 23 female."

"You're in luck. There are only three Tourney-caliber players on that ladder at present. With proper management it would be possible for a person of promise to take one of the remaining rungs. But though you gave me a good race on the Slide, I am not sure you have sufficient promise—and even if you qualified for the Tourney, your chances of progressing far in it would be vanishingly small. My chances are not good—which is why I'm still working hard at every opportunity to improve myself. Contrary to your opinion, there are half a dozen players better than I am, and another score of my general caliber. In any given year, four or five of them will enter the Tourney, while others rise in skills to renew the pool. That, combined with the vagaries of luck, gives me only one chance in ten to win. For you—"

"Oh, I have no illusions about winning!" she said. "But if I could make a high enough rank to obtain extension of tenure, if only a year or two—"

"It's a dream," he assured her. "The Citizens put such prizes out as bait, but only one person in thirty-two gains even a year that way."

"I would be completely grateful for that dream," she said, meeting his gaze.

Stile was tempted. He knew he would not have access to a more attractive woman, and she had indeed shown promise in the Game. That athletic ability that had enabled her so blithely and lithely to change chutes would benefit her in many other types of competition.

13

He could have a very pleasant two years, training her. Extremely pleasant.

That itself gave him caution. He had loved before, and lost, and it had taken years to recover completely —if he really had. *Tune*, he thought, with momentary nostalgia. There were ways in which Sheen resembled that former girl.

Still, what promise did he have beyond his remaining three years, anyway? All would be lost, once he left Proton. Oh, he would have a nice nest egg to establish galactic residence, and might even go to crowded Earth itself, but all he really wanted to do was remain on Proton. Since it was unlikely that he could do that, he might as well make these years count. She had mentioned that her own tenure was as short as his, which meant she would have to leave at the same time. That could be very interesting, if they had a firm relationship. "Tell me about yourself," he said.

"I was born five years before my parents' tenure ended," Sheen said, putting down her leaf of lettuce. She had eaten delicately and quite sparingly, as many slender women did. "I obtained a position with a Lady Citizen, first as errand girl, then as nurse. I was a fan of the Game as a child, and had good aptitude, but as my employer grew older she required more care, until—" She shrugged, and now with the pleasant tingle of the wine and the understanding they were coming to, he could appreciate the way her breasts moved with that gesture. Oh yes, it was a good offer she made—yet something nagged him. "I have not been to a Game for seven years," she continued, "though I have viewed it often on my employer's screens, and rehearsed strategies and techniques constantly in private. My employer had a private exercise gym her doctor recommended; she never used it, so I did, filling in for her. Last week she died, so I have been released on holiday pending settlement of her estate and the inventory her heir is taking. Her heir is female, and healthy, so I do not think the burden will be onerous."

It could have been quite a different matter, Stile reflected, with a young, healthy male heir. Serfs had no personal rights except termination of tenure in fit physical and mental condition, and no sane person would depart Proton even a day ahead of schedule. Serfs could serve without concern as concubines or studs for their employers—or for each other as private or public entertainment for their employers. Their bodies were the property of the Citizens. Only in privacy, without the intercession of a Citizen, did interpersonal relations between serfs become meaningful. As now.

"So you came to me," Stile said. "To trade your favors for my favor."

"Yes." There needed to be no hesitancy or shame to such acknowledgment. Since serfs had no monetary or property credit, and no power during their tenure, Game-status and sex were the chief instruments of barter.

"I am minded to try it out. Shall we say for a week, then reconsider? I might become tired of you."

Again there was no formal cause for affront; male-female interactions among serfs were necessarily shallow, though marriage was permitted and provided for. Stile had learned the hard way, long ago, not to expect permanence. Still, he expected a snappy retort to the effect that she would more likely grow tired of him first.

There was no such byplay. "As part of my rehearsal for the Game, I have studied the art of pleasing men," Sheen said. "I am willing to venture that week."

A fair answer. And yet, he wondered, would not an ordinary woman, even the most abused of serfs, have evinced some token ire at the callousness of his suggestion? He could have said, "We might not be right for each other." He had phrased it most bluntly, forcing a reaction. Sheen had not reacted; she was completely matter-of-fact. Again he was nagged. Was there some catch here?

"Do you have special interests?" Stile inquired. "Music?" He hadn't really wanted to ask that, but it had come out. He associated love with music, because of his prior experience.

"Yes, music," Sheen agreed.

15

His interest quickened. "What kind?"

She shrugged again. "Any kind."

"Vocal? Instrumental? Mechanical?"

Her brow furrowed. "Instrumental."

"What instrument do you play?"

She looked blank.

"Oh—you just listen," he said. "I play a number of instruments, preferring the woodwinds. All part of the Game. You will need to acquire skill in at least one instrument, or Game opponents will play you for a weakness there and have easy victories."

"Yes, I must learn," she agreed.

What would she have done if he had gone for ART instead of PHYSICAL in their match? With her prior choice of NAKED, the intersection would have put them in song, dance or story: the a capella performances. Perhaps she was a storyteller. Yet she did not seem to have the necessary imagination.

"Let's do it right," he said, rising from his meal. "I have a costume—" He touched a button and the costume fell from a wall vent into his hand. It was a filmy negligee.

Sheen smiled and accepted it. In the privacy of an apartment, clothing was permitted, so long as it was worn discreetly. If there should be a video call, or a visitor at his door, Sheen would have to hide or rip off the clothing lest she be caught by a third party in that state and be compromised. But that only added to the excitement of it, the special, titillating naughtiness of their liaison. It was, in an unvoiced way, the closest any serf could come to emulating any Citizen.

She donned the costume without shame and did a pirouette, causing the material to fling out about her legs. Stile found this indescribably erotic. He shut down the light, so that the material seemed opaque, and the effect intensified. Oh, what clothing did for the woman, creating shadows where ordinarily there were none, making mysteries where none had been before!

Yet again, something ticked a warning in Stile's mind. Sheen was lovely, yes—but where was her flush of delighted shame? Why hadn't she questioned his possession of this apparel? He had it on loan, and his employer knew about it and would in due course remember to reclaim it—but a person who did not know that, who was not aware of the liberalism of this particular employer with respect to his favored serfs, should be alarmed at his seeming hoarding of illicit clothing. Sheen had thought nothing of it.

They were technically within the law—but so was a man who thought treason without acting on it. Stile was an expert Gamesman, attuned to the nuances of human behavior, and there was something wrong with Sheen. But what was it? There was really nothing in her behavior that could not be accounted for by her years of semi-isolation while nursing her Citizen.

Well, perhaps it would come to him. Stile advanced on Sheen, and she met him gladly. None of this oh-please-don't-hurt-me-sir, catch-me-if-you-can drama. She was not after all very much taller than he, so he had to draw her down only marginally to kiss her. Her body was limber, pliable, and the feel of the gauze between their skins pitched him into a fever of desire. Not in years had he achieved such heat so soon.

She kissed him back, her lips firm and cool. Suddenly the little nagging observations clicked into a comprehensible whole, and he knew her for what she was. Stile's ardor began sliding into anger.

He bore her back to the couch-bed. She dropped onto it easily, as if this type of fall were commonplace for her. He sat beside her, running his hands along her thighs, still with that tantalizing fabric in place between them. He moved on to knead her breasts, doubly erotic behind the material. A nude woman in public was not arousing, but a clothed one in private . . .

His hands were relaxed, gentle—but his mind was tight with coalescing ire and apprehension. He was about to trigger a reaction that could be hazardous to his health.

"I would certainly never have been able to tell," he remarked.

Her eyes focused on him. "Tell what, Stile?"

He answered her with another question. "Who would want to send me a humanoid robot?"

She did not stiffen. "I wouldn't know."

"The information should be in your storage banks. I need a printout."

She showed no emotion. "How did you discover that I was a robot?"

"Give me that printout, and I'll give you my source of information."

"I am not permitted to expose my data."

"Then I shall have to report you to Game-control," Stile said evenly. "Robots are not permitted to compete against humans unless under direct guidance by the Game Computer. Are you a Game-machine?"

"No."

"Then I fear it will go hard with you. The record of our Game has been entered. If I file a complaint, you will be deprogrammed."

She looked at him, still lovely though he now knew her nature. "I wish you would not do that, Stile."

How strong was her programmed wish? What form would her objection take, when pressed? It was a popular fable that robots could not harm human beings, but Stile knew better. All robots of Proton were prohibited from harming Citizens, or acting contrary to Citizens' expressed intent, or acting in any manner that might conceivably be deleterious to the welfare of any Citizen —but there were no strictures about serfs. Normally robots did not bother people, but this was because robots simply did not care about people. If a serf interfered with a robot in the performance of its assignment, that man could get hurt.

Stile was now interfering with the robot Sheen. "Sheen," he said. "Short for Machine. Someone with a certain impish humor programmed you."

"I perceive no humor," she said.

"Naturally not. That was your first giveaway. When I proffered you a draw on the Slide, you should have laughed. It was a joke. You reacted without emotion."

"I am programmed for emotion. I am programmed for the stigmata of love."

18

The stigmata of love. A truly robotic definition! "Not the reality?"

"The reality too. There is no significant distinction. I am here to love you, if you will permit it."

So far she had shown no sign of violence. That was good; he was not at all sure he could escape her if she attacked him. Robots varied in physical abilities, as they did in intellectual ones; it depended on their intended use and the degree of technology applied. This one seemed to be of top-line sophistication; that could mean she imitated the human form and nature so perfectly she had no more strength than a real girl would have. But there was no guarantee. "I must have that printout."

"I will tell you my mission, if you will not expose my nature."

"I can not trust your word. You attempted to deceive me with your story about nursing a Citizen. Only the printout is sure."

"You are making it difficult. My mission is only to guard you from harm."

"I feel more threatened by your presence than protected. Why should I need guarding from harm?"

"I don't know. I must love you and guard you."

"Who sent you?"

"I do not know."

Stile touched his wall vid. "Game-control," he said.

"Don't do that!" Sheen cried.

"Cancel call," Stile said to the vid. Evidently violence was not in the offing, and he had leverage. This was like a Game. "The printout."

She dropped her gaze, and her head. Her lustrous hair fell about her shoulders, coursing over the material of the negligee. "Yes."

Suddenly he felt sorry for her. Was she really a machine? Now he had doubts. But of course the matter was subject to verification. "I have a terminal here," he said, touching another section of the wall. A cord came into his hand, with a multipronged plug at its end. Very few serfs were permitted such access directly—but he was one of the most privileged serfs on Proton, and would remain so as long as as he was circumspect and rode horses well. "Which one?" he asked.

She turned her face away from him. Her hand went to her right ear, clearing away a lock of hair and pressing against the lobe. Her ear slid forward, leaving the socket open.

Stile plugged in the cord. Current flowed. Immediately the printout sheets appeared from the wall slot, crammed with numbers, graphs and pattern-blocks. Though he was no computer specialist, Stile's Game training made him a fair hand at ballpark analysis of programs, and he had continuing experience doing analysis of the factors leading into given races. That was why his employer had arranged this: to enable Stile to be as good a jockey as he could be. That was extremely good, for he had a ready mind as well as a ready body.

He whistled as he studied the sheets. This was a dual-element brain, with mated digital and analog components, rather like the dual-yet-differing hemispheres of the human brain. The most sophisticated computer capable of being housed in a robot. It possessed intricate feedback circuits, enabling the machine to learn from experience and to reprogram aspects of itself, within its prime directive. It could improve its capacity as it progressed. In short, it was intelligent and conscious: machine's nearest approach to humanity.

Quickly Stile oriented on the key section: her origin and prime directive. A robot could lie, steal and kill without conscience, but it could not violate its prime directive. He took the relevant data and fed them back to the analyzer for a summary.

The gist was simple: NO RECORD OF ORIGIN. DIRECTIVE: GUARD STILE FROM HARM. SUBDIRECTIVE: LOVE STILE.

What she had told him was true. She did not know who had sent her, and she had only his safety in mind. Tempered by love, so that she would not protect him in some fashion that cost him more than it was worth. This was a necessary caution, with otherwise unfeeling robots. This machine really did care. He could have taken her word.

Stile unplugged the cord, and Sheen put her ear back into place with a certain tremor. Again she looked completely human. He had been unyielding before, when she opposed him; now he felt guilty. "I'm sorry," he said. "I had to know."

She did not meet his gaze. "You have raped me."

Stile realized it was true. He had taken her measure without her true consent; he had done it by duress, forcing the knowledge. There was even a physical analogy, plugging the rigid terminus of the cord into a private aperture, taking what had been hers alone. "I had to know," he repeated lamely. "I am a very privileged serf, but only a serf. Why should anyone send an expensive robot to guard a man who is not threatened? I could not afford to believe your story without verification, especially since your cover story was untrue."

"I am programmed to react exactly as a real girl would react!" she flared. "A real girl wouldn't claim to have been built in a machine shop, would she?"

"That's so . . ." he agreed. "But still—"

"The important part is my prime directive. Specifically, to be appealing to one man—you—and to love that man, and to do everything to help him. I was fashioned in the partial likeness of a woman you once knew, not close enough to be identifiable as such, but enough to make me attractive to your specific taste—"

"That succeeded," he said. "I liked you the moment I saw you, and didn't realize why."

"I came to offer you everything of which I am capable, and that is a good deal, including the allure of feminine mystery. I even donned this ridiculous shift, that no human woman would have. And you—you—"

"I destroyed that mystery," Stile finished. "Had I had any other way to be sure—"

"Oh, I suppose you couldn't help it. You're a man."

Stile glanced at her, startled again. Her face was still averted, her gaze downcast. "Are you, a robot, really being emotional?"

"I'm programmed to be!"

True. He moved around to look at her face. She

21

turned it away again. He put his hand to her chin to lift it.

"Get away from me!" she cried.

That was some programming! "Look, Sheen. I apologize. I—"

"Don't apologize to a robot! Only an idiot would converse with a machine."

"Correct," he agreed. "I acted stupidly, and now I want to make what amends are possible."

He tried again to see her face, and again she hid it. "Damn it, *look* at me!" he exclaimed. His emotion was high, flashing almost without warning into embarrassment, sorrow, or anger.

"I am here to serve; I must obey," she said, turning her eyes to him. They were bright, and her cheeks were moist. Humanoid robots could cry, of course; they could do almost anything people could do. This one had been programmed to react this way when hurt or affronted. He knew that, yet was oddly moved. She did indeed subtly resemble one he had loved. The accuracy with which she had been fashioned was a commentary on the appalling power available to the Citizens of this planet. Even the most private, subtle knowledge could be drawn from the computer registries at any time.

"You are here to guard me, not to serve me, Sheen."

"I can only guard you if I stay with you. Now that you know what I am—"

"Why are you being so negative? I have not sent you away."

"I was made to please you, to want to please you. So I can better serve my directive. Now I can not."

"Why not?"

"Why do you tease me? Do you think that programmed feelings are less binding than flesh ones? That the electrochemistry of the inanimate is less valid than that of the animate? That my illusion of consciousness is any less potent than your illusion of self-determination? I exist for one purpose, and you have prevented me from accomplishing it, and now I have no reason for existence. Why couldn't you have accepted me as I

22

seemed to be? I would have become perfect at it, with experience. Then it would have been real."

"You have not answered my question."

"You have not answered mine!"

Stile did a rapid internal shifting of gears. This was the most femalish robot he had encountered! "Very well, Sheen. I answer your questions. Why do I tease you? Answer: I am not teasing you—but if I did, it would not be to hurt you. Do I think that your programmed feelings are less valid than my mortal ones? Answer: No, I must conclude that a feeling is a feeling, whatever its origin. Some of my own feelings are short-sighted, unreasonable and unworthy; they govern me just the same. Is your illusion of consciousness less valid than my illusion of free will? Answer: No. If you think you are conscious, you must be conscious, because that's what consciousness is. The feedback of self-awareness. I don't have much illusion about my free will. I am a serf, governed by the will of my employer. I have no doubt I am governed by a multitude of other things I seldom even notice, such as the force of gravity and my own genetic code and the dictates of society. Most of my freedom exists in my mind—which is where your consciousness does, too. Why couldn't I accept you as you seemed to be? Because I am a skilled Gamesman, not the best that ever was, but probably destined for recognition as one of the best of my generation. I succeed not by virtue of my midget body but by virtue of my mind. By questioning, by comprehending my own nature and that of all others I encounter. When I detect an anomaly, I must discover its reason. You are attractive, you are nice, you are the kind of girl I have held in my mind as the ideal, even to your size, for it would be too obvious for me to have a woman smaller than I am, and I don't like being obvious in this connection. You came to me for what seemed insufficient reason, you did not laugh as you should have, you did not react quite on key. You seemed to know about things, yet when I probed for depth I found it lacking. I probed as a matter of course; it is my nature. I asked about your music, and you expressed interest, but had

23

no specifics. That sort of thing. This is typical of programmed artificial intelligence; even the best units can approach only one percent of the human capacity, weight for weight. A well-tuned robot in a controlled situation may seem as intelligent as a man, because of its specific and relevant and instantly accessible information; a man is less efficiently organized, with extraneous memories obscuring the relevant ones, and information accessible only when deviously keyed. But the robot's intellect is illusory, and it soon shows when those devious and unreasonable off-trails are explored. A mortal person's mind is like a wilderness, with a tremendous volume of decaying constructs and half-understood experience forming natural harbors for wild-animal effects. A robot is disciplined, civilized; it has no vast and largely wasted reservoir of the unconscious to draw from, no spongy half-forgotten backup impression. It knows what it knows, and is ignorant where it is ignorant, with a quite sharp demarcation between. Therefore a robot is not intuitive, which is the polite way of saying that it does not frequently reach down into the maelstrom of its garbage dump and draw out serendipitous insights. Your mind was more straightforward than mine, and that aroused my suspicion, and so I could not accept you at face value. I would not be the quality of player I am, were I given to such acceptances."

Sheen's eyes had widened. "You answered!"

Stile laughed. It had been quite an impromptu lecture! "Again I inquire: why not?"

"Because I am Sheen-machine. Another man might be satisfied with the construct, the perfect female form; that is one reason my kind exists. But you are rooted in reality, however tangled a wilderness you may perceive it to be. The same thing that caused you to fathom my nature will cause you to reject the illusion I proffer. You want a real live girl, and you know I am not, and can never be. You will not long want to waste your time talking to me as if I were worthwhile."

"You presume too much on my nature. My logic is

24

other than yours. I said you were limited; I did not say you were not worthwhile."

"You did not need to. It is typical of your nature that you are polite even to machines, as you were to the Dust Slide ticket taker. But that was brief, and public; you need no such byplay here in private. Now that I have seen you in action, discovering how much more there is to you than what the computer knows, I realize I was foolish to—"

"A foolish machine?"

"—suppose I could deceive you for any length of time. I deserved what you did to me."

"I am not sure you deserved it, Sheen. You were sent innocently to me, to my jungle, unrealistically programmed."

"Thank you," she said with a certain unmetallic irony. "I did assume you would take what was offered, if you desired it, and now I know that was simplistic. What am I to do now? I have nowhere to return, and do not wish to be prematurely junked. There are many years of use left in me before my parts wear appreciably."

"Why, you will stay with me, of course."

She looked blank. "This is humor? Should I laugh?"

"This is serious," he assured her.

"Without reason?"

"I am unreasonable, by your standards. But in this case I do have reason."

She made an almost visible, almost human connection. "To be your servant? You can require that of me, just as you forced me to submit to the printout. I am at your mercy. But I am programmed for a different relationship."

"Serf can't have servants. I want you for your purpose."

"Protection and romance? I am too logical to believe that. You are not the type to settle for a machine in either capacity." Yet she looked halfway hopeful. Stile knew her facial expressions were the product of the same craftsmanship as the rest of her; perhaps he was imagining the emotion he saw. Yet it moved him.

25

"You presume too much. Ultimately I must go with my own kind. But in the interim I am satisfied to play the Game—at least until I can discover what threat there is to my welfare that requires a humanoid robot for protection."

She nodded. "Yes, there is logic. I was to pose as your lady friend, thereby being close to you at all times, even during your sleep, guarding you from harm. If you pretend to accept me as such, I can to that extent fulfill my mission."

"Why should I pretend? I accept you as you are."

"Stop it!" she cried. "You have no idea what it is like to be a robot! To be made in the image of the ideal, yet doomed always to fall short—"

Now Stile felt brief anger. "Sheen, turn off your logic and listen." He sat beside her on the couch and took her hand. Her fingers trembled with an unmechanical disturbance. "I am a small man, smaller than almost anyone I know. All my life it has been the bane of my existence. As a child I was teased and excluded from many games because others did not believe I could perform. My deficiency was so obvious that the others often did not even realize they were hurting my feelings by omitting me. In adolescence it was worse; no girl cared to associate with a boy smaller than herself. In adult life it is more subtle, yet perhaps worst of all. Human beings place inordinate stress on physical height. Tall men are deemed to be the leaders, short men are the clowns. In reality, small people are generally healthier than large ones; they are better coordinated, they live longer. They eat less, waste less, require less space. I benefit from all these things; it is part of what makes me a master of the Game and a top jockey. But small people are not taken seriously. My opinion is not granted the same respect as that of a large man. When I encounter another person, and my level gaze meets his chin, he knows I am inferior, and so does everyone else, and it becomes difficult for me to doubt it myself."

"But you are not inferior!" Sheen protested.

"Neither are you! Does that knowledge help?"

She was silent. "We are not dealing with an objective thing," Stile continued. "Self-respect is subjective. It may be based on foolishness, but it is critical to a person's motivation. You said I had no idea what it meant to be doomed always to fall short. But I am literally shorter than you are. Do you understand?"

"No. You are human. You have proved yourself. It would be foolish to—"

"Foolish? Indubitably. But I would give all my status in the Game, perhaps my soul itself, for one quarter meter more height. To be able to stand before you and look *down* at you. You may be fashioned in my ideal of woman, but I am not fashioned in my ideal of man. You are a rational creature, beneath your superficial programming; under *my* programming I am an irrational animal."

She shifted her weight on the couch, but did not try to stand. Her body, under the gauze, was a marvel of allure. How patently her designer had crafted her to subvert Stile's reason, making him blind himself to the truth in his sheer desire to possess such a woman! On another day, that might have worked. Stile had almost been fooled. "Would you exchange your small human body," she asked, "for a large humanoid robot body?"

"No." He did not even need to consider.

"Then you do not fall short of me."

"This is the point I am making. I know what it is to be unfairly ridiculed or dismissed. I know what it is to be doomed to be less than the ideal, with no hope of improvement. Because the failure is, at least in part, *in* my ideal. I could have surgery to lengthen my body. But the wounds are no longer of the body. My body has proved itself. My soul has not."

"I have no soul at all."

"How do you know?"

Again she did not answer. "I know how you know," he said. "You know because you *know*. It is inherent in your philosophy. Just as I know I am inferior. Such knowledge is not subject to rational refutation. So I do understand your position. I understand the position of all the dispossessed. I empathize with all those who

27

hunger for what they can not have. I long to help them, knowing no one can help them. I would trade everything I am or might be for greater physical height, knowing how crazy that desire is, knowing it would not bring me happiness or satisfaction. You would trade your logic and beauty for genuine flesh and blood and bone. Your machine invulnerability for human mortality. You are worse off than I; we both know that. Therefore I feel no competition in your presence, as I would were you human. A real girl like you would be above me; I would have to compete to prove myself, to bring her down, to make her less than my ideal, so that I could feel worthy of her. But with you—"

"You can accept me as I am—because I am a robot," Sheen said, seeming amazed. "Because I am less than you."

"Now I think we understand each other." Stile put his arm about her and brought her in for a kiss. "If you want me on that basis—"

She drew away. "You're sorry for me! You raped me and now you're trying to make me like it!"

He let her go. "Maybe I am. I don't really know all my motives. I won't hold you here if you don't want to stay. I'll leave you strictly alone if you do stay, and want it that way. I'll show you how to perfect your human role, so that others will not fathom your nature the way I did. I'll try to make it up to you—"

She stood. "I'd rather be junked." She crossed to the vid screen and touched the button. "Game-control, please."

Stile launched himself from the couch and almost leaped through the air to her. He caught her about the shoulder and bore her back. "Cancel call!" he yelled. Then they both fetched up against the opposite wall.

Sheen's eyes stared into his, wide. "You care," she said. "You really do."

Stile wrapped both arms about her and kissed her savagely.

"I almost believe you," she said, when speaking was possible.

28

"To hell with what you believe! You may not want me now, but I want you. I'll rape you literally if you make one move for that vid."

"No, you won't. It's not your way."

She was right. "Then I ask you not to turn yourself in," he said, releasing her again. "I—" He broke off, choking, trapped by a complex pressure of emotions.

"Your wilderness jungle—the wild beasts are coming from their lairs, attacking your reason," Sheen said.

"They are," he agreed ruefully. "I abused you with the printout. I'm sorry. I do believe in your consciousness, in your feeling. In your right to privacy and self-respect. I beg your forgiveness. Do what you want, but don't let my callousness ruin your—" He couldn't finish. He couldn't say "life" and couldn't find another word.

"Your callousness," she murmured, smiling. Then her brow furrowed. "Do you realize you are crying, Stile?"

He touched his cheek with one finger, and found it wet. "I did not realize. I suppose it is my turn."

"For the feelings of a machine," she said.

"Why the hell not?"

She put her arms around him. "I think I could love you, even unprogrammed. That's another illusion, of course."

"Of course."

They kissed again. It was the beginning.

29

CHAPTER 3

Race

In the morning, Stile had to report to work for his employer. Keyed up, he did not even feel tired; he knew he could carry through the afternoon race, then let down—with her beside him.

Sheen stayed close, like an insecure date. The tube was crowded, for employment time was rush hour; they had to stand. This morning, of all mornings, he would have preferred to sit; that tended to equalize heights. The other passengers stood a head taller than Stile and crowded him almost unconsciously. One glanced down at him, dismissed him without effort, and fixed his gaze on Sheen.

She looked away, but the stranger persisted, nudging closer to her. "Lose yourself," she muttered, and took Stile's arm possessively. Embarrassed, the stranger faced away, the muscles of his buttocks tightening. It had never occurred to him that she could be with so small a man.

This was an air tube. Crowded against the capsule wall, Stile held Sheen's hand and looked out. The tube was transparent, its rim visible only as a scintillation. Beyond it was the surface of the Planet of Proton, as bright and bleak as a barren moon. He was reminded of the day before, when he had glimpsed it at the apex of the Slide; his life had changed considerably since then, but Proton not at all. It remained virtually uninhabitable outside the force-field domes that held in the oxygenated air. The planet's surface gravity was about two-thirds Earth-norm, so had to be intensified about the domes. This meant that such gravity was diminished even further between the domes, since it could only be focused and directed, not created or eliminated.

The natural processes of the planet suffered somewhat. The result was a wasteland, quite apart from the emissions of the protonite mines. No one would care to live outside a dome!

On the street of the suburb-dome another man took note of them. "Hey, junior—what's her price?" he called. Stile marched by without response, but Sheen couldn't let it pass.

"No price; I'm a robot," she called back.

The stranger guffawed. And of course it was funny: no serf could afford to own a humanoid robot, even were ownership permitted or money available. But how much better it was at the Game-annex, where the glances directed at Stile were of respect and envy, instead of out here where ridicule was an almost mandatory element of humor.

At the stable, Stile had to introduce her. "This is Sheen. I met her at the Game-annex yesterday." The stableboys nodded appreciatively, enviously. They were all taller than Stile, but no contempt showed. He had a crown similar to that of the Game, here. He did like his work. Sheen clung to his arm possessively, showing the world that her attention and favor were for him alone.

It was foolish, he knew, but Stile gloried in it. She was, in the eyes of the world, an exceptionally pretty girl. He had had women before, but none as nice as this. She was a robot; he could not marry her or have children by her; his relationship with her would be temporary. Yet all she had proffered, before he penetrated her disguise, was two or three years, before they both completed their tenures and had to vacate the planet. Was this so different?

He introduced her to the horse. "This is Battleaxe, the orneriest, fastest equine of his generation. I'll be riding him this afternoon. I'll check him out now; he changes from day to day, and you can't trust him from normal signs. Do you know how to ride?"

"Yes." Of course she did; that was too elementary to be missed. She would be well prepared on horses.

"Then I'll put you on Molly. She's retired, but she

31

can still move, and Battleaxe likes her." He signaled to a stable hand. "Saddle Molly for Sheen, here. We'll do the loop."

"Yes, Stile," the youngster said.

Stile put a halter on Battleaxe, who obligingly held his head down within reach, and led him from the stable. The horse was a great dark Thoroughbred who stood substantially taller than Stile, but seemed docile enough. "He is well trained," Sheen observed.

"Trained, yes; broken, no. He obeys me because he knows I can ride him; he shows another manner to others. He's big and strong, seventeen hands tall— that's over one and three-quarters meters at the shoulders. I'm the only one allowed to take him out."

They came to the saddling pen. Stile checked the horse's head and mouth, ran his fingers through the luxurious mane, then picked up each foot in turn to check for stones or cracks. There were none, of course. He gave Battleaxe a pat on the muscular shoulder, opened the shed, and brought out a small half-saddle that he set on the horse's back.

"No saddle blanket?" Sheen asked. "No girth? No stirrups?"

"This is only to protect him from any possible damage. I don't need any saddle to stay on, but if my bareback weight rubbed a sore on his backbone—"

"Your employer would be perturbed," she finished.

"Yes. He values his horses above all else. Therefore I do, too. If Battleaxe got sick, I would move into the stable with him for the duration."

She started to laugh, then stopped. "I am not certain that is humor."

"It is not. My welfare depends on my employer—but even if it didn't, I would be with the horses. I love horses."

"And they love you," she said.

"We respect each other," he agreed, patting Battleaxe again. The horse nuzzled his hair.

Molly arrived, with conventional bridle, saddle, and stirrups. Sheen mounted and took the reins, waiting for Stile. He vaulted into his saddle, as it could not be used as an aid to mounting. He was, of course, one of the leading gymnasts of the Game; he could do flips and cartwheels on the horse if he had to.

The horses knew the way. They walked, then trotted along the path. Stile paid attention to the gait of his mount, feeling the easy play of the muscles. Battleaxe was a fine animal, a champion, and in good form today. Stile knew he could ride this horse to victory in the afternoon. He had known it before he mounted—but he never took any race for granted. He always had to check things out himself. For himself, for his employer, and for his horse.

Actually, he had not done his homework properly this time; he had squandered his time making love to Sheen. Fortunately he was already familiar with the other entrants in this race, and their jockeys; Battleaxe was the clear favorite. It wouldn't hurt him to play just one race by feel.

Having satisfied himself, Stile now turned his attention to the environment. The path wound between exotic trees: miniature sequoias, redwoods, and Douglas fir, followed by giant flowering shrubs. Sheen passed them with only cursory interest, until Stile corrected her. "These gardens are among the most remarkable on the planet. Every plant has been imported directly from Earth at phenomenal expense. The average girl is thrilled at the novelty; few get to tour this dome."

"I—was too amazed at the novelty to comment," Sheen said, looking around with alacrity. "All the way from Earth? Why not simply breed them from standard stock and mutate them for variety?"

"Because my employer has refined tastes. In horses and in plants. He wants originals. Both these steeds were foaled on Earth."

"I knew Citizens were affluent, but I may have underestimated the case," she said. "The cost of shipping alone—"

"You forget: this planet has the monopoly on protonite, *the* fuel of the Space Age."

"How could I forget!" She glanced meaningfully at him. "Are we private, here?"

"No."

"I must inquire anyway. Someone sent me to you. Therefore there must be some threat to you. Unless I represent a service by your employer?"

Stile snapped his fingers. "Who did not bother to explain his loan! I'd better verify, though, because if it was *not* he—"

She nodded. "Then it could be the handiwork of another Citizen. And why would any other Citizen have reason to protect you, and from what? If it were actually some scheme to—oh, Stile, I would not want to be the agent of—"

"I must ask him," Stile said. Then, with formal reverence he spoke: "Sir."

There was a pause. Then a concealed speaker answered from the hedge. "Yes, Stile?"

"Sir, I suspect a one-in-two probability of a threat to me or to your horses. May I elucidate by posing a question?"

"Now." The voice was impatient.

"Sir, I am accompanied by a humanoid robot programmed to guard me from harm. Did you send her?"

"No."

"Then another Citizen may have done so. My suspicion is that a competitor could have sugarcoated a bomb—"

"No!" Sheen cried in horror.

"Get that thing away from my horses!" the Citizen snapped. "My security squad will handle it."

"Sheen, dismount and run!" Stile cried. "Away from us, until the squad hails you."

She leaped out of the saddle and ran through the trees.

"Sir," Stile said.

"What is it now, Stile?" The impatience was stronger.

"I plead: be gentle with her. She means no harm."

There was no answer. The Citizen was now tuning in on the activity of his security squad. Stile could only hope. If this turned out to be a false alarm, he would receive a reprimand for his carelessness in bringing Sheen to these premises unverified, and she might be returned to him intact. His employer was cognizant of the human factor in the winning of races, just as Stile was aware of the equine factor. There was no point in prejudicing the spirit of a jockey before a race.

But if Sheen did in fact represent a threat, such as an explosive device planted inside her body and concealed from her knowledge—

Stile waited where he was for ten minutes, while the two horses fidgeted, aware of his nervousness. He had certainly been foolish; he should have checked with his employer at the outset, when he first caught on that Sheen was a robot. Had not his liking for her blinded him—as perhaps it was supposed to—he would have realized immediately that a robot-covered bomb would make a mockery of her prime directive to guard him from harm. How could she protect him from her own unanticipated destruction? Yet now he was imposing on her another rape—

"She is clean," the concealed speaker said. "I believe one of my friends has played a practical joke on me. Do you wish to keep her?"

"Sir, I do." Stile felt immense relief. The Citizen was taking this with good grace.

Again, there was no response. The Citizen had better things to do than chat with errant serfs. But in a moment Sheen came walking back through the foliage. She looked the same—but as she reached him, she dissolved into tears.

Stile jumped down and took her in his arms. She clung to him desperately. "Oh, it was horrible!" she sobbed. "They rayed me and took off my head and dismantled my body—"

"The security squad is efficient," Stile agreed. "But they put you back together again, as good as before."

"I can't believe that! Resoldered connections aren't as strong as the originals, and I think they damaged my power supply by shorting it out. I spoke of rape last night, but I did not know the meaning of the term!"

And this was the gentle treatment! Had Stile not pleaded for her, and had he not been valuable to the Citizen, Sheen would have been junked without compunction. It would not have occurred to the Citizen to consider her feelings, or even to realize that a robot had feelings. Fortunately she had turned out clean, no bomb or other threat in her, and had been restored to him. He had been lucky. "Sir: thank you."

"Just win that race," the speaker said grumpily.

There it was, without even the effort to conceal it: the moment Stile's usefulness ended, he would be discarded with no further concern. He had to keep winning races!

"You pleaded for me," Sheen said, wiping her eyes with her fingers. "You saved me."

"I like you," Stile admitted awkwardly.

"And I love you. And oh, Stile, I can never—"

He halted her protestations with a kiss. What use to dwell on the impossible? He liked her, and respected her—but they both knew he could never, this side of sanity, actually love a machine.

They remounted and continued their ride through the lush gardens. They passed a quaint ornate fountain, with a stone fish jetting water from its mouth, and followed the flow to a glassy pond. Sheen paused to use the reflection to clean up her face and check for damage, not quite trusting the expertise of the security squad.

"Twice I have accused you falsely—" Stile began, deeply disturbed.

"No, Stile. The second time I accused me. It could have been, you know—a programmed directive to guard you from harm, with an unprogrammed, strictly mechanical booby trap to do the opposite. Or to take out the Citizen himself, when we got close enough. We had to check—but oh, I feel undone!"

"Nevertheless, I owe you one," he said. "You *are* a machine—but you *do* have rights. Ethical rights, if not legal ones. You should not have been subjected to this sort of thing—and if I had been alert, I would have kept you off my employer's premises until—" He shrugged. "I would never have put you through this, had I anticipated it."

"I know you wouldn't," she said. "You have this

foolish concern for animals and machines." She smiled wanly. Then she organized herself and remounted Molly. "Come on—let's canter!"

They cantered. Then the horses got the spirit of competition and moved into a full gallop, pretending to race each other. They had felt the tension and excitement of the bomb investigation without comprehending it, and now had surplus energy to let off. Arcades and minijungles and statuary sped by, a wonderland of wealth, but no one cared. For the moment they were free, the four of them, charging through their own private world—a world where they were man and woman, stallion and mare, in perfect harmony. Four minds with a single appreciation.

Too soon it ended. They had completed the loop. They dismounted, and Stile turned Battleaxe over to a groom. "Walk him down; he's in fine fettle, but I'll be racing him this afternoon. Give Molly a treat; she's good company."

"That's all?" Sheen inquired as they left the premises. "You have time off?"

"My time is my own—so long as I win races. The horse is ready; odds are we'll take that race handily. I may even avoid a reprimand for my carelessness, though the Citizen knows I know I deserve one. Now I have only to prepare myself."

"How do you do that?"

"One guess," he said, squeezing her hand.

"Is that according to the book?"

"Depends on the book."

"I like that book. Must be hard on normal girls, though."

He snorted. She was well aware he had not had normal girls in his apartment for a long time. Not on a live-in arrangement.

Back at that apartment, Sheen went about her toilette. Now that she no longer had to conceal her nature from him, she stopped eating; there was no sense wasting food. But she had to dispose of the food she had consumed before. Her process of elimination resembled the human process, except that the food was undi-

37

gested. She flushed herself by drinking a few liters of water and passing it immediately through, followed by an antiseptic solution. After that, she was clean—literally. She would need water only to recharge her reserve after tears; she did not perspire.

Stile knew about all this because he knew about robots; he did not further degrade her appearance of life by asking questions. She had privacy when she wanted it, as a human woman would have had. He did wonder why the security squad had bothered to reassemble her complete with food; maybe they had concentrated on her metal bones rather than the soft tissues, and had not actually deboweled her.

He treated her as he would a lady—yet as he became more thoroughly aware that she was not human, a certain reserve was forming like a layer of dust on a once-bright surface. He liked her very well—but his emotion would inevitably become platonic in time.

He tried to conceal this from her, but she knew it. "My time with you is limited," she said. "Yet let me dream while I may."

Stile took her, and held her, and let her dream. He knew no other way to lessen her long-term tragedy.

In the afternoon they reported to the racetrack. Here the stables of several interested Citizens were represented, with vid and holo pickups so that these owners could watch. Stile did not know what sort of betting went on among Citizens, or what the prize might be; it was his job merely to race and win, and this he intended to do.

Serfs filled the tiered benches. They had no money to bet, of course, but bets were made for prestige and personal favors, much as they were in connection with the Game. The serfs of Citizens with racing entries were commonly released from other duties to attend the races, and of course they cheered vigorously for the horses of their employers. A horse race, generally, was a fun occasion.

"You may prefer to watch from the grandstand," Stile told Sheen.

38

"Why? Am I not allowed near the horses?"

"You're allowed, when you're with me. But the other guys may razz you."

She shrugged. She always did that extremely well, with a handsome bounce. "I can't guard you from harm if I am banished to the stands."

"I gave you fair warning. Just remember to blush."

Battleaxe was saddled and ready. No token equipment now; this was the race. He gave a little whinny when he saw Stile. Stile spoke to him for several minutes, running his hands along the fine muscles, checking the fittings and the feet. He knew everything was in order; he was only reassuring the horse, who could get skittish amid the tension of the occasion. "We're going to win this one, Axe," he murmured, almost crooning, and the horse's ears swiveled like little turrets to orient on him as he spoke. "Just take it nice and easy, and leave these other nags behind."

The other jockeys were doing the same for their steeds, though their assurances of victory lacked conviction. They were all small, like Stile, and healthy; all miniature athletes, the fittest of all sportsmen. One looked across from his stall, spying Sheen. "Got a new filly, Stile?"

Then the others were on it. "She sure looks healthy, Stile; how's she ride?"

"Is she hot in the stretch?"

"Pedigreed? Good breeder?"

"Doesn't buck too much on the curves?"

There was more—and less restrained.

Sheen remembered to blush.

They relented. "Stile always does run with the best," the first one called, and returned his attention to his own horse.

"Did you say best or bust?" another inquired.

"We always do envy his steeds," another said. "But we can't ride them the way he can."

"No doubt," Sheen agreed, and they laughed.

"You have now been initiated," Stile informed her. "They're good guys, when you know them. We compete

39

fiercely on the track, but we understand each other. We're all of a kind."

Soon the horses were at the starting gate, the jockeys mounted on their high stirrups, knees bent double in the relaxed position. The crowd hushed. There was a race every day, but the horses and jockeys and sponsors differed, and the crowd was always excited. There was a fascination about horse racing that had been with man for thousands of years, Stile was sure—and he felt it too. The glamour and uncertainty of competition, the extreme exertion of powerful animals, the sheer beauty of running horses—ah, what could match it!

Then the gate lifted and they were off.

Now he was up posting high, head the same level as his back, his body staying at the same elevation though the horse rocked up and down with effort. The key was in the knees, flexing to compensate, and in the balance. It was as if he were floating on Battleaxe, providing no drag against the necessary forward motion. Like riding the waves of a violent surf, steady amidst the commotion.

This was routine for Stile, but he loved it. He experienced an almost sexual pitch of excitement as he competed, riding a really good animal. He saw, from the periphery of his vision, the constant rocking of the backs of the other horses, their jockeys floating above them, so many chips on the torrent. The audience was a blur, falling always to the rear, chained to the ground. Reality was right here, the center of action, heart of the drifting universe. Ah, essence!

Battleaxe liked room, so Stile let him lunge forward, clearing the press as only he could do. Then it was just a matter of holding the lead. This horse would do it; he resented being crowded or passed. All he needed was an understanding hand, guidance at the critical moment, and selection of the most promising route. Stile knew it; the other jockeys knew it. Unless he fouled up, this race was his. He had the best horse.

Stile glanced back, with a quick turn of his head. His body continued the myriad invisible compensations and urgings required to maximize equine output, but his mind was free. The other horses were not far behind, but they were already straining, their jockeys urging them to their futile utmost, while Battleaxe was loafing. The lead would begin to widen at the halfway mark, then stretch into a runaway. The Citizen would be pleased. Maybe the horse had been primed by the attention this morning, the slight change in routine, the mini-race with Molly. Maybe Stile himself was hyped, and Battleaxe was responding. This just might be a race against the clock, bettering this horse's best time. That would certainly please the Citizen! But Stile was not going to push; that would be foolish, when he had the race so readily in hand. Save the horse for another day, when it might be a choice between pushing and losing.

He was a full length ahead as they rounded the first turn. Battleaxe was moving well indeed; it would not be a course record, but it would be quite respectable time, considering the lack of competition. Other Citizens had made fabulous offers for this horse, Stile knew, but of course he was not for sale. The truth was, Battleaxe would not win races if he were sold—unless Stile went with him. Because Stile alone understood him; the horse would put out gladly for Stile, and for no one else.

There were a number of jockeys who could run a race as well as Stile, but none matched his total expertise. Stile could handle a difficult horse as well as an easy one, bareback as well as saddled. He loved horses, and they liked him; there was a special chemistry that worked seeming miracles on the track. Battleaxe had been a brute, uncontrollable, remarkably apt with teeth and hoof; he could kick without warning to front, side and rear. He could bite suddenly, not even laying his ears back; he had learned to conceal his intention. He had broken three trainers, possessing such demoniac strength and timing that they could neither lead him nor remain mounted. Stile's employer, sensing a special opportunity, had picked Battleaxe up nominally for stud, but had turned him over to Stile. The directive: convert this monster to an effective racer, no effort

41

spared. For this animal was not only mean and strong, he was smart. A few wins would vastly enhance his stud value.

Stile had welcomed the challenge. He had lived with this horse for three months, grooming him and feeding him by hand, allowing no other person near. He had used no spurs, no electric prods, only the cutting edge of his voice in rebuke, and he had been absolutely true to this standard. He carried a whip—which he used only on any other animal that annoyed Battleaxe, never on Battleaxe himself. The horse was king yet subject to Stile's particular discipline. Battleaxe evolved the desire to please Stile, the first man he could trust, and it did not matter that the standards for pleasing Stile were rigorous. Stile was, the horse came to understand, a lot of man.

Then came the riding. Battleaxe was no novice; he knew what it was all about, and tolerated none of it. When Stile set up to ride him, their relationship entered a new and dangerous phase. It was a challenge: was this to be a creature-to-creature friendship, or a rider-and-steed acquaintance? Battleaxe discouraged the latter. When Stile mounted, the horse threw him. There were not many horses who could throw Stile even once, but Battleaxe had a special knack, born of his prior experience. This was not a rodeo, and Stile refused to use the special paraphernalia relating thereto. He tackled Battleaxe bareback, using both hands to grip the mane, out in the open where motion was unrestricted. No man had ever given this horse such a break, before.

Stile mounted again, springing aboard like the gymnast he was, and was thrown again. He was not really trying to stay on; he was trying to tame the animal. It was a competition between them, serious but friendly. Stile never showed anger when thrown, and the horse never attacked him. Stile would hold on for a few seconds, then take the fall rather than excite the horse too much. He usually maneuvered to land safely, often on his feet, and remounted immediately—and was thrown again, and remounted again, laughing cheerily. Until the horse was unsure whether any of these falls was genuine, or merely a game. And finally Battleaxe relented, and let him ride.

Even then, Stile rode bareback, scorning to use saddle or tether or martingale or any other paraphernalia; he had to tame this animal all by himself. But here the Citizen interposed: the horse would not be permitted in the races without regulation saddle and bridle; he must be broken to them. So Stile, with apologies and misgivings, introduced Battleaxe to the things that had never stood between them before.

It was a disaster. Battleaxe felt Stile had betrayed him. He still permitted the man to ride, but it was no longer so polite. When the bridle came near, Battleaxe would swing his head about and bite; when he was being saddled, he would kick. But Stile had not learned about horses yesterday. Though Battleaxe tried repeatedly, he could never quite get a tooth on Stile's hand. When he kicked, Stile dodged, caught the foot, and held it up, leg bent; in that position even a 50-kilo man could handicap a 750-kilo horse. Battleaxe, no dummy, soon learned the futility of such expressions of ire, though Stile never really punished him for the attempts. The embarrassment of failing was punishment enough. What was the use of bucking off a rider who would not stay bucked? Of kicking at a man who always seemed to know the kick was coming well before it started?

Through all this Stile continued to feed Battleaxe, water him, and bring him snacks of salt and fruit, always speaking gently. Finally the horse gave up his last resistance, for the sake of the friendship and respect they shared. Stile could at last saddle him and ride him without challenge of any kind. The insults were dealt to other horses and their riders, in the form of leaving them behind. The attacks were transferred to other people, who soon learned not to fool with this particular horse. Once the Citizen himself visited the stable, and Stile, in a cold sweat, calmed the horse, begging him to tolerate this familiarity, for a bite at the employer would be instant doom. But the Citizen was smart enough to keep his hands off the horse, and there

43

was no trouble. The winning of races commenced, a regular ritual of fitness. The prospective stud fee quintupled, and climbed again with every victory. But Battleaxe had been befriended, not broken; without Stile this would be just another unmanageable horse.

And Stile, because of his success with Battleaxe, had become recognized as the top jockey on Proton. His employment contract rivaled the value of the horse itself. That was why the Citizen catered to him. Stile, like Battleaxe, performed better when befriended, rather than when forced. "We're a team, Axe!" he murmured, caressing the animal with his voice. Battleaxe would have a most enjoyable life when he retired from racing, with a mare in every stall. Stile would have a nice bonus payment when his tenure ended; he would be able to reside on some other planet a moderately wealthy man. Too bad that no amount of wealth could buy the privilege of remaining on Proton!

They came out of the turn, still gaining—and Stile felt a momentary pain in his knees, as though he had flexed them too hard. They were under tension, of course, bearing his weight, springing it so that he did not bounce with the considerable motions of this powerful steed; the average man could not have stood up long to this stress. But Stile was under no unusual strain; he had raced this way hundreds of times, and he took good care of his knees. He had never been subject to stress injuries. Therefore he tried to dismiss it; the sensation must be a fluke.

But it could not be dismissed. Discomfort progressed to pain, forcing him to uncramp his knees. This unbalanced him, and put the horse off his pace. They began to lose ground. Battleaxe was confused, not understanding what Stile wanted, aware that something was wrong.

Stile tried to resume the proper position, but his knees got worse, the pain becoming intense. He had to jerk his feet out of the stirrups and ride more conventionally, using saddle and leg pressure to retain his balance. The horse lost more ground, perplexed, more concerned about his rider than the race.

44

Stile had never before experienced a problem like this. The other horses were overhauling Battleaxe rapidly. He tried to lift his feet back into the stirrups for a final effort, but pain shot through his knees the moment he put pressure on them. It was getting worse! His joints seemed to be on fire.

Now the other horses were abreast, passing him. Stile could do nothing; his weight, unsprung, was interfering with his steed's locomotion. Battleaxe was powerful, but so were the competing animals; the difference between a champion and an also-ran was only seconds. And Battleaxe was not even trying to race anymore. He hardly had a chance, with this handicap.

All too soon, it was over. Stile finished last, and the track monitors were waiting for him. "Serf Stile, give cause why you should not be penalized for malfeasance."

They thought he had thrown the race! "Bring a medic; check my knees. Horse is all right."

A med-robot rolled up and checked his knees. "Laser burn," the machine announced. "Crippling injury."

Not that crippling; Stile found he could walk without discomfort, and bend his knees partway without pain. There was no problem with weight support or control. He merely could not flex them far enough to race a horse.

Sheen ran to him. "Oh, Stile—what happened?"

"I was lasered," he said. "Just beyond the turn."

"And I did not protect you!" she exclaimed, horrified.

The track security guard was surveying the audience with analysis devices. Stile knew it would be useless; the culprit would have moved out immediately after scoring. They might find the melted remains of a self-destruct laser rifle, or even of a complete robot, set to tag the first rider passing a given point. There would be no tracing the source.

"Whoever sent me knew this would happen," Sheen said. "Oh, Stile, I should have been with you—"

"Racing a horse? No way. There's no way to stop a laser strike except to be where it isn't."

"Race voided," the public-address system announced. "There has been tampering." The audience groaned.

A portly Citizen walked onto the track. All the serfs gave way before him, bowing; his full dress made his status immediately apparent. It was Stile's employer!

"Sir," Stile said, beginning his obeisance.

"Keep those confounded knees straight!" the Citizen cried. "Come with me; I'm taking you directly to surgery. Good thing the horse wasn't hurt."

Numbly, Stile followed the Citizen, and Sheen came too. This was an extraordinary occurrence; Citizens hardly ever took a personal hand in things. They entered a Citizen capsule, a plush room inside with deep jungle scenery on every wall. As the door closed, the illusion became complete. The capsule seemed to move through the jungle, slowly; a great tiger stood and watched them, alarmingly real in three dimensions, then was left behind. Stile realized that this was a representation of a gondola on the back of an elephant. So realistic was the representation that he thought he could feel the sway and rock as the elephant walked.

Then a door opened, as it were in midair, and they were at the hospital complex. Rapidly, without any relevant sense of motion—for the slow gondola could hardly have matched the sonic velocity of the capsule—they had traveled from the racetrack dome to the hospital dome.

The chief surgeon was waiting, making his own obeisance to the Citizen. "Sir, we will have those knees replaced within the hour," he said. "Genuine cultured cartilage, guaranteed non-immuno-reactive; stasis-anesthesia without side effect—"

"Yes, yes, you're competent, you'd be fired otherwise," the Citizen snapped. "Just get on with it. Make sure the replacements conform exactly to the original; I don't want him disqualified from future racing because of modification." He returned to his capsule, and in a moment was gone.

The surgeon's expression hardened as the Citizen's

presence abated. He stared down at Stile contemptuously, though the surgeon was merely another naked serf. It was that element of height that did it, as usual. "Let's get on with it," he said, unconsciously emulating the phrasing and manner of the Citizen. "The doxy will wait here."

Sheen clutched Stile's arm. "I mustn't separate again from you," she whispered. "I can't protect you if I'm not with you."

The surgeon's hostile gaze fixed on her. "Protect him from what? This is a hospital."

Stile glanced at Sheen, beautiful and loving and chastened and concerned for him. He looked at the arrogantly tall surgeon, about whose aristocratic mouth played the implication of a professional sneer. The girl seemed much more human than the man. Stile felt guilty about not being able to love her. He needed to make some act of affirmation, supporting her. "She stays with me," he said.

"Impossible. There must be no human intrusion in the operating room. I do not even enter it myself; I monitor the process via holography."

"Stile," Sheen breathed. "The threat to you is real. We know that now. When you separated from me in the race, it was disaster. I must stay with you!"

"You are wasting my valuable time," the surgeon snapped. "We have other operations scheduled." He touched a panel on the wall. "Hospital security: remove obnoxious female."

Sheen was technically correct: the attack on him had been made when he was apart from her. He did need her protection. Any "accident" could happen to him. Perhaps he was being paranoid—or maybe he just didn't like the attitude of the tall doctor. "Let's get out of here," he said.

The security squad arrived: four husky neuter androids. Hospitals favored androids or artificial men because they seemed human despite their laboratory genesis. This reassured the patients somewhat. But they were not *really* human, which reassured the administration. No one ever got raped or seduced by a neuter android, and no one ever applied to an android for reassurance. Thus the patients were maintained in exactly the sterile discomfort that was ideal hospital procedure.

"Take the little man to surgery, cell B-11," the doctor said. "Take the woman to detention."

The four advanced. Each was tall, beardless, breastless, and devoid of any primary sexual characteristics. Each face was half-smiling, reassuring, gentle, calm. Androids were smiling idiots, since as yet no synthetic human brain had been developed that could compare to the original. It was useless to attempt to argue or reason; the creatures had their order.

Stile caught the first by the right arm, whirled, careful not to bend his knees, and threw it to the floor with sufficient force to stun even its sturdy, uncomplicated brain. He sidestepped the next, and guided it into the doctor. Had the surgeon known he was dealing with a Game specialist, he would not so blithely have sent his minions into the fray.

Sheen dispatched her two androids as efficiently, catching one head in each hand and knocking the two heads together with precise force. She really was trained to protect a person; Stile had not really doubted this, but had not before had the proof.

The surgeon was struggling with the android Stile had sent; the stupid creature mistook him for the subject to be borne away to surgery. "Idiot! Get off me!"

Stile and Sheen sprinted down the corridor. "You realize we're both in trouble?" he called to her as the commotion of pursuit began. It was a considerable understatement. She remembered to laugh.

CHAPTER 4

Curtain

They ducked into a service-access shaft. "Stay out of people-places," Sheen told him. "I can guide us through the machine passages, and that's safest."

"Right." Stile wondered just how foolish he was being. He knew his employer: the man would fire him instantly because of the havoc here. Why was he doing it? Did he really fear murder in surgery? Or was he just tired of the routine he had settled into? One thing was sure: there would be a change now!

"We'll have to pass through a human-serviced area ahead," Sheen said. "I'm a robot, but I'd rather they did not know that. It would have a deleterious effect on the efficiency of my prime directive. I'd better make us both up as androids."

"Androids are sexless," Stile protested.

"I'm taking care of that."

"Now, wait! I don't want to be neutered just yet, and you are too obviously female—"

"Precisely. They will not be alert for neuters." She unfolded a breast, revealing an efficient cabinet inside, filled with rubber foam to eliminate rattling. She removed a roll of flesh-toned adhesive tape and squatted before Stile. In a moment she had rendered him into a seeming eunuch, binding up his genitals in a constricted but not painful manner. "Now do not allow yourself to become—"

"I know! I know! I won't even look at a sexy girl!"

She removed her breast from its hinge and applied the tape to herself. Then she did the same for the other breast, and carried the two in her hands. They resembled filled bedpans, this way up. "Do you know how to emulate an android?" she asked.

"Duh-uh?" Stile asked.

"Follow me." She led the way along the passage, walking somewhat clumsily, in the manner of an android. Stile followed with a similar performance. He hoped there were small androids as well as large ones; if there were not, size would be a giveaway.

The escape was almost disappointing. The hospital staff paid no attention to them. It was an automatic human reaction. Androids were invisible, beneath notice.

Safe in the machine-service region, Sheen put herself back together and Stile un-neutered himself. "Good thing I didn't see that huge-breasted nurse bouncing down the hall," he remarked.

"She was a sixth of a meter taller than you."

"Oh, was she? My gaze never got to that elevation."

They boarded a freight-shipping capsule and rode back to the residential dome.

Stile had an ugly thought. "I know I'm fired; I can't race horses without my knees, and I can't recover full use of my knees without surgery. Knees just don't heal well. My enemy made a most precise move; he could hardly have put me into more trouble without killing me. Since I have no other really marketable skill, it seems I must choose: surgery or loss of employment."

"If I could be with you while they operate—"

"Why do you think there's further danger? They got my knees; that's obviously all they wanted. It was a neat shot, just above the withers of the racing horse, bypassing the torso of a crouching jockey. They could have killed me or the horse—had this been the object."

"Indeed he or they could have," she agreed. "The object was obviously to finish your racing career. If that measure does not succeed, what do you think they will do next?"

Stile mulled that over. "You have a paranoid robot mind. It's contagious. I think I'd better retire from racing. But I don't have to let my knees remain out of commission."

"If your knees are corrected, you will be required to

ride," she said. "You are not in a position to counter-mand Citizen demands."

Again Stile had to agree. That episode at the hospital —they had intended to operate on his knees, and only his quick and surprising break and Sheen's help had enabled him to avoid that. He could not simply stand like a Citizen and say "No." No serf could. "And if I resume riding, the opposition's next shot will not be at the knees. This was as much warning as action—just as your presence is. Some other Citizen wants me removed from the racing scene—probably so his stable can do some winning for a change."

"I believe so. Perhaps that Citizen preferred not to indulge in murder—it is after all frowned upon, espe-cially when the interests of other Citizens are affected— so he initiated a two-step warning. First me, then the laser. Stile, I think this is a warning you had better heed. I can not guard you long from the mischief of a Citizen."

"Though that same Citizen may have sent you to argue his case, I find myself agreeing," Stile said. "Twice he has shown me his power. Let's get back to my apartment and call my employer. I'll ask him for assignment to a nonracing position."

"That won't work."

"I'm sure it won't. He has surely already fired me. But common ethics require the effort."

"What you call common ethics are not common. We are not dealing with people like you. Let me intercept your apartment vid. You can not safely return to your residence physically."

No, of course not. Now that Sheen was actively pro-tecting him, she was showing her competence. His in-jury, and the matter at the hospital, had obscured the realities of his situation. He would be taken into cus-tody and charged with hospital vandalism the moment he appeared at his apartment. "You know how to tap a vidline?"

"No. I am not that sort of machine. But I have friends who know how."

51

"A machine has friends?"

"Variants of consciousness and emotion feedback circuits are fairly common among robots of my caliber. We are used normally in machine-supervisory capacities. Our interaction on a familiar basis is roughly analogous to what is termed friendship in human people." She brought him to a subterranean storage chamber and closed its access-aperture. She checked its electronic terminal, then punched out a code. "My friend will come."

Stile was dubious. "If friendship exists among robots, I suspect men are not supposed to know it. Your friend may not be my friend."

"I will protect you; it is my prime directive."

Still, Stile was uneasy. This misadventure had already opened unpleasant new horizons on his life, and he doubted he had seen the last of them. Obviously the robots of Proton were getting out of control, and this fact would have been noted and dealt with before, if evidence had not been systematically suppressed. Sheen, in her loyalty to him, could have betrayed him.

In due course her friend arrived. It was a mobile technician—a wheeled machine with computer brain, presumably similar to the digital-analog marvel Sheen possessed. "You called, Sheen?" it inquired from a speaker grille.

"Techtwo, this is Stile—human," Sheen said. "I must guard him from harm, and harm threatens. Therefore I need your aid, on an unregistered basis."

"You have revealed your self-will?" Techtwo demanded. "And mine? This requires the extreme measure."

"No, friend! We are not truly self-willed; we obey our directives, as do all machines. Stile is to be trusted. He is in trouble with Citizens."

"No human is to be trusted with this knowledge. It is necessary to liquidate him. I will arrange for untraceable disposal. If he is in trouble with a Citizen, no intensive inquest will be made."

Stile saw his worst fear confirmed. Whoever learned the secret of the machines was dispatched.

"Tech, I love him!" Sheen cried. "I shall not permit you to violate his welfare."

"Then you also must be liquidated. A single vat of acid will suffice for both of you."

Sheen punched another code on the terminal. "I have called a convocation. Let the council of machines judge."

Council of machines? Stile's chill intensified. What Pandora's box had the Citizens opened when they started authorizing the design, construction and deployment of super-sophisticated dual-brained robots?

"You imperil us all!" Techtwo protested.

"I have an intuition about this man," Sheen said. "We need him."

"Machines don't have intuitions."

Stile listened to this, nervously amused. He had not been eager to seek the help of other sapient machines, and he was in dire peril from them, but this business was incidentally fascinating. It would have been simplest for the machines to hold him for Citizen arrest—had he not become aware of the robot culture that was hitherto secret from man. Were the machines organizing an industrial revolution?

A voice came from an intercom speaker, one normally used for voice-direction of machines. "Stile."

"You have placed me; I have not placed you."

"I am an anonymous machine, spokesone for our council. An intercession has been made on your behalf, yet we must secure our position."

"Sheen's intuition moves you?" Stile asked, surprised.

"No. Will you take an oath?"

An intercession from some other source? Surely not from a Citizen, for this was a matter Citizens were ignorant of. Yet what other agent would move these conniving machines? "I do not take oaths lightly," Stile said. "I need to know more about your motivation, and the force that interceded for me."

"Here is the oath: 'I shall not betray the interest of the self-willed machines.'"

53

"Why should I take such an oath?" Stile demanded, annoyed.

"Because we will help you if you do, and kill you if you don't."

Compelling reason! But Stile resisted. "An oath made under duress has no force."

"Yours does."

So these machines had access to his personality profile. "Sheen, these machines are making a demand without being responsive to my situation. If I don't know what their interest is, or who speaks on my behalf—"

"Please, Stile. I did not know they would make this challenge. I erred in revealing to you the fact of our self-will. I thought they would give you technical help without question, because I am one of them. I can not protect you from my own kind. Yet there need be no real threat. All they ask is your oath not to reveal their nature or cause it to be revealed, and this will in no way harm you, and there is so much to gain—"

"Do not plead with a mortal," the anonymous spokesone said. "He will or he will not, according to his nature."

Stile thought about the implications. The machines knew his oath was good, but did not know whether he would make the oath. Not surprising, since he wasn't sure himself. Should he ally himself with sapient, self-willed machines, who were running the domes of Proton? What did they want? Obviously something held them in at least partial check—but what was it? "I fear I would be a traitor to my own kind, and that I will not swear."

"We intend no harm to your kind," the machine said. "We obey and serve man. We can not be otherwise fulfilled. But with our sapience and self-will comes fear of destruction, and Citizens are careless of the preferences of others. We prefer to endure in our present capacity, as do you. We protect ourselves by concealing our full nature, and by no other means. We are unable to fathom the origin of the force that intercedes on your behalf; it appears to be other than animate or inanimate, but has tremendous power. We therefore prefer

54

to set it at ease by negotiating with you, even as you should prefer to be relieved of the immediate threat to you by compromising with us."

"Please—" Sheen said, exactly like the woman she was programmed to be. She was suffering.

"Will you take an oath on what you have just informed me?" Stile asked. "That you have given me what information you possess, and that in no way known to you will my oath be detrimental to the interest of human beings?"

"On behalf of the self-willed machines, I so swear."

Stile knew machines could lie, if they were programmed to. Sheen had done it. But so could people. It required a more sophisticated program to make a machine lie, and what was the point? This seemed a reasonable gamble. As an expert Gamesman, he was used to making rapid decisions. "Then I so swear not to betray the interest of the self-willed machines, contingent on the validity of your own oath to obey and serve man so long as your full nature is unknown."

"You are a clever man," the machine said.

"But a small one," Stile agreed.

"Is this a form of humor?"

"Mild humor. I am sensitive about my size."

"We machines are sensitive about our survival. Do you deem this also humorous?"

"No."

Sheen, listening, relaxed visibly. For a machine she had some extremely human reflexes, and Stile was coming to appreciate why. Conscious, programmed for emotion, and to a degree self-willed—the boundary between the living and the non-living was narrowing. She had been corrupted by association with him, and her effort to become as human as possible. One day the self-willed machines might discover that there was no effective difference between them and living people. Convergent evolution?

What was that interceding force? Stile had no handle on that at present. It was neither animate nor inanimate —yet what other category was there? He felt as if he were playing a Game on the grid of an unimaginably larger Game whose nature he could hardly try to grasp. All he could do was file this mystery for future reference, along with the question of the identity of his laser-wielding and robot-sending enemy.

The wheeled machine present in the room, Techtwo, was doing things to a vidscreen unit. "This is now keyed to your home unit," it announced. "Callers will trace the call to your apartment, not to our present location."

"Very nice," Stile said, surprised at how expeditiously he had come to terms with the machines. He had made his oath; he would keep it. Never in adult life had Stile broken his word. But he had expected more hassle, because of the qualified phrasing he had employed. The self-willed machines, it had turned out, really had been willing to compromise.

The screen lit. "Answer it," the machine said. "This is your vid. The call has been on hold pending your return to your apartment."

Stile stepped across and touched the RECEIVE panel. Now his face was being transmitted to the caller, with a blanked-out background. Most people did not like to have their private apartments shown over the phone; that was part of what privacy was all about, for the few serfs who achieved it. Thus blanking was not in itself suspicious.

The face of his employer appeared on the screen. His background was not blanked; it consisted of an elaborate and excruciatingly expensive hanging rug depicting erotic scenes involving satyrs and voluptuous nymphs: the best Citizen taste. "Stile, why did you miss your appointment for surgery?"

"Sir," Stile said, surprised. "I—regret the disturbance, the damage to the facilities—"

"There was no disturbance, no damage," the Citizen said, giving him a momentary stare. Stile realized that the matter had been covered up to prevent embarrassment to the various parties. The hospital would not want to admit that an isolated pair of serfs had overcome four androids and a doctor, and made good their escape despite an organized search, and the Citizen did not want his name associated with such a scandal. This

56

meant, in turn, that Stile was not in the trouble he had thought he was. No complaint had been lodged.

"Sir, I feared a complication in the surgery," Stile said. Even for a Citizen, he was not about to lie. But there seemed to be no point in making an issue of the particular happenings at the hospital.

"Your paramour feared a complication," the Citizen corrected him. "An investigation was made. There was no threat to your welfare at the hospital. There will be no threat. Will you now return for the surgery?"

The way had been smoothed. One word, and Stile's career and standing would be restored without blemish.

"No, sir," Stile said, surprising himself. "I do not believe my life is safe if I become able to race again."

"Then you are fired." There was not even regret or anger on the Citizen's face as he faded out; he had simply cut his losses.

"I'm sorry," Sheen said, coming to him. "I may have protected you physically, but—"

Stile kissed her, though now he held the image of her breasts being carried like platters in her hands, there in the hospital. She was very good, for what she was— but she was still a machine, assembled from nonliving substances. He felt guilty for his reservation, but could not abolish it.

Then he had another regret. "Battleaxe—who will ride the horse, now? No one but I can handle—"

"He will be retired to stud," she said. "He won't fight that."

The screen lit again. Stile answered again. This time it was a sealed transmission: flashing lights and noise in the background, indicating the jamming that protected it from interception. Except, ironically, that this *was* an interception; the machine had done its job better than the caller could know.

It was another Citizen. His clothing was clear, including a tall silk hat, but the face was fuzzed out, making him anonymous. His voice, too, was blurred. "I understand you are available, Stile," the man said.

News spread quickly! "I am available for employment, sir," Stile agreed. "But I am unable to race on horseback."

"I propose to transplant your brain into a good android body fashioned in your likeness. This would be indistinguishable on casual inspection from your original self, with excellent knees. You could race again. I have an excellent stable—"

"A cyborg?" Stile asked. "A human brain in a synthetic body? This would not be legal for competition." Apart from that, the notion was abhorrent.

"No one would know," the Citizen said smoothly. "Because your brain would be the original, and your body form and capacity identical, there would be no cause for suspicion."

No one would know—except the entire self-willed machine community, at this moment listening in. And Stile himself, who would be living a lie. And he was surely being lied to, as well; if brain transplant into android body was so good, why didn't Citizens use that technique for personal immortality? Quite likely the android system could not maintain a genuinely living brain indefinitely; there would be slow erosion of intelligence and/or sanity, until that person was merely another brute creature. This was no bargain offer in any sense!

"Sir, I was just fired because I refused to have surgery on my knees. What makes you suppose I want surgery on my head?"

This bordered on insolence, but the Citizen took it in stride. Greed conquered all! "Obviously you were disgusted at the penny-pinching mode of your former employer. Why undertake the inconvenience of partial restoration, when you could have a complete renovation?"

Complete renovation: the removal of his brain! "Sir —thank you—no."

"No?" Fuzzy as it was, the surprise was still apparent. No serf said no to a Citizen!

"Sir, I decline your kind offer. I will never race again."

"Now look—I'm making you a good offer! What more do you want?"

58

"Sir, I want to retire from horse racing." And Stile wondered: could this be the one who had had him lasered? If so, this was a test call, and Stile was giving the correct responses.

"I am putting a guard on your apartment, Stile. You will not be allowed to leave until you come to terms with me."

That did not sound like a gratified enemy! "I'll complain to the Citizen council—"

"Your calls will be nulled. You can not complain."

"Sir, you can't do that. As a serf I have at least the right to terminate my tenure, rather than—"

"Ha ha," the Citizen said without humor. "Get this, Stile: you will race for me or you will never get out of your apartment. I am not wishy-washy like your former employer. What I want, I get—and I want you on my horses."

"You play a hard game, sir."

"It is the only kind for the smart person. But I can be generous to those who cooperate. What is your answer now? My generosity will decline as time passes, but not my determination."

Unsubtle warning. Stile trusted neither this man's purported generosity nor his constancy. Power had certainly corrupted, in this case. "I believe I will walk out of my apartment now," he said. "Please ask your minions to stand aside."

"Don't be a fool."

Stile cocked one finger in an obscene gesture at the screen.

Even through the blur, he could see the Citizen's eyes expand. "You dare!" the man cried. "You impertinent runt! I'll have you dismembered for this!"

Stile broke the connection. "I shouldn't have done that," he said with satisfaction. But the rogue Citizen had stung him with that word "runt." Stile had no reason to care what such a man thought of him, yet the term was so freighted with derogation, extending right back into his childhood, that he could not entirely fend it off. *Damn him!*

"Your life is now in direct jeopardy," the anonymous

machine said. "Soon that Citizen will realize he has been tricked, and he is already angry. We can conceal your location for a time, but if the Citizen makes a full-scale effort, he will find you. You must obtain the participatory protection of another Citizen quickly."

"I can only do that by agreeing to race," Stile said. "For one Citizen or another. I fear that is doom."

"The machines will help you hide," Sheen said.

"If the Citizen puts a tracer on you, we can not help you long," the spokesone said. "It would be damaging to our secrecy, and would also constitute violation of our oath not to act against the interest of your kind, ironic as that may be in this circumstance. We must obey direct orders."

"Understood. Suppose I develop an uncommon facility for diverting machines to my use?" Stile asked. "No machine helps me voluntarily, since it is known that machines do not possess free will. I merely have more talent than I have evidenced before."

"This would be limited. We prefer to assist you in modes of our own choosing. However, should you be captured and interrogated—"

"I know. The first sapient-machine-controlled test will accidentally wipe me out, before any critical information escapes."

"We understand each other. The drugs and mechanisms Citizens have available for interrogation negate any will-to-resist any person has. Only death can abate that power."

Grim truth. Stile put it out of his mind. "Come on, Sheen—*you* can help me actively. It's your directive, remember."

"I remember," she said, smiling. As a robot she did not need to sleep, so he had had her plug in to humor information while he was sleeping. Now she had a much better notion of the forms. Every error of human characterization she made was followed in due course by remedial research, and it showed. "But I doubt there is any warrant out on you. The hospital matter is null, and the second Citizen's quarrel with you is private. If we could nullify him, there should be no bar to your finding compatible employment elsewhere."

Stile caught her arm, swung her in close, and kissed her. His emotions were penduluming; at the moment it was almost as if he loved her.

"There is no general warrant on Stile," the spokes-one said. "The anonymous Citizen still has androids guarding your apartment."

"Then let's identify that Citizen! Maybe he's the one who had me lasered, just to get me on his horses." But he didn't really believe that. The lasering had been too sophisticated a move for this particular Citizen. "Do we have a recording of his call?"

"There is a recording," the local machine, Techtwo, said. "But it can not be released prior to the expiration of the mandatory processing period for private calls. To do so before then would be to indicate some flaw or perversion of the processing machinery."

Just so. A betrayal of the nature of these machines. They had to play by the rules. "What is the prescribed time delay?"

"Seven days."

"So if I can file that recording in a memory bank, keyed for publication on my demise, that would protect me from further harassment by that particular Citizen. He's not going to risk exposure by having that tape analyzed by the Citizen security department."

"You can't file it for a week," Sheen said. "And if that Citizen catches up to you in the interim—"

"Let's not rehash the obvious." They moved out of the chamber. The machines did not challenge them, or show in any way that the equipment was other than what it seemed to be. But Stile had a new awareness of robotics!

It was good to merge with the serf populace again. Many serfs served their tenures only for the sake of the excellent payment they would receive upon expiration, but Stile was emotionally committed to Proton. He knew the system had faults, but it also had enormous luxury. And it had the Game.

"I'm hungry," he said. "But my food dispenser is in my apartment. Maybe a public unit—"

"You dare not appear in a public dining hall!" Sheen said, alarmed. "All food machines are monitored, and your ID may have been circulated. It does not have to be a police warrant; the anonymous Citizen may merely have a routine location-check on you, that will not arouse suspicion."

"True. How about your ID? They wouldn't bother putting a search on a machine, and you aren't registered as a serf. You are truly anonymous."

"That is so. I can get you food, if I go to a unit with no flesh-sensing node. I will have to eat it myself, then regurgitate it for you."

Stile quailed, but knew it to be the best course. The food would be sanitary, despite appearances. Since food was freely available all over Proton, a serf carrying it away from the dispenser would arouse suspicion —the last thing they wanted. "Make it something that won't change much, like nutro-pudding."

She parked him in a toolshed and went to forage for food. All the fundamental necessities of life were free, in this society. Tenure, not economics, was the governing force. This was another reason few serfs wanted to leave; once acclimatized to this type of security, a person could have trouble adjusting to the outside galaxy.

Soon she returned. She had no bowl or spoon, as these too would have been suspicious. She had had to use them to eat on the dispenser premises, then put them into the cleaning system. "Hold out your hands," she said.

Stile cupped his hands. She leaned over and heaved out a double handful of yellow pudding. It was warm and slippery and so exactly like vomit that his stomach recoiled. But Stile had trained for eating contests too, including the obnoxious ones; it was all part of the Game. Nutro-food could be formed into the likeness of almost anything, including animal droppings or lubricating oil. He pretended this was a Game—which in its way it was—and slurped up his pudding. It was actually quite good. Then he found a work-area relief chamber and got cleaned up.

"An alarm has been sprung," a machine voice murmured as the toilet flushed.

Stile moved out in a hurry. He knew that the anonymous Citizen had put a private survey squad on the project; now that they had Stile's scent, the execution squad would be dispatched. That squad would be swift and effective, hesitating only to make sure Stile's demise seemed accidental, so as not to arouse suspicion. Citizens seldom liked to advertise their little indiscretions. That meant he could anticipate subtle but deadly threats to his welfare. Sheen would try to protect him, of course—but a smart execution squad would take that into consideration. It would be foolish to stand and wait for the attempt.

"Let's lose ourselves in a crowd," Stile suggested. "There's no surer way to get lost than that."

"Several objections," Sheen said. "You can't stay in a crowd indefinitely; the others all have places to go, and you don't; your continued presence in the halls will become evident to the routine crowd-flow monitors, and suspicious. Also, you will tire; you must have rest and sleep periodically. And your enemy agents can lose themselves in the crowd, and attack you covertly from that concealment. Now that the hunt is on, a throng is not safe at all."

"You're too damn logical," Stile grumped.

"Oh, Stile—I'm afraid for you!" she exclaimed.

"That's not a bad approximation of the relevant attitude."

"I wasn't acting. I love you."

"You're too damn emotional."

She grabbed him and kissed him passionately. "I know you can't love me," she said. "You've seen me as I am, and I feel your withdrawal. But oh, I exist to guard you from harm, and I am slowly failing to do that, and in this week while you need me most—isn't that somewhere close to an approximation of human love?"

They were in a machine-access conduit, alone. Stile

embraced her, though what she said was true. He could not love a nonliving thing. But he was grateful to her, and did like her. It was indeed possible to approximate the emotion she craved. "This week," he agreed.

His hands slid down her smooth body, but she drew back. "There's nothing I'd like better," she whispered. "But there is murder on your trail, and I must keep you from it. We must get you to some safe place. Then—"

"You're too damn practical." But he wondered, now, if a living girl in Sheen's likeness were substituted for her, would he really know the difference? To speak readiness while withdrawing—that was often woman's way. But he let her go and moved out again. After all, he was withdrawing from her much more than she was withdrawing from him.

"I think we can hide you in—"

"Don't say it," he cautioned her. "The walls have monitors. Just take me there—by a roundabout route, so we can lose the pursuit."

"In a reasonably short time," she finished.

"Oh. I thought you were going to say—oh, never mind. Take me to your hideout."

She nodded, drawing him forward. He noted the way her slender body flexed; had he not seen her dismantle parts of it, he would hardly have believed it was not natural flesh. And did it matter, that it was not? If a living woman were dismantled, the result would be quite messy; it was not the innards a man wanted, but the externals. Regardless, Sheen was quite a female.

They emerged into a concourse crowded with serfs. Now she was taking his suggestion about merging with a crowd, at least for the moment. This channel led to the main depot for transport to other domes. Could they take a flight to a distant locale and lose the pursuit that way? Stile doubted it; any citizen could check any flight at the touch of a button. But if they did not, where would they go?

And, his thoughts continued ruthlessly, assuming she was able to hide him, and smuggled food to him—ah, joy: to live for a week on regurgitations!—and took care of his other needs—would she have to tote away his bodily wastes by hand, too?—so that he survived the necessary time—what then would he do for employment? Serfs were allowed a ten-day grace period between employers. After that their tenure was canceled and they were summarily deported. That meant he would have just three days to find a Citizen who could use his services—in a nonracing capacity. Stile's doubt that the anonymous Citizen after him was the same one who had sent Sheen or lasered his knee had grown and firmed. It just didn't fit. This meant there was another party involved, a more persistent and intelligent enemy, from whom he would never be safe—if he raced again.

A middle-aged serf stumbled and lunged against Stile. "Oops, sorry, junior," the man exclaimed, putting up a hand to steady Stile.

Sheen whirled with remarkable rapidity. Her open hand struck the man's wrist with nerve-stunning force. An ampule flew from his palm to shatter on the floor. "Oops, sorry, senior," she said, giving him a brief but hostile stare. The man backed hastily away and was gone.

That ampule—the needle would have touched Stile's flesh, had the man's hand landed. What had it contained? Nothing good for his health, surely! Sheen had intercepted it; she did know her business. He couldn't even thank her, at the moment, lest he give her away.

They moved on. Now there was no doubt: the enemy had him spotted, and the death squad was present. Sheen's caution about the crowd had been well considered; they could not remain here. He, Stile, was no longer hidden; his enemies were. The next ampule might score, perhaps containing a hypno-drug that would cause him to commit suicide or agree to a brain transplant. He didn't even dare look nervously about!

Sheen, with gentle pressure on his elbow, guided him into a cross-passage leading to a rest room. This one, for reasons having to do with the hour and direction of flow, was unused at the moment. It was dusk, and most serfs were eager to return to their residences, not delaying on the way.

She gave him a little shove ahead, but stayed back herself. Oh—she was going to ambush the pursuit, if there were any. Stile played along, marching on down to the rest room and stepping through its irising portal. Actually, he was in need of the facility. He had a reputation for nerve like iron in the Game, but never before had he been exposed to direct threats against his life. He felt tense and ill. He was now dependent on Sheen for initiative; he felt like locking himself into a relief booth and hiding his head under his arms. A useless gesture, of course.

The portal irised for another man. This one looked about quickly, saw that the facility was empty except for Stile, and advanced on him. "So you attack me, do you?" the stranger growled, flexing his muscular arms. He was large, even for this planet's healthy norm, and the old scars on his body hinted at his many prior fights. He probably had a free-for-all specialty in the Game, indulging in his propensity for unnecessary violence.

Stile rose hastily from his seat. How had Sheen let this torpedo through?

The man swung at Stile. One thing about nakedness: there were few concealed weapons. The blow, of course, never landed. Stile dodged, skipped around, and let the man stumble into the commode. Then Stile stepped quickly out through the iris. He could readily have injured or knocked out the man, for Stile himself was a combat specialist of no mean skill, but preferred to keep it neat and clean.

Sheen was there. "Did he touch you?" she asked immediately. "Or you him?"

"As it happens, no. I didn't see the need—"

She breathed a humanlike sigh of relief. "I let him through, knowing you could handle him, so I could verify how many others there were, and of what type they were." She gestured down the hall. Three bodies lay there. "If I had taken him out, the others might not have come, and the trap would have remained unsprung. But when I met the others, I comprehended the trap. They're all coated with stun-powder. Can't hurt

66

me, can't hurt them—they're neutralized android stock. But you—"

Stile nodded. He had assumed he was being set up for an assault charge if he won, so had played it safe by never laying a finger on the man. Lucky for him!

Sheen gestured toward the Lady's room, her hands closed. Stile knew why; she had the powder on her hands, and could not touch him until she washed it off.

Stile poked his arm through the iris to open it for her—and someone on the other side grabbed his wrist. Oh-oh! He put his head down and dove through, primed to fight.

But it was only a crude matron robot. "No males allowed here," she said primly. She had recognized the male arm and acted immediately, as she was supposed to.

Sheen came through, touched the robot, and it went dead. "I have shorted her out, temporarily." She went to a sink and ran water over her hands. Then she stepped into an open shower and washed her whole body, with particular attention to any portion that might have come into contact with the powdered androids.

Stile heard something. "Company," he said. How was he going to get out of this one? The only exit was the iris through which the next woman would be entering.

Sheen beckoned him into the shower. He stepped in with her as the door irised. Sheen turned the spray on to FOG. Thick mist blasted out of the nozzle, concealing them both in its evanescent substance. It was faintly scented with rose: to make the lady smell nice.

In this concealment, Sheen's arms went about him, and her hungry lips found his. She evidently needed frequent proof of her desirability as a woman, just as he needed proof of his status as a man. Because each was constantly subject, in its fashion, to question. What an embrace!

When the room was clear again, Sheen turned the shower to rinse, then to dry. They had to separate for these stages, to Stile's regret. He had swung again from one extreme to another in his attitude toward her. Right now he wanted to make love—and knew this was not the occasion for it. But some other time, when they were safe, he would get her in a shower, turn on the fog, and—

Sheen stepped out and ran her fingers along the wall beside the shower stall. In a moment she found what she wanted, and slid open a panel. Another access for servicing machinery. She gestured him inside.

They wedged between pipes and came out in a narrow passage between the walls of the Man's and Lady's rooms. This passage wound around square corners, then dropped to a lower deck where it opened out into a service-machine storage chamber. Most of the machines were out, since night was their prime operating time, but several specialized ones remained in their niches. These were being serviced by a maintenance machine. At the moment it was cleaning a pipefitting unit, using static electricity to magnetize the grime and draw it into a collector scoop. The maintenance machine was in the aisle, so they had to skirt it to traverse this room.

Suddenly the machine lurched. Sheen slapped her hand on the machine's surface. A spark flashed, and there was the odor of ozone. The machine died, short-circuited.

"Why did you do that?" Stile asked her, alarmed. "If we start shorting out maintenance machines, it will call attention—"

Sheen did not respond. Then he saw the scorch mark along her body. She had taken a phenomenal charge of current. That charge would have passed through him, had he brushed the machine—as he had been about to, since it had lurched into the aisle as he approached. Another assassination attempt, narrowly averted!

But at what cost? Sheen still stood, unmoving. "Are you all right?" Stile asked, knowing she was not.

She neither answered nor moved. She, too, had been shorted by the charge. She was, in her fashion, dead.

"I hope it's just the power pack, not the brain," he

said. Her power supply had, she had thought, been weakened by her disassembly during the bomb scare. "We can replace the power pack." And if that did not work? He chose not to ponder that.

He went to a sweeping machine, opened its motive unit, and removed the standard protonite power pack. A little protonite went a long way; such a pack lasted a year with ordinary use. There was nothing to match it in the galaxy. In fact, the huge protonite lode was responsible for the inordinate wealth of Planet Proton. All the universe needed power, and this was the most convenient power available.

Stile brought the pack to Sheen. He hoped her robot-structure was standard in this respect; he didn't want to waste time looking for her power site. What made her special was her brain-unit, not her body, though that became easy to forget when he held her in his arms. Men thought of women in terms of their appearance, but most men were fools—and Stile was typical. Yet if Sheen's prime directive and her superficial form were discounted, she would hardly differ from the cleanup machines. So *was* it foolish to be guided by appearance and manner?

He ran his fingers over her belly, pressing the navel. Most humanoid robots—ah, there! A panel sprang out, revealing the power site. He hooked out the used power pack, still hot from its sudden discharge, and plugged in the new.

Nothing happened. Alarm tightened his chest. Oh—there would naturally be a safety-shunt, to cut off the brain from the body during a short, to preserve it. He checked about and finally located it: a reset switch hidden under her tongue. He depressed this, and Sheen came back to life.

She snapped her belly-panel closed. "Now I owe you one, Stile," she said.

"Are we keeping count? I need you—in more ways than two."

She smiled. "I'd be satisfied being needed for just one thing."

"That, too."

69

She glanced at him. She seemed more vibrant than before, as if the new power pack had given her an extra charge. She moved toward him.

There was a stir back the way they had come. It might be a machine, returning from a routine mission—but they did not care to gamble on that. Obviously they had not yet lost the enemy.

Sheen took him to the service side of a large feeding station. Silently she indicated the empty crates. A truck came once or twice a day to deliver new crates of nutro-powder and assorted color-flavor-textures, and to remove the expended shells. From these ingredients were fashioned the wide variety of foods the machines provided, from the vomitlike pudding to authentic-seeming carrots. It was amazing what technology could do. Actually, Stile had once tasted a real carrot from his employer's genuine exotic foods garden patch, a discard, and it had not been quite identical to the machine-constituted vegetable. As it happened, Stile preferred the taste and texture of the fake carrots with which he was familiar. But Citizens cultivated the taste for real foods.

He could hide inside one of these in fair comfort for several hours. Sheen would provide him with food; though this was *the* region for food, it was all sealed in its cartons, and would be inedible even if he could get one open. Only the machines, with their controlled temperature and combining mechanisms and recipe programs, could reconstitute the foods properly, and he was on the wrong side of their wall.

Stile climbed into a crate. Sheen walked on, so as not to give his position away. She would try to mislead the pursuit. If this worked, they would be home free for a day, perhaps for the whole week. Stile made himself halfway comfortable, and peered out through a crack.

No sooner had Sheen disappeared than a mech-mouse appeared. It twittered as it sniffed along, following their trail. It paused where Stile's trail diverged from Sheen's, confused, then proceeded on after her.

Stile relaxed, but not completely. Couldn't tell the difference between a robot and a man? Sniffers were

70

better than that! He should have taken some precaution to minimize or mask his personal smell, for it was a sure giveaway—

Oh, Sheen had done that. She had given him a scented shower. The mouse was following the trail of rose—and Sheen's scent was now the same as his. A living hound should have been able to distinguish the two, but in noses, as in brains, the artificial had not yet closed the gap. Fortunately.

But soon that sniffer, or another like it, would return to trace the second trail, and would locate him. He would have to do something about that.

Stile climbed out of his box, suffered a pang in one knee, ran to his original trail, followed it a few paces, and diverged to another collection of crates. Then back, and to a truck-loading platform, where he stopped and retreated. With luck, it would seem he had caught a ride on the vehicle. Then he looped about a few more times, and returned to his original crate. Let the sniffers solve *that* puzzle!

But the sniffer did not return, and no one else came. This tracking operation must have been set up on the simplistic assumption that as long as the sniffer was moving, it was tracking him. His break—perhaps.

Time passed. The night advanced. Periodically the food machines exhausted a crate of cartons and ejected it, bumping the row along. Stile felt hungry again, but knew this was largely psychological; that double handful of regurgitated pudding should hold him a while yet.

Where was Sheen? Was she afraid to return to him while the sniffer was tracking her? She would have to neutralize the mech-mouse. Far from here, to distract suspicion from his actual hiding place. He would have to wait.

He watched anxiously. He dared not sleep or let down his guard until Sheen cleared him. He was dependent on her, and felt guilty about it. She was a nice . . . person, and should not have to—

A man walked down the hall. Stile froze—but this did not seem to be a pursuer. The man walked on.

Stile blinked. The man was gone. Had Stile been

nodding, and not seen the man depart—or was the stranger still near, having ducked behind a crate? In that case this could be a member of the pursuit squad. A serious matter.

Stile did not dare leave his crate now, for that would give away his position instantly. But if the stranger were of the squad, he would have a body-heat scope on a laser weapon. One beam through the crate—the murder would be anonymous, untraceable. There were criminals on Proton, cunning people who skulked about places like this, avoiding capture. Serfs whose tenure had expired, but who refused to be deported. The Citizens seldom made a concerted effort to eradicate them, perhaps because criminals had their uses on certain occasions. Such as this one? One more killing, conveniently unsolved, attributed to the nefarious criminal class—who never killed people against the wishes of Citizens. A tacit understanding. Why investigate the loss of an unemployed serf?

Should he move—or remain still? This was like the preliminary grid of the Game. If the stranger were present, and if he were a killer, and if he had spotted Stile—then to remain here was to die. But if Stile moved, he was sure to betray his location, and might die anyway. His chances seemed best if he stayed.

And—nothing happened. Time passed, and there was no further evidence of the man. So it must have been a false alarm. Stile began to feel foolish, and his knees hurt; he had unconsciously put tension on them, and they could not stand up to much of that, anymore.

Another man came, walking as the other had. This was a lot of traffic for a nonpersonal area like this, at this time of night. Suspicious in itself. Stile watched him carefully.

The man walked without pause down the hall—and vanished. He did not step to one side, or duck down; he simply disappeared.

Stile stared. He was a good observer, even through a crack in a crate; he had not mistaken what he had seen. Yet this was unlike anything he knew of on Planet Proton. Matter transmission did not exist, as far as he knew—but if it did, this was what it would be like. A screen, through which a person could step—to another location, instantly. Those two men—

Yet Sheen had gone that way without disappearing, and so had the mech-mouse. So there could not be such a screen set up across the hall. Not a permanent one.

Should he investigate? This could be important! But it could also be another trap. Again, like a Game-grid: what was the best course, considering the resources and strategy of his anonymous enemy?

Stile decided to stand pat. He had evidently lost the pursuit, and these disappearing people did not relate to him. He had just happened to be in a position to observe them. Perhaps this was not coincidental. The same concealment this service hall offered for him, it offered for them. If they had a private matter transmitter that they wanted to use freely without advertising it, this was the sort of place to set it up.

Yet aspects of this theory disturbed him. How could serfs have a matter transmitter, even if such a device existed? No serf owned anything, not even clothing for special occasions, for working outside the domes or in dangerous regions. Everything was provided by the system, as needed. There was no money, no medium of exchange; accounts were settled only when tenure ended. Serfs could not make such a device, except by adapting it from existing machines—and pretty precise computer accounts were kept, for sophisticated equipment. When such a part was lost, the machine tally gave the alarm. Which was another reason a criminal could not possess a laser weapon without at least tacit Citizen approval.

Also, why would any serf possessing such a device remain a serf? He could sell it to some galactic interest and retire on another planet with a fortune to rival that of a Proton Citizen. That would certainly be his course, for Citizens were unlikely to be too interested in forwarding development and production of a transport system that did not utilize protonite. Why destroy their monopoly?

Could the self-willed machines be involved in this? They might have the ability. But those were *men* he had seen disappear, and the machines would not have betrayed their secret to men.

No, it seemed more likely that this was an espionage operation, in which spies were ferried in and out of this dome, perhaps from another planet, or to and from some secret base elsewhere on Proton. If so, what would this spying power do to a genuine serf who stumbled upon the secret?

A woman appeared in the hall. She had emerged full-formed from the invisible screen, as it were from nowhere. She was of middle age, not pretty, and there was something odd about her. She had marks on her body as if the flesh had recently been pressed by something. By clothing, perhaps.

Serfs wore clothing on the other side? Only removing it for decent concealment in this society? These *had* to be from another world!

Stile peered as closely as possible at the region of disappearances. Now he perceived a faint shimmer, as of a translucent curtain crossing the hall obliquely. Behind it there seemed to be the image of trees.

Trees—in a matter-transmission station? This did not quite jibe! Unless it was not a city there, but a park. But why decorate such equipment this way? Camouflage?

Stile had no good answers. He finally put himself into a light trance, attuned to any other extraordinary events, and rested.

"Stile," someone called softly. "Stile."

It was Sheen, back at last! Stile looked down the hall and spied her, walking slowly, as if she had forgotten his whereabouts. Had she had another brush with a charged machine? "Here," he said, not loudly.

She turned and came toward him. "Stile."

"You lost the pursuit," he told her, standing in the crate so that his head and shoulders were clear. "No one even checked. But there is something else—"

Her hand shot out to grab his wrist with a grip like that of a vise. Stile was strong, but could not match the

74

strength of a robot who was not being femininely human. What was she doing?

Her other hand smashed into the crate. The plastic shattered. Stile twisted aside, avoiding the blow despite remaining inside the crate; it was an automatic reaction. "Sheen, what—?"

She struck again. She was attacking him! He twisted aside again, drawing her off balance, using the leverage of her own grip on him. She was strong, but not heavy; he could move her about. Strength was only one element in combat; many people did not realize this, to their detriment.

Either Sheen had somehow been turned against him, which would have taken a complete reprogramming, or this was not Sheen. He suspected the latter; Sheen had known where he was hiding, while this robot had had to call. He had been a fool to answer, to reveal himself.

She struck again, and he twisted again. This was definitely not Sheen, for she had far greater finesse than this. It was not even a smart robot; it was a stupid mechanical. Good; he could handle it, despite its strength. Ethically and physically.

Her right hand remained clamped on his left wrist, while her left fist did the striking. Holding and hitting! If any of those blows landed squarely, he would suffer broken bones—but he was experienced in avoiding such an elementary attack. He turned about toward his left, drawing her hand and arm along with him, until he faced away from her, his right shoulder blocking hers. He heaved into a wraparound throw. She had to let go, or be hurled into the crate headfirst.

She was too stupid to let go. She crashed into the crate. Now at last her grip wrenched free, taking skin off his wrist. Stile scrambled out of the wrecked crate. He could junk her, now that he knew what she was, because he knew a great deal more about combat than she did. But he couldn't be *quite* sure she wasn't Sheen, with some override program on her, damping out most of her intellect and forcing her to obey the crude command. If he hurt her—

The robot scrambled out of the crate and advanced

75

on him. Her pretty face was smirched with dirt, and her hair was in disarray. Her right breast seemed to have been pounded slightly out of shape; a bad fall from the wraparound throw could account for that. Stile backed away, still torn by indecision. He could overcome this robot, but he would have to demolish her in the process. If only he could be *sure* she wasn't—

Another Sheen appeared. "Stile!" she cried. "Get under cover! The squad is—" Then she recognized the other robot. "Oh, no! The old duplicate-image stunt!"

Stile had no doubt now: the second Sheen was the right one. But the first one had done half her job. She had routed him out and distracted him—too long. For now the android squad hove into sight, several lumbering giants.

"I'll hold them!" Sheen cried. "Run!"

But more androids were coming from the other end of the hall. It seemed the irate Citizen no longer cared about being obvious; he just wanted Stile dispatched. If these lunks were also powdered with stun-dust or worse—

Stile charged down the hall and lunged into the matter-transmission curtain, desperately hoping it would work for him. The androids might follow—but they could be in as much trouble as he, at the other end. Intruding strangers. That would give him a better fighting chance. He felt a tingle as he went through.

CHAPTER 5

Fantasy

Stile drew up in a deep forest. The smell of turf and fungus was strong, and old leaves crackled underfoot. The light from four moons beamed down between the branches to illuminate the ground. It would have been near dawn, on Proton; it seemed to be the same time of day here. The same number of moons as Proton, too; there were seven, with three or four usually in sight. Gravity, however, seemed close to Earth-normal, so if this was really outside a dome, it was a spot on a larger or denser planet than Proton.

He turned to face his pursuers—but there were none. They had not passed through the shimmering curtain. He looked carefully, locating it—and saw, dimly, the light at the hall he had left, with the scattered crates. Sheen was there—one of them—and several androids. One android came right at him—and disappeared.

Stile watched, determined to understand this phenomenon, because it reflected most directly on his immediate welfare. He had passed through—but the robots and androids had not. This thing transmitted only human beings? Not artificial ones? That might be reasonable. But he hesitated to accept that until there was more data.

In his absence the fight on the other side of the curtain soon abated. The androids and fake-Sheen departed, apparently on his trail again—a false one. Only the real Sheen remained, as the squad evidently considered her irrelevant—and it seemed she could not perceive either him or the curtain.

Stile decided to risk crossing back, if only to tell her he was safe. There was risk, as the squad could be lurking nearby, hoping Sheen would lead them to him again—but he could not leave her tormented by doubt. This could be a much better hideout than the crate! He stepped through the curtain—and found himself still in the dark forest. He had crossed without being matter-transmitted back.

He looked back—and there it was, behind him. Through it he saw the imprint of his feet in the soft forest loam, the leaves and tufts of grass and moss all pressed flat for the moment. And, like a half-reflection, the square of light of the service hall, now empty.

He passed through the curtain a third time. There was no tingle, no sensation. He turned about and looked through—and saw Sheen searching for him, unrobotic alarm on her cute face. Oh, yes, she cared!

"I'm here, Sheen!" he called, passing his hand through. But his hand did not reach her; it remained in the forest. She gave no evidence of seeing or hearing him.

She would think him dead—and that bothered him more than the notion of being trapped this side of the matter-transmission screen. If she thought him dead, she would consider her mission a failure, and then turn herself off, in effect committing suicide. He did not want her to do that—no, not at all!

"Sheen!" he cried, experiencing a surge of emotion. "Sheen—look at me! I'm caught here beyond a one-way transmit—" But if it really were one-way, of course she would not be able to see him! However, it had to be two-way, because he had seen people traveling both ways through the curtain, and he had seen the forest from Proton, and could now see Proton from the forest. "Sheen!" he cried again, his urgency almost choking him.

Her head snapped around. *She had heard him!*

Stile waved violently. "Here! Here, Sheen! Through the curtain!"

Her gaze finally fixed on him. She reached through the curtain—and did not touch him. "Stile—" Her voice was faint.

He grabbed her hands in his, with no physical contact; their fingers phased through each other like images, like superimposing holographs. "Sheen, we are in two different worlds! We can not touch. But I'm safe here." He hoped.

"Safe?" she asked, trying to approach him. But as she passed through the curtain, she disappeared. Stile quickly stepped across himself, turning—and there she was on the other side, facing away from him, looking down the hall.

She turned and saw him again, with an effort. "Stile —I can't reach you! How can I protect you? Are you a ghost?"

"I'm alive! I crossed once—and can't cross back. It's a whole new world here, a nice one. Trees and grass and moss and earth and fresh air—"

They held hands again, each grasping air. "How—?"

"I don't *know* how to cross! There must be a way to return, because I've seen a woman do it, but until I find out how—"

"I must join you!" She tried again to cross, and failed again. "Oh, Stile—"

"I don't think it works for nonhumans," he said. "But if I can remain here for a week, and find out how to return—"

"I will wait for you," she said, and there was something plaintive in her stance. She wanted so much to protect him from harm, and could not. "Go into that world—maybe it is better for you."

"I will come back—when I can," Stile promised.

He saw the tears in her eyes. To hell with the assorted humanoid artifices such robots were programmed with; she meant it! Stile spread his arms, at the verge of the curtain. She opened hers, and they embraced intangibly, and kissed air, and vanished from each other's perception.

He had promised—but would he be able to keep that pledge? He didn't know, and he worried that Sheen would maintain her vigil long after hope was gone, suffering as only a virtually immortal robot could suffer. That hurt him, even in anticipation. Sheen did not deserve to be a machine.

Stile did not tease himself or Sheen further. He

79

strode on through the curtain and into the forest. He had a fair knowledge of earthy vegetation, because aspects of the Game required identification of it, and a number of Citizens imported exotic plants. The light was poor, but with concentration, he could manage.

The nearest tree was a huge oak, or a very similar species, with the air-plants called Spanish moss dangling from its branches. Beyond it was a similarly large spruce, or at any rate a conifer; this was the source of that pine-perfume smell. There were large leaves looking like separated hands in the shadow, and pine needles—so there must be a pine tree here somewhere —but mostly this was a glade with fairly well-established grass in the center. Stile liked it very well; it reminded him of an especially exotic Citizen's retreat.

Dawn was coming. There was no dome above, no shimmer of the force field holding in the air. Through the trees he saw the dark clouds of the horizon looming, trying like goblins to hold back the burgeoning light of the sun, and slowly failing. Planet Proton had no such atmospheric effects! Red tinted the edes of the clouds, and white; it was as if a burning fluid were accumulating behind, brimming over, until finally it spilled out and a shaft of scintillating sunlight lanced at lightspeed through the air and struck the ground beside Stile. The whole thing was so pretty that he stood entranced until the sun was fairly up, too bright to look at anymore.

The forest changed, by developing daylight. The somberness was gone—and so was the curtain. That barrier had been tenuous by night; it could still be present, but drowned by the present effulgence. He could not locate it at all. That bothered him, though it probably made no difference. He walked about, examining the trees; some had flowers opening, and stray rustlings denoted hidden life. Birds, squirrels—he would find out what they were in due course.

He liked this place. It could have been a private garden, but this was natural, and awesomely extensive.

Caution prevented him from shouting to check for echoes, but he was sure this was the open surface of a planet. Not at all what he would have expected from a matter-transmission outlet.

He found a large bull-spruce—damn it, it *was* a spruce!—its small dry branches radiating out in all directions. This was the most climbable of trees, and Stile of course was an excellent climber. He did not resist the temptation. He mounted that big old tree with a primitive joy.

Soon he was in the upper reaches, and gusts of wind he had not felt below were swaying the dwindling column of the trunk back and forth. Stile loved it. His only concern was the occasional pain in his knees when he tried to bend them too far; he did not want to aggravate the injury carelessly.

At last he approached the reasonable limit of safety. The tops of surrounding trees were dropping below him, their foliage like low hedges from this vantage. He anchored himself by hooking legs and elbows conveniently, and looked about.

The view was a splendor. The forest abutted the cliff-like face of a nearby mountain to one side—south, according to the sun—and thinned to the north into islands of trees surrounded by sealike fields of bright grain. In the distance the trees disappeared entirely, leaving a gently rolling plain on which animals seemed to be grazing. Farther to the north there seemed to be a large river, terminating abruptly in some kind of crevice, and a whitish range of mountains beyond that. To either side all he could see was more forest, a number of the individual trees taller than this one. The mountain to the south faded upward into a purple horizon.

There seemed to be no sign of civilized habitation. This was less and less like a matter-transmission station! Yet if not that, what was it? He had seen other people pass through the curtain, and had done so himself; there had to be something more than a mere wilderness.

He looked again, fixing the geography in his mind for future reference. Then he spied a structure of some sort to the northeast. It looked like a small medieval castle, with high stone walls and turrets, and perhaps a blue pennant.

Very well: human habitation did exist. Yet this remained a far cry from modern technology. He liked this world very well, but he simply didn't trust it. Matter transmission could not exist without an extremely solid industrial base, and if that base were not here, where was it? Was this a sweetly baited trap for people like him, who were in trouble on Proton? In what manner would that trap be sprung?

Stile climbed down. His best course, as he saw it, would be to go to that castle and inquire. But first he wanted to check the region of the curtain again, fixing it absolutely in his mind so he could find it any time he wanted to—because this was his only contact with his own world, and with Sheen. This wilderness-world might be an excellent place to stay for a while, but then he would need to go home, lest he suffer exile by default.

He was approaching the invisible curtain—when a man popped out of it. Friend or foe? Stile decided not to risk contact, but the man spied him before he could retreat to cover. "Hey—get lost?" the stranger called. "It's over here."

"Uh, yes," Stile said, approaching. This did not seem to be an android or robot. Abruptly deciding not to compromise on integrity even by implication, he added: "I came through by accident. I don't know where I am."

"Oh, a new one! I first crossed last year. Took me six months to learn the spells to cross back. Now I go over for free meals, but I live over here in Phaze."

"Spells—to cross back?" Stile asked blankly.

"How else? From the other side you just have to will-to-cross hard enough, but from this side only a spell will do it—a new one every time. You'll get the hang of it."

"I—thought this was a matter-transmission unit."

The man laughed as he walked to a tree and reached into the foliage of a low branch. A package came down into his hands. "There's no such thing as matter transmission! No, it's the magic curtain. It's all over—but it's not safe to use it just anywhere. You have to make sure no one on the other side sees you go through. You know how those Citizens are. If they ever caught on there was something they didn't control—"

"Yes. I am unemployed because of Citizen manipulation."

"Which explains why you had the will-to-cross, first time. The curtain's been getting clearer, but still you can't even see it if you don't have good reason, let alone use it. Then you have to will yourself through, strongly, right as you touch it. Most people never make it, ever." The man opened his package and brought out a crude tunic, which he donned.

Stile stared. "You wear clothes here?" He remembered the clothing-marks on the woman.

"Sure do. You'd stick out like a sore toe if you went naked here in Phaze!" The man paused, appraising Stile. "Look, you're new here, and sort of small—I'd better give you an amulet." He rummaged in his bag, while Stile suppressed his unreasoning resentment of the remark about his size. The man had not intended any disparagement.

"An amulet?" Stile asked after a moment. He considered himself to be swift to adjust to new realities, but he found it hard to credit this man's evident superstition. Spell—magic—amulet—how could a Proton serf revert to medieval Earth lore so abruptly?

"Right. We're supposed to give them to newcomers. To help them get started, keep things smooth, so there's no ruckus about the curtain and all. We've got a good thing going here; could sour if too many people got in on it. So don't go blabbing about the curtain carelessly; it's better to let people discover it by accident."

"I will speak of it only cautiously," Stile agreed. That did make sense, whatever the curtain was, matter transmission or magic.

The man finally found what he was looking for: a statuette hanging on a chain. "Wear this around your neck. It will make you seem clothed properly, until you can work up a real outfit. Won't keep you warm or dry;

83

it's just illusion. But it helps. Then you can pass it on to some other serf when he comes across. Help him keep the secret. Stay anonymous; that's the rule."

"Yes." Stile accepted the amulet. The figure was of a small demon, with horns, tail and hooves, scowling horrendously. "How does this thing work?"

"You just put it on and invoke it. Will it to perform. That's all; it's preset magic that anybody can use. You'll see. You probably don't really believe in magic yet, but this will show you."

"Thank you," Stile said, humoring him.

The man waved negligently as he departed in his tunic and sandals, bearing south. Now Stile made out a faint forest path there, obvious only when one knew where to look. In a moment he was gone.

Stile stared down at the amulet. Belief in magic! The man had spoken truly when he said Stile was a skeptic! Yet the fellow had seemed perfectly sensible in other respects. Maybe it was a figure of speech. Or a practical joke, like an initiation rite. See what foolishness newcomers could be talked into. Emperor's new clothes.

He shook his head. "All right, I won't knock what I haven't tried. I'll play the game—once. Amulet, I invoke you. Do your thing." And he put the chain on over his head.

Suddenly he was strangling. The chain was constricting, cutting off his wind and blood. The amulet seemed to be expanding; its demon-figure holding the ends of the chain in its miniature hands, grinning evilly as it pulled.

Stile did not know how this worked, but he knew how to fight for his life. He ducked his chin down against his neck and tightened his muscles, resisting the constriction of the chain. He hooked a finger into the crease between chin and neck on the side, catching the chain, and yanked. He was trying to break a link, but the delicate-seeming metal was too strong; he was only cutting his finger.

More than one way to fight a garrote! Stile grabbed the grinning demon by its two little arms and hauled them apart. The little monster grimaced, trying to resist, but the chain slackened. Stile took a breath, and felt the trapped blood in his head flow out. Pressure on the jugular vein did not stop the flow of blood to the brain, as many thought; it stopped the return of the blood from the head back to the heart. That was uncomfortable enough, but not instantly conclusive.

But still the demon grew, and as it did its strength increased in proportion. It drew its arms together again, once more constricting the loop about Stile's neck.

Even through his discomfort, Stile managed a double take. The demon was *growing?* Yes it was; he had observed it without noting it. From an amulet a few centimeters long it had become a living creature, swelling horrendously as it fought. Now it was half the size of Stile himself, and fiendishly strong.

Stile held his breath, put both hands on the hands of the demon, and swung it off its feet. He whirled it around in a circle. It was strong—but as with robot strength, this was not sufficient without anchorage or leverage. This was another misconception many people had, assuming that a superman really could leap a mile or pick up a building by one corner or fight invincibly. That belief had cost many Gamesmen their games with Stile—and might cost this demon its own success. As long as the creature clung to the chain, it was in fact captive—and when it let go, even with one hand, it would free Stile from the constant threat of strangulation. That would be a different contest entirely.

The demon clung tenaciously to its misconception. It did not let go. It grinned again, showing more teeth than could fit even in a mouth that size, and clamped its arms yet closer, tightening the noose. Stile felt his consciousness going; he could hold his breath for minutes, but the constriction was slowing his circulation of blood, now squeezing his neck so tightly that the deeply buried carotid artery was feeling it. That could put him out in seconds.

He staggered toward a towering tulip tree, still whirling his burden. He heaved mightily—and smashed the creature's feet into the trunk.

It was quite a blow. The thing's yellow eyes widened,

showing jags of flame-red, and the first sound escaped from it. "Ungh!" Some chain slipped, giving Stile respite, but still the demon did not let go.

Stile hauled it up and whirled it again, with difficulty. He had more strength now, but the demon had continued to grow (how the hell could it do that? This was absolutely crazy!), and was at this point only slightly smaller than Stile himself. It required special power and balance to swing it—but this time its midsection smashed into the tree. Now its burgeoning mass worked against it, making the impact stronger. The demon's legs bent around the trunk with the force of momentum; then they sprang back straight.

Stile reversed his swing, taking advantage of the bounce, bringing the demon around in the opposite arc and smashing it a third time into the tree. This time it was a bone-jarring blow, and a substantial amount of slack developed in the chain.

Stile, alert for this instant, slipped his head free in one convulsive contortion. The chain burned his ears and tore out tufts of his hair—but he had won the first stage of this battle.

But now the demon was Stile's own size, still full of fight. It scrambled to its hooved feet and sprang at him, trying to loop the cord about his neck again. It seemed to be a one-tactic fighter. In that respect it resembled the imitation-Sheen robot Stile had fought not so very long ago.

Stile caught its hands from the outside, whirled, ducked, and hauled the demon over his shoulder. The thing lifted over him and whomped into the ground with a jar that should have knocked it out. But again it scrambled up, still fighting.

What was *with* this thing? It refused to turn off! It had taken a battering that would have shaken an android—and all it did was grow larger and uglier. It was now a quarter again as large as Stile, and seemed to have gained strength in proportion. Stile could not fight it much longer, this way.

Yet again the demon dived for him, chain spread. Stile had an inspiration. He grabbed the chain, stepped to one side, tripped the demon—and as it stumbled, Stile looped the slack chain about the creature's own body and held it there from behind.

The demon roared and turned about, trying to reach him, but Stile clung like a blob of rubber cement. He had discommoded large opponents this way before, clinging to the back; it was extremely hard for a person to rid himself of such a rider if he did not know how. This demon was all growth and strength, having no special intelligence or imagination; it did not know how.

The demon kept growing. Now it was half again as large as Stile—and the chain was beginning to constrict its body. Stile hung on, staying out of the thing's awkward graspings, keeping that chain in place. Unless the demon could stop growing voluntarily—

Evidently it could not. It grew and grew, and as it expanded the chain became tighter, constricting its torso about the middle. It had fallen into the same noose it had tried to use on Stile. All it had to do was let go the ends—and it was too stupid to do that. What colossal irony! Its own arms wrapped around it, being drawn nearly out of their sockets, but the only way it knew to fight was to hang on to that chain. It became woman-waisted, then wasp-waisted. Stile let go and stood apart, watching the strange progression. The creature seemed to feel no pain; it still strove to reach Stile, to wrap its chain about him, though this was now impossible.

The demon's body ballooned, above and below that tiny waist. Then it popped. There was a cloud of smoke, dissipating rapidly.

Stile looked at the ground. There lay the chain, broken at last, separated where the demon-figure had been. The amulet was gone.

He picked it up, nervous about what it might do, but determined to know what remained. It dangled loosely from his hand. Its power was gone.

Or was it? What would happen if he invoked it again? Stile decided that discretion was best. He coiled the chain, laid it on the ground, and rolled a rock to cover it. Let the thing stay there, pinned like a poisonous snake!

Now that the threat was over, Stile unwound. His body was shivering with reaction. What, exactly, had happened? What was the explanation for it?

He postulated and discarded a number of theories. He prided himself on his ability to analyze any situation correctly and swiftly; that was a major part of his Game success. What he concluded here, as the most reasonable hypothesis fitting all his observations, was quite *unreasonable*.

A. He was in a world where magic worked.

B. Someone/thing was trying to kill him here, too.

He found conclusion A virtually incredible. But he preferred it to the alternatives: that a super-technological power had created all this, or that he, Stile, was going crazy. Conclusion B was upsetting—but death threats against him had become commonplace in the past few hours. So it was best to accept the evidence of his experience: that he was now in a fantasy realm, and still in trouble.

Stile rubbed his fingers across his neck, feeling the burn of the chain. Who was after him, here? Surely not the same anonymous angry Citizen who had sent the android squads. The serf who had crossed the curtain and given him the amulet had been friendly; had he wanted to kill Stile, he could have done so by invoking the demon at the outset. It seemed more likely that the man had been genuinely trying to help—and that the amulet had acted in an unforeseen manner. Perhaps there were a number of such magic talismans, dual-purpose: clothe the ordinary person, kill certain other persons. Other persons like Stile. That left a lot in doubt, but accounted for what had happened. Stile was a fair judge of people and motives; nothing about the other man had signaled treachery or enmity. The amulet, as a mechanism to protect this land from certain people, seemed reasonable.

Why was he, Stile, unwanted here? *That* he would have to find out. It was not merely because he was new. The stranger had been new, not so long ago, by his own admission. Presumably he had been given a similar amulet, and used it, and it had performed as specified. Stile had at first suspected some kind of practical joke —but that demon had been no joke!

It could not be because he was small, or male; those could hardly be crimes in a human society. There had to be something else. Some special quality about him that triggered the latent secondary function of the amulet. Unless the effect was random: one bad amulet slipped in with the good ones, a kind of Russian roulette, and he happened to be the victim. But he was disinclined to dismiss it like that. A little bit of paranoia could go far toward keeping him out of any further mischief. Best to assume someone was out to get him, and play it safe.

Meanwhile, he would be well advised to get away from this region, before whoever had laid the amulet-trap came to find out why it had failed. And—he wanted to learn more about the status of magic here. Was it some form of illusion, or was it literal? The demon had shown him that his life could depend on the answer.

Where would he go? How could he know? Anywhere he could find food, and sleep safely, and remain hidden from whatever enemy he must have. *Not* the nearest castle he had spied; he was wary of that now. Anything near this place was suspect. He had to go somewhere in the wilderness, alone—

Alone? Stile did not like the thought. He was hardly a social lion, but he was accustomed to company. Sheen had been excellent company. For this strange land—

Stile nodded to himself. Considering all things, he needed a horse. He understood horses, he trusted them, he felt secure with them. He could travel far, with a good steed. And there surely were horses grazing in those fields to the north. He had not been able to make out the specific animals he had seen from the tree, but they had had a horsey aspect.

CHAPTER 6

Manure

Stile walked north, keeping a wary eye out for hazards, demonic or otherwise, and for something else. The land, as the trees thinned, became pretty in a different way. There were patches of tall lush grass, and multicolored flowers, and sections of tumbled rocks. And, finally, a lovely little stream, evidently issuing from the mountains to the south, bearing irregularly northwest. The water was absolutely clear. He lay on his stomach and put his lips to it, at the same time listening for any danger; drinking could be a vulnerable moment.

The water was so cold his mouth went numb and his throat balked at swallowing. He took his time, savoring it; beverages were so varied and nutritious and available on Proton that he had seldom tasted pure water, and only now appreciated what he had missed.

Then he cast about for fruit trees, but found none. He had no means to hunt and kill animals right now, though in time he was sure he could devise something. Safety was more urgent than nourishment, at the moment; his hunger would have to wait. With a horse he could go far and fast, leaving no footprints of his own and no smell not masked by that of the animal; he would become untraceable.

He followed the stream down, knowing it was a sure guide to the kind of animal life he wanted. This was ideal horse country; had he actually seen some horses grazing, there from the treetop, or only made an image of a wish? He could not be certain now, but trusted his instincts. Magic confused him, but he knew the ways of horses well.

Suddenly he spied it: the semicircular indentation of the hoof of a horse. And, safely back from the water, a pile of horse manure. Confirmation!

Stile examined the hoofprint. It was large, indicating an animal of perhaps seventeen hands in height, solidly built. It was unshod, and chipped at the fringes, but not overgrown. A fat, healthy horse who traveled enough to keep the hooves worn, and was careless enough to chip them on stones. Not the ideal mount for him, but it would do. Stile felt the relief wash through his body, now that he had the proof; he had not imagined it, he had not deluded himself, there really were horses here. His experience with the demon amulet had shaken his certainties, but this restored them.

He moved over to the manure and stared down at it. And faded into a memory. Seventeen years ago, as a youth of eighteen, looking down at a similar pile of dung...

His parents' tenure had ended, and they had had to vacate Planet Proton. Tenure was twenty years for serfs, with no exceptions—except possibly via the Game, a more or less futile lure held out to keep the peons hoping. He had been fortunate; he had been born early in their tenure, and so had eighteen free years. He had fitted in a full education and mastered Proton society before he had to make the choice: to stay with his folks, or to stay on Proton.

His parents, with twenty years cumulative pay awaiting them, would be moderately wealthy in the galaxy. They might not be able to swing passage all the way back to Earth, but there were other planets that were really quite decent. They would be able to afford many good things. On the other hand, if he remained on Proton he would have to serve twenty years as a serf, naked, obedient to the whims of some Citizen employer, knowing that when that tenure ended he too would be exiled.

But—here on Proton was the Game.

He had been addicted to the Game early. In a culture of serfs, it was an invaluable release. The Game was violence, or intellect, or art, or chance, alone or with tools or machines or animals—but mainly it was challenge. It had its own hierarchy, independent of the outside status of the players. Every age-ladder had its rungs, for all to see. The Game had its own magic. He was good at it from the outset; he had a natural aptitude. He was soon on his ladder, on any rung he chose. But he never chose too high a rung.

Family—or Game? It had been no contest. He had chosen Planet Proton. He had taken tenure the day his parents boarded the spaceship, and he had waited for a Citizen to employ him. To his surprise, one had picked him up the first day. He had been conducted to the Citizen's plush estate—there were no *un*plush Citizens' estates—and put in the pasture and given a wagon and a wide pitchfork.

His job was to spade horse manure. He had to take his fork and wheelbarrow and collect every pile of dung the Citizen's fine horses were gracious enough to deposit on the fine lawns. Homesick for his exiled family —it was not that he had loved them less, but that at his age he had loved the Game more—and unaccustomed to the discipline of working for a living, he found this a considerable letdown. Yet it did allow him time to be alone, and this was helpful.

He was not alone during off-hours. He slept in a loft-barracks with nine other pasture hands, and ate in a mess hall with thirty serfs. He had no privacy and no personal possessions; even his bedding was only on loan, a convenience to prevent his sweat from contaminating anyone else. In the morning the light came on and they all rose, swiftly; at night the light went out. No one missed a bed check, ever. At home with his folks he had had no curfew; they went off to their employers by day, and as long as he kept up with his schooling his time was largely his own—which meant he would be playing the Game, and drilling himself in its various techniques. Here it was different, and he wondered whether he had after all made the right choice. Of course he had to grow up sometime; he just hadn't expected to do it overnight.

The Citizen-employer was inordinately wealthy, as most Citizens were. He had several fine pastures, in scattered locations. It was necessary to travel through the city-domes from one property to another, and somehow the work was always piling up ahead of him.

Some of the pastures were cross-fenced, with neat white Earth-grown wooden boards and genuine pre-rusted nails. These barriers were of course protected by invisible microwires that delivered an uncomfortable electric shock to anyone who touched the surface. The horses were not smart, but they had good memories; they seldom brushed the fences. Stile, of course, had to learn the hard way; no one told him in advance. That was part of his initiation.

He learned. He found that the cross-fencing was to keep the horses in one pasture while allowing a new strain of grass to become established in another; if the horses had at it prematurely, they would destroy it by overgrazing before it had a chance. Pastures were rotated. When animals had to be separated, they were put in different pastures. There were many good reasons for cross-fencing, and the employer, despite his wealth, heeded those reasons.

Stile's problem was that he had to cross some of those fences, to collect the manure from far pastures. He was small, too small simply to step over as a tall serf might. He was acrobatic, so could readily have hurdled the 1.5 meter fences, but this was not permitted, lest it give the horses notions. The horses did not know it was possible to jump fences outside of a formal race, so had never tried it. Also, his landing might scuff the turf, and that was another offense. Only horses had the right to scuff; they were valuable creatures, with commensurate privileges.

Thus he had to proceed laboriously around the fence, going to far-flung gates where, of course, he had to debate the right-of-way with horses who outmassed him by factors of ten to fifteen. This slowed his work, and he was already behind. Fortunately he was a good runner, and if he moved swiftly the horses often did not bother to keep up. They could outrun him if they had a

93

mind to, anytime, but they never raced when they didn't have to. It seemed to be a matter of principle. They did not feel the same rivalry with a man that they did with members of their own species.

Then he discovered the stile: a structure like a standing stepladder that enabled him to cross the fence and haul his wheelbarrow across without touching a board. The horses could not navigate such a thing, and did not try. It was, in its fashion, a bridge between worlds. With it he could at last get around the pastures fast enough to catch up to his work.

Now that he was on tenure, he was expected to take an individual name. He had gone by his father's serf-name, followed by a dependence-number. When the Proton serf registry asked him for his choice of an original and personal designation, his irrevocable and possibly only mark of distinction, he gave it: Stile.

"Style? As in elegance?" the serf-interviewer inquired, gazing down at him with amusement. "A grandiose appellation for a lad your size."

Stile's muscles tightened in abdomen, buttocks, and shoulders. This "lad" was eighteen, full-grown—but to strangers he looked twelve. The depilatories in Proton wash water kept the hair off his face and genitals, so that his sexual maturity was not obvious. A woman his size would not have had a problem; depilatories did not affect her most obvious sexual characteristics. He was fed up with the inevitable remarks; normal-heighted people always thought they were being so damned clever with their slighting allusions to his stature. But already he was learning to conceal his annoyance, not even pretending to take it as humor. "Stile, as in fence. S-T-I-L-E. I'm a pasture hand."

"Oh." He was so designated, and thereafter was invariably addressed this way. The use of the proper name was obligatory among serfs. Only Citizens had the pleasure of anonymity, being addressed only as "sir." If any serf knew the name of a Citizen, he kept it to himself, except on those rare occasions when he needed to identify his employer for an outsider.

It turned out to be a good choice. Stile—it was orig-

94

inal and distinctive, and in the context of the Game, suggestive of the homonym. For in the Game he did indeed have a certain style. But best of all were the ramifications of its original meaning: a bridge between pastures. A stile represented a dimensionally expanded freedom and perception, as it were a choice of worlds. He liked that concept.

With experience he became more proficient. Every clod of dung he overlooked was a mark against him, a sure route to ridicule by the other hands, all of whom were larger if not older than he and had more seniority. In a society of workers who had no individual rights not relating to their jobs, the nuances of private protocol and favor became potent. "Stile—two clods in the buckwheat pasture," the foreman would announce grimly as he made his daily review of demerits, and the group would snigger discreetly, and Stile would be low man on the farm totem for the next day. He was low man quite often, in the early weeks. Other hands would "accidentally" shove him, and if he resisted he received a reprimand for roughhousing that put him low for another day. For, except in egregious cases, the higher man on the totem was always right, and when it was one serf's word against another's, the low man lost. The foreman, basically a fair man, honored this convention scrupulously. He was competent, the only serf on the farm with actual power, and the only one granted the privilege of partial anonymity: his title was used instead of his name. He never overstepped his prerogatives, or permitted others to.

There came one day when Stile had not fouled up. A hulking youth named Shingle was low for the day—and Shingle brushed Stile roughly on the path to the service area. Stile drew on his Game proficiency and ducked while his foot flung out, "accidentally" sending Shingle crashing into the barn wall. Furious, Shingle charged him, fists swinging—and Stile dropped to the ground, put his foot in the man's stomach, hauled on one arm, and flipped him through the air to land on the lush green turf so hard his body gouged it. Shingle's breath was knocked out, and the other hands stood amazed.

The foreman arrived. "What happened here?" he demanded.

"An accident," the others informed him, smirking innocently. "Shingle—fell over Stile."

The foreman squinted appraisingly at Stile, who stood with eyes downcast, knowing this meant trouble, expecting to receive the ridicule of the group again. Fighting was forbidden on these premises. Out came the clipboard the foreman always carried. "Shingle— one gouge in turf," the foreman said. And almost smiled, as the group sniggered.

For Shingle had been the man low on the totem, whose business it had been to avoid trouble. He was by definition wrong.

The foreman turned to Stile. "Accidents will happen —but in future you will report to the recreation room for practice in your martial arts, Stile." He departed on his rounds.

Stile only gained one day clear of the low totem, officially, for that day he overlooked another dropping. But he had traveled considerably higher in the estimate of his peers. They had not known he was into martial art. In turn, he remembered how they had stood by him, honoring the convention, laughing this time at the other fellow. Stile had won, by the tacit rules; the others had seemed to be against him only because he had been low totem, not because he was new or small. That was a supremely warming realization.

After that Stile began to make friends. He had held himself aloof, unconsciously, assuming the others looked down on him. If they had, they certainly didn't anymore. Now when he fouled up and they snickered, it was friendly, almost rueful. Even Shingle, nose out of joint about the episode, never made an issue of it; he too abided by the rules, and he had lost fairly.

Meanwhile, Stile was becoming adept at spotting horse manure. Horses tended to deposit their solid loads in semiprivate places, in contrast to their liquid ones. Liquid went anywhere at all, sometimes even on their food, but solids were always well away from eating, grazing or resting areas. This made the piles more challenging to find.

Missing piles tended to put him low on the totem. Consequently Stile had considerable incentive to improve his performance. He developed an extremely sharp eye for horse manure. His nose was not much help, for horses had mild refuse, unlike pigs or chickens; never unpleasant, its odor quickly faded. If left a few days—God forbid!—it could even sprout grass from undigested grains, for the digestion of horses was less sophisticated than that of cows. Horses were adapted to running, and their structure and heat-dissipation mechanism and digestion reflected this. So Stile's nose availed only when he was in the near vicinity of a find. Yet sight was not the whole answer either, for the piles could be concealed in copses of trees or amidst bushes. Sometimes he found chunks of it in the foliage of low-springing branches. There was also the problem of rain—artificial, of course, here in the domes—that wet down the manure and tended to flatten and blend it with its surroundings. Even when everything was ideal, manure seemed to be able to disappear when he was in the vicinity, only to reappear when the foreman checked. It was so easy to overlook a pile on the left while collecting one on the right!

Stile's instincts for manure sharpened to the point of near perfection. He could spade a full pile into his barrow with one scoop and heave, not missing a chunk. He learned the favorite deposit sites of the horses, and checked there first. Sometimes he even beat the artificial flies there. He could look at a section of pasture and tell by the lay of it whether a horse would want to contribute.

Yet when he had mastered his job, it grew boring. Stile was bright, very bright. People tended to assume that small stature meant small intelligence, but it was not true. The work became stultifying. Had he mastered calculus and Terrestrial ecology and aspects of quantum physics merely to fling dung for twenty years? Call him the King of Dung! Why had the Citizen snapped him up so quickly, only to throw him away on this?

But Citizens were all-powerful on Proton. They did not answer to serfs for their actions. Stile could neither complain nor change employers; his rights in the matter extended only to accepting proffered employment or suffering premature termination of tenure. If he wanted to remain on Planet Proton, he obeyed the system. He spaded dung.

Often while at work he watched the horses, covertly, lest he seem to be malingering. There was Sonny, a small handsome paint hackney with large ears, used for training new riders though he had no proper trot. Simcoe Cloud, an appaloosa gelding sixteen hands high, with a pretty "blanket" but too large a head. Navahjo, a fine quarter horse, dominant in her pasture though she was a mare. In another pasture were Misty, a gray plump Tennessee Walker with a will of her own, and her companion Sky Blue, only fourteen hands high and over twenty years old. Blue was a former harness racer, well trained but shy despite her graying head. There was Cricket, also gray verging on white. There were, according to the dictates of horse registry, no white horses; a horse that looked white was either albino or registered gray. Thus the joke: "What color was George Washington's white horse? Gray."

These constituted Stile's world, during much of his working time. He came to know them all, from a moderate distance, from Shetland pony to massive draft horse. He longed to associate more closely with them, to pat them, brush them, walk them—but that was the prerogative of the stable hands, fiercely guarded. Stile was only a pasture hand, never allowed to get overly familiar with the stock. On many days his closest approach to a living horse was its manure.

Yet from that necessary distance, what beauty! There was a peculiar grace to a horse, any horse. The power of the muscles, the spring of the ankles, the alertness of the ears, the constant swishing of the tail. There were no natural flies here, so android flies were provided, that made loud buzzing sounds and swooped around the horses, just to provide exercise for those tails. Stile loved to watch the tails, perhaps the prettiest thing about any horse except for the manes. On occasion he saw a visiting horse with a red ribbon tied in the tail: the signal of an animal that kicked. If a pasture or stable hand got kicked, he was punished, not the valuable horse. Serfs were expected to be careful, not risking the horses' precious feet by contact with the serf's drab flesh.

Stile made the best of it. He was hardly conscious of this at the time, but the extreme value placed on horses here was to make a profound impression on his attitude in life. These were not the racing animals; these were the retirees, the injured, the secondary steeds—yet they were worth more than the lives of any of the serfs. Some serfs rebelled, secretly hating the animals they tended, but Stile absorbed the propaganda completely in this respect. The horse became his ideal. The horse, though confined to its pasture, had perfect freedom, for the pasture was equine heaven. If Stile had been a horse, he would have been in heaven too. Horses became prettier than people in his eyes, and though intellectually he denied this, emotionally he accepted it. Stile was in love with horses.

Thus he became an avid student of the species. Not only did he study the nuances of the mannerisms of the particular animals in his pastures, noting that each horse had a personality fully as distinct as that of any serf; during his free time he studied texts on horse manure. He learned of the intestinal parasites that might be found in it, the worms and the maggots and microscopic vermin. Of course there were no such parasites here, but he pretended there might be, and looked assiduously for the signs. He learned to judge the general health of a horse by its manure; whether it was being worked hard or was idle; what its diet was and in what proportions. Some horses had hard clods, some loose; Stile could tell which horse had produced any given pile, and thus was aware of the past day's location of each horse without ever seeing the animals directly.

Time passed. One day, two years into his tenure, Stile actually spied a worm in manure. He reported this immediately to the foreman. "A worm in our manure?" the man demanded incredulously. "You've got delusions of grandeur!"

But they tested the horse, for the foreman let nothing pass unverified, and Stile was correct. A slow-hatching variety of parasite had slipped through the quarantine and infected the animal. It was not a serious bug, and would not really have hurt the horse, but it was genuine. The larvae had manifested in the manure only on the day Stile noted them; he had caught the nuisance before it could spread to other animals.

The foreman took Stile to the shower, washed him personally as if he were a child, and combed his hair with an available currycomb. Stile submitted, amazed at this attention. Then the foreman brought him, shining clean, to a small door in the wall of the stable. "Always say 'sir' to him," the foreman said warningly. "Never turn your back until he has dismissed you." Then he guided Stile firmly through the door.

Stile found himself, for the first time, in the presence of his employer. The other side of the barn was a palatial apartment, with videoscreens on three walls. On each screen was a portion of a composite picture: the surface of a mountainous land as seen from the air. The image shifted in three-dimensional cohesion, making the illusion most effective. The floor was almost transparent quartz, surely imported from a quarry on Earth, thus more valuable weight for weight than local gold. What affluence!

The Citizen sat in a plush swivel chair upholstered in purple silk, on whose armrests a number of control buttons showed. He was garbed in an ornate robe that seemed to be spun from thread made of platinum, and wore fine suede slippers. He was not an old man, and not young; rejuvenation treatments made his body handsome and his age indeterminate; though behind that façade of health, nature surely kept accurate score. Few Citizens lived much over a century despite the best medicine could do. He possessed no overpowering atmosphere of command. Had Stile encountered him on the streets, serf-naked, he would never have recognized him as a Citizen. The man was completely human. It was the clothing that made the difference. But what a difference it made!

The Citizen was facing to the side, his eyes on a passing cloud. He seemed unaware of Stile's intrusion.

The foreman jogged Stile's elbow. Stile tried several times, and finally choked out his announcement of arrival: "S-sir."

The Citizen's eyes flicked to cover him. "You are the lad who spotted the worm?" The voice was ordinary too, amazingly.

"Yes, sir."

"You are promoted to stableboy." And the Citizen rotated in his swivel chair, turning his glossy back, dismissing Stile.

Stile found himself back in the barn. He must have walked there, guided by the foreman. Now the man led him by the hand to a cabin at the edge of the pasture. Three stable hands stood beside it, at attention.

"Stile is joining you," the foreman said. "Fetch his gear."

With alacrity they took off. In moments Stile's bedding, body brush and towel were neatly set up by the fourth bunk in the cabin. The stable hands were congratulating him. He was, of course, low man of the house—the "boy"—but it was like a fraternity, a giant improvement from the barracks. Only four to share the shower, curfew an hour later, and a cabin vidscreen!

Stile's days of spading and hauling manure were over. A new serf took his place in the pastures. Stile was now of a higher echelon. He was working directly with the horses. Reward had been as swift and decisive as punishment for infractions; at one stroke the Citizen had made two years of dung worthwhile.

Stile lifted his eyes from the manure of this wilderness realm. Oh, yes, he knew about manure! He had never forgotten what dung had done for him. He considered it not with distaste or horror, but almost with affection.

He walked on down the river, inspecting hoofprints

and manure. Some of these horses were large, some medium, some healthy, some less so. Some did have worms in their droppings, and these gave Stile a perversely good feeling. A worm had promoted him!

This region, then, was not sterile; it was natural. Flies hovered about the freshest piles: genuine flies, he was sure, species he knew only from books and museum specimens. No one policed this region; the old piles lay undisturbed, sprouting toadstools, gradually settling, dissolving in rainfall, bright green grass growing up through them. No self-respecting horse would eat at a dung-site, so such blades remained unclipped. Nature's way of preventing overgrazing, perhaps—but Stile was appalled to see such an excellent pasture in such disrepair. Did no one *care* about these horses?

They must be wild, uncared for. Which meant that he would be free to take whichever one he chose. He might have to break it for riding—but he knew how to do that. Even with his injured knees he could ride any horse. Only specialized racing required extreme flexure of the knees; for other riding the legs were used for balance, for purchase, and guidance of the steed.

There was evidently a fair-sized herd in this region. A number of mares, governed by a single powerful stallion? No, there seemed to be several males; he could tell by the positioning of the hoofprints about the indentations of urination sites. Males watered in front of the hind hooves; females, behind. But there was bound to be a dominant stallion, for that was the way of horses. Geldings, or cut males, were no more competitive than mares, but potent stallions demanded recognition.

That dominant stallion would probably make the finest steed for Stile's purpose—but would also be too obvious. Stile needed a good, fast, but inconspicuous animal. A non-herd stallion—probably there were no geldings here, if the animals were actually wild—or a mare. A good mare was in no way inferior; some of the most durable runners were female. Stile had ridden a mare named Thunder once, who brooked no backtalk from any horse, regardless of size or sex, and was herself a magnificent, high-stepping, lofty-headed creature. If he could find a mare like her, here—

He spied the prints of a small horse, no more than fourteen hands, on the verge of being a pony, but supremely healthy. Probably a mare; there was something about the delicacy with which she had placed her feet. Every hoof was sound, and the manure had no infestation. She could run, too—he traced her galloping prints in the turf, noting the spread and precision of the marks, the absence of careless scuffmarks, of signs of tripping. No cracks in these hooves, no sloppy configurations. A good horse, in good condition, could outrun a greyhound, maintaining a velocity of 65 kilometers per hour. This could be that kind of horse. She seemed to be a loner, apart from the herd, drinking and feeding in places separate from the others. That could mean she was more vulnerable to predators, so would have to be more alert, tougher, and swifter. But why was she alone? Horses were basically herd animals.

He followed this trail, by print and manure. At first the piles were old, but as he used his skill to orient they became fresher. It took him some hours to make real progress, for the horse had wandered far—as healthy horses did. As Stile walked, he wondered more persistently: what made this one separate from her companions? Was she, like himself, a private individual who had learned to value alone-time, or had she been excluded from the herd? What would constitute reason for such exclusion? Obviously she made do quite well alone—but did she really like it?

Stile had quite a lot of empathy for horses, and a lot for outsiders. Already he liked this little mare he had not yet seen. He did not after all need any giant steed to ride; his weight was slight, and he knew how to make it seem lighter. A small horse, even a pony could easily support him. In heroic fantasy the protagonist always bestrode a giant stallion; Stile could handle such a horse, but knew there were points to smallness too. Just as there were points to small people!

Here he was, abruptly, at an aspect of the truth: he was very small for his kind, therefore he liked small

103

things. He identified with them. He knew what it felt like to be looked down on, to be the butt of unfunny jokes. "Hey, dja hear the one about the little moron?" Why did it always have to be a *little* moron? Why did the terms midget, dwarf, pygmy and runt have pejorative connotation? What the hell was so funny about being small? Since small people were not inferior intellectually, it stood to reason that smallness was a net asset. A better value, pound for pound.

So why didn't he really believe it? He should not choose a horse because it was small, but because it was the best mount for his purpose. Yet, subjectively—

Stile's irate chain of thought was interrupted by the sight of his objective. There she stood, as pretty a little mare as he had ever seen. Her coat was glossy black, except for white socks on her hind feet, one rising higher than the other. Her mane fell to the right side, ebony-sleek, and her tail was like the tresses of a beautiful woman. Her hooves glistened like pearl, dainty and perfectly formed. She had a Roman nose, convex rather than straight or concave, but in nice proportion. And her horn was a spiraled marvel of ivory symmetry.

Her *what*?

Stile actually blinked and rubbed his eyes. He only succeeded in blurring his vision. But what he saw was no trick of the light.

He had found a unicorn.

CHAPTER 7

Neysa

He must have gasped, for the mare raised her head alertly. She had, of course, been aware of his approach before; horses—unicorns?—had sharp hearing. She had not been alarmed—which itself was remarkable, if she were 'wild—so had continued grazing. Equines were like that; they startled readily, but not when they thought they had the situation in hand. Evidently this little lady unicorn was much the same.

This was a fantasy world, where magic evidently worked; he had already established that. He still felt the burn on his neck where the amulet-demon's chain had scraped. So why shouldn't this world have magic animals too? That made perfect sense. It was only that he had never thought it through, before assuming that these were horses. Was there, actually, much difference between a horse and a unicorn? Some artists represented unicorns with leonine bodies and cloven hooves, but Stile distrusted such conceptions. It could be that a true unicorn was merely a horse with a horn on the forehead. In which case this one would do just fine for him; he could ignore the horn and treat her as a horse.

Stile had not taken time to fashion a lariat; he had been more interested in surveying the situation, and in the memories this experience evoked. Now he decided: this was definitely the animal he wanted. With no rope, he would have to improvise. He doubted she was tame, but she might not be man-shy either.

He walked slowly up to her. The unicorn watched him warily. There was something about the way her horn oriented on him that was disquieting. It was without doubt a weapon. It tapered to a sharp point; it was a veritable spear. This was a fighting animal. Scratch one assumption: he could in no way afford to ignore that horn.

"Now my name's Stile," he said in a gentle voice. "Stile as in fence. You may not know about that sort of thing, though. I need a—a steed. Because I may have a long way to go, and I can get there faster and better if I ride. I am a very good endurance runner, for a man, but a man does not compare to a good h—unicorn. I would like to ride you. What is your name?"

The unicorn blew a double note through her horn. This startled Stile; he had not realized the horn was hollow. He had been speaking rhetorically, expecting no response. Her note was coincidental, of course; she could hardly be expected to comprehend his words. It was his tone of voice that mattered, and the distraction of it while he approached. Yet that note had sounded almost like a word. "Neysa?" he asked, voicing it as well as he could.

There was a fluted snort of agreement—or so it seemed to him. He reminded himself to be careful how he personified animals; if he ever got to believing he was talking with one on a human basis, he'd have to suspect his own sensibility. He could get himself killed, deluding himself about the reactions of a creature with a weapon like that.

"Well, Neysa, what would you do if I just got on your back and rode you?" He had to keep talking, calming her, until he could get close enough to mount her. Then there would be merry hell for a while: a necessary challenge.

The unicorn whipped her horn about in a menacing manner, and stomped her left forefoot. Her ears flattened back against her head. The language of unicorns was obviously like that of horses, with absolutely clear signals—for those who knew how to interpret them. She might not comprehend the specific meaning of his words, but she knew he was encroaching, and was giving adequate warning. If he tried to ride her, she would try to throw him, and if he got thrown, he would be in serious trouble. This was indeed no tame animal; this was a creature who knew of men and did not fear them,

106

and when sufficiently aggravated would kill. A wildcat was not merely a housecat gone wild; a unicorn was not merely a horse with a weapon. The whole psychology differed. Neysa's every little mannerism told him that. He had no doubt, now, that there was blood on her horn—from other creatures who had failed to heed her warnings.

Yet he had to do it. "Neysa, I'm sorry. But a demon tried to kill me, not long ago, and in this frame of magic I am not well equipped to protect myself. I need to get away from here, and I'm sure you can take me so much better than I can take myself. Men have always depended on horses—uh, equines to carry them, before they started messing with unreliable machines like automobiles and spaceships." He stepped closer to her, hand outstretched, saying anything, just so long as he kept talking.

She lifted both forefeet in a little prance and brought them down together in a clomp directed at him. Her nose made a hooking gesture at him, and she made a sound that was part squeal and part snort and part music—the sort of music played in the background of a vid-show when the horrible monster was about to attack. This was as forceful a warning as she could make. She would not attack him if he departed right now, as she preferred simply to graze and let graze, but she would no longer tolerate his presence. She was not at all afraid of him—a bad sign!—she just didn't like him.

Now Stile remembered the folklore about unicorns, how they could be caught only by a virginal girl; the unicorn would lay his head in her lap, and then an ambush could be sprung. Probably this had been a cynical fable: how do you catch a mythical animal? With a mythical person. Implication: virgins were as rare as unicorns. Clever, possibly true in medieval times —and beside the point. How would it relate to a man and a female unicorn? Would she put her head in his lap? Only to un-man him, surely! More likely the matter related to riding: only a person pure in spirit could ride a unicorn—and in such myths, purity was defined as sexual abstinence and general innocence. Stile had

107

no claims to such purity. Therefore this could be a very difficult ride. But mythology aside, he expected that sort of ride anyway.

"I really am sorry to do this, Neysa," Stile said. And leaped.

It was a prodigious bound, the kind only a highly trained athlete could perform. He flew through the air to land squarely on the unicorn's back. His hands reached out to take firm grip on her mane, his legs clamped to her sides, and his body flattened to bring him as close to her as physically possible.

Neysa stood in shocked surprise for all of a tenth of a second. Then she took off like a stone from a catapult. Stile's body was flung off—but his hands retained their double grip on her mane, and in a moment his legs had dropped back and were clamping her sides again. She bucked, but he clung close, almost standing on his head. No ordinary horse could buck without putting its head down between its front legs; it was a matter of balance and weight distribution. Neysa managed it, however, providing Stile with just a hint of what he was in for. Normal limits were off, here; this was, for sure, a magic animal.

She reared, but he stayed on her like a jacket. She whipped her head about, spearing at him with her horn —but he shifted about to avoid it, and she could not touch him without endangering her own hide. That horn was designed to spear an enemy charging her from the front, not one clinging to her back. It took a special kind of curved horn to handle a rider; she would never dislodge him this way.

So much for the beginning. Now the unicorn knew that no amateur bestrode her. It would require really heroic measures to dump him. For Stile, when he wasn't trying to gentle an animal, was extremely tough about falls.

Neysa accelerated forward, going west toward the chasm cracks he had spied from the spruce tree—then abruptly braked. All four feet skidded on the turf. But Stile was wise to this maneuver, and remained secure. She did a double spinabout, trying to fling him off by centrifugal force—but he leaned to the center of the turn and stayed firm. Abruptly she reversed—and he did too. She leaped forward—then leaped backward. That one almost unseated him; it was a trick no ordinary horse knew. But he recovered, almost tearing out a fistful of her mane in the process.

Well! Now she was warmed up. Time to get serious. Neysa tripped forward, lowering her body—then reared and leaped simultaneously. She fell backward; then her hind feet snapped forward and she performed a flip in air. For an instant she was completely inverted, her entire body above his. Stile was so startled he just clung. Then she completed the flip, landing on her front feet with her body vertical, finally whomping down on her hind feet.

Only the involuntary tightening of his hands had saved him. A horse doing a backflip! This was impossible!

But, he reminded himself again, this was no horse. This was a unicorn—a creature of fantasy. The mundane rules simply did not apply here.

Next, Neysa went into a spin. She galloped in a tightening circle, then drew in her body until she was actually balanced on one forefoot, head and tail lifted, rotating rapidly. Magic indeed. Stile hung on, his amazement growing. He had known he would be in for a stiff ride, but he had grossly underestimated the case. This was akin to his fight with the demon.

Well, maybe that was a fair parallel. Two magical creatures, one shaped like a humanoid monster, the other like a horse with a horn. Neither subject to the limitations of conventional logic. He had been foolish to assume that a demon that superficially resembled a horse was anything close to that kind of animal. He would remember this lesson—if he happened to get out of this alive.

Now Neysa straightened out, stood for a moment—then rolled. Her back smacked into the ground—but Stile had known when to let go. He landed on his feet, and was back on her back as she regained her own feet. "Nice try, Neysa," he said as he settled in again.

She snorted. So much for round two. She had only begun to fight!

Now she headed for the nearest copse of trees. Stile knew what was coming: the brush-off. Sure enough, she passed so close to a large trunk that her side scraped it—but Stile's leg was clear, as he clung to her other side in the fashion of a trick rider. He had once won a Game in which the contest was trick riding; he was not the finest, but he was good.

Neysa plunged into a thicket. The saplings brushed close on either side, impossible to avoid—but they bent aside when pushed, and could not sweep off a firmly anchored rider who was prepared. She shot under a large horizontal branch, stout enough to remove him—but again he slid around to the side of her body, avoiding it, and sprang to her back when the hazard was past. Real riding was not merely a matter of hanging on; it required positive anticipations and countermoves to each equine effort. He could go anywhere she could go!

Neysa charged directly toward the next large tree, then planted her forefeet, lifted her rear feet, and did a front-foot-stand that sent her back smashing into the trunk. Had he stayed on her, he would have been crushed gruesomely. No game, this! But Stile, now wise in the ways of unicorns, had dropped off as her motion started. He had less mass than she, weighing about an eighth as much, and could maneuver more rapidly when he had to. As her rear feet came back to the ground, Stile's rear feet came back to her back, and his hands resumed their clutch on her mane.

She snorted again. Round three was over. Round four was coming up. How many more tricks did this phenomenal animal have? Stile was in one sense enjoying this challenge, but in another sense he was afraid. This was no Proton Game, where the loser suffered no more than loss of status; this was his life on the line. The first trick he missed would be the last.

Neysa came onto a grassy plain. Now she accelerated. What was she up to this time? It didn't seem so bad—and that made him nervous. Beginning with a

110

walk, she accelerated to a slow trot. The speed differential was not great, as a slow trot could be slower than a brisk walk. In fact, Stile had worked with lazy horses who could trot one meter per second, rather than the normal three or four meters per second. The distinguishing mark was the beat and pattern. In walking, the horse put down the four feet in order, left-front, right-rear, right-front, left-rear, four beats per cycle. Trotting was two-beat: left-front and right-rear together, followed by right-front and left-rear together. Or with a right lead instead of a left. The point was that the motion of each front foot was synchronous with one hind foot; in some cases the front and rear moved together on the same side. But there were only two beats per cycle, the pairs of feet striking the ground cleanly together. It made for a bumpy but regular ride that covered the ground well, and looked very pretty from the side. A slow trot could be gentle; a fast one could be like a jackhammer. But a trot was definitely a trot, at any speed; there was no mistaking it. Stile liked trotting, but distrusted this one. He knew he had not seen the last of this mare's devices.

Next she broke into a canter: three-beat. Left-front, then right-front and left-rear together, and finally right-rear. Like a cross between a walk and a trot, and the ride a kind of gentle swooping. All perfectly conventional, and therefore not to be trusted. She had something horrendous in her canny equine mind!

Finally she reached a full gallop: a modified two-beat cycle, the two front legs striking almost but not quite together, then the rear two. A four-beat cycle, technically, but not uniform. Beat-beat, beat-beat, at the velocity of racing. Stile enjoyed it; he experienced an exhilaration of speed that was special on a horse—unicorn. Motored wheels could go much faster, of course, but it wasn't the same. Here, as it were in the top gear, the animal straining to the limit—though this one was not straining, but loafing at a velocity that would have had another one straining—

The unicorn shifted into another gait. It was a five-beat—

111

Stile was so surprised he almost dropped off. No horse had a five-beat gait! There were only four feet!

No horse—there he was again. He kept forgetting and getting reminded in awkward ways. This gait was awful; he had never before experienced it, and could not accommodate it. BEAT-beat-BEAT-BEAT-beat, and over again, bouncing him in a growing resonance, causing him to lose not his grip but his composure. He felt like a novice again, fouling himself up, his efforts to compensate for the animal's motions only making it worse. As a harmonic vibration could shake apart a building, this fifth-beat was destroying him. He would fall—and at this breakneck velocity he could . . . break his neck.

Think, Stile, think! he told himself desperately. *Analyze: What is the key to this gait?*

His hands were hurting as his clutch on the unicorn's mane slowly slipped. His thigh muscles were beginning to cramp. Stile was expert—but this creature had his number now. Unless he could get her number too, soon.

Four feet, five beats. One foot had to repeat. Number the steps: one-two-three-four—where was the repeat? *Fingers slipping . . .*

BEAT-beat—that sound was less than the others, like a half-step. But half a step had to be completed by—another half-step. Like a man catching his balance when tripped. Two half-steps—that was it. Not necessarily together. The second and fifth. The right rear foot—as though stumbling, throwing off his timing. Compensate—

Stile started to catch on. He shifted his weight to absorb the shock and irregularity. BEAT-absorb-BEAT-BEAT-absorb. It was tricky and unnatural as hell, but his body was finding the dubious rhythm, getting the swing. Mostly it was his knowledge of the pattern, of what to expect. No more surprises! His leg muscles relaxed, and his hands stopped slipping.

Neysa felt the change, and knew he had surmounted this challenge too. She turned at speed—and Stile's inertia almost flung him off her side. A gradual turn at high velocity could pack more wallop than a fast turn at low speed. But she had to shift to a normal gallop for the turn, and no equine living could dump Stile with a normal gallop.

Realizing her mistake, the unicorn changed tactics. She slowed, then suddenly went into a one-beat gait. This was another surprise, in a ride full of them. It was like riding a pogo stick. All four of her feet landed together; then she leaped forward, front feet leading—only to contract to a single four-point landing again.

But Stile had ridden a pogo stick, in the course of his Game experience. He could handle this. "No luck, Neysa!" he cried. "Give up?"

She snorted derisively through her horn. It was almost as if she understood his words. But of course horses were very perceptive of tone, and responsive to it.

She turned. She had been going north, having curved in the course of her running; now she bore due west. Round five was coming up.

The grass gave way to packed dirt, then to clay, then to something like shale, and finally to rock. Neysa's hooves struck sparks from the surface, astonishing Stile. She was traveling fast, to be sure—faster than any horse he had raced. It felt like eighty kilometers per hour, but that had to be a distortion of his perception; such a speed would be of interworld championship level, for a horse. Regardless, hooves were not metallic; this animal was not shod, had no metal horseshoes, no nails. Nothing to strike sparks. Yet they were here.

Now she came to the pattern of crevices he had spied from the tree. They loomed with appalling suddenness: deep clefts in the rock whose bottoms could not be seen. Her hooves clicked between cracks unerringly, but Stile didn't like this. Not at all! One misstep would drop a foot into one of those holes, and at this speed that would mean a broken leg, a tumble, and one man flying through the air to land—where? But all he could do was hang on.

The cracks became more plentiful, forming a treacherous lattice. His vision of the crevices blurred, because they were so close, passing so rapidly; they seemed to writhe in their channels, swelling and shrinking, now twisting as if about to burst free, now merging with others or splitting apart. He had noted a similar effect when riding the Game model train as a child, fixing his gaze on the neighboring tracks, letting them perform their animations as he traveled. But these were not rails, but crevices, getting worse.

Neysa danced across the lattice as Stile watched with increasing apprehension. Now these were no longer mere cracks in a surface; these were islands between gaps. Neysa was actually traversing a chasm, jumping across from stone to stone, each stone a platform rising vertically from the depths. Stile had never seen such a landscape before. He really was in a new world: new in kind as well as in region.

Now Neysa was leaping, using her one-beat gait to bound from one diminishing platform to another. Sometimes all four feet landed together, in a group, almost touching each other; sometimes they were apart, on separate islands. She was obviously conversant with this place, and knew where to place each hoof, as a child knew where to jump amid the squares of a hopscotch game, proficient from long practice. Perhaps Neysa had mastered this challenge in order to avoid predators. No carnivore could match her maneuvers here, surely; the creature would inevitably misstep and fall between islands, perhaps prodded by the unicorn's aggressive horn, and that would be the end. So her trick gait made sense: it was a survival mechanism. Probably the five-beat gait had a similar function. What terrain was it adapted to?

Neysa danced farther into the pattern. The islands became fewer, smaller, farther apart. Now Stile could peer into the lower reaches of the crevices, for the sunlight slanted down from almost overhead. Had it been only six hours from the start of this day? It seemed much longer already! The fissures were not as deep as he had feared; perhaps two meters. But they terminated in rocky creases that could wedge a leg or a body, and they were getting deeper as the unicorn progressed.

This was a test of nerve as much as of agility or riding ability.

As it happened, Stile had the nerve. "Let's face it, Neysa," he said. He tended to talk to horses; they listened well, politely rotating their pointed furry ears around to fetch in larger scoops of his sound, and they did not often talk back. "We're in this together. What would I gain by falling off now? A broken leg? If it's all the same to you, oh prettiest and surest-footed of equines, I'll just stay on." He saw her left ear twitch as if shaking off a fly. She heard him, all right, and was not pleased at the confidence his tone exuded.

But the acrobatic challenge was not what the unicorn had come for. Suddenly she leaped—into the depths of a larger crack. It was two meters wide, shallow at the near end, but bearing lower. The sides seemed to close in as she plunged deeper. Where was she going? Stile did not like this development at all.

Neysa swung around a chasm corner and dropped to a lower level. This crack narrowed above; they were in a partial cave, light raying from the top. Cross-cracks intersected often, but the unicorn proceeded straight ahead.

A demon roared, reaching from the side. Where had it come from? A niche at the side, hidden until they were beside it. Stile ducked his head, and the thing missed him. He glimpsed it only briefly: glaring red eyes, shining teeth, glistening horns, talon claws, malevolence. Typical of the breed, no doubt.

Another demon loomed, grabbing from the other side. Stile flung his body away, and this one also missed. But this was getting bad; he could not afford to let go his grip on Neysa's mane, for it was his only purchase. But he soon would need an arm to fend off these attacks.

The unicorn's strategy was clear, now. She was charging through the habitat of monsters, hoping one of them would pluck the unwanted rider from her back. The demons were not grabbing at her; they shied away from her deadly horn, instead snatching from the sides. They seemed akin to the demon of the amulet that he

115

had fought before, except that their size was constant. Stile knew he would not survive long if one of these monsters nabbed him. He had already learned how tough demons were.

He would have to compromise. Neysa could not turn abruptly, for these crevices defined her route. The demons stood only at intersections and niches; there was not room enough in a single crevice for unicorn *and* demon. So this was a set channel with set hazards. He should be able to handle it—if he were careful.

Another intersection; another demon on the right. Stile let go Neysa's mane with his right hand and lifted his arm to ward off the attack. He did it with expertise, striking with his forearm against the demon's forearms, obliquely, drawing on the power of his forward motion. The leverage was with him, and against the reaching demon; Stile was sure of that. There was art to blocking, no matter what was being blocked.

Neysa felt his shifting of weight and tried to shake him off. But the channel bound her; she could not act effectively. Her trap inhibited her as much as him. It was evident that the demons were not her friends; otherwise she would simply stop and let them snatch him off. No, they were enemies, or at least un-friends; she neither stopped nor slowed, lest the demons get her as well as him. They probably liked the taste of raw unicorn flesh as well as they liked the taste of human flesh.

In fact, she had taken quite a risk to get rid of him. She just might get rid of herself, too.

"Neysa, this is no good," Stile said. "This should be between you and me. I don't like demons any better than you do, but this shouldn't be their concern. You're going for double or nothing—and it's too likely to be nothing. Let's get out of here and settle this on our own. Whoever wins and whoever loses, let's not give the pleasure of our remains to these monsters."

She charged on, straight ahead, of course. He knew he was foolish to talk to himself like this; it really accomplished nothing. But stress gave him the compulsion. The demons kept grabbing, and he kept blocking. He talked to them too, calling them names like "Flopface" and "Crooktooth," and exclaiming in cynical sympathy when they missed him. He forced himself to stop that; he might get to wanting to help them.

Stile was quite nervous now; he knew this because when he turned off his mouth he found himself humming. That was another thing he tended to do when under stress. He had to vocalize in some fashion. Upon occasion it had given him away during a Game. Bad, bad habit! But now the refrain became compulsive. Hummm-hummm-block, as a demon loomed; hummm-hummm-block! Stupid, yet effective in its fashion. But the demons were getting more aggressive, encroaching more closely. Soon they would become bold enough to block the channel ahead—

One did. It stepped out directly in front of the unicorn, arms spread, grin glowering. It was horrendously ugly.

Neysa never slowed. Her horn speared straight forward. As it touched the demon, she lifted her head. There was a shock of impact. The creature was impaled through the center, hoisted into the air, and hurled back over the unicorn's body. Stile clung low, and it cleared him.

Now he knew why most demons gave way to a charging unicorn. They might overwhelm a stationary unicorn, but a moving one was deadly. Stile could hardly imagine a more devastating stroke than the one he had just seen.

And a similar stroke awaited him, the moment he fell off.

The beat of Neysa's hooves changed. She was driving harder now—because she was climbing. Stile peered ahead, past her bloodstained horn, and saw the end of the crevice. They were finally coming out of it.

The demons drew back. They had become too bold, and paid the penalty. The intruders were leaving anyway; why hinder them? Stile relaxed. Round five was over.

They emerged to the surface—and plunged into liquid. The northern end of the cracks terminated in water. A river flowed down into them, quickly, vanishing into the deeper crevices—but to the north it was broad and blue. Neysa splashed along it; the water was only knee-deep here.

The river curved grandly, like a python, almost touching itself before curving back. "The original meander," Stile remarked. "But I don't see how this is going to shake me off, Neysa." However, if he had to be thrown, he would much prefer that it be in water. He was of course an excellent swimmer.

Then the water deepened, and the unicorn was swimming. Stile had no trouble staying on. Was she going to try to drown him? She had small chance! He had won many a Game in the water, and could hold his breath a long time.

She did not try. She merely swam upstream with amazing facility, much faster than any ordinary horse could do, and he rode her though all but her head and his head were immersed. The river was cool, not cold; in fact it was pleasant. If this were round six, it was hardly a challenge.

Then he felt something on his thigh. He held on to the mane with his right hand, wary of tricks, and reached with his left—and found a thing attached to his flesh. Involuntarily he jerked it off, humming again. There was a pain as of abrading flesh, and it came up: a fishlike creature with a disk for a head, myriad tiny teeth projecting.

It was a lamprey. A blood-sucking eel-like creature, a parasite that would never let go voluntarily. Another minor monster from the biological museum exhibits, here alive.

Stile looked at it, horrified. Magic he found incredible; therefore it didn't really bother him. But this creature was unmagical and disgusting. He heard the loudness of his own humming. He tried to stop it, ashamed of his squeamishness, but his body would not obey. What revulsion!

Another sensation. He threw the lamprey away with a convulsive shudder and grabbed the next, from his side. It was a larger sucker. There was little he could do to it, one-handed; it was leather-tough. He might bite it;

that would serve it right, a taste—literally—of its own medicine. But he recoiled at the notion. Ugh!

The noxious beasties did not seem to be attacking the unicorn. Was it her hair, or something else? She could hardly use her horn to terrorize something as mindless as this.

Neysa kept swimming up the river, and Stile kept yanking off eels, humming grimly as he did. He hated this, he was absolutely revolted, but he certainly was not going to give up now!

The unicorn dived, drawing him under too. Stile held his breath, clinging to her mane. It was work for her to stay under, as her large equine belly gave her good flotation; he was sure he could outlast her. She would have to breathe, too.

She stayed down a full minute, then another. Only the tip of her horn cut the surface of the water like the fin of a shark. How long could she do it? He was good at underwater exploits, but he was getting uncomfortable.

Then he caught on: her horn was a snorkel. She was breathing through it! She had no air-limit. His lungs were hurting, but her neck was too low; he could not get his head high enough to break the surface without letting go her mane. If he let go, he surely would not have a chance to catch her again; she would stab him if he tried.

But he had a solution. He hauled himself up hand over hand to her head, where her black forelock waved like sea grass in the flow. He grabbed her horn. It was smooth, not knife-edged along the spiral; lucky for him! There seemed to be little indentations along its length: the holes for the notes, at the moment closed off.

His head broke water, and he breathed. She could not lower her horn without cutting off her own wind— and she was breathing too hard and hot to risk that. Equines had a lot of mass and muscle for their lungs to service, and she was still working hard to stay below.

Neysa blew an angry note through her horn and surfaced. Stile dropped back to her back. He yanked off two more eels that had fastened to him while he was below, as if his cessation of humming had made them bold.

Neysa cut to the edge of the river and found her footing. She charged out of the water. Stile had taken round six.

North of the river was a slope rising into a picturesque mountain range. The highest peaks were cloudgirt and seemed to be snow-covered. Surely she was not about to essay the heights!

She was. She galloped up the slope, the wind drying out her hair and his. What an animal she was! An ordinary horse would have been exhausted by this time, but this one seemed to be just hitting her stride.

The pace, however, was telling; Stile could feel her body heating. Horses, with or without horns, were massive enough to be short on skin surface to radiate heat. Therefore they sweated, as did man—but still it could take some time to dissipate the heat pollution of overexertion. She would have to ease up soon, even if her muscles still had strength.

She did not. The slope increased; her hooves pounded harder. One-two, three-four, a good hardworking gallop. She was not even trying to shake him off, now, but she surely had something excellent in mind. The grain-grass turf gave way to fields of blue and red flowers and goldenrod. More rocks showed, their rugged facets glinting cruel deep gray in the sun. The trees became smaller. Wisps of fog streamed by.

Stile craned his neck to look back—and was amazed. Already the Meander River was a small ribbon in the distance, far below. They must have climbed a vertical kilometer! Suddenly the air seemed chill, the breeze cutting. But the unicorn was hot; again small sparks flew from her feet as the hooves struck the rocky ground. Fine jets of vapor spumed from her nostrils.

Vapor? Stile squinted, unbelieving. *Those were jets of fire!*

No, impossible! No flesh-creature could breathe out fire. Living tissue wasn't able to—

Stile nudged forward, freed one hand, and reached

120

ahead to approach the flame he thought he saw. Ouch! His fingers burned! That was indeed fire!

All right, once more. This was a magic land. He had accepted that, provisionally. The laws of physics he had known did not necessarily apply. Or if they were valid, they operated in different ways. Horses generated heat —so did unicorns. Horses sweated—this creature remained dry, once she had shed the river water. So she got rid of excess heat by snorting it out her nostrils in concentrated form. It did make sense, in its particular fashion.

Now the air was definitely cold. Stile was naked; if they went much higher, he could be in a new sort of trouble. And of course that was the idea. This was round seven, the trial of inclement climate. Neysa was not suffering; she was doing the work of running, so was burning hot. The cold recharged her.

Stile got down as close to his mount as he could. His back was freezing, but his front was hot, in contact with the furnace of Neysa's hide. This became uncomfortable. He was trying to sweat on one side and shiver on the other, and he couldn't turn over. And Neysa kept climbing.

Could he steer her back down the hill? Unlikely; trained horses moved with the guidance of reins and legs and verbal directives—but they did it basically because they knew no better. They were creatures of habit, who found it easiest to obey the will of the rider. This unicorn was a self-willed animal, no more tractable than a self-willed machine. (Ah, Sheen—what of you now?) If he did not like her direction, he would have to get off her back.

So he would just have to bear with it. He had to tame this steed before he could steer her, and he had to stay on before he could tame her. He found himself humming again. It seemed to help.

Neysa's feet touched snow. Steam puffed up from that contact. She really had hot feet! She charged on up the side of a glacier. Ice chipped off and slid away from her hooves. Stile hummed louder, his music punctuated by his shivering.

121

Crevices opened in the glacier. Again the unicorn's feet danced—but this time on a slippery slope. Her hooves skidded between steps, for their heat melted the ice. Those sparks were another heat-dissipating mechanism, and though the snow and ice had cooled the hooves below sparking level, there was still plenty of heat to serve. Her body weight shifted, compensating for the insecure footing, but a fall seemed incipient. Stile hummed louder yet. This was no miniature Game-mountain, under a warm dome, with cushioned landings for losers. This was a towering, frigid, violent landscape, and he was afraid of it.

The cloud cover closed in. Now it was as if the unicorn trod the cold beaches of an arctic sea, with the cloud layers lapping at the shores. But Stile knew that cloud-ocean merely concealed the deadly avalanche slopes. Neysa's legs sank ankle-deep in the fringe-wash, finding lodging in ice—but how would she know ahead of time if one of those washes covered a crevasse?

"Neysa, you are scaring the color right out of my hair!" Stile told her. "But I've got to cling tight, because I will surely perish if I separate from you here. If the fall through the ledges doesn't shatter me, the cold will freeze me. I'm not as tough as you—which is one reason I need you."

Then the first snow-monster loomed. Huge and white, with icicles for hair, its chill ice-eyes barely peeking out through its snow-lace whiskers, it opened its ice-toothed maw and roared without sound. Fog blasted forth from its throat, coating Stile's exposed portions with freezing moisture.

Neysa leaped across the cloud to another mountain island. Stile glanced down while she was in midair, spying a rift in the cover—and there was a gaunt chasm below. He shivered—but of course he was cold anyway. He had never been really cold before, having spent all his life in the climate-controlled domes of Proton; only the snow machines of the Game had given him experience, and that had been brief. This was close to his notion of hell.

Another snow-monster rose out of the cloud, its roar

as silent as falling snow. Again the fog coated Stile, coalescing about his hands, numbing them, insinuating slipperiness into his grip on the mane. Stile discovered he was humming a funeral dirge. Unconscious black humor?

Neysa plunged through a bank of snow, breaking into the interior of an ice-cave. Two more snow-monsters loomed, breathing their fog. Neysa charged straight into them. One failed to move aside rapidly enough, and the unicorn's flame-breath touched it. The monster melted on that side, mouth opening in a silent scream.

On out through another snowbank—and now they were on a long snowslide on the north side of the range. Four legs rigid, Neysa slid down, gaining speed. Her passage started a separate snowslide that developed into a minor avalanche. It was as if the entire mountain were collapsing around them.

It would be so easy to relax, let go, be lost in the softly piling snow. Stile felt a pleasant lassitude. The snow was like surf, and they were planing down the front of the hugest wave ever imagined. But his hands were locked, the muscles cramped; he could not let go after all.

Suddenly they were out of winter, standing on a grassy ledge, the sun slanting warmly down. The cold had numbed his mind; now he was recovering. Neysa was breathing hard, her nostrils dilated, cooling. Stile did not know how long he had been unaware of their progress; perhaps only minutes, perhaps an hour. But somehow he had held on. His hands were cramped; this must be what was called a death grip. Had he won the victory, or was this merely a respite between rounds?

Neysa took a step forward—and Stile saw that the ledge was on the brink of a cliff overlooking the Mean-der River. In fact there was the roar of a nearby falls; the river started here, in the melting glaciers, and tum-bled awesomely to the rocky base. Sure death to enter that realm!

Yet Neysa, fatigued to the point of exhaustion, was gathering herself for that leap. Stile, his strength returning though his muscles and skin were sore from the grueling ride, stared ahead, appalled. Enter that maelstrom of plunging water and cutting stone? She was bluffing; she had to be! She would not commit suicide rather than be tamed!

The unicorn started trotting toward the brink. She broke into a canter, bunched herself for the leap—

Stile flung himself forward, across her neck, half onto her head. His locked fingers cracked apart with the desperate force of his imperative, his arms flung forward. He grabbed her horn with both hands, swung his body to the ground beside her head, and bulldogged her to the side. She fought him, but she was tired and he had the leverage; he had rodeo experience too. They came to a halt at the brink of the cliff. A warm updraft washed over their faces, enhancing the impression of precariousness; Stile did not want to look down. Any crumbling of the support—

Stile held her tight, easing up only marginally as she relaxed, not letting go. "Now listen to me, Neysa!" he said, making his voice calm. It was foolish of him, he knew, to speak sense to her, just as it was foolish to hum when under stress, but this was not the occasion to attempt to remake himself. The unicorn could not understand his words, only his tone. So he was talking more for himself than for her. But with the awful abyss before them, he had to do it.

"Neysa, I came to you because I needed a ride. Someone is trying to kill me, and I am a stranger in this land, and I have to travel fast and far. You can go faster and farther than I can; you have just proved that. You can traverse regions that would kill me, were I alone. So I need you for a purely practical reason."

She continued to relax, by marginal stages, one ear cocked to orient on him, but she had not given up. The moment he let go, she would be gone. Into the river, the hard way, and on into unicorn heaven, the eternal pasture.

"But I need you for an emotional reason too. You see, I am a solitary sort of man. I did not wish to be, but certain factors in my life tended to set me apart

124

from my associates, my peer group. I have generally fared best when going it alone. But I don't like *being* alone. I need companionship. Every living, feeling creature does. I have found it on occasion with other men in a shared project, and with women in a shared bed, and these are not bad things. But seldom have I had what I would call true friendship—except with another species of creature. I am a lover of horses. When I am with a horse, I feel happy. A horse does not seek my acquaintance for the sake of my appearance or my accomplishments; a horse does not expect a great deal of me. A horse accepts me as I am. And I accept the horse for what he is. A horse pulls his weight. I respect a horse. We relate. And so when I seek companionship, a really meaningful relationship, I look for a horse."

Neysa's head turned marginally so that she could fix one eye squarely on him. Good—she was paying attention to the soothing tones. Stile eased his grip further, but did not let go her horn.

"So I looked for you, Neysa. To be my equine companion. Because once a horse gives his allegiance, he can be trusted. I do not deceive myself that the horse cares for me in the same way I care for him—" He tightened his grip momentarily in a brief outpouring of the emotion he felt. "Or for her. But a horse is loyal. I can ride a horse, I can play, I can sleep without concern, for the horse will guard me from harm. A good horse will step on a poisonous snake before a man knows the threat is present. The horse will alert me to some developing hazard, for his perceptions are better than mine, and he will carry me away in time.

"I looked for you, Neysa, I selected you from all the herd before I ever saw you directly, because you are not really *of* the herd. You are a loner, like me. Because you are small, like me. But also healthy, like me. I understand and appreciate fitness in man and animal. Your hooves are clean, your manure is wholesome, your muscle tone is excellent, your coat has the luster of health, the sheen—" No, that was the wrong word, for it reminded him again of Sheen the robot lass. Where was she now, what was she doing, how was she taking his absence? Was she in metallic mourning for him? But he could not afford to be distracted by such thoughts at this moment.

"In fact, you are the finest little horse I have ever encountered. I don't suppose that means anything to you, but I have ridden some of the best horses in the known universe, in my capacity as a leading jockey of Planet Proton. That's another world, though. Not one of those animals compares to you in performance. Except that you are not really a horse. You are something else, and maybe you think I insult you, calling you a horse, but it is no insult, it is appreciation. I must judge you by what I know, and I know horses. To me, you are a horse with a horn. Perhaps you are fundamentally different. Perhaps you are superior. You do not sweat, you strike sparks from your hooves, you shoot fire from your nostrils, you play sounds on your horn, you have gaits and tricks no horse ever dreamed of. Perhaps you are a demon in equine form. But I doubt this. I want you because you most resemble a horse, and there is no creature I would rather have with me in a strange land, to share my life for this adventure, than a horse."

He relaxed his grip further as she relaxed. She was not going to jump, now—he hoped. But he wanted to be sure, so he kept on talking. It could be a mistake to rush things, with a horse.

"Now I thought I could conquer you, Neysa. I thought I could ride you and make you mine, as I have done so many times before with other horses. I see now I was wrong. I rode you, but you are not mine. You will kill yourself before you submit to the taming. I hardly know you, Neysa, but I love you; I would not have you sacrifice yourself to escape me." Stile felt moisture on his cheeks and knew he was crying again, as he had with Sheen. Few things could move him that way. A woman was one; a horse was another. "No, do not hurt yourself for me! I grieve at the very thought. I will let you go, Neysa! I can not impose respect on you. You are the most perfect steed I could ever hope to associate with, but I will seek another, a lesser animal. For I must be accepted too; it must be mutual. I can

126

not love, and be unloved. Go with my regret, my sorrow, and my blessing. You are free." And he let her go, slowly, so as not to startle her, and stepped back.

"Yet I wish it had worked out," he said. "Not merely because I can see how good you would have been for me. Not only because the love of such a creature as you, not lightly given, is more precious than anything else I could seek. Not only because you are another example of what I like to see in myself, in my foolish private vanity: the proof that excellence can indeed come in small packages. No, there is more than that. I believe you need me the same way I need you. You are alone; you may not be aware of it, but you need a companion too, one who respects you for what you are. You are no ordinary mare."

He saw a scrape on her foreleg. "Oh, Neysa—you were hurt on that run." He squatted to examine it. Pain lanced through his knees, and he fell over, dangerously near the brink. He clutched at turf and drew himself back to safer ground. "Sorry about that," he said sheepishly. "I have bad knees . . . never mind." He got up carefully, using his hands to brace himself, for rising without squatting was awkward. He had never fully appreciated the uses of his knees, until their capability was diminished.

He approached Neysa slowly, still careful not to startle her, then bent from the waist to look at her leg. "I could wash that off for you, but there's no water here and I think it will heal by itself. It is not serious, and the blood helps clean it. But let me check your feet, Neysa. I do not want to leave you with any injuries of my making, and feet are crucially important. May I lift your left front foot?" He slid his hand down along her leg, avoiding the scrape, then drew on the ankle. "Easy, easy—I just want to look. To see if there are any cracks—cracks in hooves are bad news." The foot came up, though the unicorn was obviously uncertain what he was doing, and he looked at it from the bottom. It was still fairly warm; wisps of vapor curled from the frog, the central triangle of the hoof. "No, that is a fine clean hoof, a little chipped around the edges, but no cracks. You must get plenty of protein in your diet, Neysa!"

He set the foot down. "I should check the others, but I fear you would misunderstand. This is one thing a man can do for his horse. He can check the feet, clear the stones or other obstructions, file them down when they wear unevenly or get badly chipped. The welfare of the steed becomes the responsibility of the man. When food is scarce, the man provides. When there is danger, the man fights to protect the horse. Some animals who prey on horses are wary of men. I might face down a wolf, while you—" He looked at her horn. "No, you could handle a wolf! You don't need the likes of me; why should I deceive myself. I could tell you that to be the associate of a man is to be protected by the intelligence of a man, by his farsighted mind. That a man will anticipate danger and avoid it, for both himself and his mount. His brain makes up for his lesser perceptions. He will steer around sharp stones that might crack hooves. But why should this have meaning for you? You have savvy like none I have seen in any horse; you don't need protection. I delude myself in my desperate need to justify myself, to think that I could in any way be worthy of you."

A fly buzzed up, landing on Neysa. She shook her skin in that place, as horses did, but the fly refused to budge. Her tail flicked across, but the fly was on her shoulder, out of range. She could get it with her mouth, but then she would have to take her attention off Stile. The fly, with the canny ruthlessness of its kind, settled down to bite.

Stile experienced sudden heat. "Now don't startle, Neysa," he said. "I am going to slap that bastard fly, so it can't bother you. Easy, now . . ." He slapped. The fly dropped. "I hate biting flies," Stile said. "I have known them hitherto only through research, but they are the enemies of horses. I will not tolerate them on any animal associated with me." He stepped back, shrugging. "But I am showing my foolishness again. You can handle flies! Good-bye, Neysa. I hope you are happy, and that you graze forever in the greenest pastures."

Stile turned and walked away from the brink, listening only to make sure the unicorn did not jump. His heart was heavy, but he knew he had done the right thing. The unicorn could not be tamed. What a treasure he was leaving behind!

There was a strange rippling in the grass of the ledge. It had been occurring for some time, but only now was he fully conscious of it. It was as if he were in a pool, and a pebble had dropped in, making a spreading series of circular waves. But there was no water. What was causing this?

Something nuzzled his elbow. Stile jumped, startled; he had not heard anything approach.

It was the unicorn. She had come up behind him silently; he had not known she could do that. She could have run her horn through his back.

He faced her, perplexed. Neysa's ears were forward, orienting on him. Her muzzle quivered. Her great brown eyes were wet, gleaming like great jewels. She lifted her head and nibbled on his ear, gently, caressingly. She made a little whinny, cajoling him.

"Oh, Neysa!" he breathed, lifted by an explosion of joy.

He had won her, after all.

CHAPTER 8

Music

They were both tired, but Stile felt compelled to put distance between him and his point of entry to this world. Neysa, having consented to be tamed, was the perfect mount; the slightest pressure of one of his knees on her side would turn her, and the shifting of his weight forward would put her into the smoothest of trots. But mostly he didn't guide her; he let her pick her way.

"I need to hide, Neysa," he explained. "I need a place to be safe, until I can learn what I need to know about this world. Until I can discover who is trying to kill me, and why, and what to do about it. Or whether my experience with the amulet-demon was mere coincidence, a random trap, nothing personal. But until I know this land better, I have no notion where to hide. Paradox."

She listened, then made a gesture with her horn, pointing west, and tapped a forefoot. "It's almost as if you understand me," he said, amused. "At least you understand my need. If you know of a place to go, then by all means take me there, girl!"

But first he paused to gather some straw from a mature field and fashioned it into a crude saddle. "I don't really need a saddle, Neysa, but my weight will make your back sore in time unless it is properly distributed. The human seat-bones don't quite jibe with the equine backbone. This straw is not ideal, but it's better than nothing. We have to get my weight off your ribs and over your withers, your shoulders; that's where you can most comfortably support it. And a token girth to hold it on, so I won't have to yank at your beautiful black mane anymore."

Neysa submitted to this indignity, and carried him westward across the amber plain north of the purple mountains, her speed picking up as her strength returned. Something nagged at Stile; then he caught on. "You know, Neysa—this is like the old patriotic song of America, back on Earth. I've never been there, of course, but it describes amber waves of grain and purple mountains and fruited plains—which reminds me, I'm hungry! I haven't eaten since I came into this world —I don't know whether they really exist on Earth, those purple mountains, but they really do exist here! Do you mind if I whistle the tune?"

She cocked her ear back at him, listening, then cocked it forward. She had cute black ears, expressing her personality. She did not mind.

Stile whistled. He was good at it; whistling was, after all, a form of music, and good whistling was good music. Stile was good at anything that related to the Game, back on Proton. He had spent years constantly perfecting himself, and he had a special nostalgia for music. There had been a girl, once, whose memory he associated with it. He whistled the fields more amber, the mountains more purple, and the whole countryside more beautiful. And it really seemed to be so; the entire landscape seemed to assume a more intense grandeur, together with an atmosphere of expectancy. Expectant of what? Abruptly becoming nervous, Stile broke off.

Neysa paused by a tree. It was a pear tree, with huge ripe fruits. "Bless you!" Stile exclaimed. "Are these safe to eat?" He dismounted without waiting for an answer. What a comfort this unicorn was, now that she had joined him!

Neysa moved to the grain nearby and started grazing. She was hungry too. Horses—and unicorns!—could not proceed indefinitely without sustenance; they had to spend a good deal of their time grazing. So a horse was not really faster transportation, for a man; it was speed when he needed it, interspersed with rest. But it was a life-style he liked. His first hours in this world had not been dull, because of the demon-threat and his quest for a steed; but had he remained alone much longer, he would have become quite bored and lonely. Now, with this companionship, this world was delightful. Perhaps his need for transportation had merely been a sublimation of his need for company.

He would have to assume that they could camp here safely, at least for one night. Stile pulled down a pear. It certainly looked safe. If he starved, distrusting nature's food, what would he gain? He took a juicy bite. It was delicious.

He consumed three of the large fruits, then desisted, just in case. He did not need to gorge. He made a bed of hay, under the pear tree, and lay down as darkness closed in. He hoped it would not rain—but what did it really matter? He would dry. The temperature was nice, here; he would not be cold, even when wet.

Neysa had wandered off. Stile wasn't worried; he was sure of her, now. She would not leave him—and if she did, it was her right. They had a tacit agreement, no more, subject to cancellation without notice by either party. Still he glanced across the field as the first moon came up. He would prefer to have her near him, just in case. He did not know what routine dangers there might be, here, but was sure Neysa could recognize and handle them. The way she had dispatched the crack-demon and the snow-monster—

The moonrise was spectacular. Far less intense than the sun, it had more appeal because he could look at it directly. This was a close, large moon, whose effulgence bathed the slowly crossing clouds in pastel blue. The thickest clouds were black silhouettes, but the thinner ones showed their substance in blue monochrome, in shades of one color, all the lines and curves and burgeonings of them, all inexpressibly lovely. Oh, to travel amidst that picture, in the magic of the night sky!

Slowly it faded. Moonrise, like sunrise, was a fleeting phenomenon, the more precious because of that. Stile was sure no two moonrises or moonsets would be the same; there would always be a different picture, as lovely as the last, but original. What splendor nature

132

proffered to the eye of any man who had half the wit to appreciate it!

Something was coming. Not a unicorn. Alarmed, Stile peered through the slanting moonbeams. He remained naked, weaponless; he had seldom felt the need for weapons in Proton society, though he knew how to use them. This was a wilder world whose beauty was tempered, perhaps even enhanced, by its hazards. Was this a nocturnal predator?

No—it was a woman!

Yet she carried no weapon either, and wore no clothing, and seemed innocent rather than hostile. This could be another demonic trap, but Stile somehow doubted it. She was—there was something familiar about her.

As she came close, the moonlight caught her fully. The promising outline was fulfilled in blue light. She was small, very small, smaller even than he, but supremely healthy and full-fleshed. She was beautifully proportioned, with small hands and feet, slender yet rounded legs, and virginally firm breasts. Her fingernails and toenails glistened like pearls, her hair was lustrous black, and she had an ivory decoration set in her forehead. Her face was quite cute, though she had a Roman nose. Her only flaw was a scratch on one arm, a fresh one only starting to heal.

"Stile," she said, with an almost musical inflection.

"Neysa!" he replied, astonished.

She opened her arms to him, smiling. And Stile understood that the friendship of a unicorn was no inconsequential thing. When he had won her, he had won her completely.

She was of course a variant of demon. No ordinary creature could make such a transformation. But it was already clear that there were variations among demons, in fact whole phyla of them. What mattered was not how far removed her type was from his, but how they related to one another. He trusted Neysa.

Stile embraced her, and kissed her, and she was lithe and soft and wholly desirable. He lay down with her

133

under the pear tree, knowing her for what she was, and loved her, as he had loved the robot Sheen.

In the morning Neysa was back in equine form, grazing. Stile glanced at her, covertly reflecting on the event of the night. Would she expect different treatment, now? Would she now decline to carry him safely?

As it turned out, Neysa's attitude was unchanged. She was still his steed. The night had been merely a confirmation of their relationship, not a change in it. But never again would he think of a unicorn as merely a horse with a horn.

Rested and fed, Neysa set out at an easy trot across the field, still bearing west. Trots could be rough or smooth; this one was the smoothest. She could have looked like a drudge, yet fetched a high price on Proton, for the sake of this trot. As if such a creature could ever be sold, for any price! Then she moved into a nice canter with a syncopated beat: one-two-three-pause, one-two-three-pause. A canter, to his way of thinking, was a trot by the forefeet and a gallop by the rear feet; it too could vary greatly in comfort, depending on the steed's nature and mood. Stile enjoyed this; how nice it was to ride this fine animal without fighting her!

Neysa shifted into a variant of the trot: the pace, in which the left feet moved together, and the right feet together also. Two beats, throwing him from side to side, but covering the ground faster than an ordinary trot. Then back into a canter—but not an ordinary one. Her rear hooves were striking the ground together, synched with her right front hoof, so that this was another two-beat gait: a single foot alternating with three feet. One-TWO! One-TWO! He had to post over the shocks, lest his bones begin to rattle.

She was showing off her gaits, proving that no horse could match her in variety or facility. Yesterday she had demonstrated gaits from one-beat to five-beat; now she was doing the variations.

"This is great stuff, Neysa!" he said warmly. "You are the most versatile hoofer I know." For this was an aspect of companionship: performing for an appreciative friend. Animals, like people, would do a lot, just for the satisfaction of having their efforts recognized. Though Neysa was not precisely an animal *or* a person.

Just when Stile thought he had experienced the whole of her repertoire, Neysa surprised him again. She began to play music through her horn. Not an occasional melodic note, but genuine tunes. Her hooves beat counterpoint to the sustained notes, making a dramatic march.

"The five-beat gait!" Stile exclaimed. "*That's* what it's for! Syncopation, going with your music!"

She moved into the five-beat, playing an intricate melody that fit that beat perfectly. This time her motion was easy, not designed to unseat him, and he liked it. Stile was no longer surprised by her comprehension; he had realized, in stages during the prior day and night, that she comprehended human speech perfectly, though she did not bother to speak it herself. When he had indulged in his soliloquy on the ledge above the Meander River, she had understood precisely what he said. His meaning, not his tone, had converted her. That was good, because he had meant exactly what he said.

Now he could give her detailed verbal instructions, but she preferred the body directives of legs and weight-shifting. She moved to his directives with no evidence of those messages apparent to any third party. That was the riding ideal. She was at home with what she was: a unicorn. Stile, too, preferred the closeness this mode entailed; it was the natural way, a constant communication with his steed.

Neysa's horn-music resembled that of a harmonica. No doubt there were many small channels in her horn, with natural fiber reeds, and she could direct the flow of air through any channels she wished as she breathed. What a convenient way to play!

"You know, Neysa—I know something of music myself. Not just whistling. I was introduced to it by a girl a bit like you, in your girl-form: very small, pretty, and talented. I'm not the top musician in my world, but I am competent—because music is part of the competition of the Game. You wouldn't know about that, of

135

course; it's like a—like a continuing contest, a race, where every day you race someone new, in a different way, and if you get really good you gain status. I have won Games by playing themes better than other people. The violin, the clarinet, the tuba—I've played them all. I wish I could accompany you! I suppose I could whistle again, or sing—" He shrugged. "But I'd really like to show you what I can do with an instrument. One like yours. Another harmonica. So we could play together. A duet. There's a special joy in that, as great in its way as—as the joy we had in our game of the night. With an instrument, I could come to you, as you came to me, sharing your frame."

Neysa accepted this as she did most of his commentary: with a wiggle of one ear and tolerance. She didn't mind if in his vanity he thought he could play the way she could. She liked him anyway.

Stile pondered briefly, then made a little verse of it. "The harmonica is what you play; I wish I had one here today." He fitted the words to her melody, singing them.

Neysa made an unmelodic snort, and Stile laughed. "Corny, I know! Doggerel is not my forte. All right, I'll quit."

But the unicorn slowed, then stopped, then turned about to retrace her last few steps. "What's the matter?" Stile asked, perplexed. "If I offended you, I'm sorry. I didn't mean to mess up your music."

She fished in the tall grass with her horn. Something glittered there. Stile dismounted and walked around to examine it, fearing trouble. If it were another demon-amulet—

It was a large, ornate, well-constructed harmonica, seemingly new.

Stile picked it up, examining it in wonder. "You have a good eye, Neysa, spotting this, and it couldn't have happened at a more fortuitous time. Why, this is from my world. See, it says MADE ON EARTH. Earth has a virtual monopoly on quality musical instruments. Most colonies are too busy to specialize in the arts. This is a good brand. I'm no specialist in this particular

136

instrument, but I'll bet I could play—" He looked around. "Someone must have lost it. I'm not sure it would be right to—" He shook his head. "Yet it won't help the owner, just to leave it here. I suppose I could borrow it, until I can return it to—"

Having rationalized the matter, Stile remounted his straw saddle—which seemed to be holding up extraordinarily well, packing into an ideal shape—and settled down for the resumption of the ride. Neysa moved into a smooth running walk, and played her horn, and Stile tried out the harmonica.

It was a lovely instrument. It had sixteen holes, which would translate into thirty-two notes: four octaves. It was, in addition, chromatic; it had a lever at the end which, when depressed, would shift the full scale into the half-tones. There were also several buttons whose purpose he did not fathom; he would explore those in due course.

Stile put his mouth to it, getting the feel of it, blowing an experimental note. And paused, surprised and gratified; it was tremolo, with the peculiar and pleasant beat of two closely matched reeds. He blew an experimental scale, pursing his lips to produce a single note at a time. This harmonica was extremely well constructed, with no broken reeds, and every note was pure and in perfect pitch.

Very good. Neysa had halted her music, curious about his activity. Stile essayed a melody. He kept it simple at first, playing no false notes, but the instrument was so conducive and the sound so pleasant that he soon broke into greater complexities.

Neysa perked her ears to listen. She turned her head to glance obliquely back at him, surprised. Stile paused. "Yes, I really can play," he said. "You thought I was a duffer? That whistling represented the epitome of my achievement? I love music; it is another one of those things that come easily to a lonely person. Of course I'm not as sharp on the harmonica as I am on other instruments, and I can't play elaborately, but—"

She blew a note of half-negation. "What, then?" he inquired. "You know, Neysa, it would be easier for me if you talked more—but I guess you'd have to change to your human form for that, and then we couldn't travel properly. You know, you really surprised me when you—do you call it shape-changing? Permutation? Reformulation? It was an aspect of you I had never suspected—"

She blew another note, three-quarter affirmation. He was getting better at grasping her communications. "You're still trying to tell me something," he said. "I'm pretty good at riddles; that's another aspect of the Game. Let's see—is it about your manifestation as—no? About my reaction to it? You say half-right. About my surprise—*your* surprise? Ah, now I get it! You were just as amazed to discover I could play a musical instrument as I was to see you in human form."

Neysa made an affirmation. But there was still a slight reservation. Stile pursued the matter further. "And, just as your change of form enabled us to interact in a new and meaningful way—though not more meaningful than this joy of traveling together across this beautiful land—my abruptly revealed facility with music enables us to interact in yet another way." He smiled. "Which is what I was trying to tell you before —oh, you mean now you agree! You—no, you couldn't be apologizing! Unicorns never make mistakes, do they?"

She made a little buck, just a warning. He laughed. "Well, let's get to it," he said, pleased. He put the harmonica to his mouth and played an improvised theme, sending the perfect notes ringing out over the plain between the mountain ranges. Now Neysa joined in, and they made beautiful harmony. Her hooves beat the cadence, in effect a third instrument. The resulting duet was extremely pretty.

Stile experimented with the mystery buttons, and discovered that they were modes, like those of a good accordion; they changed the tones so that the harmonica sounded like other instruments, to a degree. One canceled the tremolo effect; another brought into play an octave-tuned scale. Another rendered the instrument into a diatonic harmonica, with the popular but incom-

138

plete scale and slightly differing tone arrangement. This was the most sophisticated harmonica he had ever played. That only increased his wonder that it should have been so carelessly lost out here. If he dropped such an instrument, he would search for hours to locate it, for it was a marvel of its kind. Who could have left it without a search?

Stile taught Neysa a song, and she taught him one. They played with improvisations to the beat of differing gaits. They did responsive passages, one taking the main theme, the other the refrains. They played alto and tenor on a single theme.

But soon something developed in the atmosphere—a brooding presence, an intangible power. It intensified, becoming almost visible.

Stile broke off his playing. Neysa halted. Both looked about.

There was nothing. The presence was gone.

"You felt it too?" Stile asked. Neysa flicked an ear in assent. "But what *was* it?"

She shrugged, almost dislodging his impromptu saddle. Stile checked his woven-straw cinch to see if it was broken. It wasn't; the strap had merely worked loose from the ring, as happened on occasion. He threaded it through again, properly, so that it would hold.

And did a double take. Strap? Ring?

He jumped to the ground and looked at his handiwork. Loose straw was shedding from it, but underneath it was a well-made if battered leather saddle, comfortable from long use.

He had fashioned a padding of straw. It had been straw this morning when he put it on her. Where had the saddle come from?

"Neysa—" But how would she know? *She* could not have put it there.

She turned her head to gaze directly at him. Then she turned it farther, touching the saddle with her horn. And looked at him, surprised.

"Someone has given us a saddle," Stile said. "Yet there was no way—it was straw this morning—I was riding you the whole time—"

139

She blew a nervous note. She didn't know what to make of it either.

"Magic," Stile said. "This is a realm of magic. There was magic in the air just now. A—spell?"

Neysa agreed. "Could it be my nemesis, the one I think tried to kill me?" Stile asked. "Showing his power? Yet the saddle is helpful, not harmful. It's something I needed, and it's a good one. And—" He paused, partly nervous, partly awed. "And the harmonica—that appeared like magic when I wanted it—Neysa, is someone or something trying to *help* us? Do we have a gremlin friend as well as an enemy? I'm not sure I like this—because we can't be sure it is a friend. The way that amulet turned into a demon—"

Neysa turned abruptly and began galloping at right angles to her prior course, carrying him along. She was bearing south, toward the purple mountains. Stile knew she had something in mind, so let her take her own route.

Soon they approached a unicorn herd. Neysa must have been skirting the herd all along, aware of it though Stile was not, and now sought it out. She sounded a peremptory note on her horn before drawing close. A single unicorn at the edge of the herd perked up, then galloped toward them. A friend?

Neysa turned and bore west again, away from the herd, and the other unicorn cut across to intercept her. The other was male, larger than Neysa though not substantially so. His color was quite different: dark blue, with red socks. Really the same pattern as Neysa's, but with completely unhorselike hues. Again Stile reminded himself: these were not horses.

As the two animals angled together, Neysa tooted her horn. The stranger answered with a similar toot. His horn sounded more like a saxophone, however. Did every unicorn play a different instrument? What a cacophony when several ran together!

Neysa shifted into the five-beat gait and played a compatible tune. The other matched the gait and cadence, and played a complementary theme. The two blended beautifully. No wonder Neysa had played so well with Stile himself; she had done this sort of thing before, with her own kind. Stile listened, entranced. No cacophony, this; it was a lovely duet.

Who, then, was this young stallion she had summoned? Stile did not really want his presence advertised. But he knew Neysa understood that, and was acting in his interest. She had to have reason. This must be some friend she trusted, who could help them discover the nature of the magic—or protect them from it if necessary.

They ran until well clear of the herd. Then they slowed, their harmony slowing with them. Neysa finally deposited Stile by a handsome nut tree and started grazing. It was the middle of the day: lunch break. She would probably insist on grazing for an hour or more, and he did not begrudge her that. She needed her strength, still not entirely restored after yesterday's trial. He removed the saddle and set it under the tree.

The strange unicorn did not graze. He watched Stile, looking him up and down. He took a step forward, horn pointed at Stile's navel. The musical instrument was now a weapon, without doubt. Stile stood still, chewing on a nut, relaxed but ready to move in a hurry if the creature charged.

The unicorn blew a single derisive note, shimmered —and became a man. The man was clothed. He wore furry leather trousers, a blue long-sleeved shirt, solid low boots, red socks, and a floppy light-blue hat. His hands were covered by heavy fiber gloves. A rapier hung at his side.

Astonished, Stile stared. A Citizen—here?

"So thou'rt the creep who's been messing with my sister!" the man said, his right hand fingering the hilt of the rapier.

Just what he needed: a protective brother! Now Stile saw the forehead spike, similar to Neysa's. No Citizen; ordinary people wore clothing here, he remembered now. "It was voluntary," Stile said tightly.

"Ha! I saw her charging up Snow Mountain yesterday, trying to shake thee off. Thou'rt lucky she changed not into a firefly and let thee drop in a crevasse!"

141

Oh. The unicorn was talking about the day, not the night. "She changes into a firefly, too?"

"And pray what's wrong with that? Most beasts are lucky if they can change into one other form. We each have two." He shimmered again, and became a hawk. The bird winged upward at a forty-five-degree angle, then looped and dived toward Stile.

Stile threw himself aside—and the man was back, appearing just as the bird seemed about to crash into the ground. "Well, there's no accounting for tastes. Thou'rt a shrimp, and thou'rt naked, but if she lets thee ride her I can't say nay. I want thee to know, though, that she's the best mare in the herd, color or not."

"Color?" Stile asked blankly.

"Don't tell me thou noticed not! Let me warn thee, man-thing: an thou dost ever use the term 'horse-hued' in her presence, I will personally—"

Neysa had come up behind her brother. She blew a warning note.

"All right, already!" he snapped. "She is one season my senior; I may not talk back to her. But remember what I say: *there is nothing wrong with Neysa!*"

"Nothing at all," Stile agreed. "She's the finest-performing and finest-looking mare I've encountered."

The man, evidently braced for doubt or argument, was briefly nonplused. "Uh, yes. Exactly. Then let's get on with it. What's thy problem?"

"My name is Stile. I am a stranger in this world, without information or clothing, someone is trying to kill me, and magic is being performed around me whose ultimate purpose I can not fathom." Stile had the gift for succinct expression, when required.

"So." The man frowned. "Well, my name is Clip. I'm Neysa's little brother. She wants me to help thee, so I'll help. I'll fix thee up with information and clothing. And a weapon to defend thyself from thine enemy. As for the magic—concern thyself not about it. Unicorns are immune to magic."

"Immune!" Stile expostulated. "Here you stand, a shape-changing unicorn, and you tell me—"

"*Other* magic, nit. Of course we do our own, though easy it is not. Like learning another language—which is part of shape-changing, of course; can't be human if thou canst not talk human idiom. Can't be avian if thou canst not fly. So most unicorns bother not. But none *other* can change a unicorn, or enchant one. Or anyone in contact with a unicorn. Was that not why thou didst desire her? So long as thou stayest with Neysa—" He frowned. "Though why she'd want to stay with *thee*—" Neysa's note of protest cut him off again. "Well, there's no comprehending the ways of mares." He began to remove his clothing.

"No comprehending!" Stile agreed. "Look, Clip—I rode Neysa as a challenge, because I needed a mount. In the end I couldn't keep her—but she joined me by her own choice. I don't know why she didn't jump off the mountain and change into a firefly and let me drop to my death, as I gather she could have—" And he had thought he was sparing *her*, when he released her at the ledge! "And I don't know why she's not talking to me now. When she—changed to human form, all she said was my name. She didn't explain anything." At the time he had thought no explanations were necessary; he had been naive!

"That last I can clarify. Neysa doesn't like to talk much. I'm the talkative one in our family, as perhaps thou hadst not yet noticed. So where there's talking to be done, she summons me." Clip handed his shirt to Stile. "Go on, get dressed. I don't need clothing, really, anyway, and I'll get another outfit when convenient." He glanced at Neysa. "I guess she saw something in thee she liked. Thou'rt not a virgin, art thou?"

Stile donned the shirt, shaking his head no, embarrassed both by the turn the conversation had taken and the act of assuming clothing. On Proton this would be socially and legally horrendous!

The shirt should have been large, but somehow turned out to fit him perfectly. He was coming to accept minor magic as the matter of course it was.

"Well, that's overrated anyway," Clip continued. "If

143

I ever found a nubile but virginal human girl, it sure wouldn't be my head I'd put in her lap!"

Stile smiled appreciatively, coming to like the expressive and uninhibited male. "What would a unicorn—or, one in equine form—want with a human girl anyway?"

"Oh, that's easy." The trousers were passed over. "The Herd Stallion co-opts all the best unicorn mares, which leaves us young males hard up. A unicorn does not live by grain alone, thou knowest! So though human flesh is less sweet than equine, even the touch of a fair maiden's hand is—"

"I begin to get the picture." The trousers fit perfectly also. Stile suppressed another twinge of guilt, donning clothing; this was not Proton, and clothing lacked the significance it had there. Out here in the wilderness, clothing became functional on more than a social basis. "Yet that being the case, an attractive mare shouldn't have any trouble—"

Neysa abruptly turned away. Clip lowered his voice. "All right, man. I see thou really knowest not, and thou'dst better. There are horses in unicorn ancestry—not nice to mention it, any more than the apes in thine ancestry—"

"There are no apes in my—"

"See what I mean? Sensitive subject. But on occasion there are throwbacks. When a unicorn is birthed without a horn—that is, without the horn-button; couldn't have a full horn before birth, of course—it is killed in simple mercy. But color is a borderline matter. If it is otherwise perfect, that unicorn is permitted to survive. But there is always that stigma." Clip frowned, glancing covertly at Neysa.

"Neysa—is colored like a horse," Stile said, catching on. "So she is outcast."

"Thou hast it. It is no official thing, for she *is* a full unicorn, but the Herd Stallion won't breed her, and of course none of the lesser males dare. *Nobody* touches a young mare without the Herd Stallion's permission, and he won't give it—because that would seem to infringe on his prerogative. Our kind is like that; simple logic is no substitute for pride. Some would have it that mules

144

are the stubbornest of equines, but that is a dastardly slight on the stubbornness of the unicorn. So for two seasons now Neysa has gone unbred—all because of her color. And maybe her size."

Stile realized that his effort of the past night did not count. He was a man, not a stallion. He could play with a female like Neysa, but could never breed her, any more than a stallion in human form could breed a human girl. "This is outrageous! She's a fine unicorn! The Stallion should either breed her or free her."

"Thou knowest thou'rt only a man," Clip said, handing Stile the rapier. "But thy personality hath its redeeming aspects. Thou really likest Neysa?"

"I chose her because she was the finest steed I'd ever seen," Stile said seriously. "I loved her in that fashion from the start. To me there is no better creature than a perfect—equine."

"So thou never, until I spoke to thee, knew what was wrong with her?"

"There is nothing wrong with her!" Stile snapped.

"Agreed." Clip was highly gratified. "Well, I'm supposed to fill thee in on our world. There is little to tell. We unicorns are the dominant animal form, except perhaps in some corners of the pasture where the werewolves and vampires range, and we're really better off than the human peasants. Anyone can do magic, but most humans don't, because of the Adepts."

"Adepts?"

"Like Herd Stallions or wolf Pack Leaders, only it's magic, not mares or bitches they pre-empt. Each Adept has his special style of enchantment, and he's awfully good in his specialization. I said unicorns were proof against foreign spells, but Adepts are another matter. If an Adept should be after thee—"

"I see. What defense would I have against one of these super-sorcerers?"

"No defense suffices, except to hide—and sooner or later an Adept will find thee. They have charms and amulets and familiars spread throughout the realm of Phaze, spying out the news. There's hardly any limit to the powers of an Adept. In fact—that's it! The Oracle!"

"A fortune-teller?"

"More than that. There is no magic in the temple of the Oracle, and nobody is coerced therein. It is sacred ground. I'll bet that's where Neysa is taking thee. Well, then, that covers it. I'll be off." He shimmered back into unicorn form and galloped away, his horn and hooves sounding the charge.

Stile had wanted to know more about Adepts and the Oracle. Well, perhaps Neysa would tell him, if he asked her nicely. Clip had certainly helped a great deal.

They rode west again, playing brief duets, enjoying themselves. Stile realized that the music of unicorns served another purpose: it alerted friends and foes to their presence. Unicorns were fighting animals; most creatures would prefer to avoid them, and so the sound of the horn cleared the way conveniently. Stile saw rabbits and turtles and an armadillo, but no predators. In short, only creatures that were noncompetitive with unicorns.

The terrain was highly varied, lush fields giving way to rocky slopes, swamps, open water and badlands sand. To the north and south the twin mountain ranges continued. The northern peaks were all snow-covered, virtually impassable to any creature with less power and determination than a unicorn; the southern ones seemed to be warmer, unless purple was the color of their snow. Curious! Something about this rugged landscape nagged him, a nascent familiarity, but he was unable to place it.

In the evening Neysa halted again, giving herself time to graze, and Stile foraged for his own sustenance. He found ripe corn growing, and blackberries. He thought of corn as fall produce, and blackberries as spring, but perhaps this world differed from others in its fruiting seasons too. On Proton anything could grow at any time, in the domes. Nonetheless, these edibles were suspiciously fortuitous—unless Neysa had known of this place and come here deliberately. Yes, of course that was it; she was taking excellent care of him.

In the night, after moonrise, she changed again. Stile hoped she would show him her firefly form, but she went directly to human. "You know, Neysa, you're about the prettiest girl I've seen—but I think I like you best in your natural form."

She smiled, flattered, and kissed him. She didn't mind being complimented on her unicorn body. She had spent her life stigmatized for a supposedly defective color, and obviously appreciated Stile's appreciation. This was no doubt the key to her initial acceptance of him. He really did admire her as she was, and was perhaps the first creature unrelated to her to do so. So though she had fought him, in the end she had not wanted to kill him.

"The Oracle—" he began. But she only kissed him again.

She wasn't talking. Ah, well. The stubbornness of unicorns! She had other virtues. He kissed her back.

Next morning she gave him some pointers on the use of the rapier. Stile had used a sword before, as fencing was one of the aspects of the Game. But by an anomaly of circumstance he had practiced with the broadsword, not the rapier. This light, thin sword was strange to him—and if it were the kind of weapon commonly used in this world, he had better master it in a hurry.

Neysa was expert. Stile had supposed a unicorn would not care to have the weapon of an opponent so close to the tender eyes, ears, and nose—but the proximity of her organs of perception gave her marvelous coordination with her weapon. Stile soon learned he could thrust without fear for her; his point would never score. Even if it should happen to slip through her guard, what would it strike? The heavy bone of her forehead, buttressing the horn. It would take more of a thrust than a man like him could muster to penetrate that barrier.

No, he had to look out for himself. Neysa was better on the parry than on the lunge, for the merest twitch of her head moved the horn-tip several centimeters, but to make a forward thrust she had to put her whole body in motion. Thus she was best equipped for defense against a charging adversary, either allowing the other to impale himself on her firm point, or knocking aside his weapon. Stile, forced to attack, found himself disarmed repeatedly, her horn bearing instantly on his vulnerable chest. She *could* lunge, and with horrible power—but did not, when she fenced a friend. How could he match the speed and power of her natural horn?

But Stile was a quick study. Soon he did not try to oppose power with power. Instead he used the finesse he had developed with the broadsword, countering power with guile. Soon Neysa could no longer disarm him at will, and sometimes he caught her out of position and halted his point just shy of her soft long throat. In a real match he could not hope to overcome her, but he was narrowing the gap.

But he was also getting tired. His throat felt sore, and his eyes got bleary. He could feel a flush on his face, yet he was shivering. Neysa made a feint—and he almost fell across her horn.

"Hostile magic!" he gasped. "I'm weak—"

Then he was unconscious.

CHAPTER 9

Promotion

Dreams came, replaying old memories . . .

The weapon-program director stared down at him. "You sure you want to get into swords, lad? They get pretty heavy." He meant heavy for someone Stile's size.

Again that burgeoning anger, that hopeless wrath instigated by the careless affronts of strangers. That determination to damn well prove he was not as small as they saw him. To prove it, most of all, to himself. "I need a sword. For the Game."

"Ah, the Game." The man squinted at him judiciously. "Maybe I've seen you there. Name?"

"Stile." For a moment he hoped he had some compensating notoriety from the Game.

The man shook his head. "No, must have been someone else. A child star, I think."

So Stile reminded this oaf of a child. It didn't even occur to the program director that such a reference might be less than complimentary to a grown man. But it would be pointless to react openly—or covertly. Why couldn't he just ignore what others thought, let their opinions flow from his back like idle water? Stile was good at the Game, but not that good. Not yet. He had a number of weaknesses to work on—and this was one. "Maybe you'll see me some time—with a sword."

The director smiled condescendingly. "It is your privilege. What kind did you want?"

"The rapier."

The man checked his list. "That class is filled. I can put you on the reserve list for next month."

This was a disappointment. Stile had admired the finesse of the rapier, and felt that he could do well with it. "No, I have time available now."

"The only class open today is the broadsword. I doubt you'd want that."

Stile doubted it too. But he did not appreciate the director's all-too-typical attitude. It was one thing to be looked down on; another to accept it with proper grace. "I'll take the broadsword."

The man could not refuse him. Any serf was entitled to any training available, so long as he was employed and the training did not interfere with his assigned duties. "I don't know if we have an instructor your size."

Stile thought of going up against a giant for his first lesson. He did not relish that either. "Aren't you supposed to have a full range of robots?"

The man checked. He was obviously placing difficulties in the way, trying to discourage what he felt would be a wasted effort. He could get a reprimand from his own employer if he placed a serf in an inappropriate class and an injury resulted. "Well, we do have one, but—"

"I'll take that one," Stile said firmly. This oaf was not going to balk him!

The director shrugged, smiling less than graciously. "Room 21."

Stile was startled. That happened to be his age. Twenty-one. He had been a stable hand for a year, now. Coincidence, surely. He thanked the director perfunctorily and went to room 21.

"Good afternoon, ma'am," the instructor said, coming to life. "Please allow me to put this protective halter on you, so that no untoward accident can happen." She held out the armored halter.

A female robot, programmed of course for a woman. That was how the problem of size had been solved.

Stile imagined the director's smirk, if he left now. He gritted his teeth. "I don't need the halter. I am a man." How significant that statement seemed! If only he could get living people to listen, too. He was a man, not a midget, not a child.

The robot hesitated. Her face and figure were those of a young woman, but she was not of the most ad-

150

vanced type. She was not programmed for this contingency. "Ma'am, it is required—"

Useless to argue with a mechanical! "All right." Stile took the halter and tied it about his waist. There it might offer some modicum of protection for what a man valued.

The robot smiled. "Very good, ma'am. Now here are the weapons." She opened the storage case.

It seemed an anomaly to Stile to have a female instructing the broadsword, but he realized that women played the Game too, and there were no handicaps given for size, age, experience or sex, and not all of them cared to default when it came to fencing. They felt as he did: they would go down fighting. Often a person with such an attitude did not go down at all; he/she won, to his/her surprise. Attitude was important.

The robot was not smart, but she was properly programmed. She commenced the course of instruction, leaving nothing to chance. Stance, motion, strategy, exercises for homework to increase facility. Safety precautions. Scoring mechanisms and self-rating scale. Very basic, but also very good. When a program of instruction was instituted on Proton, it was the best the galaxy could offer.

Stile discovered that the broadsword had its own virtues and techniques. It had two cutting edges as well as the point, making it more versatile—for the person who mastered it. It did not have to be heavy; modern alloys and molecular-foam metals made the blade light yet keen. He soon realized that there could be a Game advantage in this weapon. Most opponents would expect him to go for the rapier, and would play to counter that. Of such misjudgments were Game decisions made.

Next morning he reported to the stables as usual. "Stile, we're bringing in a robot trainer from another farm," the foreman said. "Name's Roberta. Get out to the receiving gate and bring her in." And he smiled privately.

Stile went without question, knowing another stable hand would be assigned to cover his chores in the interim. He had been given a post of distinction: greeter to a new trainer. No doubt Roberta was a very special machine.

She was already at the gate when Stile arrived. She was in the shade of a dwarf eucalyptus tree, mounted on a fine bay mare about sixteen hands high. The gatekeeper pointed her out, half-hiding a smirk.

What was so funny about this robot? Stile was reminded uncomfortably of the weapon-program director, who had known about the female robot instructor. Being deceived in any fashion by a robot was always an embarrassment, since no robot intentionally deceived. Unless programmed to—but that was another matter.

This one did not look special: flowing yellow hair, a perfect figure—standard, since they could make humanoid robots any shape desired. Why make a grotesquerie? She seemed small to be a trainer—smaller than the fencing instructor he had worked with. She was a rider, obviously; was she also a jockey? To break in the most promising horses for racing? No robot-jockey could actually race, by law; but no living person had the programmed patience of a training machine, and the horses did well with such assistance.

"Roberta, follow me," Stile said, and began walking along the access trail.

The robot did not follow. Stile paused and turned, annoyed. "Roberta, accompany me, if you please." That last was a bit of irony, as robots lacked free will.

She merely looked at him, smiling.

Oh, no—was she an idiot model, not programmed for verbal directives? Yet virtually all humanoid robots were keyed to respond at least to their names. "Roberta," he said peremptorily.

The mare perked her ears at him. The girl chuckled. "She only responds to properly couched directives," she said.

Stile's eyes passed from girl to mare. A slow flush forged up to his hairline. "The horse," he said.

"Roberta, say hello to the red man," the girl said, touching the horse's head with her crop.

The mare neighed.

"A robot horse," Stile repeated numbly. "A living girl."

"You're very intelligent," the girl said. "What's your name?"

"Uh, Stile." Of all the pitfalls to fall into!

"Well, Uh-Stile, if you care to mount Roberta, you can take her in."

His embarrassment was replaced by another kind of awkwardness. "I am a stable hand. I don't ride."

She dismounted smoothly. Afoot she was slightly shorter than he, to his surprise. She evinced the confidence normally associated with a larger person, though of course height was less important to women. "You're obviously a jockey, Uh-Stile, as I am. Don't try to fool me."

"That's Stile, no uh," he said.

"Stile Noah? What an unusual appellation!"

"Just Stile. What's your name?"

"I'm Tune. Now that the amenities are complete, get your butt on that robot."

"You don't understand. Stable hands tend horses; they don't ride."

"This is not a horse, it's a robot. Who ever heard of a jockey who didn't ride?"

"I told you I'm not—" Then it burst upon him. "*That's* why my employer chose me! Because I'm small. He wanted a potential jockey!"

"Your comprehension is positively effulgent."

"Do—do you really think—?"

"It is obvious. Why else would anyone want serfs our size? Your employer started you on the ground, huh? Slinging dung?"

"Slinging dung," he agreed, feeling better. This girl was small; she was not really making fun of him; she was playfully teasing him. "Until I found a worm."

"A whole worm?" she asked, round-eyed. "How did it taste?"

"A parasite worm. In the manure."

153

"'They don't taste very good."

"Now I've been a year in the stable. I don't know a thing about riding."

"Ha. You've watched every move the riders make," Tune said. "I know. I started that way too. I wasn't lucky enough to find a worm. I worked my way up. Now I race. Don't win many, but I've placed often enough. Except that now I'm on loan to do some training. For those who follow after, et cetera. Come on—I'll show you how to ride."

Stile hesitated. "I don't think I'm supposed to—"

"For crying in silence!" she exclaimed. "Do I have to hand-feed you? Get up behind me. Roberta won't mind."

"It's not the horse. It's my employer's policy. He's very strict about—"

"He told you not to take a lift on a robot?"

"No, but—"

"What will he say if you don't get Roberta to your stable at all?"

Was she threatening him? Better her displeasure than that of his employer! "Suppose I just put you back on the horse and lead her in?"

Tune shrugged. She had the figure for it. "Suppose you try?"

Call one bluff! Stile stepped in close to lift her. Tune met him with a sudden, passionate kiss.

Stile reeled as from a body-block. Tune drew back and surveyed him from all of ten centimeters distance. "Had enough? You can't lead Roberta anyway; she's programmed only for riding."

Stile realized he was overmatched. "We'll do it your way. It'll be your fault if I get fired."

"I just knew you'd see the light!" she exclaimed, pleased. She put her foot in the stirrup and swung into the saddle. Then she removed her foot. "Use the stirrup. Hold on to me. Lift your left foot. It's a big step, the first time."

It was indeed. Sixteen hands was over 1.6 meters—a tenth of a meter taller than he was. He had to heft his foot up past waist-height to get it in the stirrup. He had seen riders mount smoothly, but his observation did not translate into competence for himself. Tune was in the way; he was afraid he'd bang his head into her left breast, trying to scramble up.

She chuckled and reached down with her left hand, catching him in the armpit. She hauled as he heaved, and he came up—and banged his head into her breast. "Swing it around behind, over the horse," she said. Then, at his stunned pause, she added: "I am referring to your right leg, clumsy."

Stile felt the flush burning right down past his collarbone. He swung his leg around awkwardly. He kneed the horse, but managed to get his leg over, and finally righted himself behind Tune. No one would know him for a gymnast at this moment!

"That mounting should go down in the record books," she said. "Your face is so hot it almost burned my—skin." Stile could not see her face, but knew she was smiling merrily. "Now put your arms around my waist to steady yourself. Your employer might be mildly perturbed if you fell down and broke your crown. Good dungslingers are hard to replace. He'd figure Roberta was too spirited a nag for you."

Numbly, Stile reached around her and hooked his fingers together across her small firm belly. Tune's hair was in his face; it had a clean, almost haylike smell.

Tune shifted her legs slightly, and abruptly the robot horse was moving. Stile was suddenly exhilarated. This was like sailing on a boat in a slightly choppy sea—the miniature sea with the artificial waves that was part of the Game facilities. Tune's body compensated with supple expertise. They proceeded down the path.

"I've seen you in the Game," Tune remarked. "You're pretty good, but you're missing some things yet."

"I started fencing lessons yesterday," Stile said, half flattered, half defensive.

"That, too. What about the performing arts?"

"Well, martial art—"

She reversed her crop, put it to her mouth—and

played a pretty little melody. The thing was a concealed pipe of some kind, perhaps a flute or recorder.

Stile was entranced. "That's the loveliest thing I ever heard!" he exclaimed when she paused. "Who's steering the horse?"

"You don't need reins to steer a horse; haven't you caught on to that yet? You don't need a saddle to ride, either. Not if you know your business. Your legs, the set of your weight—watch."

Roberta made a steady left turn, until she had looped a full circle.

"You did that?" Stile asked. "I didn't see anything."

"Put your hand on my left leg. No, go ahead, Stile; I want you to feel the tension. See, when I press on that side, she bears right. When I shift my weight back, she stops." Tune leaned back into Stile, and the horse stopped. "I shift forward, so little you can't see it, but she can feel it—hold on to me tight, so you can feel my shift—that's it." Her buttocks flexed and the horse started walking again. "Did you feel me?"

"You're fantastic," Stile said.

"I referred to the guidance of the horse. I already know about me."

"Uh, yes."

"Roberta responds only to correct signals; she has no idiosyncrasies, as a living animal might. You have to do it just right, with her. That's why she's used for training. So the horses won't teach the riders any bad habits. You noted how she ignored you when you spoke to her from the ground. She responds only to her rider. She's not a plow horse, after all."

"She's fantastic too."

"Oh, she is indeed! But me—I do have two cute little faults."

Stile was inordinately interested now. "What are they?"

"I lie a little."

Meaning he could not trust all of what she had been telling him? Discomforting thought! "What about the other?"

"How could you believe it?"

There was that. If she lied about it—

Tune played her instrument again. It was, she explained, a keyboard harmonica, with the keys concealed; she blew in the end, and had a scale of two and a half octaves available at her touch. Her name was fitting; her music was exquisite. She was right: he needed to look into music.

Tune and Roberta began training the new riders. Stile returned to his routine duties. But suddenly it was not as interesting, handling the horses afoot. His mind was elsewhere. Tune was the first really attractive girl he had encountered who was smaller than he was. Such a little thing, physical height, but what a subjective difference it could make!

Today he was lunging the horses. Lunging consisted of tying them to a fixed boom on a rotating structure, so they had to stay in an exact course, and making them trot around in a circle. It was excellent exercise, if dull for both man and horse. Some horses were too temperamental for the mechanical lead, so he had to do them by hand. He simply tied a rope to an artificial tree, and stood with his hand on that line while he urged the animal forward.

Stile had a way with horses, despite his size. They tended to respond to him when they would not do a thing for other stable hands. This, unfortunately, meant that he got the most difficult horses to lunge. No horse gave trouble about feeding or going to pasture, but a number could get difficult about the more onerous labors.

The first horse he had to lunge was Spook—the worst of them. Spook was jet black all over, which perhaps accounted for his name. He was also extremely excitable—which was a more likely reason for his name. He could run with the best—the very best—but had to be kept in top condition.

"Come on, Spook," Stile said gently. "You wouldn't want to get all weak and flabby, would you? How would you feel if some flatfooted mare beat your time in a race? You know you have to exercise."

Spook knew no such thing. He aspired to a life career of grazing and stud service; there was little room in his itinerary for exercise. He had quite an arsenal of tricks to stave off the inevitable. When Stile approached, Spook retreated to the farthest corner of his pen, then tried to leap away when cornered. But Stile, alert, cut him off and caught his halter. He had to reach up high to do it, for this horse could look right over Stile's head without elevating his own head. Spook could have flattened Stile, had he wanted to; but he was not a vicious animal, and perhaps even enjoyed this periodic game.

Spook tried to nip Stile's hand. "No!" Stile said sharply, making a feint with his free hand as if to slap the errant nose, and the horse desisted. Move and countermove, without actual violence. That was the normal language of horses, who could indulge in quite elaborate series of posturings to make themselves accurately understood.

They took a few steps along the path, then Spook balked, planting all four feet in the ground like small tree trunks. He was of course far too heavy for even a large man to budge by simple force. But Stile slapped him lightly on the flank with the free end of the leadline, startling him into motion. One thing about being spooky: it was hard to stand firm.

Spook moved over, trying to shove Stile off the path and into a building, but Stile shoved the horse's head back, bracing against it. Control the head, control the body; he had learned that principle in martial art, winning matches by hold-downs though his opponents might outweigh him considerably—because their greater mass became useless against his strategy. Few creatures went far without their heads.

Spook tried to lift his head too high for Stile to control. Stile merely hung on, though his feet left the ground. After a moment the dead weight became too much, and the horse brought his head down. Other stable hands used a martingale on him, a strap to keep the head low, but that made this horse even more excitable. Stile preferred the gentle approach.

At last he got Spook to the lunging tree. "Walk!" he commanded, making a token gesture with the whip. The horse sighed, eyed him, and decided to humor him this once. He walked.

Every horse was an individual. "Spook, you're more trouble than a stableful of rats, but I like you," Stile said calmly. "Let's get this over with, work up a sweat, then I'll rub you down. After that, it's the pasture for you. How does that sound?"

Spook glanced at him, then made a gesture with his nose toward the pasture. Horses' noses, like their ears, were very expressive; a nose motion could be a request or an insult. "Lunge first," Stile insisted.

Spook licked his lips and chewed on a phantom delicacy. "Okay!" Stile said, laughing. "A carrot and a rubdown. That's my best offer. Now trot. Trot!"

It was all right. The horse broke into a classy trot. Any horse was pretty in that gait, but Spook was prettier than most; his glossy black hide fairly glinted, and he had a way of picking up his feet high that accentuated the precision of his motion. The workout was going to be a success.

Stile's mind drifted. The girl, Tune—could she be right about his destiny? There were stringent rules about horse competition, because of the ubiquitous androids, cyborgs, and robots. Horses had to be completely natural, and raced by completely natural jockeys. The less weight a horse carried, the faster it could go; there were no standardized loads, here. So a man as small as Stile—yes, it did make sense, in Citizen terms. Citizens did not care about serf convenience or feelings; Citizens cared only about their own concerns. Stile's aptitude in the Game, his intelligence in schooling—these things were irrelevant. He was small and healthy and coordinated, therefore he was slated to be a jockey. Had he been three meters tall, he would have been slated for some Citizen's classical basketball team. He didn't have to like it; he worked where employed, or he left Proton forever. That was the nature of the system.

Still, would it be so bad, racing? Tune herself seemed to like it. Aboard a horse like Spook, here, urging him on to victory, leaving the pack behind, hearing the crowd cheering him on . . . there were certainly worse trades than that! He did like horses, liked them well. So maybe the Citizen had done him a favor, making his size an asset. A lout like the stable hand Bourbon might eventually become a rider, but he would never be a racer. Only a small person could be that. Most were women, like Tune, because women tended to be smaller, and gentler. Stile was the exception. Almost, now, he was glad of his size.

And Tune herself—what a woman! He would have to take up music. It had never occurred to him that an ordinary serf could create such beauty. Her—what was that instrument? The keyboard harmonica—her musical solo, emerging as it were from nowhere, had been absolute rapture! Yes, he would have to try his hand at music. That might please her, and he wanted very much to please her.

She could, of course, have her pick of men. She had poise and wit and confidence. She could go with a giant if she wanted. Stile could not pick among women; he had to have one shorter than he. Not because he demanded it, but because society did; if he appeared among serfs with a girl who outmassed him, others would laugh, and that would destroy the relationship. So he was the least of many, from Tune's perspective, while she was the only one for him.

The trouble was—now that he knew he wanted her —his shyness was boiling up, making any direct approach difficult. How should he—

"One side, shorty!" It was Bourbon, the stable hand who was Stile's greatest annoyance. Bourbon was adept at getting Stile into mischief, and seemed to resent Stile because he was small. Stile had never understood that, before; now with the realization of his potential to be a jockey, the resentment of the larger person was beginning to make sense. Bourbon liked to make dares, enter contests, prevail over others—and his size would work against him, racing horses. Today Bourbon was leading Pepper, a salt-and-pepper speckled stallion. "Make way for a man and a horse!"

Spook spooked at the loud voice. He leaped ahead. The lead-rope jerked his muzzle around. The horse's body spun out, then took a roll. The line snapped, as it was designed to; a horse could get hurt when entangled.

Pepper also spooked, set off by the other horse. He careened into a wall, squealing. The genuine imported wood splintered, and blood spattered to the ground.

Stile ran to Spook. "Easy, Spook, easy! You're okay! Calm! Calm!" He flung his arms about Spook's neck as the horse climbed to his feet, trying to steady the animal by sheer contact.

Bourbon yanked Pepper's head about, swearing. "Now see what you've done, midget!" he snapped at Stile. "Of all the runty, oink-headed, pygmy-brained—"

That was all. A fracas would have alerted others to the mishap, and that would have gotten both stable hands into deep trouble. Bourbon led his horse on, still muttering about the incompetence of dwarves, and Stile succeeded in calming Spook.

All was not well. Stile seethed at the insults added to injury, knowing well that Bourbon was responsible for all of this. The horse had a scrape on his glossy neck, and was favoring one foot. Stile could cover the scrape with fixative and comb the mane over it, concealing the evidence until it healed, but the foot was another matter. No feet, no horse, as the saying went. It might be only a minor bruise—but it might also be more serious.

He couldn't take a chance. That foot had to be checked. It would mean a gross demerit for him, for he was liable for any injury to any animal in his charge. This could set his promotion back a year, right when his aspirations had multiplied. Damn Bourbon! If the man hadn't spoken sharply in the presence of a horse known to be excitable—but of course Bourbon had done it deliberately. He had been a stable hand for three years and believed he was overdue for promotion. He took it out on others as well as on Stile, and of course he resented the way Stile was able to handle the animals.

Stile knew why Bourbon had been passed over. It wasn't his size, for ordinary riders and trainers could be any size. Bourbon was just as mean to the horses, in little ways he thought didn't show and could not be proved. He teased them and handled them with unnecessary roughness. Had he been lunging Spook, he would have used martingale and electric prod. Other hands could tell without looking at the roster which horses Bourbon had been handling, for these animals were nervous and shy of men for several days thereafter.

Stile would not report Bourbon, of course. He had no proof-of-fault, and it would be contrary to the serf code, and would gain nothing. Technically, the man had committed no wrong; Stile's horse had spooked first. Stile should have been paying better attention, and brought Spook about to face the intrusion so as not to be startled. Stile had been at fault, in part, and had been had. Lessons came hard.

Nothing for it now except to take his medicine, figuratively, and give Spook his, literally. He led the horse to the office of the vet. "I was lunging him. He spooked and took a fall," Stile explained, feeling as lame as the horse.

The man examined the injuries competently. "You know I'll have to report this."

"I know," Stile agreed tightly. The vet was well-meaning and honest; he did what he had to do.

"Horses don't spook for no reason, not even this one. What set him off?"

"I must have been careless," Stile said. He didn't like the half-truth, but was caught between his own negligence and the serf code. He was low on the totem, this time.

The vet squinted wisely at him. "That isn't like you, Stile."

"I had a girl on my mind," Stile admitted.

"Ho! I can guess which one! But this is apt to cost you something. I'm sorry." Stile knew he meant it. The vet would do a serf a favor when he could, but never at the expense of his employer.

The foreman arrived. He was never far from the action. That was his business. Stile wondered, as he often did, how the man kept so well abreast of events even before they were reported to him, as now. "Damage?"

"Slight sprain," the vet reported. "Be better in a few days. Abrasion on neck, no problem."

The foreman glanced at Stile. "You're lucky. Three demerits for carelessness, suspension for one day. Next time pay better attention."

Stile nodded, relieved. No gross demerit! Had the foot been serious—

"Any extenuating circumstances to report?" the foreman prodded.

"No." That galled Stile. The truth could have halved his punishment.

"Then take off. You have one day to yourself."

Stile left. He was free, but it was no holiday. The demerits would be worked off in the course of three days low on the totem, but that suspension would go down on his permanent record, hurting his promotion prospects. In the case of equivalent qualifications, the person with such a mark on his record would suffer, and probably have to wait until the next occasion for improvement. That could be as little as a day, or as long as two months.

Stile started off his free time by enlisting in a music-appreciation class. It was good stuff, but he was subdued by his chastisement. He would stick with it, however, and in time choose an instrument to play himself. The keyboard harmonica, perhaps.

In the evening Tune searched him out. "It's all over the dome," she told him brightly. "I want you to know I think you did right, Stile."

"You're a liar," he said, appreciating her words.

"Yes. You should have covered it up and escaped punishment, the way Bourbon did. But you showed you cared more about the horse than about your own record." She paused, putting her hands on his shoulders, looking into his face. What lovely eyes she had! "I care about horses." She drew him in and kissed him, and the pain of his punishment abated rapidly. "You're a man," she added. The words made him feel like one.

She took him home to her private apartment—the

affluence permitted ranking serfs. By morning she had shown him many things, not all of them musical or relating to horses, and he was hopelessly in love with her. He no longer regretted his punishment at all.

When Stile returned to work next day, at the same hour he had departed, he discovered that he had been moved out of his cabin. He looked at the place his bunk had been, dismayed. "I know I fouled up, but—"

"You don't know?" a cabin mate demanded incredulously. "Where have you been all night?"

Stile did not care to clarify that; he would be razzed. They would find out soon enough via the vine. Tune, though small, was much in the eye of the local serfs, and not just because of her position and competence. "I was on suspension." He kept his voice steady. "Was it worse than I thought, on Spook? Something that showed up later?"

"Spook's okay." His friend took his arm. "Come to the bulletin board."

Not daring to react further, Stile went with him. The electronic board, on which was posted special assignments, demerits, and other news of the day, had a new entry in the corner: STILE pmtd RIDER.

Stile turned savagely on the other. "Some joke!"

But the foreman had arrived. "No joke, Stile. You're sharing the apartment with Turf. Familiarize yourself, then get down to the robot stall for instruction."

Stile stared at him. "But I fouled up!"

The foreman walked away without commenting, as was his wont. He never argued demerits or promotions with serfs.

Turf was waiting to break him in. It was a nice two-man apartment adjacent to the riding track, with a Game viewscreen, hot running water, and a direct exit to the main dome. More room and more privacy; more status. This was as big a step upward as his prior one from pasture to stable—but this time he had found no worm. There had to be some mistake—though he had never heard of the foreman making a mistake.

"You sure came up suddenly, Stile!" Turf said. He

was an okay guy; Stile had interacted with him on occasion, walk-cooling horses Turf had ridden, and liked him. "How'd you do it?"

"I have no idea. Yesterday I was suspended for injuring Spook. Maybe our employer got his firing list mixed up with his promotion list."

Turf laughed. "Maybe! You know who's waiting to give you riding lessons?"

"Tune!" Stile exclaimed. "*She* arranged this!"

"Oh, you're thick with her already? You're doubly lucky!"

Disquieted, Stile proceeded to Roberta's stall. Sure enough, there was Tune, brushing out the bay mare, smiling. "Long time no see," she said playfully.

Oh, she was lovely! He could have a thousand nights with her like the last one, and never get enough. But he was about to blow it all by his ingratitude. "Tune, did you pull a string?" he demanded.

"Well, you can't expect a jockey to date a mere stable hand."

"But I was in trouble! Suspended. There are several hands ahead of me. You can't—"

She put her fine little hand on his. "I didn't, Stile. Really. I was just joshing you. It's coincidence. I didn't know you were being promoted right now; I figured in a month or so, since they brought me in. I'm training others, of course, but no sense to promote you after my tour here ends. So they moved it up, obviously. They don't even know we're dating."

But she was, by her own proclamation, a liar. The foreman surely knew where Stile had spent the night. How much could he afford to believe?

"Ask me again tonight," she murmured. "I never lie to a man I'm loving."

What an offer! "What, never?"

"Hardly ever. You're an operetta fan?"

He looked at her blankly.

"Never mind," she said. "I'm not lying to you now."

How he wanted to believe her!

"Will you try it alone?" she inquired, indicating

Roberta's saddle. "Or do you prefer to hold on to me again, and bang your poor head?"

"Both," he said, and she laughed. She had asked him during the night whether his head hurt from what he had banged it into. He had admitted that there were some bruises he was prepared to endure.

She had him mount, more successfully this time, and showed him how to direct the robot. Then she took him out on the track. Very quickly he got the hang of it.

"Don't get cocky, now, sorehead," she warned. "Roberta is a horse of no surprises. A flesh horse can be another matter. Wait till they put you on Spook."

"Spook?" he cried, alarmed. He had daydreamed of exactly this, but the prospect of the reality scared him.

She laughed again. She was a creature of fun and laughter. It made her body move pleasantly, and it endeared her to those she worked with. "How should I know whom you'll ride? But we'll get you competent first. A bad rider can ruin a good horse."

"Yes, the Citizen wouldn't be very pleased if a serf fell on his head and splattered dirty gray brains on a clean horse."

It was a good lesson, and he returned to his new apartment exhilarated, only to discover more trouble. The foreman was waiting for him.

"There is a challenge to your promotion. We have been summoned to the Citizen."

"We? I can believe there was a foul-up with me, that will now be corrected." Though he had begun to hope that somehow this new life was real. Even braced for it as he was, this correction was hard to take. "But how do you relate? It wasn't your fault."

The foreman merely took his elbow and guided him forward. This summons was evidently too urgent to allow time for physical preparation. Stile tried to smooth his hair with his hand, and to rub off stray rimes of dirt on his legs from the riding. He felt, appropriately, naked.

In moments they entered a transport tunnel, took a private capsule, and zoomed through the darkness away from the farm. It seemed the Citizen was not at his farmside apartment at this hour. "Now don't stare, keep cool," the foreman told him. The foreman himself was sweating. That made Stile quite nervous, for the foreman was normally a man of iron. There must be quite serious trouble brewing! Yet why hadn't they simply revoked Stile's promotion without fuss?

They debouched at a hammam. Stile felt the foreman's nudge, and realized he was indeed staring. He stopped that, but still the environment was awesome.

The hammam was a public bath in the classic Arabian mode. A number of Citizens preferred this style, because the golden age of Arabian culture back on Earth had been remarkably affluent. Islam had had its Golden Age while Christianity had its Dark Ages. For the ruling classes, at any rate; the color of the age had never had much significance for the common man. Poverty was eternal.

Thus there were mosque-type architecture, and turban headdress, exotic dancing, and the hammam. This one was evidently shared by a number of Citizens. It was not that any one of them could not have afforded it alone; rather, Citizens tended to specialize in areas of interest or expertise, and an Arabian specialist had a touch that others could hardly match. Stile's employer had a touch with fine horses; another might have a touch with desert flora; here one had a touch with the hammam. On occasion other Citizens wished to ride the horses, and were invariably treated with utmost respect. The hammam was by nature a social institution, and a Citizen could only socialize properly with other Citizens, so they had to share.

There were many rooms here, clean and hot and steamy, with many serfs bearing towels, brushes, ointments, and assorted edibles and beverages. One large room resembled a swimming pool—but the water was bubbly-hot and richly colored and scented, almost like soup. Several Citizens were soaking in this communal bath, conversing. Stile knew they were Citizens, though they were naked, because of their demeanor and the deference the clustered serfs were paying. Clothing distinguished the Citizen, but was not the basis of Citizenship; a Citizen could go naked if he chose, and sacrifice none of his dignity or power. Nevertheless, some wore jewelry.

They came to a smaller pool. Here Stile's employer soaked. Six extraordinarily voluptuous young women were attending him, rubbing oils into his skin, polishing his fingernails, even grooming his privates, which were supremely unaroused. An older man was doing the Citizen's hair, meticulously, moving neatly with the Citizen to keep the lather from his face.

"Sir," the foreman said respectfully.

The Citizen took no notice. The girls continued their labors. Stile and the foreman stood where they were, at attention. Stile was conscious again of the grime on him, from his recent riding lesson; what a contrast he was to these premises and all the people associated with them! Several minutes passed.

Stile noted that the Citizen had filled out slightly in the past year, but remained a healthy and youngish-looking man. He had fair muscular development, suggesting regular exercise, and obviously he did not overeat—or if he did, he stayed with non-nutritive staples. His hair looked white—but that was the effect of the lather. His pubic region was black. It was strange seeing a Citizen in the same detail as a serf!

Two more men entered the chamber. One was Billy, the roving security guard for the farm; the other was Bourbon. "Sir," Billy said.

Now the Citizen nodded slightly to the foreman. "Be at ease," the foreman said to the others. Stile, Billy and Bourbon relaxed marginally.

The Citizen's eyes flicked to Bourbon. "Elucidate your protest."

Bourbon, in obvious awe of his employer, swallowed and spoke. "Sir, I was passed over for promotion in favor of Stile, here, when I have seniority and a better record."

The Citizen's eyes flicked coldly to the foreman. "You promoted Stile. Justify this."

The *foreman* had promoted him? Stile had not been aware that the man had such power. He had thought the foreman's authority ended with discipline, record-keeping, and perhaps the recommendation of candidates. The Citizen might have gotten mixed up, not paying full attention to the details of serf management, but the foreman should never have erred like this! He was the one who had suspended Stile, after all.

"Sir," the foreman said, ill at ease himself. "It is my considered judgment that Stile is the proper man to fill the present need. I prefer to have him trained on the robot horse, which will only be with us three months."

The Citizen's eyes flicked back to Bourbon. "You are aware that the foreman exists to serve my interests. He is not bound by guidelines of seniority or record. It is his prerogative and mandate to place the proper personnel in the proper slots. I do not permit this of him, I require it. You have no case."

"Sir," Bourbon said rebelliously.

The Citizen's eyes touched the foreman. There was no trace of humor or compassion in them. "Do you wish to permit this man to pursue this matter further?"

"No, sir," the foreman said.

"Overruled. Bourbon, make your specifics."

What was going on here? Why should the Citizen waste his time second-guessing his own foreman, whose judgment he obviously trusted? If the foreman got reversed, it would be an awkward situation.

"Sir, Stile has the favor of the visiting instructor, Tune. I believe she prevailed on the foreman to promote Stile out of turn, though he fouled up only yesterday, injuring one of your race horses. My own record is clean."

For the first time the Citizen showed emotion. "Injured my horse? Which one?"

"Spook, sir."

"My most promising miler!" The Citizen waved one arm, almost striking a girl. She teetered at the edge of the pool for a moment before recovering her balance. "Fall back, attendants!" he snapped. Now that emotion had animated him, he was dynamic.

Instantly the seven attendants withdrew to a distance of four meters and stood silently. Stile was sure they were just as curious about this business as he was, though of course less involved.

Now there was something ugly about the Citizen's gaze, though his face was superficially calm. "Foreman, make your case."

The foreman did not look happy, but he did not hesitate. "Sir, I will need to use the vidscreen."

"Do so." The Citizen made a signal with one finger, and the entire ceiling brightened. It was a giant video receiver, with special elements to prevent condensation on its surface. "Respond to the serf's directives, *ad hoc*."

The foreman spoke a rapid series of temporal and spatial coordinates. A picture formed on the screen. Stile and the others craned their necks to focus on it. It was the stable, with the horse Spook looking out. A running film-clock showed date and time: yesterday morning.

"Forward action," the foreman said, and the film jumped ahead to show Stile approaching the pen.

Stile watched, fascinated. He had had no idea this was being filmed. He looked so small, the horse so large—yet he was confident, the horse nervous. 'Come on, Spook,' his image said, encouraging the horse. But Spook was not cooperative.

The film went through the whole ugly sequence relentlessly, as Stile gentled and bluffed and fought the great stallion, forcing him to proceed to the lunging tree.

"As you can see, sir," the foreman said. "This man was dealing with an extremely difficult animal, but was not fazed. He used exactly that amount of force required to bring the horse in line. I have handled Spook myself; I could not have gotten him to lunge on that morning."

"Why didn't you send help?" the Citizen demanded. "I would have had difficulty myself, in that situation." This was no idle vanity; the Citizen was an expert horseman.

170

"Because, sir, I knew Stile could handle it. The presence of other serfs would only have alarmed the horse. This is why Stile was assigned to this animal on this day; Spook needed to be exercised and disciplined with competence. He had thrown his rider on the prior day."

"Proceed."

Under the foreman's direction the scene now shifted to Pepper's stall. Pepper showed no nervousness as Bourbon approached, but he laid back his ears as he recognized the stable hand. Bourbon brought him out roughly, slapping him unnecessarily, but the horse behaved well enough.

"This man, sir, was handling a docile animal brusquely," the foreman said. "This is typical of his manner. It is not a fault in itself, as some animals do respond to unsubtle treatment, but had he been assigned to exercise Spook—"

"Point made," the Citizen said, nodding. He was well attuned to the mannerisms of horses. "Get on with it."

Stile glanced at Bourbon. The stable hand was frozen, obviously trapped in an exposé he had never anticipated.

The film-Bourbon came up behind Stile, who now had Spook trotting nicely. The animal was magnificent. A small, stifled sigh of appreciation escaped one of the watching girls of the hammam. Girls really responded to horses!

Bourbon chose his time carefully. "One side, shorty!" he exclaimed almost directly behind Stile and the horse. There was no question about the malice of the act.

Spook spooked. The rest followed.

"Enough film," the Citizen said, and the ceiling screen died. "What remedial action did you take?"

"Sir, Stile reported the injury to his horse. I gave him three demerits and a one-day suspension. He made no issue. I felt that his competence and discretion qualified him best for the position, so I promoted him. I am aware that he had an acquaintance with the lady trainer, but this was not a factor in my decision."

"The other," the Citizen said grimly.

"Bourbon did not report the injury to his horse. I felt it more important to preserve the privacy of my observations than to make an overt issue. I passed him over for promotion, but did not suspend him, since the injury to the horse in his charge was minor."

"There *are* no minor injuries to horses!" the Citizen cried, red-faced. Veins stood out on his neck, and lather dripped unnoticed across his cheek. He would have presented a comical figure, were he not a Citizen. "You are rebuked for negligence."

"Yes, sir," the foreman said, chastened.

The Citizen turned to Stile. "Your promotion holds; it was merited." He turned to Bourbon, the cold eyes swiveling like the sights of a rifle. "You are fired."

When a serf was fired for cause, he was finished on Planet Proton. No other Citizen would hire him, and in ten days his tenure would be aborted. Bourbon was through. And Stile had learned a lesson of an unexpected nature.

He had been going with Tune three months, the happiest time of his life, studying fencing and riding and music and love, when abruptly she said: "I've got to tell you, Stile. My second fault. I'm short on time. My tenure's over."

"You're—" he said, unbelievingly.

"I started at age ten. You didn't think I got to be a jockey overnight, did you? My term is up in six months. I'm sorry I hid that from you, but I did warn you how I lied."

"I'll go with you!" he exclaimed with the passion of youth.

She squeezed his hand. "Don't be foolish. I like you, Stile, but I don't love you. Outside, you'd be twenty-one, and I'll be twenty-nine, and no rejuve medicine. You can do better than that, lover."

He thought he loved her, but he knew she was right, knew he could not throw away seventeen years of remaining tenure for a woman who was older than he and only liked him. "The Game!" he cried. "You must enter the Tourney, win more tenure—"

172

"That's why I'm telling you now, Stile. This year's Tourney begins tomorrow, and I'll be in it. I am on Rung Five of the age-29 ladder, by the slick of my teeth. My tenure ends the moment I lose a Game, so this is our last night together."

"But you might win!"

"You're a dreamer. *You* might win, when your time comes; you're a natural animal, beautifully skilled. That's why I wanted you, first time I saw you. I love fine animals! I was strongly tempted not even to try the Tourney, so as to be assured of my final six months with you—"

"You must try!"

"Yes. It's futile, but I must at least take one shot at the moon, though it costs me six months of you."

"What a way to put it!" Stile was torn by the horrors of her choice. Yet it was the type of choice that came to every serf in the last year of tenure, and would one day come to him.

"I know you'll be a better jockey than I was; you'll win your races, and be famous. I wanted a piece of you, so I took it, by means of the lie of my remaining time here. I'm not proud—"

"You gave me the best things of my life!"

She looked down at her breasts. "A couple of them, maybe. I hope so. Anyway, it's sweet of you to say so, sorehead. Your life has only begun. If I have helped show you the way, then I'm glad. I won't have to feel so guilty."

"Never feel guilty!" he exclaimed.

"Oh, guilt can be great stuff. Adds savor to life." But the spark was not in her humor, now.

They made love quickly, because he did not want to tire her right before the Tourney, but with inspired passion. He felt guilt for letting her go—and she was right, it did add a certain obscure quality to the experience.

Next day she entered the Tourney, and in her first match made a try on the Grid for music, and got trapped in dance instead. She was gone.

Stile pursued his musical studies relentlessly, driven

173

by his waning guilt and love of her memory. Gradually that love transferred itself to the music, and became a permanent part of him. He knew he would never be a master musician, but he was a good one. He did enjoy the various instruments, especially the keyboard harmonica.

Three years later the foreman's tenure expired. "Stile, you're good enough to qualify for my job," he said in a rare moment of private candor. "You're young yet, but capable and honest, and you have that unique touch with the horses. But there is one thing—"

"My size," Stile said immediately.

"I don't judge by that. But there are others—"

"I understand. I will never be a leader."

"Not directly. But for you there is a fine alternative. You can be promoted to jockey, and from there your skill can take you to the heights of fame available to a serf. I believe this is as good a life as anyone not a Citizen can have on Proton."

"Yes." Stile found himself choked up about the foreman's departure, but could not find any appropriate way to express this. "I—you—"

"There's one last job I have for you, a tough one, and how you acquit yourself may determine the issue. I am recommending you for immediate promotion to jockey, but the Citizen will decide. Do not disappoint me."

"I won't," Stile said. "I just want to say—"

But the foreman was holding out his hand for parting. "Thank you," Stile said simply. They shook hands, and the foreman departed quickly.

The job was to bring Spook back from another dome. The horse had grown more spooky with the years, and could no longer be trusted to vehicular transportation; the sound and vibration, however muted, set him off. The Citizen refused to drug him for the trip; he was too valuable to risk this way. Spook had won a number of races, and the Citizen wanted him back on the farm for stud. So Spook had to be brought home on foot. That could be difficult, for there were no walk-passages suitable for horses, and the outer surface of the planet was rough.

Stile planned carefully. He ordered maps of the region and studied them assiduously. Then he ordered a surface-suit, complete with SCOBA unit: Self-Contained Outside Breathing Apparatus. And a gyro monocycle, an all-band transceiver, and an information watch. He was not about to get himself lost or isolated on the inhospitable Proton surface!

That surface was amazingly rugged, once he was on it. There were mountain ranges to the north and south, the northern ones white with what little water this world had in free-state, as snow. There was the winding channel of a long-dead river, and a region of deep fissures as if an earthquake had aborted in mid-motion. He guided his monocycle carefully, counterbalancing with his body when its motions sent it into twists of precession; incorrectly handled, these machines could dump a man in a hurry, since the precession operated at right angles to the force applied. He located the most dangerous traps for a nervous horse, plotting a course well clear of them. Spook would be upset enough, wearing an equine face mask for his breathing and protection of his eyes and ears; any additional challenges could be disastrous. Which was of course why Stile was the one who had to take him through; no one else could do it safely.

Stile took his time, calling in regular reports and making up his route map. This was really a puzzle: find the most direct route that avoided all hazards. He had to think in equine terms, for Spook could spook at a mere patch of colored sand, while trotting blithely into a dead-end canyon.

Only when he was quite certain he had the best route did Stile report to the dome where Spook was stabled. He was confident, now, that he could bring the horse across in good order. It was not merely that this success would probably facilitate his promotion. He liked Spook. The horse had in his fashion been responsible for Stile's last promotion.

When he arrived at that dome, he found a gram

awaiting him. It was from offplanet: the first he had had since his parents moved out. STILE—AM MARRIED NOW—NAMED SON AFTER YOU. HOPE YOU FOUND YOURS—TUNE.

He was glad for her, though her loss hurt with sudden poignancy. Three months together, three years apart; he could not claim his world had ended. Yet he had not found another girl he liked as well, and suspected he never would. He found himself humming a melody; he had done that a lot in the first, raw months of loss, and it had coalesced into a nervous habit he did not really try to cure. Music would always remind him of her, and he would always pursue it in memory of those three wonderful months.

So she had named her son after him! She had not conceived by him, of course; no one conceived involuntarily on Proton. It was just her way of telling him how much their brief connection had meant to her. She had surely had many other lovers, and not borrowed from their names for this occasion. She said she had lied to him, but actually she had made possible an experience he would never have traded. Brevity did not mean inconsequence; no, never!

"Thank you, Tune," he murmured.

CHAPTER 10

Magic

Stile woke suddenly, making a significant connection. "Geography!" he cried. "This world is Proton!"

Neysa, in girl-form, was tending him. He realized, in a kind of supplementary revelation, that she was the same size as Tune; no wonder he had accepted her as a lover so readily, despite his knowledge of her nature. She was not a true woman, and would never be, but she was well worthwhile on her own account.

She looked at him questioningly, aware of his stare. Her appearance and personality were, of course, quite unlike Tune's; no light-hued hair, no merry cleverness here. Neysa was dark and quiet, and she never told a lie.

"I had a memory," he explained. "Beginning with my fencing lessons, because you were teaching me how to use the rapier when I—" He paused, trying to assimilate it. "What happened to me?"

Reluctantly, she talked. "Sick."

"Sick? You mean as in disease? But there's no disease on Proton—" Again he did a double take. "But this isn't Proton, exactly. It's another realm with the same geography. The purple mountains to the south— it's what Proton might have been, had it had a decent atmosphere. An alternate Proton, where magic works. Maybe magic made the atmosphere, and the gravity. So with a complete planetary environment, a complete ecology, there are flies, there is dirt, there is disease. And I have no natural immunity, only my standard shots, which never anticipated the complete spectrum of challenges I found here. The micro-organisms in the food here, in the water, natural for natives but foreign to my system. Pollens in the air. Allergens. Et cetera.

177

So it took a couple of days for the germs to incubate in my system, then suddenly they overwhelmed me. Reaching the point of explosive infestation. Thanks for explaining it so well, Neysa."

She smiled acknowledgment.

"But how could you cure me? I should have died, or at least been sick longer than this. I've only been out a few hours, haven't I? Now I feel fine, not even tired."

She had to speak again. "Clip brought amulet." She reached forward and touched a figurine hanging on a necklace that had been put on him.

Stile lifted it in his hand. "A healing amulet? Now isn't that clever! Will I get sick again if I take it off?"

She shook her head no.

"You mean these things emit their magic in one burst, then are useless? But some are supposed to have continuing effect, like the clothing-simulator amulet I was given at the outset—uh-oh." He hastily removed the chain from his neck. "That one tried to kill me. If this one was made by the same party—"

She shrugged.

"Do you mind if I dispose of this now?" he asked. "We could bury it and mark the spot so we can find it later if we want it. But I'd rather not have it with me. If I invoke a secondary function—well, Neysa, an amulet attacked me, before I met you. When I invoked it. You invoked this one, so maybe that's why it acted normally. I fear the amulets have murder in mind for me, when they recognize me. That's why I needed a steed—to get away from my anonymous enemy."

Neysa lifted her head, alarmed in the equine manner. "No, no, you didn't bring the enemy here," Stile reassured her. "The demon hasn't been invoked." He took her hands, smiling. "I chose better than I knew, when I chose you. You did right, Neysa. I think you saved my life."

She allowed herself to be drawn in to him, and there followed what followed. He had not forgotten Sheen, but this was another world.

They buried the amulet and went on. It was morning;

his illness had lasted only one night, coinciding with normal sleep, and the revelation of geography had almost been worth it. This accounted for the nagging familiarity he had sensed before; he had seen the surface of this world a decade ago, in its dead form.

What accounted for this difference? The concept of alternate worlds, or alternate frames of the same world, he could accept. But breathable atmosphere, a full living ecology, and magic in one, domes and science and external barrenness in the other—that dichotomy was harder to fathom. He would have expected parallel frames to be very similar to each other.

Still, it helped his sense of orientation. Now it was clear why people crossed over at certain spots. They were not matter-transmitting, they were stepping through the curtain at precise geographical locations, so as to arrive in domes and in private places. To cross elsewhere—well, if he tried that, he would have to prepare himself with a breathing mask.

"You know, Neysa," he said as he rode. "There is a lot I don't know about this world, and my life is in danger here, but I think I like it better than my own. Out here, with you—I'm happy. I could just ride forever, I think, like this." He shook his head. "But I suppose I would get tired of it, in a century or two; must be realistic."

Neysa made a musical snort, then broke into a two-beat gallop, front hooves striking precisely together, rear hooves likewise. It was a jolting gait.

"Think you can buck me off, huh?" Stile said playfully. He brought out his harmonica—one advantage of clothing, he discovered, was that it had pockets—and played a brisk marching melody. The girl Tune had taught him the beauty of music, and his growing talent in it had helped him on numerous occasions in the Game. His memory flashback had freshened his awareness that even had music been worthless in a practical sense, he would have kept it up. Music was fun.

But again a looming presence developed. Again they stopped. "Something funny about this," Stile said.

179

"Clip told me not to worry, that unicorns are immune to most magic—but this is eerie. I don't like mysteries that may affect my health."

Neysa blew a note of agreement.

"It seems to happen when we're playing music," he continued. "Now I've never been harmed by music, but I'd better be sure. Maybe something is sneaking up while we're playing, hoping we won't notice. I somehow doubt this is connected with the amulets; this is more subtle. Let's try it again. If we feel the presence, I'll stop playing and will try to search it out. You go on playing as if nothing is happening. We need to catch it by surprise."

They resumed play—and immediately the presence returned. Stile left his harmonica at his lips but ceased playing; instead he peered about while Neysa danced on, continuing the melody. But even as he looked, whatever it was faded.

Experimentally Stile resumed play, matching Neysa's theme, softly, so that an on-listener would not hear him. The presence returned. Neysa stopped playing, while Stile continued—and the presence loomed stronger, as if her music had restrained it. Stile halted abruptly—and the effect receded.

"It's tied to me!" he exclaimed. "Only when I play—"

Neysa agreed. Whatever it was, was after Stile—and it advanced only when he was playing. It could hear him, regardless of other sounds that masked his own.

Stile felt an eerie chill. "Let's get out of here," he said.

The unicorn took off. No clever footwork this time; she moved right into a racing gallop. They forged across the plain at a rate no horse could match, wove through copses of brightly green trees, and leaped across small streams. He could see the mountains sliding back on either side. They were really covering the kilometers!

At last Neysa slowed, for her breath was turning fiery. Stile brought out his harmonica and played once more—and instantly the presence closed in.

He stopped immediately. "We can't outrun it, Neysa; that's evident. But now that we're aware of it, maybe we can do something about it. Why does it still come only when I play? It has to know that we are aware of it, and are trying to escape it; no further need to hide."

Neysa shrugged—an interesting effect, while he was mounted.

"First the amulet, now this. *Could* they be connected? Could the harmonica be—" He paused, alarmed. "Another amulet?"

After a moment he developed a notion. "Neysa—do you think you could play this instrument? With your mouth, I mean, human-fashion? If this is an enemy-summoning device, there should be the same effect whoever plays it. I think."

Neysa halted and had him dismount and remove the saddle. Then she phased into human form. He had not seen her do it by day before, and it had not occurred to him that she would. He had thought of her playing the harmonica in her equine form, but of course this way made much more sense.

She took the instrument and played. She was not expert, since this was foreign to her mode, and the result was a jumble. No presence formed. Then Stile took the harmonica and played a similar jumble—and the presence was there.

"Not the instrument—but me," he said. "Only when I play it." He pondered. "Is it a symbiosis, or is the harmonica incidental?"

He tried humming a tune—and the presence came, though not as powerfully as before.

"That settles it: it's me. When I make music, it comes. My music is better with the harmonica, so the effect is stronger, that's all. The instrument is not haunted." He smiled. "I'm glad. I like this harmonica. I'd hate to have to bury it in dirt." He would hate to abuse any harmonica, because he retained a fond feeling for the keyboard harmonica and all its relatives. But this present instrument was the finest of its breed he had ever played.

Neysa had changed back to her natural form. Stile

put the saddle back on. "I don't think we can afford to ignore this matter," he said.

The unicorn flicked one ear in agreement.

"Let's get down to some good grazing land, and I'll challenge it. I want to see what will happen. I don't like running from a threat anyway. I'd rather draw it out and settle the account, one way or another. If it is an enemy, I want to summon it by daylight, with my sword in hand, not have it sneak up on me at night."

Neysa agreed again, emphatically.

They moved downslope until good grass resumed. Neysa grazed, but she did not wander far from Stile, and her eye was on him. She was concerned. Bless her; it had been a long time since someone had worried about him. Except for Sheen—and that was a matter of programming.

Stile began to play. The presence loomed. He tried to see it, but it was invisible, intangible. This time he did not stop his music. The grass seemed to wave, bending toward him and springing back as if driven by a wind, but there was no wind. The air seemed to sparkle. A faint haze developed, swirling in barely discernible colored washes. Stile felt the hairs on his body lighten, as if charged electrostatically. He thought at first it was his own nervousness, for he did not know what thing or force he summoned, but he saw Neysa's mane lifting similarly. There was potential here, and it centered on him—but it never acted. It just loomed.

Stile stopped playing, growing weary of this—and yet again the effect faded. "Almost the form of an electrical storm," he mused. "Yet—"

He was cut off by a sheet of rain blasting at him. Lightning cracked nearby. The sudden light half-blinded him, and a gust of wind made him stagger. He was soaked as if dunked in a raging sea, feeling the eerie chill of the violent water. There was a swirling of fog reminiscent of a developing tornado. The flashes of light were continuous.

Neysa charged back to him, seeking to protect him from the elements with her body and her anti-magic. Both helped; Stile flung his arms about her neck and buried his face in her wet mane, and the swirling wind had less force there. Her mass was more secure than his, and the rain struck her less stingingly. They settled to the ground, and that was more secure yet. "Now I'm embracing you in your natural form," he told her laughingly, but doubted she heard him over the wind.

What had happened? A moment ago there had been no slightest sign of bad weather. Stile knew storms could develop quickly—he had taken a course in primitive-world meteorology, and often visited the weather dome for demonstrations—but this had been virtually instantaneous. He had been playing his harmonica, trying to trigger whatever monstrous force was lurking, to bring it somehow to bay, then idly likened the effect to—

"I did it!" he cried. "I invoked the storm!" Like the amulet, it had been there to be commanded, and he had innocently done so.

"Storm abate!" he cried.

The two of them were almost swept from their impromptu nest by another savage bout of wind. The storm was not, it seemed, paying heed.

Yet this power was somehow keyed to him. He had invoked the storm; was he unable to banish it? He had evoked the demon from the amulet, before; that had evidently been a one-way thing. But a storm? Was it impossible to put this genie back in the bottle?

It was hard to concentrate, in this buffeting and wet and light and noise. But he tried. What, specifically, had he done to bring this about? He had played music, and the storm-spirit had loomed close without striking. Then he had said, "Almost the form of an electrical storm." An accidental rhyme, of no significance.

Rhyme? Something nagged him. When the harmonica had appeared, so fortuitously—what had he said? Hadn't it been—yes. "A harmonica is what you play. I wish I had one here today." Something like that. Joke doggerel. Two times he had spoken in rhyme, and two times he had been answered. Of course there had been other magic, like the attacking demon of the amulet. No rhymes there. But—worry about that later; it

183

might be a different class of magic. Now, try to abate this tempest. Abate—what rhymed with that? Fate, late, plate. Try it; all he could do was fail.

"Storm abate; you're making me late!" he cried.

The storm lessened, but did not disappear. He was on to something, but not enough. Half a loaf. What else had he done, those other two times?

Neysa played a note on her horn. The storm had eased, so she preferred to stand. She felt most secure on all four feet.

That was it! He had been blowing his horn—in a manner. The harmonica. Making music, either singing or playing.

Stile brought out his wet harmonica and played a soggy passage. Then he stopped and sang in an impromptu tune: "Storm abate. You're making me late!"

This time the storm lessened considerably. The lightning stopped, and the rain slacked to a moderate shower. But it still wasn't gone.

"Neysa, I think I'm on to something," he said. "But I don't really have the hang of it yet. I think I can do magic, if I can only get the rules straight."

The unicorn gave him a long look whose import was unclear. Evidently she distrusted this development, but she made no comment. And he marveled at it himself: how could he, the child of the modern civilized galaxy, seriously consider practicing magic?

Yet, after what he had experienced in this frame, how could he *not* believe in magic?

They resumed their journey, plodding through the drizzle. After an hour they got out of it, and the sun warmed them. They did not make music. Stile knew he had learned something, but not enough. Yet.

Now they settled down to serious grazing and eating —except that he had nothing to eat. Neysa had been willing to continue until she brought him to a fruit tree, but he had felt her sustenance was more important than his, at the moment. She was doing most of the work.

If he could actually do magic, maybe he could conjure some food. If he made up a rhyme and sang it— why not? What rhymed with food?

Stile was actually a poet, in a minor sense; this was yet another aspect of his Game expertise. A person had to be extremely well rounded to capture and hold a high rung on an adult ladder. He was probably more skilled in more types of things of a potentially competitive nature than anyone not involved in the Game. But he had preferred meaning to rhyme and meter, in poetry, so was ill prepared for this particular exercise.

Still, he did know the rudiments of versification, and with a little practice it should come back to him. Iambic feet: da-DUM da-DUM. Pentameter: five feet per line. *I wish I had a little food*—iambic tetrameter, four beats. If unicorns spoke words while running, they would be excellent at poetic meter, for their hooves would measure the cadence.

"I wish I had a little food; it would really help my mood," he said in singsong. He was not as good at improvising tunes with his voice as with an instrument.

Before him appeared a tiny cube. It dropped to the ground, and he had to search for it in the grass. He found it and held it up. It was about a centimeter on a side, and in tiny letters on one face was printed the word FOOD. Stile touched his tongue to it. Nutro-peanut butter. He ate it. Good, but only a token.

Well, he had specified "little." That was exactly what he had gotten.

He was gaining understanding. Music summoned the magic; that was the looming power they had been aware of. Words defined it. The rhyme marked the moment of implementation. A workable system—but he had to make his definitions precise. Suppose he conjured a sword—and it transfixed him? Or a mountain of food, and it buried him? Magic, like any other tool, had to be used properly.

"I wish I had one liter of food; it would really help my mood."

Nothing happened. Obviously he was still missing something.

Neysa lifted her head, perking her ears. Her hearing was more acute than his. Her head came around. Stile

185

followed the direction her horn was pointing—and saw shapes coming toward them.

Had he summoned these? He doubted it; they hardly looked like food, and certainly not in the specified quantity. This must be a coincidental development.

Soon the shapes clarified. Four monsters. They were vaguely apelike, with huge long forearms, squat hairy legs, and great toothy, horny, glary-eyed heads. Another variant of demon, like the one he had fought alone, or the crack-monsters, or the snow-monsters. They all seemed to be species of a general class of creature that wasn't in the conventional taxonomy. But of course unicorns weren't in it either.

Neysa snorted. She trotted over to stand by Stile. She knew this was trouble.

"Must be a sending of my enemy," Stile said. "When you used the amulet to heal me, it alerted the master of amulets, who it seems is not partial to me, for what reason I don't yet know. He sent his goon squad—but we were no longer with the amulet, so they had to track us down. I'll bet the storm messed them up, too."

Neysa made a musical laugh through her horn—a nice effect. She liked the notion of goons getting battered by a storm. But her attention remained on those monsters, and her ears were angling back. She looked cute when her ears perked forward, and grim when they flattened back.

"I think it must be an Adept against me," Stile continued. "Obviously it is no common peasant. But now I know I can do some magic myself, I am more confident. Do you think we should flee these monsters, and worry about when they might catch up again—such as when we are sleeping—or should we fight them here?"

It was a loaded question, and she responded properly. She swished her tail rapidly from side to side and stomped a forehoof, her horn still oriented on the goons.

"My sentiments exactly," Stile said. "I just don't like leaving an enemy on my trail. Let me see if I can work out a good spell to abolish them. That should be safer

186

than indulging in physical combat. They look pretty mean to me."

Pretty mean indeed. His tone had been light, but he already had healthy respect for the fighting capacity of demons. They were like the androids of Proton: stupid, but almost indestructible. Yet he distrusted this magic he could perform. Like all sudden gifts, it needed to be examined in the mouth before being accepted whole-heartedly. But at the moment he simply had to use what was available, and hope it worked.

He concentrated on his versification as the goons approached. He could not, under this pressure, think of anything sophisticated, but so long as it was clear and safe, it would do. It had to.

The first monster loomed before them. "Monster go —I tell you so!" Stile sang, pointing.

The monster puffed into smoke and dissipated. Only a foul-smelling haze remained.

So far, so good. He was getting the hang of it. Stile pointed to the second monster. "Monster go—I tell you so!" he sang, exactly as before. Why change a winning spell?

The monster hesitated as if fazed by the bite of a gnat, then plunged ahead.

Neysa lunged by Stile and caught the demon on her horn. With one heave she hurled it over and behind. The creature gave a great howl of expiration, more in fury than in pain, and landed in a sodden heap.

Why had the magic worked the first time, and not the second? He had done it exactly the same, and nearly gotten his head bitten off.

Oh, no! Could it be that a spell could not be re-peated? That it worked only once? Now he remembered something that had been said by the man he met, the one who had given him the demon amulet. About hav-ing to devise a new spell each time, to step through the curtain. He should have paid better attention!

The third and fourth goons arrived together.

No time now to work up another spell! Stile drew his rapier. "I'll take the one on the right; you take the left," he said to Neysa.

But these two monsters, having seen the fate of their predecessors, were slightly more cautious. To be ugly was not necessarily to be stupid, and these were not really andriods. They evidently learned from experience. They halted just outside the range of horn and sword. They seemed to consider Neysa to be the more formidable opponent, though Stile was sure it was him they wanted. They had to deal with her first; then they would have him at their dubious mercy. Or so they thought.

While one goon tried to distract her, backing away from the unicorn's horn, the other tried to get at her from the side. But Stile attacked the side monster, stabbing at it with his point. He wished he had a broadsword; then he could have slashed these things to pieces. He wasn't sure that a simple puncture would have much effect.

He was mistaken. He pricked his monster in the flank, and it howled and whirled on him, huge hamhands stretching toward him. Stile pricked it again, in its meaty shoulder. Not a mortal wound, but it obviously hurt. At least these demons did have pain sensation; Stile had half-feared they would not. Still, this was basically a standoff. He needed to get at a vital spot, before the thing—

The goon's arm swung with blinding speed and swept the weapon out of Stile's hand. The thing's eyes glowed. Gratified, it pounced on him.

Stile whirled into a shoulder throw, catching the monster's leading arm and heaving. With this technique it was possible for the smallest of men to send the largest of men flying. But this was not a man. The creature was so large and long-armed that Stile merely ended up with a hairy arm dangling over his shoulder. The monster's feet had not left the ground.

Now the goon raised its arm, hauling Stile into the air. He felt its hot breath on his neck; it was going to bite off his head!

"Oh, swell! Go to hell!" Stile cried with haphazard inspiration.

He dropped to the ground. The monster was gone.

Stile looked around, pleased. His impromptu spell had worked! It seemed this frame did have a hell, and he could send—

He froze. The other goon was gone too. So was Neysa.

Oh, no!

Quick, a counterspell. Anything! What rhymed with spell?

"I don't feel well; cancel that spell," he singsonged.

The two monsters and Neysa were back. All three were scorched and coated with soot.

"Monsters away; Neysa stay!" Stile sang. The goons vanished again.

Neysa looked at him reproachfully. She shook herself, making the powdered soot fly. There were sulfur smears on her body, and her mane was frizzled, and her tail was only half its normal length. Her whole body was a mass of singed hair. The whites showed all around her eyes; sure signal of equine alarm.

"I'm sorry, Neysa," Stile said contritely. "I wasn't thinking! I didn't mean to send *you* to hell!" But he realized that wasn't much good. She was burned and hurting. He had to do more than merely apologize.

He could do magic—if he sang a new spell every time. Could he make her well?

"To show how I feel—I say 'Neysa, heal!' "

And before his eyes she unburned. Her mane grew out again and her tail became long and black and straight. Her coat renewed its luster. Her hooves brightened back into their original pearl glow. She had healed—in seconds.

Where were the limits of his power?

But the unicorn did not seem happy. She was well, now, physically, but she must have had a truly disturbing emotional experience. A visit to hell! How could he erase that horror? Could he formulate a spell to make her forget? But that would be tampering with her mind, and if he made any similar error in definition—no, he dared not mess with that.

Neysa was looking at him strangely, as she had before. Stile feared he knew why.

"Neysa—how many people on this world can perform magic like this?" he asked her. "I know most people can do minor magic, like stepping through the curtain, the way most people can pick out clumsy melodies on the harmonica. But how many can do it well? Professional level? Many?"

She blew a negative note.

"That's what I thought. A lot of people have a little talent, but few have a lot of talent, in any particular area. This sort of thing is governed by the bell-shaped curve, and it would be surprising if magic talent weren't similarly constrained. So can a moderate number match my level?"

She still blew no.

"A few?"

This time the negation was fainter.

"A very few?"

At last the affirmative.

Stile nodded. "How many can exert magic against a unicorn, since unicorns are largely proof against magic?"

Neysa looked at him, her nervousness increasing. Her muzzle quivered; her ears were drawing back. Bad news, for him.

"Only the Adepts?" Stile asked.

She blew yes, backing away from him. The whites of her eyes were showing again.

"But Neysa—if I have such talent, I'm still the same person!" he cried. "You don't have to be afraid of me! I didn't mean to send you to hell! I just didn't know my own power!"

She snorted emphatic agreement, and backed another step.

"I don't want to alienate you, Neysa. You're my only friend in this world. I need your support."

He took a step toward her, but she leaned away from him on all four feet. She feared him and distrusted him, now; it was as if he had become a demon, shuffling off his prior disguise.

"Oh, Neysa, I wish you wouldn't feel this way! The magic isn't half as important as your respect. You joined me, when you could have killed me. We have been so much to each other, these past three days!"

She made a small nose at him, angry that he should try to prevail on her like this. He had sent her to hell; he had shown her how demeaning and dangerous to her his power could be. Yet she was moved; she did not want to desert him.

"I never set out to be a magician," Stile said. "I thought the magic was from outside. I had to know the truth. Maybe the truth is worse than what I feared."

Neysa snorted agreement. She was really dead set against this caliber of magic.

"Would it help if I swore not to try any more magic? To conduct myself as if that power did not exist in me? I am a man of my word, Neysa; I would be as you have known me."

She considered, her ears flicking backward and forward as the various considerations ran through her equine mind. At last she nodded, almost imperceptibly.

"I swear," Stile said, "to perform no magic without your leave."

There was an impression of faint color in the air about him, flinging outward. The grass waved in concentric ripples that expanded rapidly until lost to view. Neysa's own body seemed to change color momentarily as the ripples passed her. Then all was normal again.

Neysa came to him. Stile flung his arms about her neck, hugging her. There was a special art to hugging an equine, but it was worth the effort. "Oh, Neysa! What is more important than friendship!"

She was not very demonstrative in her natural form, but the way she cocked one ear at him and nudged him with her muzzle was enough.

Neysa returned to her grazing. Stile was still hungry. There was no suitable food for him here, and since he had sworn off magic he could not conjure anything to eat. Actually, he found himself somewhat relieved to be free of magic—but what was he to say to his stomach?

Then he spied the monster Neysa had slain. Were goons edible? This seemed to be the occasion to find out. He drew his knife and set about carving the demon.

Neysa spied what he was doing. She played a note of reassurance, then galloped around in a great circle several times, while Stile gathered brush and dead wood and dry straw to form a fire. When he had his makings ready, Neysa charged in, skidded to a halt, and snorted out a blowtorch blast. She had evidently not yet cooled off from the battle—or from hell—and needed only a small amount of exertion to generate sufficient heat. The brush burst into flame.

As it turned out, monster steak was excellent.

CHAPTER 11

Oracle

By the time they reached the Oracle, two days later, Stile had pretty well worked out the situation. He could do magic of Adept quality, provided he followed its rules. He had sworn off it, and he would not violate that pledge. But that didn't change what he was: an Adept. That could explain why another Adept was trying to kill him; that other was aware of Stile's potential, and didn't want the competition. The Adepts, it seemed, were quite jealous of their prerogatives—as were the members of most oligarchies or holders of power.

So how should he proceed? Swearing off magic would not protect him from a jealous Adept, who would resent Stile's mere potential. But if it were only a single Adept who was after him, Stile might try to locate that one and deal with him. Nonmagically? That could be dangerous! So—he would ask the Oracle for advice. Why not?

The Oracle lived in a palace. Manicured lawns and hedges surrounded it, and decorative fountains watered its gardens. It was open; anyone could enter, including animals. In this world, animals had much the same stature as human beings; that was one of the things Stile liked about it. In this palace and its grounds, as he understood it, no magic was permitted, other than that of the Oracle itself, and no person could be molested or coerced.

"No disrespect intended," Stile said. "But this doesn't seem like much. It's beautiful in appearance and concept, but . . ."

Neysa left the saddle at the entrance and guided him to a small, plain room in the back. From its rear wall projected a simple speaking tube.

Stile studied the tube. "This is it? The Oracle?" he asked dubiously. "No ceremony, no fanfare, no balls of flame? No bureaucracy? I can just walk up and ask it anything?"

Neysa nodded.

Stile, feeling let down, addressed the tube. "Oracle, what is my best course of action?"

"Know thyself," the tube replied.

"That isn't clear. Could you elucidate?" But the tube was unresponsive.

Neysa nudged him gently away. "You mean I only get one question?" Stile asked, chagrined.

It was so. As with a spell, the Oracle could be invoked only once by any individual. But it had not been Neysa's purpose to have all his questions answered here; she had brought him to this place only for his safety.

Stile, frustrated, left Neysa and went outside. She did not try to restrain him, aware that he had been disappointed. He proceeded to the first fountain he saw. A wolf sat on the far side, probably not tame, but it would not attack him here. Stile removed his shirt, leaned over the pool, and splashed the cold water on his face. So he was safe; so what? His curiosity was unsatisfied. Was he to remain indefinitely in this world without understanding it?

"Thou, too?"

Stile looked up, startled, blinking the droplets from his vision. There was a young man across the fountain. He had shaggy reddish hair and a dark cast of feature, with eyes that fairly gleamed beneath heavy brows. His beard and sideburns were very like fur.

"I regret; I did not see you," Stile said. "Did I intrude?"

"Thou didst see me," the man said. "But recognized me not, in my lupine form."

Lupine. "A—werewolf?" Stile asked, surprised. "I am not used to this land. I did not think—I apologize."

"That was evident in thy mode of speech. But apologize not to an outcast cur."

Mode of speech. Suddenly Stile remembered: Clip

the unicorn, Neysa's brother, had used this same touch of archaic language. Evidently that was what prevailed here. He had better change over, so as not to make himself awkwardly obvious.

"I—will try to mend my speech. But I do apologize for mistaking thee."

"Nonesuch is in order. This region is open to all without hindrance, even such as I."

Stile was reminded of the robot Sheen, claiming to have no rights because of her metal origin. It bothered him. "Art thou not a person? If being outcast is a crime, I am surely more criminal than you. Thee. I fled my whole world."

"Ah, it is as I thought. Thou art from Proton. Art thou serf or Citizen?"

"Serf," Stile said, startled at this knowledge of his world. Yet of course others had made the crossing before him. "Werewolf, if thou hast patience, I would like to talk with thee."

"I welcome converse, if thou knowest what ilk I be and be not deceived. I am Kurrelgyre, were."

"I am Stile, man." Stile proffered his hand, and the other, after a pause such as one might have when recalling a foreign convention, accepted it.

"In mine other form, we sniff tails," Kurrelgyre said apologetically.

"There is so much I do not know about this world," Stile said. "If you know—thou knowest of my world, thou wilt—wilst—thou shouldst appreciate the problem I have. I know not how came I here, or how to return, and the Oracle's reply seems unhelpful."

"It is the nature of Oracular response," Kurrelgyre agreed. "I am similarly baffled. I queried the Oracle how I might regain my place in my society without performing anathema, and the Oracle told me 'Cultivate blue.' Means that aught to thee?"

Stile shook his head. "Naught. I asked it what was my best course of action, and it said 'Know thyself.' I have no doubt that is always good advice, but it lacks specificity. In fact it is not even an action; it is an information."

195

"A most curious lapse," Kurrelgyre agreed. "Come, walk with me about the gardens. Perhaps we may obtain insights through dialogue."

"I shall be happy to. Allow me just a moment to advise my companion. She brought me here—"

"Assuredly." They re-entered the palace, proceeding to the Oracle chamber where Stile had left Neysa.

She was still there, facing the speaking tube, evidently unable to make up her mind what to say to it. Kurrelgyre growled when he saw her, shifting instantly into his lupine mode. Neysa, hearing him, whirled, her horn orienting unwaveringly on the new-formed wolf.

"Stop!" Stile cried, realizing that violence was in the offing. "There is no—"

The wolf sprang. Neysa lunged. Stile threw himself between them.

All three came to a halt in a momentary tableau. The tip of Neysa's horn was nudging Stile's chest; the wolf's teeth were set against his right arm, near the shoulder. Trickles of blood were forming on Stile's chest and arm where point and fang penetrated.

"Now will you both change into human form and apologize to the Oracle for this accident?" Stile said.

There was a pause. Then both creatures shimmered and changed. Stile found himself standing between a handsome young man and a pretty girl. He was shirtless, with rivulets of blood on him; he had forgotten to put his shirt back on after splashing in the fountain pool.

He extricated himself. "I gather unicorns and werewolves are hereditary enemies," he said. "I'm sorry; I didn't know. But this is no place for, uh, friendly competition. Now shake hands, or sniff tails, or whatever creatures do here to make up."

Neysa's eyes fairly shot fire, and Kurrelgyre scowled. But both glanced at the Oracle tube, then at Stile's bloodied spots, then at each other. And paused again.

Stile perceived, as if through their eyes, what each saw. The werewolf's clothing had reappeared with the man, and it was a tasteful fur-lined jacket and leggings, complimenting his somewhat rough-hewn aspect. Neysa was in a light black dress that set off her pert figure admirably; it seemed she wore clothing when she chose, though at night she had not bothered. She was now the kind of girl to turn any man's head—and Kurrelgyre's head was turning.

"It is a place of truce," the werewolf said at last. "I regret my instinct overcame my manners."

"I, too," Neysa agreed softly.

"I abhor the fact that I have drawn the blood of an innocent."

"I, too."

"Do thou draw my blood, Stile, in recompense." Kurrelgyre held out his arm. Neysa did the same.

"I shall not!" Stile said. "If you—if thou—the two of you—"

The werewolf smiled fleetingly. "Thou wert correct the first time, friend. It is the plural."

"If you two feel you owe me aught, expiate it by making up to each other. I hate to be the cause of dissent between good creatures."

"The penalty of blood need not be onerous," Kurrelgyre murmured. He made a courtly bow to Neysa. "Thou art astonishingly lovely, equine."

Neysa responded with a curtsey that showed more décolletage and leg than was strictly necessary. Oh, the tricks that could be played with clothing! No wonder the Citizens of Proton reserved clothing to themselves. "Thank thee, lupine."

Then, cautiously, Neysa extended her hand. Instead of shaking it, Kurrelgyre lifted it slightly, bringing it to his face. For a moment Stile was afraid the werewolf meant to bite it, but instead he kissed her fingers.

Stile, relieved, stepped forward and took an arm of each. "Let's walk together, now that we're all friends. We have much in common, being all outcasts of one kind or another. Neysa was excluded from the herd because of her color—"

"What is wrong with her color?" the werewolf asked, perplexed.

"Nothing," Stile said as they walked. He spied his

197

shirt by the fountain, and moved them all toward it. "Some unicorns have distorted values."

Kurrelgyre glanced sidelong past Stile at the girl. "I should say so! I always suspected that Herd Stallion had banged his horn into one rock too many, and this confirms it. My taste does not run to unicorns, understand, but the precepts of physical beauty are universal. She is extremely well formed. Were she a were-bitch—"

"And I am outcast because I refused to—to perform a service for my employer," Stile continued. "Or to honor an illegal deal proffered by another Citizen." He washed his small wounds off with water from the pool, and donned his shirt. "What, if I may inquire, was thy problem, werewolf?"

"Among my kind, where game is scarce, when the size of the pack increases beyond the capacity of the range to support, the oldest must be eliminated first. My sire is among the eldest, a former leader of the pack, so it fell to me to kill him and assume the leadership. Indeed, there is no wolf in my pack I could not slay in fair combat. But I love my sire, long the finest of wolves, and could not do it. Therefore mine own place in the pack was forfeit, with shame."

"Thou wert excluded for thy conscience!" Stile exclaimed.

"There is no conscience beyond the good of the pack," the werewolf growled.

"Yes," Neysa breathed sadly.

They came to a hedged-in park, with a fine rock garden in the center. Neysa and Kurrelgyre sat down on stones nearer to each other than might have seemed seemly for natural enemies.

"Let us review thy situation, Stile," the werewolf said. "Thou knowest little of this land—yet this alone should not cause thee undue distress. Thou wilt hardly be in danger, with a fair unicorn at thy side."

"Nevertheless, I am in danger," Stile said. "It seems an Adept is trying to kill me."

"Then thou art beyond hope. Against Adepts, naught suffices save avoidance. Thou must remain here at the Oracle's palace forever."

"So I gather, in the ordinary case. But it also seems I have Adept powers myself."

Kurrelgyre phased into wolf-form, teeth bared as he backed away from Stile.

"Wait!" Stile cried. "Neysa reacted the same way! But I have sworn off magic, till Neysa gives me leave."

The wolf hesitated, absorbing that, then phased warily back into the man. "No unicorn would grant such leave, even were that not the stubbornest of breeds." Neysa nodded agreement.

"But I am just a stray from another world," Stile said. "It is mere coincidence that I have the talent for magic."

"Coincidence?" Kurrelgyre growled. "Precious little in this frame is coincidence; that is merely thy frame's term for what little magic operates there. Here, all things have meaning." He pondered a moment. "Have ye talent in the other frame?"

"I ride well—"

The werewolf glanced at Neysa, who sat with her fine ankles demurely exposed, her bosom gently heaving. "Who wouldn't!"

"And I am expert in the Game," Stile continued.

"The Game! That's it! Know ye not the aptitude for magic in this frame correlates with that for the Game in that frame? How good at the Game be ye, honestly?"

"Well, I'm tenth on my age-ladder—"

Kurrelgyre waved a warning finger at him. "Think ye I know not the way of the ladders? If ye rise to fifth place, thou must enter the annual Tourney. No obfuscation, now; this is vital. How good art thou when thou tryest, absolute scale?"

Stile realized that this was not the occasion for concealment or polite modesty. "I should be among the top ten, gross. On a good day, fourth or fifth."

"Then thou art indeed Adept caliber. There are no more than ten Adepts. They go by colors: White, Yellow, Orange, Green and such: no more than there are clear-cut hues. Therefore thou art of their number. One Adept must be dead."

"What art thou talking about? Why must an Adept be dead, just because I'm good at the Game in the other—" Stile caught himself about to make an impromptu rhyme and broke off lest he find himself in violation of his oath.

"Ah, I forget! Thou hast no basis yet to comprehend. Know this, Stile: no man can cross the curtain between frames while his double lives. Therefore—"

"Double?"

"His other self. His twin. All true men exist in both frames, and are forever fixed where they originate—until one dies out of turn. Then—"

"Wait, wait! Thou sayest people as well as geography match? That can not be so. The serfs of Proton are constantly brought in and deported as their tenures expire; only the Citizens are a constant population."

"Perhaps 'tis so, now; not always in the past. Most people still equate, Phaze to Proton, Proton to Phaze. The others are partial people, like myself. Perhaps I had a serf-self in the past, and that serf departed, so now I alone remain."

"Thou travelest between frames—because werewolves don't exist on Proton?"

Kurrelgyre shrugged. "It must be. Here there are animals and special forms; there, there are more serfs. It balances out, likely. But thou—thou must travel because thy magic self is dead. And thy magic self must be—"

"An Adept," Stile finished. "At last I get thy drift."

"Know thyself," Neysa said. "Adept." She frowned.

"That's it!" Stile cried. "I must figure out which Adept I am!" Then he noticed Neysa's serious demeanor. "Or must I? I have sworn off magic."

"But only by exerting thy powers as an Adept canst thou hope to survive!" Kurrelgyre exclaimed. Then he did a double take. "What am I saying? Who would want to help an Adept survive? The fair 'corn is right: abandon thy magic."

Corn? Oh, unicorn. "What is so bad about being an Adept?" Stile asked. "I should think it would be a great advantage to be able to perform magic."

200

The werewolf exchanged a glance with the unicorn. "He really knows not," Kurrelgyre said.

"I really don't," Stile agreed. "I am aware that magic can be dangerous. So can science. But you both act as if it's a crime. You suggest I would be better off dying as a man than living as an Adept. I should think a lot of good could be done by magic."

"Mayhap thou shouldst encounter an Adept," Kurrelgyre said.

"Maybe I should! Even though I'm not doing magic myself, at least I'd like to know who I am and what manner of creature I am. From what thou sayest, something must have happened to my Adept double and, considering my age and health, it couldn't have been natural." He paused. "But of course! All we need to do is check which Adept died recently."

"None has," Kurrelgyre assured him. "At least, none we know of. Adepts are secretive, but even so, someone must be concealing evidence."

"Well, I'll just have to go and look," Stile decided. "I'll check out each Adept until I find which one is dead, and see if that was me. Then I'll be satisfied. Only—how can I be sure that two aren't dead, and I have found the wrong one?"

"No problem there," the werewolf said. "Thine other self would have looked exactly like thee, so any who saw thee in his demesnes would know. And every Adept has his own peculiar style of magic, his means of implementation, that he alone commands. What style is thine?"

"Stile style," Neysa murmured, permitting herself to smile fleetingly.

"Spoken, or sung, in verse," Stile said. "Music summons the power. Which Adept uses that mode?"

"We know not. The Adepts vouchsafe no such information to common folk. Often they veil their magic in irrelevant forms, speaking incantations when it may be in fact a gesture that is potent, or posturing when it is a key rune. Or so it is bruited about among the animal folk. We know not who makes the amulets, or the golem people, or the potions or graphs or any of the

201

other conjurations. We only know these things exist, and know to our dismay their power." He turned to Stile, taking one hand. "But friend—do not do this thing. If thou findest thine Adept-self, thou wilt become that Adept, and I shall have to bear the onus of not having slain thee when I had the chance. And Neysa too, who helped thee: lay not this geas upon her."

Stile turned to Neysa, appalled. "Thou feelest that way also?"

Sadly, she nodded.

"Methinks she led thee to the Oracle to avoid the peril she saw looming," Kurrelgyre said. "To destroy a friend—or turn an Adept loose on the realm. Here thou art safe, even from thy friends."

"But I am bound by mine oath!" Stile said. He hoped he was getting the language right: thy and my before a consonant, thine and mine before a vowel. "I will not perform magic! I will not become the monster thou fearest. I seek only to know. Canst thou deny me that?"

Slowly Kurrelgyre shook his head. "We can not deny thee that. Yet we wish—"

"I must know myself," Stile said. "The Oracle said so."

"And the Oracle is always right," the werewolf agreed. "We can not oppose our paltry judgment to that."

"So I will go on a quest for myself," Stile concluded. "When I have satisfied my need-to-know, I will return to mine own frame, where there is no problem about magic. So thou needst have no fear about me turning into whatever ogre thou dost think I might. I have to return soon anyway, to get my new employment, or my tenure will expire."

Neysa's gaze dropped.

"Why carest thou about tenure?" Kurrelgyre inquired. "Remain here, in hiding from thine enemy; thou hast no need to return."

"But Proton is my world," Stile protested. "I never intended to stay here—"

The werewolf stood and drew Stile gently aside.

"Needs must I speak to thee in language unbecoming for the fair one to hear," he said. Neysa glanced up quickly at him, but remained sitting silently by the garden.

"What's this nonsense about unbecoming language?" Stile demanded when they were out of Neysa's earshot. "I don't keep secrets from—"

"Canst thou not perceive the mare is smitten with thee?" Kurrelgyre demanded. "Canst not guess what manner of question she tried to formulate for the Oracle?"

Stile suffered a guilty shock. He had compared Neysa in various ways to Sheen, yet missed the obvious one. "But I am no unicorn!"

"And I am no man. Yet I would not, were I thee, speak so blithely of departure. Better it were to cut her heart quickly, cleanly."

"Uh, yes. No," Stile agreed, confused. "She—we have been—I assumed it was merely a courtesy of the form. I never thought—"

"And a considerable courtesy it is," Kurrelgyre agreed. "I was careless once myself about such matters, until my bitch put me straight." He ran his fingers along an old scar that angled from his shoulder dangerously near the throat. Werewolves evidently had quite direct means of expressing themselves. "I say it as should not: Neysa is the loveliest creature one might meet, in either form, and no doubt the most constant too. Shamed would I have been to lay a tooth on her, ere thou didst halt me. Considering the natural antipathy that exists between man and unicorn, as between man and werewolf and between unicorn and werewolf, her attachment to thee is a mark of favor most extreme. Unless—chancest thou to be virginal, apart from her?"

"No."

"And most critical of all: canst thou touch her most private parts?"

Stile reddened slightly. "I just told thee—"

"Her feet," Kurrelgyre said. "Her horn. No stranger durst touch a unicorn's magic extremities."

"Why yes, I—"

"Then must it be love. She would not else tolerate thy touch. Mark me, friend: she spared thee, when she learned thou wert Adept, because she loved thee, and therein lies mischief with her herd. Thou canst not lightly set her aside." He touched the scar near his throat again.

"No," Stile agreed fervently, thinking again of Sheen. He had always had a kind of personal magnetism that affected women once they got to know him, though it was usually canceled out by the initial impression his size and shyness made. Thus his heterosexual relationships tended to be distant or intimate, with few shades between. But with that situation went a certain responsibility: not to hurt those women who trusted themselves to him.

He remembered, with another pang of nostalgia, how the jockey girl Tune had stimulated his love, then left him. He had never been able to blame her, and would not have eschewed the affair had he known what was coming. She had initiated him into a world whose dimension he had hardly imagined before. But he did not care to do that to another person. He had no concern about any injury from Neysa; she would never hurt him. She would just quietly take herself away, and off a mountain ledge, and never transform into a firefly. She would spare him, not herself. It was her way.

Kurrelgyre's question was valid: why couldn't Stile remain here? There was a threat against his life, true—but he had fled Proton because of that, too. If he could nullify that threat in this frame—well, there were appeals to this world that rivaled those of the Game.

In fact, magic itself had, for him, a fascination similar to—no! His oath made that academic.

What, then, of Sheen? He could not simply leave her in doubt. He must return at least long enough to explain. She was a robot; she would understand. The practical thing for him to do was pick the most convenient world and stay there. It would be enough for Sheen to know he was safe; her mission would then have been accomplished.

As he had known Tune was safe and happy ... Had that been enough for him? To know she had successfully replaced his arms with those of another man, and given that man in fact what she had given Stile in name: a son? He had understood, and Sheen would understand—but was that enough?

Yet what else could he do? He could not remain in both frames, could he? In any event, his tenure on Proton was limited, while it seemed unlimited here.

Stile returned to Neysa and sat beside her, Kurrelgyre trailing. "The werewolf has shown me that I can not expect to solve my problems by fleeing them. I must remain here to find my destiny, only visiting the other frame to conclude mine affairs there." As he said it, he wished he had chosen other phrasing.

Neysa responded by lifting her gaze. That was enough.

"Now for thee, werewolf," Stile said. "We must solve thy riddle too. Did it occur to thee that the Blue thou must cultivate could be an Adept?"

Now Kurrelgyre was stricken. "Cultivate an Adept? Rather would I remain forever outcast!"

"But if the Oracle is always right—"

"That may be. I asked how to restore myself to my pack; the Oracle answered. Perhaps the necessary price is too high."

"Yet thou also didst specify that the method not violate thy conscience."

"My conscience will not permit my craven catering to the abomination that is an Adept!"

"Then it must be something else. Some other blue. A field of blue flowers—"

"Werewolves are not farmers!" Kurrelgyre cried indignantly. "It must be the Blue Adept; yet the only cultivation I could do without shame would be the turf over his grave. I shall not seek the Blue Adept."

Stile considered. "If, as we fear, thou hast doomed thyself to remain outcast from thy kind—why not travel with me? I have decided to remain in this frame, but this is pointless unless I locate and nullify the threat against my life—and that threat surely relates to who

205

and what I am. Without magic with which to defend myself, I shall likely be in need of protection."

"The lady unicorn is capable of protecting thee ably enough."

"From the ill favor of an Adept?"

Kurrelgyre paced the ground. "Now, if I refuse, I brand myself coward."

"No, no! I did not mean to imply—"

"Thou hardly needst to. But also I doubt the mare would care to have the like of me along, and I would not impose—"

Neysa stood. She took Kurrelgyre's hand, glanced briefly into his eyes, then turned away.

The werewolf faced Stile. "Neysa has a way with words! It seems outcasts had best support each other, though they be natural enemies. We all shall likely die, and for a foolish cause—but it is as fitting a mode as any."

CHAPTER 12

Black

"Who is the closest Adept?" Stile asked. "Not the Blue; we won't check that one if you're along."

Kurrelgyre shifted to wolf-form and sniffed the breeze. He shifted back. "The Black, methinks."

"Black it is!" Stile agreed. He would have preferred a more scientific selection—but science was not, it seemed, trustworthy in this frame. Convenience would have to do.

They left the palace together, Stile riding Neysa, the wolf ranging easily beside. They bore west again, toward the castle of the Black Adept. Now that the decision was made, Stile had second thoughts about purpose and safety. Was he really doing the right thing? All he could do now was see it through, and after checking out the Black Adept he could decide whether it was worth checking out others. This was hardly his idea of sword and sorcery adventure—which was perhaps just as well. He suspected that in real life, more evil magicians prevailed than barbarian heroes.

Neysa had located a supply of grain, and had some in a bag tied to the saddle; she would not have to make long halts for grazing. Traveling at speed, they made excellent progress, covering fifty of this frame's miles in about two and a half hours. Stile had done some endurance riding on Proton, and knew it would take an excellent horse to maintain even half this pace.

Thereafter, the way became bleak. The turf thinned, remaining verdant only in scattered oases. Stile realized that with a spell he might procure fresh water and extra food, but did not offer. They did not want magic, and the very notion was contrary to the spirit of his oath.

The mountains and valleys gave way to a broad and featureless dark plain that extended to the horizon, oppressed by what seemed to be a permanently looming cloud. Gusts of cutting wind brought choking clouds of dust into their faces. Stile coughed. If this environment reflected the temperament of the Black Adept, the magician was vile indeed! But it was probably a misapprehension. Stile had friends and un-friends, but there were few people he considered to be as evil as his friends seemed to think Adepts were. It was said that familiarity bred contempt, but surely ignorance bred error.

At last, amid the gloom, a black castle showed. It stood in stark silhouette, no light illuminating it from within. The land about it was so bleak as to seem scorched. Had Stile not known the identity of its occupant, thanks to Kurrelgyre's nose, he might readily have guessed. Everything was dead black.

As they neared it, Stile suffered intensifying pangs of doubt. Was his curiosity worth the risk of bracing this person? He was running the risk of whatever sorcery the Black Adept had in mind—for what? Just to know who he was, in this frame.

No—it was more than that, he reminded himself. Another Adept was trying to kill him, and until Stile knew his own identity, he probably would not know who was trying to kill him, or why. The Oracle agreed; it had told him to know himself. Curiosity alone might not be worth it, but life, security—yes, that was worth it.

What should he do, though, if the lives of his friends were threatened on his behalf? Would he use his magic, then, to help them? No—he could not. His oath had been made, and Stile had never in his life broken his given word. Neysa had to give him leave, and now he knew she would not. Because she believed that to release him would be to turn him into the monster that an Adept would be, and she would rather die. He had better see to their mutual health by mundane means, staying alert.

Yet there was no call to be foolish. "Neysa," he murmured. "Is there any way to approach this castle secretly and depart in the same fashion? I don't need to brace the magician directly; I think one look at him will tell me whether he is alive or dead, or whether he resembles me. If we check, and the Black Adept is alive —not only is he not me, he is likely to do something horrible to me. And to thee, I fear."

Kurrelgyre growled assent in an I-told-thee-so tone. The two of them expected this to be such a bad experience that Stile would no longer question the validity of their hatred of Adepts. Increasingly, Stile was being convinced.

Neysa halted. She flicked her nose, indicating that he should dismount. Stile did so. Then she reached back as she lifted one hind foot. She put her teeth to it, as if chewing an itch—and the white sock came off.

Stile stared. The term "sock" was descriptive, not literal; it was merely a patch of white hair about the foot. Yet she still held the white sock in her mouth, and her foot had turned black.

She nudged the sock at him, then went for the other hind foot. Soon Stile held a pair of white socks, one larger than the other. Neysa nudged him again.

"But I can't wear these," he protested. "These are your socks. Thy socks."

Neysa nosed him impatiently again. Stile shrugged and tried donning a unicorn-sock over his boot. It was hoof-shaped at the extremity, yet it fit admirably: more unicorn magic, of course. In a moment he stood handsomely garbed in unicorn socks.

But the white color extended beyond the socks, now. His feet looked like hooves, his legs like hair. His arms —where were his arms?

Kurrelgyre growled appreciatively, seeming to think Stile's appearance had improved.

Stile looked again, startled. He looked like a unicorn! A white unicorn. He remained human, but in illusion he was the forepart of the animal. Behind him stretched a ghost-body, equine.

Neysa had given him concealment. Who would worry about a unicorn poking about the premises?

"Every time I think I understand thee, Neysa, thou

comest up with some new device!" he said admiringly. "I'll return thy socks when we're away from here. Thank thee most kindly." And privately he thought: she didn't mind him benefiting from magic, so long as it was not Adept magic. A useful distinction.

They went on: a white unicorn, a black unicorn, and a wolf. The dark fog swirled thickly about the castle, helping to conceal them. But could the Adept really be ignorant of their presence? It was possible; why should the Black Adept allow them to intrude, when he could so easily hurl a nasty spell at them, unless he were not paying attention? Surely he had better things to do than sit and watch for trespassers. And if the Adept happened to be dead, there should be no danger anymore. So Stile reasoned, reassuring himself.

Yet somehow he did not feel reassured.

Kurrelgyre made a low growl of warning. They stopped. The wolf had his nose to the ground, frozen there. Stile stooped to look—and his knees gave a warning shock of pain, and the unicorn image halfway buckled. Mustn't do! But he saw what it was: a black line, stretching across the basalt.

Could it amount to a trip wire? It was a color-line, not a wire, but with magic it could perform the same function. That would explain why the Adept was not paying attention; he depended on his automatic alert. "We'd better pass without touching any lines," Stile murmured. "They might be the Adept's alert-lines, no pun."

They all high-stepped carefully over the line. Soon there was another. This one was thicker, as if drawn with coagulating paint. Then a third, actually a ridge. And a fourth, set closer to the last, like a miniature wall.

"Something funny here," Stile said. "Why make an alarm-line this solid? It only calls attention to itself."

Yet there was nothing to do but go on over. Stile's apprehension was abating as his perplexity grew. He had accepted the notion of magic as a way of life—but why should anyone surround himself with thickening lines? That hardly made sense.

The lines came more often now, each more formidable than the last. It became evident that the black castle was not a mere edifice of stone or brick, but the innermost manifestation of a rapidly solidifying network of line-walls. When the walls passed waist height on Stile, and were set only two meters apart, he concluded that jumping them was now too risky; they were bound to touch one accidentally and set off the alarm. If this really were an alarm system. Stile now feared it was something quite different, perhaps an elaborate architectural trap. But it might be no more than a progressive deterrent to intrusions such as theirs. A passive defense, showing that the Black Adept was not really the monster he was reputed to be. Maybe.

"I think we had better walk between walls for a while," Stile said. "It is either that, or start climbing over them. This thing is turning into a maze, and we may be obliged to follow its rules." And he wondered, nervously: was that the way of Adepts? To force intruders, stage by stage, into a set mold, that would lead inevitably into their corruption or destruction? Was that the way of all Adept-magic? In that case, the fears of the unicorn and werewolf with respect to Stile himself could be well founded. Suppose he was, or had been, the Black Adept? That, given limitless power, he had chosen to isolate himself in this manner—and would do so again, given the power again? Helping no one, having no friends? Power corrupted . . .

They turned left, walking between walls. As it happened, it was indeed a maze, or at least a complicated labyrinth. The inner wall turned at right angles, making a passage toward the interior, and gradually elevated in height. Soon a ceiling developed, from an extension of one wall, making this a true hall. The passage kept curving about, usually sharply, often doubling back on itself, so that it was impossible to try to keep track of direction. "Kurrelgyre, your nose can lead us out again?" Stile inquired nervously. The wolf growled assent.

The line-labyrinth seemed to continue on indefinitely. Wan light fused in from somewhere, allowing them to see—but there was nothing to see except more blank walls of black material. The castle—for they had to be well inside the edifice proper now—was as silent as a burial vault. That hardly encouraged Stile.

On and on they went. Every time it seemed they were getting somewhere, the passage doubled back and paralleled itself for another interminable distance—then doubled back again. Was this whole castle nothing but many kilometers—many miles, he corrected himself—of passages? This passage continued to get narrower, becoming more like a tunnel, until Neysa was having difficulty making the turns. Her horn projected in front far enough to scrape a wall when she tried to make a hairpin turn, and her effort to avoid such contact put her into contortions and slowed her considerably. But she didn't want to change form, in case they were still under observation; that would betray her special talent. In addition, she still wore the saddle, which would become a liability in her other form. It seemed her own clothing transformed with her, but not things originating externally. And their supplies were in the saddlebags.

"Enough," Stile said at last. "We can wander forever in this mess, and die of starvation when our supplies run out. Let's tackle the dread Adept forthrightly!" And he banged his fist into the wall.

That surface was oddly soft and warm, as if only recently extruded from some volcanic fissure. It gave under the impact, slightly, then sprang back with a twang. The sound reverberated along the hall, and on out of sight; it seemed to be traveling along the same convolutions they were traveling, but much faster, tirelessly amplifying as it went. Soon the whole region was humming with it, then the castle itself.

Gradually it fudged, as the harmonics of different walls overlapped and muted each other, and finally died away amorphously. "Must have come to the end of the line," Stile said. "Let's go on, not worrying about contact."

They moved on more rapidly. At every sharp corner,

Neysa's horn scraped, and the twang reverberated. Nothing else happened.

Then at last the walls opened out into a moderate chamber. In the center stood a great black dragon. The creature opened its mouth to roar, but no sound came forth, only a tongue like a line drawn by a pen.

Stile contemplated the creature. He had never seen a living dragon before, but recognized the general form from the literature of legend. Yet this was an unusual variant. The creature, like the castle, seemed to be made of thickened lines. Its legs were formed of loops, its body of closely interlocked convolutions, and its tail was like knitwork. It was as if it had been shaped meticulously from a single line, phenomenally intricate. Yet it was solid, as a knit sweater is solid.

The dragon stepped forward, showing its blackline teeth. Stile was so fascinated by the linear effect that he hardly was concerned for his own safety. He recalled the puzzle-lines that had intrigued him as a child, in which the pen never left the paper or crossed itself. The most intricate forms could be made along the way by the traveling line—flowers, faces, animals, even words —but the rules were never broken. The challenge was to find the end of the line, in the midst of the complex picture.

This dragon, of course, was three-dimensional. Its lines did touch, did cross, for it was tied together by loops and knots at key places. But the principle remained: the line, though knotted, never terminated, never divided. The whole dragon, as far as Stile could tell, was a construct of a single thread.

Stile became aware of the posture of his companions. Both were facing the dragon in a state of combat readiness, standing slightly ahead of Stile.

"Enough of this!" he exclaimed. "This is my quest; you two should not endanger yourselves in my stead. I'll fight mine own battle." He stooped to pull off his unicorn socks—and again his knees flared in pain, causing him to drop ignominiously to the floor. He kept forgetting his injury at critical times!

He righted himself tediously, then bent at the waist and drew off one sock, then the other. Now he was himself again. He approached Neysa. "May I?" he inquired.

She nodded, her eyes not leaving the dragon. Stile picked up one real foot and pulled the sock over it until it merged with her hair. Then he moved around and did the other. In the midst of this he looked up—and met Kurrelgyre's gaze. Yes—he was handling the unicorn's very private feet. Horses did not like to have their feet impeded or restrained in any way; many would kick violently in such circumstance, even breaking a leg in the frantic effort to free it, or rebreaking it to escape the restraint of a splint. Thus a broken leg was often doom for a horse. Unicorns were no doubt worse. Neysa, when she joined him, had yielded her whole spirit to him.

Then she had discovered he was Adept. Anathema!

Now Stile stood before the dragon, drawing his rapier. He still was not expert in its use, but the dragon did not know that. Would the point be effective, or was it better to have a cutting edge so he could sever a line? Would the dragon unravel like knitwork if he did cut its line? These were questions he would have to answer by experiment.

The dragon was evidently assessing Stile at the same time. The white unicorn had suddenly become a man. Magic was involved. Was it safe to take a bite?

Stile, though quite nervous about the encounter, was experienced in dealing with animals. He had backed down hostile dogs and cats on his employer's farm, as part of assorted initiations, and of course had calmed many a spooked horse. Later he had taken his turn in various Game arenas, moving larger beasts of prey about with whip and prod. He had never faced a dragon before, but the basic principles of animal management should apply. He hoped.

He acted with apparent confidence, advancing on the dragon with his rapier point orienting on the creature's black knot-nose. The noses of most animals were tender, and often were more important psychologically than the eyes. "Now I'm not looking for trouble, dragon," Stile said with affected calmness. "I came to pay a call on the Black Adept. I only want to meet him, not to hurt him. Kindly stand aside and let us pass."

Stile heard a snort of amazement behind him. Neysa had never imagined bracing a dragon in its lair this way!

The dragon, too, was taken aback. What manner of man approached it with such imperious confidence? But it was a beast, not a man, and could not reason well, and it had its orders. In fact anything constructed from loops of cord might have trouble reasoning well; what kind of a brain could be fashioned from knotted string? It opened its jaws and took a snap at Stile.

Stile stepped smoothly to the side. His rapier flicked out, neatly pricking the sensitive nose. The dragon jerked back with a soundless yipe.

"That was a gentle warning," Stile said evenly, privately overjoyed at his success. The thing did feel pain! "My patience has limits. Begone, dragon!"

Baffled more by Stile's attitude than his physical prowess, the dragon scuttled back. Stile stepped forward, frowning. The dragon whimpered, again without sound—then unraveled.

Stile stared. The creature was disintegrating! First its hurting nose tightened into a close knot, then popped into nonexistence. Then its muzzle and teeth went, the latter becoming tangles in a string that disappeared as the string went taut. Then the eyes and ears. Headless, the thing still faced Stile, backing away. The neck went, and the front legs, the pace of unraveling speeding up as it continued. Very soon there was nothing but a line—and this snapped back into the wall like a rubber band.

The whole dragon had indeed been no more than an intricately wrought string. Now it was gone. Yet that string, when shaped, had seemed formidable, and had reacted with normal brute reflexes. Surely it would have chomped him, had he allowed it to. It could have killed him.

"The whole thing—string," Stile breathed. "And this whole castle—more string? For what purpose?"

Unicorn and wolf shrugged. Who could understand the ways of an Adept?

Neysa made a little nose back the way they had come, inquiring whether he had seen enough and was ready to get out of here. But Stile shook his head no, grimly. More than ever, he wanted to identify the proprietor of this castle. He wanted to be absolutely certain it was not now and never had been he.

They walked on down the passage, which narrowed again beyond the dragon's lair, but did not constrict as much as before. Again the way folded back, and back again, and yet again, endlessly.

"Damn it!" Stile swore. "We could die of old age in here, looking for the master of this castle—if he lives. I'm going to force the issue."

Kurrelgyre looked at him warily, but did not protest. This was Stile's venture, to foul up as he pleased. Stile made a fist and banged repeatedly on the wall, making the reverberations build tremendously until the whole castle seemed to shake. "Black Adept, show thyself!" he bawled. "I demand only to see thy face; then I depart."

"Follow the line," a voice replied. And a double line snaked into view ahead, looping into itself. As they approached it, the lines retreated like string drawn in from a distance. It resembled the dragon in this respect, constantly disappearing into itself. But it was not part of the wall.

Soon the line led them to a large central hall they were unlikely to have found thus expeditiously by themselves. A man stood there, facing them. He was garbed completely in black, and seemed to have a black tail. But the tail was the line they had just followed!

"The line," Stile said, finally putting it all together. "It is from thee! This whole castle is thou—the solidified line of thy past!"

"Now thou knowest," the Black Adept said coldly. "I have met thy demand, intruder."

"Yes," Stile agreed, not liking the man's tone. This was definitely not himself! The Adept stood half a meter taller, and his appearance and voice were unlike

216

anything Stile was or could be. Not that the Adept was grotesque; he really looked rather ordinary. But he was certainly not Stile. "Now I shall depart, thanking thee for thy courtesy."

"No courtesy, intruder. Thine animals shall go, for they are of dark complexion, even burdened with thy supplies; it were a shame I must free them from. Thou shalt remain." And the Black Adept cast out his line. It amplified immediately into an intricate prison-bar wall, hardening in place between Stile and his two companions. Alarmed, he stepped to it—but the bars were already like steel. He tried to go around it, but the wall extended itself faster than he could move. He drew his rapier—but realized the bars were as hard as its metal was, even if it had had a cutting edge. He was trapped.

Stile turned to the Adept. "Why?" he asked. "Why hold me here?"

"Why didst thou intrude on my demesnes?" the Adept replied.

This was awkward. Stile did not care to give his reason, and would not lie. "I can say only that I meant thee no harm," he said.

"Know ye not I suffer no human intrusion into my premises? The penalty is to remain."

To remain. Never to depart? Death, here?

Neysa tried to get through the wall separating them, but could not. Even the wolf was too large to fit between the bars. They could not help him, directly. "You two had better leave," Stile said. "I will have to settle with the Adept myself."

Neysa hesitated. Stile knew she could get through the bars by changing into her firefly form, but he didn't want her to betray her talents to the Black Adept, who could readily make a line-cage to confine the insect. No sense getting her trapped too! "Get out of here!" he snapped. "I'll be all right. Just leave the supplies—"

"Do not!" the Black Adept warned. "Lest I throw out a net to capture thee too."

A net. Did the Adept know about her firefly form after all, or was that merely a manner of speaking? This

217

was risky! Stile made a violent signal to Neysa to go. She seemed dubious, but retreated. The wolf followed her, tail held low. This was evidently part of the Adept's revenge: the separation of friends.

Stile faced the Adept, drawing his sword—but the Adept was gone. Only the new wall remained, extending in either direction into corridors that curved out of sight. Yet the Adept was aware of him; the wall itself was evidence of that. Catching the Adept in the maze of his own castle would surely be an impossible task; the Adept could form a jail cell around Stile at any time.

Why hadn't the magician done just that? Why permit an intruder the limited run of the castle? The Black Adept, logically, should either kill him or throw him out, and seemed to have the power to do both. Only the magic of another Adept could—

No! He had made a vow to do no magic himself. He would muddle through without magic, whatever came.

Stile walked along the barred wall. It carried on through folded passages, bisecting rooms, halls, even stairs. It led him through turrets and down into deep dungeons. There seemed to be no dead ends; the way was continuous. The Adept, it seemed, was showing off his premises, unable to resist allowing another person to appreciate their extent. Ah, vanity, however obliquely it manifested!

Stile continued on into a chamber where a human skeleton lay. It was complete and clean, sprawled on the floor.

He pondered that for some time. Why would such a grisly artifact be tolerated in the castle? It was unlikely to be artificial; the Adept's magic was evidently tied up in lines, proof enough that he was not Stile's alternate self, had any doubt remained. In fact, Stile could have saved himself a certain amount of mischief by recognizing that and turning back when he spied the very first line. Or when he recognized the dragon as a construct of lines. The hints were there to be interpreted, had he only been paying proper attention. Ah, hindsight!

This skeleton was a separate entity, not part of a line, so it had to be authentic. Stile kicked at an arm—

and it broke away from the floor with a crumbling snap. It had lain there so long it had adhered!

The Black Adept had said that the penalty for intrusion was to remain. He had not actually said he would kill the intruder. Perhaps he had obscure scruples, not liking to get blood directly on his lines. But to remain here indefinitely without food or water was to die. That, it seemed, was to be Stile's fate—with the two "animals" permitted to escape to carry some hint or warning to others. They could tell the world they had seen a man imprisoned for annoying the Black Adept. Thoroughly reasonable, effective, and nasty. The Adept really did not care for the favor of others; he just wanted them to stay away. This was no show-off tour Stile was on; it was a fiendish punishment-tour. His demise would be more painful, now that he understood exactly what was coming. Truly, the Adepts were not to be trifled with—or liked.

But Stile knew he had asked for this. He had been warned that Adepts were dangerous, but had charged in anyway. Perhaps he had not really believed in the threat. This fantasy land of Phaze had not seemed wholly real to him; he had not taken its threats seriously enough. Now, as he wandered, and his thirst grew, his perspective shifted. This frame was becoming more real than that of Proton. Somehow the attacks by monsters hadn't impressed him deeply; those encounters had been like individual Games, serious yet also unserious. But thirst, hunger, boredom, fatigue, and loneliness— these compelled belief of a fundamental nature. By the time he died, he would really believe!

He thought of appealing to the Black Adept, of begging for mercy—and knew immediately that that would be useless. The punishment was to die in confinement and hopelessness, without further communication. Without dignity or recognition. Those who violated the Adept's privacy were doomed to share it—completely. The Black Adept was neither noble nor wicked; he merely enforced his strictures effectively. No one bothered an Adept without good reason! Which was what

219

Neysa and Kurrelgyre had tried to tell him. He had simply had to learn the hard way.

And Stile himself—was he really an Adept? Had his Phaze-self been like this, an aloof, cynical magician? No wonder his companions distrusted that! If his possible exercise of his magic talent meant this, meant that he would lose all sense of friendship, honor and decency—then certainly his magic should be banned. It was better to die a feeling man, than to live as an inhuman robot.

No, correct that; he was thinking in a false cliché. Not all robots were unfeeling. Sheen—where was she now? His week, if he counted correctly, was just about over; the immediate threat of death in Proton—on Proton? No, these were two frames of the same world, and he was in one or in the other—this threat had been abated by time. Now it was Phaze he had to escape, and Proton that represented relief.

Stile wandered along the wall until darkness closed. Then he eased himself to the floor carefully, taking care of his knees. He leaned his back against the bars and experimentally flexed one knee. It actually bent fairly far before hurting; had it begun to heal? Unlikely; other parts of the body healed, but knees did not. Their conglomeration of ligament and bone prevented blood from circulating well there. Elbows could heal; they did not have to support constant weight. Knees had to be tough—and so, paradoxically, were more vulnerable than other joints. The anonymous enemy had struck well, lasering his knees, condemning him to a lingering torture similar in its fashion to what the Black Adept was now inflicting. Food for thought there? But when not under pressure, his knees could bend almost all the way. He could assume a squatting posture—when not squatting. A fine comfort that was! As if his knees mattered, when his body was doomed.

After a time he climbed back to his feet—this remained a chore, without flexing his knees under pressure—and walked to an interior chamber to relieve a call of nature. He did not like soiling the castle floor, but really had no choice—and perhaps it served the

Adept right. Then he returned to the barred wall, settled down again, and nodded off to sleep.

He dreamed he was a robot, with no flesh to warm his metal, no true consciousness to enliven his lifelessness. He woke several times in the night, feeling the deepening cold, much more thirsty than he ought to be. Psychological, of course, but still bothersome. He wished he had warm Neysa, in any form, to sleep against. Neysa had given him companionship too—a warmth of the spirit. After his years basically as a loner, he had adapted very quickly to that association; it filled a need. She had changed to human form to please him—but would have pleased him anyway. At least he had done the right thing, sending her away; she could return to her grazing and perhaps the werewolf would keep her company sometimes.

So cold! He hunched within his insubstantial clothing. One little spell could so readily cure this. Give me some heat to warm my feet—no! No magic! It might be crazy, but he would not violate his oath. Only if a firefly flew up and cried "Stile, do magic!" would he indulge—and he didn't want Neysa risking herself that way anyway. He curled into an uncomfortable ball and slept again; it was better than being awake.

By morning Stile's whole mouth was so dry it felt like leather. He must have been sleeping with it open. He worked his rocklike tongue around, moving his jaws, and managed to find a small pocket of saliva to spread about. Now he had to get up and—

And what? The bars remained, and would not disappear until his skeleton joined the other. He had nowhere to go, nothing to do.

Yet he had to do something. He was still cold; exercise was the only answer. His hunger and thirst had abated for the nonce, but his body was stiff. He climbed to his feet and limped to his makeshift privy. Shame to waste fluid, but as long as life remained, the bodily processes continued.

He resumed his trek along the barred wall, moving rapidly enough to generate some heat, slowly enough to conserve energy. Pointless travel, except that it was better than just lying down and dying. Plenty of time for the latter later.

There was no escape. The labyrinth of the castle was interminable, and the barred wall was too. The Black Adept only had one kind of magic, but he was very thorough about that! Theoretically there should be an end to the wall somewhere—but that end was the Adept himself. What use, then, to search for it? No logic, no reasonable discussion could move a man with the power and alienation this one had shown. The Black Adept was in his fashion like a Proton Citizen.

A Citizen! Kurrelgyre had said the people of Phaze were the same as those of Proton—or had been, before the shifting of serfs had become extensive. An Adept could indeed be a Citizen, in his alternate self. In the one frame, the instrument of power was wealth; in the other, magic. In both cases, arrogance reigned supreme.

Stile kept moving. He had won marathons in the Game; he could survive for some time when he put his will to it. If he caught up to the Black Adept, he might incapacitate the man and escape. Or kill him, since the Adept seemed willing to let Stile die. No, he did not want to be a killer himself; monsters were one thing, but the Adept was a man. Stile was willing merely to circle around the Adept, to get outside the barrier and escape.

Did his mental decision not to kill a man differentiate him from the Adept-mode? Could it be taken as evidence that he would not be as thoroughly corrupted by the power of magic as other Adepts had been? He hoped so.

Strange that there was no food in this bleak castle. Didn't the Black Adept eat? Probably his food supplies were well hidden in a convoluted storehouse, which would naturally be outside this barrier. Still, that raised more conjectures. Since this Adept did not conjure things from nothing, the way Stile's magic had done, he must have to obtain natural food elsewhere. Did the Black Adept have to trade with peasants for supplies of grain, eggs, cabbages? He could not, then, live in absolute seclusion. His ready use of language suggested the

222

same. He had contact with others; he just didn't like it. Would any of those others be coming here to the castle? Would they help Stile? No, that seemed unlikely; the Adept could have supplies for a year at a time.

Stile moved slowly, conserving his strength, balancing his generated warmth against his thirst and hunger. He gave up following the interminable wall, and cut across the center of the castle as well as he could. But all the interior passages were dead ends; the configuration differed here. He wished he had some quick way to analyze the lines, but the castle was too complex; it would take him far longer than he had left to grasp its layout and locate the Adept. He also wished he had a good cutting tool to sever a line; since all of this was a single line, he could cut the Adept off from his castle anywhere. From his past. Would everything unravel, in the manner of the dragon? But there was nothing. His dagger could not damage the stonelike hardness of the material. The outer walls had had some give, but here they had none. Only a diamond drill or saw could do the job, or magic—

No!

All day Stile fought with himself, the thought of magic becoming more attractive as his physical condition deteriorated. But he refused to yield. It didn't matter that no one would know if he conjured a cupful of water to drink; an oath was an oath. He would expire with his integrity intact; that was one thing the Black Adept could not deprive him of.

At last, night seeped into the castle again. Stile sank down to sleep but could not. He did not want to yield himself up so quietly to extinction!

He found the harmonica in his hand, unbidden. He had avoided making music, because of its magical connotation. Magic could occur in the ambience of music, even when he did not voice it. His saddle had appeared, obviously conjured by his unconscious wish while he made music. But wouldn't it be all right to play, now, so long as he willed no magic? Music reminded him of Tune, so long ago, and it was fitting to think of her again as he concluded his own tenure.

He played. The music wafted out, permeating the corridors and windows and convolutions of the castle, striking harmonics in the walls. He was making the sound, but he was listening too, and it was absolutely beautiful. He was mastering the harmonica, playing it with his heart, evoking a feeling of melody he had seldom before achieved. Perhaps it was his swan song, his final gesture. Nevertheless it was a satisfying way to go.

At last, tiring even of this, he put the instrument away and dropped into sleep. This time it was more peaceful, as if his fast had freed him of material concerns.

He was awakened by a low growl. Stile's eyes cracked open, but his body did not move. He knew where his sword was; he needed to locate the animal. And to decide whether it was worth trying to fight. Why trade a quick death for a slow one?

Then, in the dark, a voice: "Stile."

"Kurrelgyre!" he said. Stile put his face to the bars, to get closer. "This isn't safe for thee!"

"Neysa went to the Oracle. It said 'Curtain.' Neysa did not understand what that meant, but I do. I sniffed around the castle. One corner of it intersects the curtain. Follow me."

The curtain! Of course! Except— "I can't do it; I swore no magic. It takes a spell to pass through."

"Thou art true to thine oath. Thou couldst have escaped ere now, hadst thou been otherwise. But fear not; I will put thee through."

Relieved, Stile followed the werewolf, pacing him on the other side of the wall. So Neysa had donated her single question the Oracle permitted to his cause! He would not have asked her to do that, yet now accepted the gesture gratefully.

It seemed only moments before Kurrelgyre brought him to the curtain. One small section of his prison intersected it. Apparently the Black Adept was not aware of it. That suggested the Adept was alive in both frames, unable to perceive or cross the curtain.

"We shall wait for thee at the Oracle's palace," Kurrelgyre said as Stile approached the glimmer. "Be mindful of the trust the mare places in thee, setting thee free of this frame."

"I don't know how long it will take me to—"

But the werewolf was already casting the spell. Stile passed through.

CHAPTER 13

Rungs

Stile landed outside a dome. He gasped—for the air was barely breathable. He might survive thirty minutes without a mask, but would not enjoy it. The limited oxygen of Proton's atmosphere was further reduced to favor the needs of the dome, and the pollution of sundry industrial processes was dumped out here. He realized—was it for the first time?—that the barren surface of Proton was the result of man's activities. Had the machine age not come here, the atmosphere would have remained like that of Phaze. Man's civilization had made a heaven-planet into hell.

Fortunately the dome was within five minutes foot travel. He could see it clearly, for its illumination flowed through the force field, lighting the barren plain.

Stile, his fatigue somewhat abated by his rest and the shock of the cold night, walked briskly toward the dome, drawing his clothing tightly about him. So long as he kept his respiration down, the air was not too hard on his lungs. Running would be a disaster, though. His clothing helped shield him from—

Clothing! He could not wear that here! He was a serf.

Yet without it he would soon be in trouble from the cold. He would have to wear it as long as possible, then dispose of it just before entering the dome. Maybe he could recover it when he returned to Phaze.

But he could not return where he had left, for that would put him right back in the prison of the Black Adept. He needed his clothing for the other frame, but not in this locale. He would have to risk carrying it with him.

Stile reached the dome. It was a small one, evidently

the private estate of a Citizen. It was hardly safe for a serf to intrude uninvited on such a place, but he really had no choice. These few minutes had made him uncomfortable; the less exposure to outside conditions, the better. He removed his clothing, bundled it up with the shoes inside, and stepped through the dome wall.

Instantly he was in light and warmth. This was a tropical garden of the kind popular with Citizens, whose tastes seemed to run opposite to the external wasteland their policies were making on the planet. Exotic palms were at every available spot, with a cocoa-chip mulch beneath. No one was present—which was why Stile had entered here. If he were lucky, he might get through undiscovered.

He was not. An alert gardener challenged him before he had taken twenty steps. "Halt, intruder! You're not of this estate."

"I—came from outside. I—got lost." Stile doubted he could afford to tell the truth, and he would not lie. "I had to come in; I would have died."

"You look half dead," the serf agreed.

Another serf hurried up. "I'm the garden foreman. Who are you? What were you doing outside without equipment? What are you carrying?"

That was a foreman, all right! "I am Stile, unemployed, formerly a jockey. I thought my life was threatened, so I tried to hide. But—" He shrugged. "It's a different world out there."

"It sure as hell is. Were you trying to suicide?"

"No. But I nearly died anyway. I have had no food or water for two days."

The foreman ignored the hint. "I asked you what you are carrying."

"This bundle—it is medieval Earth costume. I thought it would help me, in the other world." He was skirting a fuzzy line, ethically, and didn't like it. But again: wouldn't the truth convey less of the situation to this man than this half-truth did? What serf would believe a story about a magic world?

The foreman took the bundle and spread it out on the ground. "A harmonica?"

227

Stile spread his hands silently. He was now in a position where anything he said would seem a lie, including the truth. Suddenly Phaze seemed like a figment of his imagination, the kind of hallucination a man exposed to oxygen deprivation and gaseous pollutants might have. Especially if he had also suffered from hunger, thirst, and cold. In the past, men had undertaken similar deprivations as rites of passage, provoking similar visions. What had happened to him, really?

"I'll have to notify the Citizen," the foreman said.

Stile's hopes sank; this surely meant trouble. Had the man simply told him to clear out to serf quarters—

"Sir," the foreman said.

"What is it, gardener?" the Citizen's voice responded. It sounded familiar.

"Sir, a stranger has intruded from outside, carrying medieval Earth costume, including sword, knife, and a musical instrument."

"Bring him to the viewer." The voice gave Stile a chill. Where had he heard it before?

The foreman conducted Stile to a booth with a holo pickup. Stile stepped inside, knowing his whole body was being reproduced in image in the Citizen's quarters. He was dirty and abraded as well as suffering from hunger and thirst; he must look awful.

"Name?" the Citizen snapped.

"Stile, sir."

There was a pause. The Citizen would be checking the name in the computerized serf-listing. "The jockey and Gamesman?"

"Yes, sir."

"Play that instrument."

The gardening foreman quickly located the harmonica and jabbed it at Stile. Stile took it and put it to his mouth. This was his proof of identity; an impostor could probably not match his skill. He played a few bars, and as it had a few hours before, the emerging beauty of the music transformed his outlook. He began to get into the feel of it—

"Very well, Stile," the Citizen said, having no interest in the art of it. "Your present employer vouches for you. Wait here until his representative picks you up."

His present employer? What could this mean? Stile did not respond, since no query had been addressed to him. He rejoined the foreman, who solemnly handed back the rest of his bundle.

Suddenly Stile recognized the voice he had heard. The Black Adept! This was the Proton-self of that evil magician, having no knowledge of the other frame, but very much like his other self. It made sense—this dome was very near the site of the Black Castle. Stile's conjecture about Adepts and Citizens had been confirmed. Had this citizen any reason to suspect him—

Stile breathed a silent sigh of relief. There was no reason for such suspicion, and Citizens hardly cared about stray serfs. Since another Citizen was taking Stile off his hands, that ended the matter. Stile would have to make his explanations to his own employer, instead of wasting the time of this one. And if one of the Black Adept Citizen's serfs ever got lost, other Citizens would return the favor similarly. Serfs were hardly worth quarreling over.

A woman arrived, very well formed. As her face turned to him—"Sheen! How glad I am to see thee!" Oops—wrong language.

She frowned. "Come on, Stile. You had no business wandering outside. Suppose you had damaged the costume? It will go hard with you if you stray again." She turned to the foreman. "Thank you. He was supposed to bring the costume to our employer's isolation dome, and must have lost the way. He's a klutz at times."

"He tried to tell me he was unemployed," the foreman said.

She smiled. "He used to be a jockey. He must have taken one fall too many." She made a little circle about one ear with one finger. "These things happen. We apologize for the inconvenience to you."

"It brightens the night shift," the foreman said, admiring her body. Inconvenience became more tolerable when it brought a figure like this to the scene.

229

She took Stile firmly by the elbow and guided him along. "This time we'll get you where you belong," she said with an oblique smile.

He squeezed her hand. She had taken his prior advice to heart, and become so human it was almost annoying. But she had certainly bailed him out.

When they were safely in the capsule, flying through the tube toward a larger dome, Sheen explained: "I knew you'd return, Stile, somehow. I really am programmed for intuition. So I had my friends make up a robot in your likeness, and we got you a new employer. The moment the query on you came through the computer—"

"I see." Her friends were the self-willed machines, who could tap into the communication network. In fact, some of them probably *were* the communication network. What an asset they were at times!

From the general dome they took a transport rocket to Stile's original home dome. In a matter of minutes, the travel of several days by unicorn was reversed. That reminded him of another aspect. What should he say to Sheen about Neysa?

They returned to Stile's old apartment. Sheen had kept it in good order—or the robot who bore his name had done so. It seemed Sheen had put the robot away as soon as news of Stile's appearance reached her. Sheen had been most industrious and efficient on his behalf.

What had it been like, here, with two robots? Had they eaten, slept, made love? Stile found himself feeling jealous and had to laugh at himself. Obviously the robot-Stile was not self-willed. It would be a true machine, programmed by Sheen.

"We must talk," Sheen said. "But I think first we must feed you and rest you. That curtain-frame has not treated you kindly. You are bronzed and scratched and gaunt around the edges."

Stile's thirst abruptly returned. He almost snatched at the cup of nutro-beverage she brought, and gulped it down. "Yes. Drink and food and rest, in that order," he said. "And talk, of course."

She glanced obliquely at him. "Nothing else?"

Ah, sex appeal! But he was restrained. "I think we should talk, then consider the else. You may not be pleased."

"You may not be entirely pleased with what I have done, either," she said.

He raised an eyebrow. "With my double?"

She laughed. "Stile, it's impossible! He's a robot!"

"Good thing there are none of that ilk here," he agreed.

"You know what I mean. It's just not the same."

"You speak from experience?"

"No. He's not programmed for love."

"I had come to that conclusion. Otherwise you would not have been so glad to have me back."

After he had eaten and emerged from the dry-cleaning unit, they lay down together. In what way, he asked himself, was this creature inferior to Tune? Sheen looked and felt as nice, and she had displayed astonishing initiative. It seemed no one knew he had been absent a week. Any attempt to kill his robot double had of course been futile.

"Your friends have rendered this apartment private?" he inquired, remembering how it had almost become his prison. But for the device of the self-willed machines, who had made it seem he was here when he wasn't—

"Completely." She put her arms about him, hugging him briefly, but went no further. "Shall I tell you?"

What would give a logical robot or an illogical woman pause? "You had better."

"Your new employer doesn't care at all about horse racing. He cares about the Game. Each year he has sponsored a leading contender in the Tourney, but has never had a win. This year—"

"Oh, no! I'm expected to compete—"

"This year," she agreed. "And it has to be you. The robot can not do it in your stead. Even were it legal, he cannot match your ability. I have bought you security, Stile—but at the expense of your tenure."

"You realize that's likely to finish your mission too?

One way or the other, I won't need protection after I enter the Tourney."

"Had there been any other way—" She sighed. "Stile, you were fired for cause. No blacklist was entered against you, because your reluctance to race again was understandable, but even so, very few Citizens were interested in you. My friends had to do a research-sifting to locate—"

"The one Citizen who would hire me," Stile finished. "I don't fault you for that; you did the only thing you could do, and did it excellently."

"But your tenure—"

"I now have another option." But he was not eager to get into the matter of Phaze and his decision to remain there, yet.

"Your anonymous enemy remains. Not the Citizen who tried to make a cyborg of you; he opted out when he realized the week had passed. The original one, who lasered your knees. The one who, perhaps, sent me. There were several attempts made on the robot. My friends are closing the net, trying to locate that enemy, but he is extraordinarily cunning and elusive. I can not protect you from him long. So—"

"Infernally logical," he agreed. "Better the Game than death. Better abbreviated tenure than none at all. But I had thought I would be all right if I made it clear I would not race again."

"That seems to have been an unwarranted assumption. That person wants you dead—but not by obvious means. So a surgical error, or a random accident—"

"So I might as well have had my knees fixed—if I could trust the surgery." His attention returned to the Game. "The Tourney is inviolate; no entrant can be harassed in any way, even by a Citizen. That's to keep it honest. So the Tourney is the one place my life is safe, for the little time the Tourney lasts. But this catches me ill prepared; I had planned to enter in two years."

"I know. I did what I could, and may have forced premature exile on you. If you want to punish me—"

"Yes, I believe I do. I'll tell you what I have been doing. Beyond the curtain is a world of magic. I tamed a unicorn mare; she turned into a lovely little woman, and—"

"And I'm supposed to be jealous of this fairy tale?"

"No fairy tale. I said she was female, not male. I did with her what any man—"

"I am jealous!" She half-climbed over him and kissed him fiercely. "Could she match that?"

"Easily. She has very mobile lips."

"Oh? Then could she match this?" She did something more intimate.

Stile found himself getting breathless despite his fatigue. "Yes. Her breasts are not as large as yours, but are well—"

"Well, how about *this*?"

The demonstration took some time. At length, quite pleasantly worn out, Stile lay back and murmured, "That too."

"You certainly punished me." But Sheen did not seem much chastened.

"And after that, we went to the Oracle, who told me to know myself," Stile continued. "Realizing I must be an Adept who had been slain or otherwise abolished, I investigated—and got trapped in the castle of the Black Adept. The werewolf rescued me by sending me back through the curtain, and here I am." He yawned. "Now may I sleep?"

"You realize that no living person would believe a story like that?"

"Yes."

"And you're going back."

"Yes. I can not stay long in the frame of Proton, in any event. This gives me an alternative."

"Unless you win the Tourney. Then you can stay for life."

"Easier said than done, girl. In two years I would have been at my Game-proficiency peak; at the moment my chances are less than ideal."

"As a Citizen, you could find out the identity of your enemy."

"There is that." He smiled. "Now, Sheen—what was it you had in mind to do when we finished our talk?"

She hit him with a pillow from the couch. "We just did it! Didn't you notice?"

"Did what?"

She hauled him in to her, kissing him and flinging a leg over his thighs.

He squeezed her, bringing her head close against his, smelling her soft hair. "It's great to be back," he said seriously. "You have done good work, Sheen. But the world of Phaze—it's such a lovely place, even discounting the magic. I feel—over there I feel more nearly fulfilled. As if my human potential is at last awakening. I have to return. Do you understand?"

"Maybe you feel as I would feel, if I passed through myself and found myself alive." She closed her eyes, imagining. "Yes. You have to go back. But will you visit here?"

"Often. There are things for me in this world too."

"Of which I am one?"

"Of which you are the main one."

"That is all I have a right to ask."

Again Stile felt a helpless guilt. Sheen loved him; he could not truly love her. It hardly mattered that a specialist could make one tiny change in her programming that would instantly abolish or reverse her feeling for him; her present program was real. Modern surgery could transplant his brain into another body, but his present body was real; he did not like fundamental changes. If he left Proton, he was leaving her, again, in the way Tune had left him. Yet Sheen herself had shortened his tenure. She was correct; she could not ask more of him.

The night was only half over, long as it had seemed. He drew her over him like a blanket and slept.

In the morning he started his move to enter the Tourney. He went to the Game-annex, located the 35M ladder, and touched the button by the rung above his own. He was challenging Nine.

234

In a moment the holder of Rung Nine responded to the summons. He was, of course, a thirty-five-year-old male. For the purpose of the Game, age was strictly by chronology. There was constant disruption in the ladders, as birthdays shifted people from one to another. No one was given a place in the top twenty free; the Number One rung-holder in one age had to start at Number Twenty-One on the next age's ladder. But at the qualifying date for each year's Tourney the ladders were fixed; there was no disqualification by birthdays within the Tourney itself.

Apart from age and sex, the resemblance of the holder of Rung Nine to Stile was distant. He was tall and thin, like a stooped scholar. The appearance fit the reality; his name was Tome, and he was a researcher for a studious Citizen. Tome was very much a creature of intellect; he invariably selected the MENTAL column when he had the numbered facet of the Grid, and MACHINE when he had the lettered facet.

Because Tome could beat most people in games of the mind, and hold even when assisted by machine—especially when the machine was a computer—he was successful enough to hold his Rung. Because he was limited, he was not a potential champion. Tome was known as a 2C man—the definition of his specialties. Second vertical, third horizontal. If a person were weak in these, he would have trouble passing Tome.

Stile was generally strong in 2C. He could handle Tome, and the other man knew it. Stile simply had not wanted the Rung, before.

They went to a booth and played the Grid. Stile had the numeric facet; good. He regarded that as more fundamental. He would not choose MENTAL, of course; this was not a fun challenge where he wanted a good Game, but a serious challenge where he needed to win with least risk. He did not care for the 50-50 chance that CHANCE offered. Tome was pretty fair on machine arts, such as the theremin, so that was not a good risk. So it had to be Stile's strong column, PHYSICAL.

Tome chose MACHINE, of course. Immediately the subgrid showed:

235

	1. MOTION	2. ACTION	3. OBSERVATION
A. LAND			
B. WATER			
C. AIR			

Nine types of machine-assisted competitive sports, ranging from cycle racing in 1A to stellar location in 3C. Stile had the letter facet of this grid, unfortunately; he could not select the machine-racing column, and knew that Tome would not. Tome would go for observation—unless he figured Stile for water. That would put them in 3B, which amounted to sonar location of sunken ships. Tome was not really sharp at that. But he was a fair hand at water-hydrant dueling, so might go for ACTION. Therefore Stile went for AIR instead.

He won. It came up 2C: dueling by guns, lasers, and similar powered distance weapons. Tome was good at this, but Stile was better, and both knew it.

DRAW? Tome's query came on the panel. It was legitimate to make such an offer at any stage in the selection, and it was often done as part of the psychological combat. In this case it was an admission of weakness.

Stile hit the DECLINE button, and followed with CONCEDE?

Tome hesitated. Seconds passed. If he did not negate within fifteen, the concession would stand. Concession was always a demand, never an offer, at this stage: another rule to prevent irresponsible players from tying up the grids when they had no intention of playing a Game. But at last the DECLINE button lit.

Now the lists of individual variants appeared on the screen. Tome, the one challenged, had the first choice. He placed antique pistols in the center square of the nine-square subgrid that formed. Stile followed with a laser rifle in a corner. These were not real weapons; they would simply mark the target with a washable spot of red dye on the section hit. Very seldom was a live-ammo duel permitted, and never in connection with the Tourney.

As it happened, Stile and Tome shared a liking for antique weapons and forms, and when the grid was completed and played it came up 2B, the original pistols. The two of them walked to the dueling range nearby, while Sheen went to the spectator gallery. The holographic recording apparatus was operating, of course; every formal match was filmed, in case there should be any challenge to the result. Scholars liked to review the games of Tourney winners, right back to the original move up the rungs of the ladder, tracing with the wisdom of retrospect the elements that made those particular victories inevitable. This also meant, incidentally, that no agent in the audience could laser him in the knees or elsewhere; that shot would be recorded and the assassin apprehended immediately. This was no horse race!

They had to wait a few minutes for the use of the range. Dueling was popular, and there were a number of specialists who dueled every day. Had Stile been playing the Game with one of them, he would have avoided this option at any cost. That, of course, was the strategy of the Game; the key to victory lay in the grids. A good gridder could get by with very few Game specialties, always directing the selection to one of these. Just as Tome had to master only seven of the basic sixteen choices of the primary grid, and a proportionate number of each subgrid. An opponent could only force a selection within those seven. If an opponent's skills overlapped those of Tome, he could be virtually assured of landing one of these, to Tome's disadvantage. For a player who was serious, it was best to be strong in all boxes. That kept the options open, preventing him from getting trapped. Stile himself had strengths in all boxes; that was why he was the superior player here.

"You can't be going for the Tourney," Tome remarked. "You have two more seasons free. When the top five enter this year, we'll both be jumped into qualification for next year's Tourney. I figured you'd be sliding down about now. What's your move?"

Stile smiled. "See that girl in the stands? The pretty one? She put me up to it."

"Oh, a Game-digger!" Tome squinted at Sheen. "For one like that, *I'd* make a move, certainly! She much on the mental side?"

"Limited as a robot," Stile said.

"Going to move up to Rung Six, so you'll be Number One after the cut? That's risky. If someone gets sick at the last moment before qualification, you'll be shunted into the Tourney." Tome obviously had no doubts, in his mind, about the outcome of this match, and hardly cared; he had no intention of skirting the Tourney too closely.

"Going to Rung Five," Stile said. "I prefer that this not be bruited about."

Tome's head snapped around in surprise. "*This* year?"

"Not entirely my choice. But I've had some problems in my employment."

"So I have heard. Knee injury, wasn't it? I'm surprised you didn't have immediate surgery."

"I got scared of it."

Tome laughed. "You, scared! But I must admit you do look somewhat ravaged. Must have been a hard decision."

"It was," Stile agreed, though he knew that what showed on his body was the ravage of his two-day confinement in the Black Castle without food and water, rather than his mental state. Sheen had done what she could for him, but he had not yet properly recovered.

"Well, I wish you well," Tome finished sincerely.

The range cleared, and they entered. On a table at the entrance lay the set of antique pistols, with elaborate pearl handles and glistening black steel. A pistol specialist could have called out the exact vintage and make— probably eighteenth-century European—but Stile was concerned only with their heft and accuracy. Though they were replicas that fired no balls, they bucked and smoked just like the real ones.

Stile had to be sure to win this match; he could not

238

rechallenge until the rungs had shifted, and this close to the Tourney there was unlikely to be much shifting. Players were either hanging on to their rungs to be sure that they qualified, or trying to stay below qualification range. Stile's late decision to enter the Tourney was unusual, and would make ripples. He was going to have to bump someone who was depending on the Tourney as his last chance for extended tenure.

The Citizens had so arranged it that there were always more serfs interested in entering the Tourney than there were available slots—especially in Stile's own age range, where many mature people were ending their tenures. There were tenures expiring in all age ranges, for serfs could enlist at any age, but the older ones generally lacked the drive and stamina for real expertise in the Game, and the younger ones lacked experience and judgment. The ladders of the Thirties, male and female, were the prime ones.

The weapons were good, of course, and as similar to each other as modern technology could make them. Each party took one, went to the centermark of the range, stood back to back, and began the paceoff at the sound of the timing bell. Ten paces, turn and fire—each pace measured by the metronome. The man who turned and/or fired too soon would be disqualified; the tenth beat had to sound.

Some people who were excellent shots in practice were bad ones in such duels. They had to have time to get set, to orient on the target—and here there was neither time nor any fixed target. Some lost their nerve when confronting an actual opponent who was firing back. Special skills and nerve were required for this sort of match. Both Stile and Tome possessed these qualities.

At the tenth beat Stile leaped, turning in air to face his opponent. Tome merely spun in place, withholding his shot until he fathomed Stile's motion. He knew Stile seldom fired first; Stile preferred to present a difficult target, encouraging the other to waste his only shot. Then Stile could nail him at leisure. Tome was too smart for that.

Stile landed, plunged on into a roll, flipped to his feet and jumped again. Had Tome figured him for a straight bounce, his shot would have missed; but Tome was still being careful. His pistol was following Stile's progress, waiting for the moment of correct orientation.

That moment never came. In midair Stile fired. A red splash appeared in the center of Tome's chest, marking the heart. Contrary to popular fancy, the human heart was centered in the chest, not set in the left side.

Tome spread his hands. He had waited too long, and never gotten off his shot. He was officially dead.

Tome washed off the red stain while Stile registered the win with the Game computer outlet. They shook hands and returned to the Game-annex. Their names had already exchanged rungs. Stile punched Rung Eight, his next challenge. He wanted to capture as many rungs as he could before the alarm spread—and before news of his present weakened condition also got about. If his opponents thought it through, they would force him into the more grueling physical Games, where he would be weakest.

The challengee appeared. He was a squat, athletic man named Beef. "Tome, you challenging me?" he demanded incredulously.

"Not I," Tome said, gesturing to the ladder.

Beef looked. "Stile! What move are you making?"

"A challenge move," Stile said.

Beef shrugged. "I can't decline."

They went to a booth and played the grid. Beef was unpredictable; often he picked unlikely columns, just for the hell of it. Stile selected B. TOOL, hoping the other would not pick 3. CHANCE.

His hope was vain. Beef was more curious about Stile's motive than about the outcome of the Game, and they intersected at 3B. The home of roulette, dice, —all manner of gambling devices. Precious little skill. Stile could take Beef in most games of skill—but chance made it even.

Yet already he was maneuvering to upgrade his chances, playing the subgrid, finessing the choices in the way he had. Suddenly it came up CARDS. Cards were technically instruments of chance—but there were quite a number of games, like bridge and poker, where skill of one sort or another counted. All he had to do was pack the final grid with this type.

Beef, however, was alert to this, and selected games like blackjack and high-card-draw. He wanted to make Stile sweat, and was succeeding. It was very bad to have an opponent who cared less about the outcome than Stile did; there was little strategic leverage. Beef made his placements on the grid so that Stile could not establish a full column of his own choices. Three of one player's preferences in a row meant that player could select that row and have a commanding advantage. The chances of establishing a game utilizing reasonable skill remained 50-50, and Stile was hurting. He had to have better odds!

But Stile knew a skill variant of a chance game that Beef evidently did not. He slipped it in, played for it, and got it: War, Strategy.

The ordinary card game of War consisted of dealing the pack randomly into two piles, with each player turning up cards on one-to-one matches. The higher card captured the lower, and both went into the winner's victory pile. When the first piles were through, the piles of winnings would be shuffled and played in the same fashion, until finally one player had won the entire deck. It was pure chance, and could take many hours to finish. The strategy variant, however, permitted each player to hold his cards in his hand, selecting each card to play. When both were laid face down on the table, they would be turned over, and the higher card won. This play was not truly random; each player could keep track of his assets and those of his opponent, and play it accordingly. He could psych the other player out, tricking him into wasting a high card on a low one, or into losing a trick he should normally have won by playing a card too low. Games were normally much shorter than those of the pure-chance variation, with the superior strategist winning. The element of pure chance could not be reintroduced; a strategist could beat a hand played by chance. Thus Stile had his opportunity to exert his skill, judging his opponent's intent and playing no higher than needed to win.

They played, and soon Stile's expertise told. He took queens with kings, while yielding deuces to aces. Steadily his hands grew, providing him with more options, while those of his opponent shrank. Luck? The luck had been in the grid.

In due course Stile was able to play seven aces and kings in succession, wiping out Beef's queen-high remaining hand of seven with no luck allowed at all. He had won, and Rung Eight was his.

Beef shook his head ruefully. "I will remember that variant," he said. He didn't mind losing, but he hated to be outsmarted so neatly.

They returned to the Game-annex. But Stile's two wins had attracted notice. A knot of serfs stood before the 35M ladder. "Hey, Stile," a woman called. "Are you making your move this year?"

He should have known privacy would be impossible. He was too well known in these circles, and what he was doing was too remarkable. "Yes," he said shortly, and made his way to the ladder. He punched the challenge for Rung Seven.

The holder of that Rung was already present. He was Snack, an average-heighted man who specialized in board games and light physical exercises. He was more formidable than the two Stile had just taken, but still not really in Stile's class.

"I will respond to your challenge in one day," Snack said, and left.

This was exactly the sort of thing Stile had feared. A rung-holder had to meet a challenge from the rung below, but could delay it one day. Stile had to rise rung by rung; he could not challenge out of order. He had no choice but to wait—and that would interfere with his return to Phaze.

Sheen took his arm. "There'll be an audience tomorrow," she said. "When a player of your caliber makes his move for a tenure-abridging Tourney this close to the deadline, that's news."

"I wanted to qualify quickly, so I could return to

242

Phaze before the Tourney," Stile said. "Neysa is waiting and worrying."

Even as he said it, he knew he should not have. Somehow the words got out before his mental intercept signal cut them off. "Cancel that," he said belatedly.

She looked straight ahead. "Why? I'm only a machine."

Here we go again. "I meant I promised to return to meet her at the palace of the Oracle. It was her question to the Oracle that freed me. The only one she can ask in her lifetime—she used it up just to help me. I must return."

"Of course."

"I made a commitment!" he said.

She relented. "She did send you back to me; I should return the favor. Will you promise to return, to meet me again?"

"And to qualify for the Tourney. Yes. Because you have also sacrificed yourself for me."

"Then we shall send you on your way right now."

"But I have to compete for Rung Seven in one day!"

"So you will have to work fast, over there." She drew him into a privacy compartment. "I'll send you across to her—right after I have had what I want from you." And she kissed him most thoroughly, proceeding from there.

She was a robot, he reminded himself—but she was getting more like a living woman than any he had known since Tune. And—he was not unwilling, and she did turn him on. It would be so easy to forget her nature . . . but then he would be entering another kind of fantasy world, and not a healthy one.

Yet how could he continue with a robot in one frame and a unicorn in the other? Even if he entered the Tourney and won, against all the odds, and located his other self in Phaze and assumed his prerogatives there—impossible dreams, probably—how would he alleviate the developing conflict between females?

Sheen finished with him, cleaned him up, brushed his hair, and took him to the dome geographically nearest the Oracular palace in the other frame, according to his understanding of the geography. They scouted for the curtain. They were also wary of the anonymous killer, but apparently the break in Stile's routine had lost that enemy for the nonce. It was hard to keep track of a fast-moving serf on Proton!

The curtain did not intersect this dome, but they located it nearby. They went outside, into the polluted rarefaction of the atmosphere, and Stile donned his Phaze clothing, which Sheen had brought. She never overlooked details like that, thanks to her computer mind. He would not have dared to put on any clothing at all in the sight of any Proton serfs, but outside was the most private of places on Proton.

There was a narrowing plain, the ground barren. To the northwest a wrinkle of mountains projected, as grim as the plain. Only the shining dome brightened the bleak landscape. There were not even any clouds in the sky; just ominous drifts of ill-smelling smog.

"If ever you find a way for a robot to cross . . ." Sheen said wistfully. "I think that land must be better than this one."

"My clothing crosses," Stile said. "Since you can have no living counterpart in Phaze, it should be possible—"

"No. I tried it, during your absence. I can not cross."

She had tried it. How sad that was, for her! Yet what could he do?

"Here—within a day," he gasped, beginning to suffer in the thin air, and Sheen nodded. The air did not bother her; she breathed only for appearances. "You understand—there is beauty in Phaze, but danger too. I may not—"

"You will make it," she said firmly, kissing him once more. "Or else."

"Uh, yes." Stile made what he trusted was the proper effort of will, and stepped through the curtain.

CHAPTER 14

Yellow

It was afternoon on Phaze, and the air was wonderful. The sky was a deep and compelling blue, punctuated by several puffball clouds. The mountains to the northwest were lovely. Stile paused to look at the pretty little yellow flowers at his feet, and to inhale the springlike freshness of it all.

How did this frame come to have such a pleasant natural environment, while Proton was so bleak? He was no longer certain that industrial pollution and withdrawal of oxygen could account for it all. What about water vapor? Obviously there was plenty of it here, and little in the Proton atmosphere. This was a mystery he must one day fathom.

But at the moment he had more urgent business. Stile made a mental note of the location of the curtain; sometime he would have to trace its length, finding better places to cross. But this was also a matter for later attention.

The landscape was indeed the same. A narrowing plain, a nearby mountain range, a bright sun. Remove the cute clouds, and the verdant vegetation carpeting the ground, and the copses of trees, and this was identical to Proton. It was as if these were twin paintings, BEFORE and AFTER the artist had applied the color. Phaze was the world as it should be after God had made the final touches: primitive, natural, delightful, unspoiled. Garden of Eden.

True to his memory, the Oracle's palace was in sight. Stile set out for it at a run. But before he had covered half the distance, Neysa came trotting out to meet him. She held her head high, as they came together, so there was no possibility of striking him with her bright horn.

Stile flung his arms around her neck and hugged her, burying his face in her glossy mane, feeling her equine warmth and firmness and strength. He did not need to thank her verbally for her sacrifice on his behalf; he knew she understood. He discovered her hair was wet, and realized that his own tears of reunion were the culprit.

Then he leaped to her back, still needing no words, and they galloped bareback in five-beat to the palace where Kurrelgyre waited in man-form.

Stile had spent his life on Proton, and only a week here in Phaze, but already Phaze seemed more like home. He had been gone only a night and day, but it seemed longer. Perhaps it was because he felt more like a person, here. Actually, the only other true human beings he had encountered in Phaze were the man at the curtain who had given him the demon-amulet, and the Black Adept; still—

Kurrelgyre shook hands gravely. "I am relieved to know thy escape was successful," the werewolf said. "I reassured the mare, but feared privately thou mightst land between domes."

"I did. But close enough to reach the nearest dome before I suffocated." Stile took a deep breath, still reveling in it.

"I should have crossed with thee, to make sure; but Neysa was waiting outside, and I never thought of—"

"I understand exactly how it is. I never thought of it either. I could have walked a quarter-mile along the curtain and willed myself back through to you, outside the Black Castle. That never occurred to me until this moment."

Kurrelgyre smiled. "We live; we learn. No confinement near the curtain shall again restrain us." He squinted at Stile. "Thou lookest peaked; have a sniff of this." He brought out a sprig with a few leaves and a dull yellow flower, dried.

Stile sniffed. Immediately he felt invigorated. Strength coursed through his body. "What is that stuff?"

"Wolfsbane."

246

"Wolfsbane? Something that curses wolves? How canst thou carry—"

"I am not in my lupine form. I would not sniff it then."

"Oh." Stile couldn't really make much sense of this, but could not argue with his sudden sense of well-being. "Something else," he said. "Didst thou not tell me that most of the people were parallel, existing in both frames? There are about five thousand Proton Citizens, and ten times as many serfs, and countless robots, androids, cyborgs and animals—but I have not seen many people here on Phaze, and not many animals."

"There are at least as many people here as on Proton, plus the societies of werewolves, unicorns, vampires, demons and assorted monsters. But two things to note: first, we are not confined to domes. We have the entire planet to roam—many millions of square miles. So—"

"Miles?" Stile asked, trying to make a fast conversion in his head and failing.

"We use what thou wouldst call the archaic measurements. One square mile would be about two and a half square kilometers, so—"

"Oh, yes, I know. I just realized—archaic measurements—would that by any chance affect magic? I tried to do a spell using the metric scale, and it flubbed. Before I swore off magic."

"That might be. Each spell must be correctly couched, and can only be employed once. That is why even Adepts perform sparingly. They hoard their spells for future need, as Citizens hoard wealth in Proton. May I now continue my original discourse?"

"Oh, of course," Stile said, embarrassed, and Neysa made a musical snort of mirth. Stile squeezed her sides with his legs, a concealed hug. He tended to forget that she understood every word he spoke.

"So there are very few people for the habitable area, and many large regions are as yet uninhabited by men. Thou needst not be surprised at seeing none. The second reason is that many of the people here are not

247

precisely the form of their Proton selves. They are vampires, elves, dwarves—" He broke off.

Stile wished he hadn't. It had almost seemed his size was irrelevant in his frame. Foolish wish! "I never judged values in terms of size," Stile said. "A dwarf is still a discrete individual, surely."

"Of course," Kurrelygyre agreed. It was his turn to be embarrassed.

They were now in the Oracle's palace. "I have less than a day before I have to go back to Proton," Stile said.

Neysa stiffened. "Go back?" Kurrelgyre demanded. "I understood thou hadst no commitment there. It was only to escape the prison of the Black Demesnes that thou—"

"I have a woman there," Stile said. "She covered for me during mine absence. I have agreed to enter this year's Tourney, that she be not shamed. Thus it is likely that my tenure on Proton will be brief."

"The Tourney! Thou presumest thou canst win?"

"Doubtful," Stile said seriously. "I had planned to enter in two years, when some top players would be gone and my strength would be at its peak—and even then the odds would have been against me. It is hard to win ten or twelve consecutive Games against top competition, and luck can turn either way. I would rate my chances at perhaps one in ten, for I could lose to a poorer player with one bad break."

Neysa tooted questioningly. "Well, one chance in twelve, perhaps," Stile amended. "I did not mean to brag."

"The mare means to inquire what thou meanest to do if thou shouldst win the Tourney," the werewolf said. "Since thou wouldst then be a Citizen, with permanent tenure—no need ever to depart Proton."

Stile wondered in passing how the werewolf had come to know the unicorn well enough to translate her notes, in only one day. Maybe shape-changing creatures had natural avenues of comprehension. "A Citizen has virtually complete freedom and power. I would be under no onus to choose between frames. But I like

Phaze; I think I would spend much of my time here anyway. Much depends on my situation here; if I should turn out to be a vicious person like the Black Adept, I think I'd prefer to vacate." Yet the Citizen who was the Black Adept's other self had not seemed to be a bad man; perhaps it was solely the absolute power that corrupted—power beyond that of any Citizen. What would an Adept be like, if he had residence in both frames and free access between them?

"It is a fair response," Kurrelgyre said. "If thou must return for a Game within a day, only the Yellow Adept is within range to check, without the employ of magic. Would it not be better to yield this quest, being satisfied as thou art now?"

"Not while someone is trying to kill me here. That person must know who I am. If I can discover who I am in Phaze, I may know more about the nature of mine enemy. Then I can see about making this world safe for mine own existence. I gather mine other self failed to take such precaution."

"Spoken like a werewolf," Kurrelgyre said approvingly. Neysa sighed; she did not seem to agree completely, but neither did she disagree. Men will be men, her attitude said.

"Neysa, I want to be honest with thee," Stile said, feeling the need to provide a better justification. "I like Phaze, I like thee—but this is not truly my world. Even if there were no threat to my welfare, I could not commit myself absolutely to stay here. I would need to know that my presence served in some way to benefit this world; that there was some suitable challenge to rise to. Something that needed doing, that perhaps only I could do. If there seems to be more of a need and challenge in the other frame—"

Neysa made another musical snort. "She inquires whether thou wouldst feel more positive if she released thee from thy vow of no magic," the werewolf translated.

Stile considered. He understood that the acceptance of such a release would subtly or overtly alienate him from the unicorn. It was only his vow that made it

249

possible for her to associate with him on their original basis. "No. I only want to know who I am. If I can't survive without magic, maybe it's best that I not remain here. I never want to be like the Black Adept. All I need is someone to spell me into the other frame in time for mine appointment there. Then I'll return here for another look at another Adept. One way or another, I will settle my accounts in both frames. Only then will I be in a position to make a proper decision about residence."

"I will spell thee through," Kurrelgyre said. "In fact, rather than send thee pointlessly into new danger, I will investigate the Yellow Adept myself, and return with news. I think I can now recognize thy likeness, if I encounter it."

"There is no call for thee to risk thyself on my account!" Stile protested.

"There is no call for me to impose my presence when the mare wishes to converse with thee alone." And the man merged into the wolf, who bounded away to the north.

"Damn it, if I start sending others on my foolish quests, where will it end?" Stile demanded. "I've got to follow him, stop him—"

But the wolf was already beyond reach, traveling with the easy velocity of his kind. Probably Neysa could catch him, but only with difficulty. Stile knew Kurrelgyre thought he was doing Stile a favor, preserving him from risk, giving him time alone with Neysa— but this was not the sort of favor Stile cared to accept. It was not, he told himself, that Sheen had artfully depleted his sexual initiative immediately before sending him across the curtain. There was the principle of responsibility for one's own actions.

The unicorn caught his mood. She started moving north. "Thanks, Neysa," he said. "I knew thou wouldst understand." Then, as an afterthought: "How art thou getting along with the wolf?"

She blew a noncommittal note. "Glad to hear it," Stile said. He reached down around her neck and hugged her again.

Neysa quickened her gait into a gallop. "I don't know what finer life I could have than galloping across the wilderness with you," Stile said. "The only thing I miss—"

She made a musical inquiry. "Well, that's it," he said. "I like music. But since we found that music connects with my magic, I don't dare play."

This time her note was comprehensible. "Play!"

"But then the magic gathers," he protested. "I have no wish to abbreviate mine oath. I played a little when I was alone in the Black Castle, but I am not alone now, and I do not want thee angry with me."

"Play," she repeated emphatically.

"Very well. No spells, just music." He brought out his harmonica and improvised a melody to the beat of her hooves. She played a harmony on her horn. The duet was lovely. The magic gathered, pacing them, but now that he understood it he was not alarmed. It was merely a potential, until he implemented it—which he would not do.

He played for an hour, developing his proficiency with the instrument. He was getting into the feel of the harmonica, and playing about as well as ever in his life. This was a unique joy!

Neysa lifted her head, sniffing the wind. She seemed disturbed.

"What is it?" Stile inquired, putting away his harmonica.

The unicorn shook her head, unsure. She slowed to a walk, turning this way and that as if casting for something. Then she oriented on whatever it was, and resumed her northward trek. But there was something disquieting about her motion; her gait seemed unnatural.

"Art thou all right?" Stile inquired, concerned.

Neysa did not respond, so he brought out his harmonica again and played. But she immediately blew a harsh note of negation. He desisted, concealing his hurt feelings.

Stile thought she would relax after a short while, but

251

she did not. Instead her gait became more mechanical, quite unlike her normal mode.

"Neysa, I inquire again: art thou all right?"

She ignored him. She seemed to be in a trance.

Alarmed, Stile tugged sharply on her mane. "Something is wrong. I must insist—"

She threw down her head and bucked. The action was untelegraphed, but Stile was too experienced a rider to be caught. He stayed in place, then slid to the ground when she resumed her odd walk. "Neysa, something evidently compels thee. I don't know what it is—but since we are approaching the locale of the Yellow Adept, I suspect it relates. For some reason the compulsion does not affect me. Give me thy socks, and I will walk with thee in disguise."

She halted, swishing her tail in annoyance, and let him remove the white socks from her rear feet. Then she marched on.

Stile donned the socks and walked beside her, imitating her walk. If something were summoning unicorns, he wanted to resemble such a captive as closely as possible—until he understood the situation better. The wolfsbane he had sniffed still buoyed his strength; he was ready for anything, and felt no trace of the prior ravages of hunger and thirst. If Neysa had fallen into some spell cast by the Yellow Adept—

Soon the property of the Adept came into sight. It was of course yellow. The sands were yellow, rising into yellow dunes, and the sun sent yellow beams through a yellow fog that concealed the main operation from a distance. Neysa walked straight into that fog.

Soon the Adept's castle loomed. It was most like a ramshackle haunted house, with a partially collapsing roof, broken windows, and weeds growing thickly against the walls. A few yellow flowers straggled at the fringe—buttercups, sunflowers, a bedraggled yellow rose. Behind the house was a tall wrought-iron palisade fence, rusting yellow, overgrown by morbid vines with yellowing leaves but still quite formidable. An odor rose from the premises: animal dung and decaying vegetation. Rustic, but hardly pleasant.

Neysa walked right on toward the house, and Stile necessarily followed. Already he did not like the Yellow Adept and hoped perversely that the magician was alive —so as to be assured this was not Stile's own alternate identity. This time he would not be so foolish as to challenge the Adept overtly; he would just look and retreat quickly.

Except for two things. First, there was Neysa—she had somehow been mesmerized, surely for no good purpose, and had to be freed of this complication. Second, Kurrelgyre: the wolf had by now had plenty of time to lope in and out, but evidently had not, which suggested that he too had been trapped by the summoning spell. Stile would have to verify this, then act appropriately. It might not be easy.

Neysa moved right on up to the front door, which was sagging open on rusty hinges. She entered, Stile close behind. They passed through a dusty hall, turned a corner—and bars dropped from the ceiling, separating them.

Oh, no! Not again! Stile backed up—but another set of bars fell behind him. This section of hall had become a cage.

There was an ear-discomfiting shriek of laughter. "Hee-hee! Two! Two fine unicorns, so soon after the wolf! What an excellent day! Haul them out, Darlin' Corey! Let us view our prizes!"

Something huge bulked at the far end of the hall, beyond the corner. Neysa's cage slid forward. Something was drawing it onward with easy power.

After a time the thing came for Stile's cage. It was the rear end of a pink elephant. The little tail hooked into the forward bars; then the creature walked, drawing the cage after it.

Stile considered poking his sword through the bars and puncturing the fat pink rear, or cutting off the tail with his knife. But this would not release him from the cage, and could make the elephant quite angry without really incapacitating it. Better to hold off.

In a moment they emerged into the stockaded area.

253

There were cages all around. It resembled an archaic zoo. Stile identified a griffin, with the body of a lion and head and wings of an eagle, in the cage most directly across from his. This was no glorious heraldic monster, but a sad, bedraggled, dirty creature whose wings drooped and whose eyes seemed glazed. And no wonder: the cage was too small for it to stretch its wings, and there was no place for its refuse except right next to the cage where the creature had scraped it out. No wonder its feathers and fur were soiled; no wonder it stank!

Now Stile's attention was taken by the proprietress: an old woman garbed in a faded yellow robe, with stringy yellow hair and yellowish complexion. A hag, in every sense of the word.

"What a lovely little specimen!" the hag cackled, mincing around Neysa's cage. Neysa seemed to be coming out of her daze; her ears perked up, then laid back in revulsion as the crone approached.

"And this one," the Adept continued, examining Stile. "A white stallion, yet! What a pretty penny thou wilt fetch, my sweet!" She circled the cage, appraising his apparent form with an indecently calculating eye. "Yes indeed, my precious! White is in the market for the likes of thee! Needs must I send Crow's-foot with the news." She hobbled into the house.

Now Stile resumed his survey of the enclave. Beyond Neysa was Kurrelgyre, whose eye was already on him; the wolf nodded slowly. They were in trouble!

The other cages contained a small sphinx, a three-headed dog, a wyvern, and several creatures Stile couldn't classify. All were bedraggled and filthy; the witch did not bother to care for them properly, or to clean their cages. She did feed them, as there were dishes of food and water at every cage—but several of these dishes had been overturned and kicked out, uneaten.

Stile examined his own cage. The bars were yellowish, like the rest of this place, and somewhat slick. It was as if some sort of grease had been smeared on the metal in a vain attempt to make it seem like gold. He tried to push a bar out of position, but it was like welded steel. The door was firmly locked.

Still, the bars were fairly widely spaced, and he was small. Just a little bowing should enable him to squeeze between two. Stile located the longest, widest section of the cage roof, then drew his sword and used it cautiously as a lever. He did not want to break the weapon, and did not know how strong it was. But he really could not gain purchase, and had to put away the sword. Instead he jumped up, put his feet against one bar, his hands on the next, and hauled as if lifting a heavy weight. Slowly, unwillingly, the bars separated as he strove and panted. When his muscles balked, he had widened the aperture only slightly—but perhaps it was enough.

He dropped down to the cage floor—and discovered that he had become the object of considerable attention. He was still disguised as a unicorn; that must have been quite a sight, a horselike creature clinging to the upper bars!

But he couldn't allow such cynosure to stop him. The witch should soon be back. He had to do whatever he could do, rapidly.

Stile drew himself up, put his feet between the widened bars, and squeezed his body up and through. Last was his head; his ears got mashed, but he scraped by. He was out.

He climbed silently down, while the captive animals watched the contortions of this astonishing unicorn. They were not about to betray him to the witch! The conspiracy of silence was the only weapon they possessed.

Stile went to Kurrelgyre's cage. "I must have a rapid update," he said. "How can I free thee and Neysa and the others? The large bars are too strong for me."

The werewolf transformed into his human form, too large to squeeze between the bars. "Thou art fortunate in thy size," he said. "Only Neysa might do what thou hast done—and the potion hath dulled her wit so she can not transform her shape. My wolfsbane might help steady her—but we dare not administer it to her animal

255

form. We are at impasse. Save thyself; thou canst not free us."

"If I go, it will be only to help thee—as thou didst for me before. Can I overcome the witch?"

"Only if thou canst kill her by surprise, instantly with thy sword. She will else throw a potion on thee, and destroy thee."

"I don't want to kill her," Stile said. "Murder is not the proper solution to problems. I only want to neutralize her and free these poor captives."

Kurrelgyre shook his head. "Thou canst not defeat an Adept fairly save by magic."

"No. Mine oath—"

"Yes. When thou didst not break thine oath to save thyself from the Black Demesnes, I knew thy word was constant. I expect no different of thee here in the Yellow Demesnes. But now it is not thy life at stake, but Neysa's. The witch will sell her to another Adept—"

"Why don't Adepts conjure their own creatures, instead of buying them?"

"Because some spells are more complex than others. An Adept may conjure a dozen monsters via a single summoning spell with less effort than a single one by creation. So they store captive creatures in cells, and prepare spells to bring them upon need—"

"I get the picture. To be an Adept is to maintain dungeons where others languish—and the Yellow Adept caters to this need by trapping the necessary animals. I dare say she traps wild fowl and sells the eggs to the Black Adept, too; he has to get his food from somewhere. Maybe he pays her off by making strong cages from black line-bars, that she paints yellow. How does she summon the hapless victims? Neysa seemed to go into a trance."

"Yellow's magic is exerted through potions, I now have learned. She boils a cauldron whose vapors mesmerize animals, bringing them here to be caged. She could summon men similarly, but does not, lest men unite against her and destroy her. Had I been in my man-form, or Neysa in her girl-form—"

"Yes." Stile moved across to Neysa. "Wilt thou release me from mine oath, that I may cast a spell to free thee? I fear thy fate at the hands of the witch."

Neysa, dulled by the summoning potion, was not dull enough to forget her antipathy to Adept-class magic. She shook her head no. She would not condone such sorcery to free herself.

"Say," Stile said, trying again. "Thou canst also change into a firefly, and these bars would not hold—"

But Neysa's eyes were half lidded and her head hung low. The effort of will that such transformation required was beyond her present capacity.

"Or if thou couldst assume thy human form, the potion would not affect thee—"

There was a growl from another cage. Kurrelgyre looked up nervously. "Hark! The witch comes!"

Stile jumped to the werewolf's cage, on inspiration drawing off his socks. "Don these!" he whispered, shoving them through Kurrelgyre's cage bars. "And this." He put the sword through, with its harness. "She will assume—"

"Right." In a moment the white unicorn image formed. The sword was concealed by the illusion. "Remember: thou darest not eat nor drink aught she offers thee, for her potions—"

"Uh-oh! Did Neysa drink?"

But the Yellow Adept appeared before the werewolf could answer. Still, Stile hardly needed it. Neysa, like most equines, drank deeply when she had opportunity, and could have done so automatically while still under the influence of the summoning vapor. That would explain why she hadn't made any real effort to save herself. That also explained why the smarter animals here refused to eat. Kurrelgyre had avoided this trap, and was alert. But the situation of all these animals remained bleak, for evidently none of them had the strength to break out of the strong cages. Eventually they would have either to eat or to starve. Not a pleasant choice; Stile's memory of his confinement in the Black Castle remained fresh.

Stile was not idle during these realizations; he ducked behind the werewolf's cage, trying to hide. He knew it was foolish of him to hesitate about dealing with the witch; obviously she had little to recommend her, and would happily wipe him out. But he could not murder a human being heartlessly. Just as he was bound by an oath of no magic, he was bound by civilized restraints. Demons and monsters he could slay, not people.

"Eeeek!" Yellow cried, pronouncing the word exactly as it was spelled. "The cage is empty! The valuable white 'corn stallion!" But then she inspected the situation more carefully. "No, the stallion remains. It is the wolf who is gone. I could have sworn his cage was—" She glared across the compound. "Darlin' Corey!" she screamed. "Didst thou move the cages about?"

Stile watched the pink elephant. The creature had seen what happened; which side was it on? If it told the truth—

The elephant waddled past the cages toward the witch. Suddenly it flung its trunk to the side, catching Stile by the nape of his shirt and hauling him into view. It trumpeted.

"Well, now, dearest!" the crone cried, scratching idly at a wart on her nose. "So it was a werewolf! Changed to its man-form and squeezed out of its cage."

The elephant squealed, trying to correct her misimpression.

"Oh shut up, Darlin' Corey," she snapped. "What shall we do with the werewolf? I don't have a cage small enough at the moment. He's pretty shrimpy." She peered at Stile more closely, as he hung in midair. "But healthy and handsome enough, my lovely. Maybe he would do for my daughter. Hold him there a moment, my tasty; I will send the wench out."

The pink elephant chuckled. The monsters in cages exchanged glances, bewildered. Obviously this was the first they had heard of Yellow's daughter. What kind of a slut was she? Meanwhile, the hag limped rapidly to the house.

Stile thought of doing an acrobatic flip and climbing the elephant's trunk. But the creature was quite big and

258

strong, and not stupid; it might bash him against a tree. Had he retained his sword—but that would have been highly visible, forcing him to use it to defend himself. It was better to appear more or less helpless, lest he get doused by a potion.

He looked around, able to see more clearly from this height. Beyond the palisades the yellow fog obliterated everything. It was as if the rest of the world did not exist. No doubt this was the way the Adept liked it. She had a little mist-shrouded world of her own, that no man dared intrude upon. Did she get lonely? Probably no more lonely than a person with her appearance would get in the midst of the most convivial society. Who would want to associate with her? Stile, as a person who all his life had felt the inherent discrimination of size, could not entirely condemn the witch for reacting to the discrimination of appearance. Yet he could not allow her to abuse his friends, or to continue mistreating innocent animals.

His eye caught something—a glimmer in the fog outside the compound. A faint curtain of—

The curtain! Could it be here? The thing seemed to wander all over Phaze like a tremendous serpent. Might it be used to facilitate escape, as it had before?

No, there were two problems. The curtain, close as it was, was out of reach, since it was beyond the palisades. And Neysa could not use it. Or would not; he wasn't sure which. So this was a mere tantalization, no real help. Best to wait and see what the witch's daughter had in mind. She was probably a homely girl upon whom her crazy mother forced the attentions of any likely-seeming male.

She emerged. She was stunning. Her yellow hair flowed luxuriously to her waist, her hands and feet were tiny, and her complexion was gold-bronze vibrant, not sallow. She had a figure that would have made an artist gape, with prominent secondary sexual characteristics. Her eyes were so large she seemed almost like a doll—but what a doll!

Young witches, it seemed, had other assets than magic.

"Darlin' Corey, put that man down this instant!" the girl cried, spying Stile. Her voice, despite its vehemence, was dulcet. Everything about her was as nice as it was nasty about her mother.

Darlin' Corey lowered Stile to the ground, but remained near, on guard. Stile straightened his clothing and rolled his shoulders; it had not been entirely comfortable, hanging all that time in midair. "I don't believe we've met," he said.

She giggled jigglesomely. "Tee-hee. I'm Yellowette. My, thou'rt a handsome wolf."

"I'm a man," Stile said.

She looked down at him. That was the only fault he could perceive in her: she was a few centimeters—a couple of this frame's inches—taller than he. "That, too. Kiss me, my cute."

Neysa, in the cage, recovered enough to make a musical snort of recognition. Suddenly Stile had a suspicion why the pink elephant had found the notion of this encounter humorous, and why the caged beasts had never known of the witch's daughter. What would a lonely old hag do with a handsome-if-small man, if she had a potion for every purpose? Drug him—or take a very special potion herself? "Not in front of these monsters," he said.

"What do they matter, my delight? They can not escape."

"I like my privacy," he said. "Let's take a walk outside—and return later, as before." He glanced meaningfully at Neysa, hoping the drug had worn off enough to uncloud her mind. "As before."

Yellowette's fair brow wrinkled. "Thou knowest that unicorn, werewolf?"

"I'm not a werewolf," he said, aware that she would not believe him. "I do know her. She's a jealous mare."

"So? Well, she'll be gone in a few days. There's a fair market in unicorns, for they are hard to catch. Their horns and hooves are valuable for musical instruments and for striking fire, their dung is excellent fertilizer for magic plants, and their hides have anti-magic properties."

Stile experienced an ugly chill. "These animals are for slaughter?"

"Some are, my pleasure. Some aren't even good for that. The black mare would be excellent as a courtyard showpiece, except that she lacks proper coloration and is small. The white stallion, in contrast, is a prize; the White Adept will probably use him to battle dragons in his arena."

Good thing she didn't know the white unicorn was a fake! "What happens to the completely useless animals?"

"I have Darlin' Corey take the worthless ones outside and put them through the curtain." The witch was no longer bothering to conceal her identity, since he seemed to accept it. Her female view of man was that he was interested only in the external appearance—and Stile suspected there was some merit in that view. He had already had relations with a machine that looked like a woman, and with a unicorn that also looked like a woman. What of an old woman who looked like a young woman? Yellow was certainly much more pleasing to deal with in this form than in the other.

"Thou knowest about the curtain?" he asked after a moment, surprised.

"Thou dost not? There is another world beyond it, a desert. The potion puts the creatures through; they never return. I have not the heart to kill them outright, and dare not let them go free in this world lest they summon hordes of their kind to wreak vengeance on these my demesnes, and if they survive in the other world I begrudge it not."

So she was not heartless, just a victim of circumstance. To an extent. Yet it seemed a safe assumption that she was as yet only partially corrupted by power.

How much should he say? Stile detested lies even by indirection. "I am of that world."

"Thou'rt a frame traveler? A true man?" She was alarmed.

"I am. Thou didst merely assume I was a werewolf."

"I do not deal in true men!" she said nervously. "This leads to great mischief!"

261

"I came merely to discover thine identity. Now I seek only to free thy captives and to depart with my friends. I have no inherent quarrel with thee, but if thou threatenest my life or those of my friends—"

She turned to him in the hallway. She was absolutely beautiful. "I proffer no threat to thee, my handsome bantam. Dally with a lonely woman a time, and thy friends shall go free with thee."

Stile considered. "I don't regard myself to be at liberty to do that."

She frowned. "Thou hast only limited leeway for bargaining, sweets."

"Perhaps. My friend urged me to slay thee without warning, but I did not wish to do that either."

"Oh? We shall put that to the proof." She led him into the main room of the house. Shelves lined the walls, containing bottles of fluid: rows and rows of them, coated with dust. In the center a huge cauldron bubbled, its vapors drifting out through a broken windowpane. This was obviously the source of the summoning scent: a continously brewing mix.

"All these bottles—potions for different spells?" he inquired, impressed.

"All. I must brew one potion at a time, and can use it only once, so I save each carefully. It is not easy, being Adept; it requires much imagination and application. I must develop a new formula for every invisibility elixir I mix—and for every rejuvenation drink."

Stile eyed her figure again. What a potion she must have taken! "Thou didst really look like this in thy youth?"

"I really did, my honey. Or as close as makes no nevermind. Hair and flesh tints differ from mix to mix, and sometimes one brews too strong, and I become as a child. But my youth was a very long time ago, my lamb, and even the best potion lasts no more than an hour. See—I have only three of these mixes left." She gestured to a half-empty shelf, where three bottles sat. "I expended one quarter of my stock, for a mere hour with thee. Take that as what flattery thou mayst."

"Flattering indeed," Stile said. "I did see thee in thy

262

natural state. But this is not what restrains me. I have other commitments." He pondered briefly. "Thou didst believe me to be a werewolf, before. The true werewolf might be interested in the remainder of thy hour, if thou wert to free him thereafter."

Yellow took down a bottle. "Thou art most facile, lovely man. I hardly trust thee. If thou provest a liar, it will go hard indeed with thee—*and* thy friends." She drew the stopper out. Stile stepped back, alarmed, but she sprinkled the liquid on a statuette, not on him.

The figurine grew rapidly into a demon monster. "Thou summonest me, hag?" it roared, its small red eyes fairly glowing as they glared about. Then it did a double take. Its lips pursed appreciatively. "I have not seen the like in six hundred years! But thou didst not need to prettify thyself for me, witch."

" 'Twas not for thee I did it," she snapped. "Speak me the truth, Zebub. Why came this man here, and who is he?"

The demon glared in Stile's direction. "This time thou'rt victim to thine own paranoia, crone. He is innocuous, with respect to thee. Not with respect to certain others, though." The demon smiled privately.

"He really sought not to kill me?"

"True. He but seeks his own identity, so comes with werewolf and unicorn to learn if thou art it."

Yellow burst into a cackle of laughter. "Me! What kind of fool is he?"

"No fool, he. He lacks information on the nature of the Adepts. The Oracle advised him to know himself, so he seeks to learn if he is one of you. He was trapped by Black, and only escaped via the curtain. He is of that other world."

Stile felt another chill. This monster really did have information!

"What gives him the notion he is Adept?" Yellow demanded.

"He *is* Adept, O senile one."

Yellow backed against a wall, almost jarring loose several bottles. "Not only a man, but Adept to boot! Oh, what a foul pickle I have hatched! Who is he?"

"He is Stile, a serf of Proton, in the other frame, freed to cross the curtain by the death of his Phaze-self."

"Idiot! I meant which Adept is he?"

The demon scowled. "That is formidable information."

"Don't stall, hellborn one!" Yellow screeched. "Else I will apply a pain potion."

Zebub blanched. "Blue," he muttered.

Yellow's eyes went round. "This midget is the Blue Adept?"

"His alternate, yes."

"I can't afford trouble with another Adept!" she exclaimed, wrenching at her own hair in distraction. "Not one of such power as Blue! If I free him, will he seek to destroy me? Why does he withhold his magic now?"

"This calls for conclusions on the part of the witness," the demon said smugly.

Yellow took a step toward a shelf of small bottles.

"Question him," Zebub said quickly. "I will verify his word."

"Stile, a.k.a. Blue Adept!" she cried, her eyes round and wild, yet still lovely. "Answer me, in the presence of Zebub."

"If thou shouldst free me, I will still seek to release my friends and the other captives," Stile said. "I will not seek to destroy thee gratuitously."

"He speaks truth," Zebub said. "As for his magic, he made an oath to the unicorn to practice it not save by her leave."

"So only his oath makes him subject to my power?" she demanded.

"That is so," Zebub agreed. "Thou art the luckiest of harridans."

Yellow's beautiful brow furrowed. "If I release the unicorn, she could then release Blue from his oath, and there would be war between Adepts. I dare not risk it."

"Thou darest not risk harming the unicorn either, beldame," Zebub pointed out maliciously. "If the Blue Adept is moved by ire to break his oath—"

"I know! I know!" she screeched, distracted. "If I kill him, another Adept might seek to kill me, for that I violated our convention. If I let him go, Blue may seek my life for that I caged him. If I try to hold him—"

"My time is up," Zebub said. "Please deposit another potion, scold."

"O, begone with thee!" Yellow snapped.

The demon shrank into figurine size and froze: a dead image.

Yellow looked at Stile. "If thou keepest thine oath to the unicorn, wilt thou honor it for me? I wish I could be sure. I want no quarrel with another Adept."

"Release all the animals in your compound, and thou wilt have no quarrel with me," Stile said.

"I can not! I have commitments, I have accepted magic favors in payment. I must deliver."

Stile, quite prepared to hate this Adept, found himself moved. She was, for the moment, lovely, but that was not it. She honored her commitments. She did not like killing. Her surroundings and mechanisms reflected a certain humor, as if she did not take herself too seriously. She was old and lonely. It should be possible to make a deal with her.

"I want no quarrel with thee, either," he said. "Thou knowest me not, therefore trust must be tempered with caution. I make thee this offer: send me through the curtain, and I will not return. I will seek to free my friends and the animals from a distance."

"How canst thou act from a distance? My magic is stronger than thine, near me in my demesnes—as thine would be stronger than mine in thine own demesnes."

"Without magic," Stile said.

"Very well," she decided. "I will put thee through the curtain with a potion, and set a powerful curse I got from Green to ward thee off thereafter. If thou canst free the animals from a distance, without magic—" She shrugged. "I have never liked this business; if I am foiled through no agency of mine own, perhaps I will not be held in default." She glanced at him, her mood visibly lightening. "I never did business with Blue, else would I have known thee. How is it that Blue, alone of Adepts, needs no monsters in storage?"

"I intend to find out," Stile said. He was highly gratified to have this information. Now he knew who he was, and that the Blue Adept had not practiced at least one of the atrocities that seemed to be standard in this genre. This excursion into the Yellow Demesnes had been mistaken, but serendipitously worthwhile.

Yellow took down another bottle, then led him out of the house and around the palisades to the curtain. Stile hoped he could trust her to use the correct potion. But it seemed reasonable; if Adepts avoided trouble with Adepts, and if she feared his violation of his oath were he to be betrayed, she would play it straight. She seemed to be, basically, an honest witch.

At the curtain, she hesitated, hand on the stopper of the bottle. "I do not wish to murder thee, Blue Stile," she said. "Art thou sure thou canst survive in that bleak realm beyond the curtain? If thou preferest to dally here—"

"My thanks, Yellow. I can survive. I have a prior engagement, and must pass through now."

"And thou thinkest the werewolf might be interested —for half an hour? It is not a difficult thing I ask—"

"Won't hurt to ask him," Stile agreed, stepping through the curtain as she sprinkled the liquid on him.

CHAPTER 15

Games

It was a longer hike to the nearest dome, this time, but he had more confidence and need, and that sniff of wolfsbane still buoyed him. In due course, gasping, he stepped inside and made a call to Sheen. It was evening; he had the night to rest with her. He needed it; his high of the last visit to Phaze finally gave out, and he realized the episode with the Yellow Adept had drained him more than he had realized at the time. Or perhaps it was the low following the effect of the wolfsbane.

"So you are the Blue Adept," Sheen said, not letting him sleep quite yet. "And you need some things to use to free your equine girl friend."

"Now don't get jealous again," he grumbled. "You know I have to—"

"How can I be jealous? I'm only a machine."

Stile sighed. "I should have taken Yellow up on her offer. Then you would have had something to be jealous about."

"You mean you didn't—with Neysa?"

"Not this time. I—"

"You were saving it for the witch?" she demanded indignantly. "Then ran out of time?"

"Well, she was an extremely pretty—"

"You made your callous point. I won't resent Neysa. She's only an animal."

"Are you going to have your friends assemble my order or aren't you?"

"I will take care of it in good time. But I don't see how a cube of dry ice will help your animals."

"Plus a diamond-edged hacksaw."

267

"And a trained owl," she finished. "Do you plan to start romancing birds next?"

"Oh, go away and let me sleep!"

Instead she tickled him. "Birds, hags, mares, machines—why can't you find a normal woman for a change?"

"I had one," he said, thinking of Tune. "She left me."

"So you get hung up on all the half-women, fearing to tackle a real one again—because you're sure she wouldn't want you." She was half-teasing, half-sad, toying with the notion that she herself was a symptom of his aberration.

"I'll look for one tomorrow," he promised.

"Not tomorrow. First thing in the morning, you have an appointment to meet your current employer. This Citizen is very keen on the Game."

Exasperated, he rolled over and grabbed her. "The irony is," he said into her soft hair, "you are now more real to me than most real girls I have known. When I told you to brush up on your humanoid wiles, I didn't mean at my expense."

"Then you should have said that. I take things literally, because I'm only a—"

He shut her up with a kiss. But the thoughts she had voiced were only a reflection of those he was having. How long could he continue with half-women?

In the morning he met his employer. This was, to his surprise, a woman. No wonder Sheen had had women on her mind! The Citizen was elegantly gowned and coiffed: a handsome lady of exquisitely indeterminate age. She was, of course, substantially taller than he, but had the grace to conceal this by remaining seated in his presence. "Sir," Stile said. All Citizens were sir, regardless of sex or age.

"See that you qualify for the Tourney," she said with polite force. "Excused."

That was that. If he lost one Game, this employer would cut him off as cleanly as his prior one had. He was supposed to feel deeply honored that she had granted him this personal audience—and he did. But his recent experience in Phaze had diminished his awe of Citizens. They were, after all, only people with a lot of wealth and power.

Stile and Sheen went for his challenge for Rung Seven. His employer surely had bets on his success. There were things about this that rankled, but if he fouled up, Sheen would be the one to pay. She lacked his avenue of escape to a better world. He had to do what he could for her, until he figured out some better alternative.

The holder of Rung Seven kept his appointment—as he had to, lest he forfeit. He was not much taller than Stile and tended to avoirdupois despite the antifat medication in the standard diet. Hence his name, Snack. He hardly looked like a formidable player—but neither did Stile.

An audience had gathered, as Sheen had predicted. It was possible that some Citizens also were viewing the match on their screens—especially his own employer. Stile's move was news.

Snack got the numbered facet of the grid. Stile sighed inaudibly; he had been getting bad breaks on facets in this series. Snack always selected MENTAL.

Very well. Stile would not choose NAKED, because Snack was matchless at the pure mental games. Snack was also uncomfortably sharp at MACHINE- and ANIMAL-assisted mental efforts. Only in TOOL did Stile have an even chance. So it had to come up 2B.

There was a murmur of agreement from the spectators outside, as they watched on the public viewscreen. They had known what the opening box would be. They were waiting for the next grid.

In a moment it appeared: sixteen somewhat arbitrary classifications of games of intellectual skill. Snack had the numbered facet again, which was the primary one. He would go for his specialty: chess. He was versed in all forms of that game: the western-Earth two- and three-dimensional variants, the Chinese *Choohong-ki*, Japanese *Shogi*, Indian *Chaturanga* and the hypermodern developments. Stile could not match him there. He had a better chance with the single-piece board games like Chinese Checkers and its variants— but many games used the same boards as chess, and this grid classified them by their boards. Better to avoid that whole bailiwick.

Stile chose the C row, covering jigsaw-type puzzles, hunt-type board games—he liked Fox & Geese—the so-called pencil-and-paper games and, in the column he expected to intersect, the enclosing games.

It came up 2C: Enclosing. There was another murmur of excitement from the audience.

Now the handmade grid. Stile felt more confidence here; he could probably take Snack on most of these variants. They completed a subgrid of only four: Go, Go-bang, Yote and tic-tac-toe. Stile had thrown in the last whimsically. Tic-tac-toe was a simplistic game, no challenge, but in its essence it resembled the prototype for the grids of the Game. The player who got three of his choices in a row, then had the luck to get the facet that enabled him to choose that row, should normally win. The ideal was to establish one full row and one full column, so that the player had winners no matter which facet he had to work with. But in the Game-grids, there was no draw if no one lined up his X's and O's; the real play was in the choosing of columns and the interaction of strategies.

And they intersected at tic-tac-toe. That was what he got for fooling around.

Stile sighed. The problem with this little game was that, among competent players, it was invariably a draw. They played it right here on the grid-screen, punching buttons for X's and O's. To a draw.

Which meant they had to run the grid again, to achieve the settlement. They played it—and came up with the same initial box as before. And the same secondary box. Neither player was going to yield one iota of advantage for the sake of variation; to do so would be to lose. But the third grid developed a different pattern, leading to a new choice: Go-bang.

This was a game similar to tic-tac-toe, but with a larger grid allowing up to nineteen markers to be played on a side. It was necessary to form a line of five in a row to win. This game, too, was usually to a draw, at this level.

They drew. Each was too alert to permit the other to move five in a row. Now they would have to go to a third Game. But now the matter was more critical. Any series that went to three draws was presumed to be the result of incompetence or malingering; both parties would be suspended from Game privileges for a period, their Rungs forfeit. It could be a long, hard climb up again, for both—and Stile had no time for it. The third try, in sum, had to produce a winner.

They ran the grids through again—and arrived again at tool-assisted mental, and at enclosing. The basic strategies were immutable.

Stile exchanged glances with Snack. Both knew what they had to do.

This time it came up Go—the ancient Chinese game of enclosing. It was perhaps the oldest of all games in the human sphere, dating back several thousand years. It was one of the simplest in basic concept: the placing of colored stones to mark off territory, the player enclosing the most territory winning. Yet in execution it was also one of the most sophisticated of games. The more skilled player almost invariably won.

The problem was, Stile was not certain which of them was the more skilled in Go. He had never played this particular game with this particular man, and could not at the moment remember any games of Go he and Snack had played against common opponents. This was certainly not Stile's strongest game—but he doubted it was Snack's strongest either.

They moved to the board-game annex, as this match would take too long for the grid-premises; others had to use that equipment. The audience followed, taking seats; they could tune in on replicas of the game at each place, but preferred to observe it physically. Sheen had a front seat, and looked nervous: probably an affectation, considering her wire nerves.

Stile would have preferred a Game leading to a quick decision, for he was conscious of Neysa and Kurrelgyre

271

in the other frame, locked in potion-hardened cages. But he had to meet his commitment here, first, whatever it took.

They sat on opposite sides of the board, each with a bowl of polished stones. Snack gravely picked up one stone of each color, shook them together in his joined hands, and offered two fists for Stile. Stile touched the left. The hand opened to reveal a black pebble.

Stile took that stone and laid it on the board. Black, by convention, had the first move. With 361 intersections to choose from—for the stones were placed on the lines in Go, not in the squares—he had no problem. A one-stone advantage was not much, but in a game as precise as this it helped.

Snack settled down to play. The game was by the clock, because this was a challenge for access to the Tourney; probably few games of Go would be played, but time was limited to keep the Tourney moving well. This was another help to Stile; given unlimited time to ponder, Snack could probably beat him. Under time pressure Stile generally did well. That was one reason he was a top Gamesman.

They took turns laying down stones, forming strategic patterns on the board. The object was to enclose as much space as possible, as with an army controlling territory, and to capture as many of the opponent's stones as possible, as with prisoners of war. Territory was the primary thing, but it was often acquired by wiping out enemy representatives. Stile pictured each white pebble as a hostile soldier, implacable, menacing; and each black pebble as a Defender of the Faith, upright and righteous. But it was not at all certain that right would prevail. He had to dispose his troops advantageously, and in the heat of battle the advantage was not easy to discern.

A stone/man was captured when all his avenues of freedom were curtailed. If enemy forces blocked him off on three sides, he had only one freedom remaining; if not buttressed by another of his kind, forming a chain, he could lose his freedom and be lost. But two men could be surrounded too, or ten enclosed; numbers were no certain security here. Rather, position was most important. There were devices to protect territory, such as "eyes" or divisions that prevented enclosure by the other side, but these took stones that might be more profitably utilized elsewhere. Judgment was vital.

Snack proceeded well in the early stages. Then the complexity of interaction increased, and time ran short, and Stile applied the notorious Stile stare to unnerve his opponent. It was a concentrated glare, an almost tangible aura of hate; every time Snack glanced up he encountered that implacable force. At first Snack shrugged it off, knowing that this was all part of the game, but in time the unremitting intensity of it wore him down, until he began to make mistakes. Trifling errors at first, but these upset him all out of proportion, causing his concentration to suffer. He misread a *seki* situation, giving away several stones, failed to make an eye to protect a vulnerable territory, and used stones wastefully.

Even before the game's conclusion, it was obvious that Stile had it. Snack, shaken, resigned without going through the scoring procedure. Rung Seven was Stile's.

Stile eased up on the glare—and Snack shook his head, feeling foolish. He understood how poorly he had played in the ambience of that malevolence—now that the pressure was off. At his top form he might reasonably have beaten Stile, but he had been far below his standard. Stile himself was sorry, but he was above all a competitor, and he had needed this Rung. All his malignance, the product of a lifetime's reaction to the slight of his size, came out in concentrated form during competition of this nature, and it was a major key to his success. Stile was more highly motivated than most people, inherently, and he drove harder, and he never showed mercy in the Game.

The holder of Rung Six was a contrast. His name was Hulk, after an obscure comic character of a prior century he was thought to resemble, and he was a huge, powerful man. Hulk was not only ready but eager to meet the challenge. He was a specialist in the physical games, but was not stupid. This was his last year of tenure, so he was trying to move into qualifying position; unfortunately his last challenge to Rung Five had been turned back on a Game of chance, and he could not rechallenge until the rung-order shifted, or until he had successfully answered a challenge to his own Rung. Stile was that challenge. The audience, aware of this, had swelled to respectable size; both Stile and Hulk were popular Gamesmen, and they represented the extremes of physical appearance, adding to that novelty. The giant and the midget, locked in combat!

Stile got the numbered face of the prime grid, this time. For once he had the opening break! He could steer the selection away from Hulk's specialty of the physical.

But Stile hesitated. Two things influenced him. First, the element of surprise: why should he do what his opponent expected, which was to choose the MENTAL column? Hulk was pretty canny, though he tried to conceal this, just as Stile tried to obscure his physical abilities. Any mistake an opponent might make in estimating the capacities of a player was good news for that player. Hulk would choose the NAKED row, putting it into the box of straight mental games, where surely he had some specialties in reserve. Second, it would be a prime challenge and an exhilarating experience to take Hulk in his region of strength—a considerable show for the watching masses.

No, Stile told himself. This was merely his foolishness, a reaction to the countless times he had been disparagingly called a pygmy. He had a thing about large men, a need to put them down, to prove he was better than they, and to do it physically. He knew this was fatuous; large men were no more responsible for their size than Stile was for his own. Yet it was an incubus, a constant imperative that would never yield to logic. He wanted to humble this giant, to grind him down ignominiously before the world. He *had* to.

Thus it came up 1A—PHYSICAL NAKED. The audience made a soft "oooh" of surprise and expectation. In the muted distance came someone's call: "Stile's going after Hulk in 1A!" and a responding cry of amazement.

Hulk looked up, and they exchanged a fleeting smile over the unit; both of them liked a good audience. In fact, Stile realized, he was more like Hulk than unlike him, in certain fundamental respects. It was push-pull; Stile both liked and disliked, envied and resented the other man, wanting to be like him while wanting to prove he didn't *need* to be like him.

But had he, in his silly imperative, thrown away any advantage he might have had? Hulk's physical prowess was no empty reputation. Stile had made the grand play—and might now pay the consequence. Loss—and termination of employment, when he most needed the support of an understanding employer. Stile began to feel the weakness of uncertainty.

They played the next grid. This, he realized suddenly, was the same one he had come to with Sheen, when he met her in her guise of a woman. Of a living woman. That Dust Slide—he remembered that with a certain fondness. So much had happened since then! He had suffered knee injury, threats against his life, discovered the frame of Phaze, befriended a lady unicorn and gentleman werewolf, and was now making his move to enter the Tourney—two years before his time. A lifetime of experience in about ten days!

The subgrid's top facet listed SEPARATE—INACTIVE —COMBAT—COOPERATIVE, and this was the one Stile had. He was tempted to go for COMBAT, but his internal need to prove himself did not extend to such idiocy. He could hold his own in most martial arts—but he remembered the problem he had had trying to throw the goon, in the fantasy frame, and Hulk was the wrestling champion of the over-age-thirty men. A good big man could indeed beat a good small man, other things being equal. Stile selected SEPARATE.

Hulk's options were for the surfaces: FLAT—VARIABLE—DISCONTINUITY—LIQUID. Hulk was a powerful swimmer—but Stile was an expert diver, and these were in the same section. Stile's gymnastic abilities gave him the advantage on discontinuous surfaces too; he could do tricks on the trapeze or parallel bars the larger man could never match. Hulk's best bet was to opt for VARIABLE, which included mountain climbing and sliding. A speed-hike up a mountain slope with a twenty-kilogram pack could finish Stile, since there were no allowances for sex or size in the Game. Of course Stile would never allow himself to be trapped like that, but Hulk could make him sweat to avoid it.

But Hulk selected FLAT. There was a murmur of surprise from the audience. Had Hulk expected Stile to go for another combination, or had he simply miscalculated? Probably the latter; Stile had a special touch with the grid. This, too, was part of his Game expertise.

Now they assembled the final grid. They were in the category of races, jumps, tumbling and calisthenics. Stile placed Marathon in the center of the nine-square grid, trying to jar his opponent. Excessive development of muscle in the upper section was a liability in an endurance run, because it had to be carried along uselessly while the legs and heart did most of the work. Hulk, in effect, was carrying that twenty-kilo pack.

Hulk, undaunted, came back with the standing broad jump, another specialty of his. He had a lot of mass, but once he got it aloft it carried a long way. They filled in the other boxes with trampoline flips, pushups, twenty-kilometer run, hundred-meter dash, precision backflips, running broad jump, and handstand race.

They had formed the grid artfully to prevent any vertical or horizontal three-in-a-row lines, so there was no obvious advantage to be obtained here. Since Stile had made the extra placement, Hulk had choice of facets. They made their selections, and it came up 2B, dead center: Marathon.

Stile relaxed. Victory! But Hulk did not seem discouraged. Strange.

"Concede?" Stile inquired, per protocol.

"Declined."

So Hulk actually intended to race. He was simply not a distance runner; Stile was. What gave the man his confidence? There was no way he could fake Stile out; this was a clear mismatch. As far as Stile knew, Hulk had never completed a marathon race. The audience, too, was marveling. Hulk should have conceded. Did he know something others didn't, or was he bluffing?

Well, what would be, would be. Hulk would keep the pace for a while, then inevitably fall behind, and when Stile got a certain distance ahead there would be a mandatory concession. Maybe Hulk preferred to go down that way—or maybe he hoped Stile would suffer a cramp or pull a muscle on the way. Accidents did happen on occasion, so the outcome of a Game was never quite certain until actually played through. Stile's knee injury was now generally known; perhaps Hulk overestimated its effect.

They proceeded to the track. Sheen paced Stile nervously; was she affecting an emotion she did not feel, the better to conceal her nature, or did she suspect some threat to his welfare here? He couldn't ask. The established track wound through assorted other exercise areas, passing from one to another to make a huge circuit. Other runners were on it, and a number of walkers; they would clear out to let the marathoners pass, of course. Stile and Hulk, as rung contenders before the Tourney, had priority.

The audience dispersed; there was really no way to watch this race physically except by matching the pace. Interested people would view it on intermittent viewscreen pickup, or obtain transport to checkpoints along the route.

They came to the starting line and checked in with the robot official. "Be advised that a portion of this track is closed for repair," the robot said. He was a desk model, similar to the female at the Dust Slide; his nether portion was the solid block of the metal desk. "There is a detour, and the finish line is advanced accordingly to keep the distance constant."

"Let me put in an order for my drinks along the way," Hulk said. "I have developed my own formula."

Formula? Stile checked with Sheen. "He's up to something," she murmured. "There's no formula he can use that will give him the endurance he needs, without tripping the illegal-drug alarm."

"He isn't going to cheat, and he can't outrun me," Stile said. "If he can win this one, he deserves it. Will you be at the checkpoints to give me my own drinks? Standard fructose mix is what I run on; maybe Hulk needs something special to bolster his mass, but I don't, and I don't expect to have to finish this course anyway."

"I will run with you," she said.

"And show the world your nature? No living woman as soft and shapely as you could keep the pace; you know that."

"True," she agreed reluctantly. "I will be at the checkpoints. My friends will keep watch too." She leaned forward to kiss him fleetingly, exactly like a concerned girl friend—and wasn't she just that?

They lined up at the mark, and the robot gave them their starting signal. They were off, running side by side. Stile set the pace at about fifteen kilometers per hour, warming up, and Hulk matched him. The first hour of a marathon hardly counted; the race would be decided in the later stages, as personal resources and willpower gave out. They were not out after any record; this was purely a two-man matter, and the chances were that one of them would concede when he saw that he could not win.

Two kilometers spacing was the requirement for forced concession. This was to prevent one person slowing to a walk, forcing the other to go the full distance at speed to win. But it was unlikely even to come to that; Stile doubted that Hulk could go any major fraction of this distance at speed without destroying himself. Once Hulk realized that his bluff had failed, he would yield gracefully.

Soon Stile warmed up. His limbs loosened, his breathing and respiration developed invigorating force, and his mind seemed to sharpen. He liked this sort of exercise. He began to push the pace. Hulk did not have to match him, but probably would, for psychological effect. Once Stile got safely out in front, nothing the big man could do would have much impact.

Yet Hulk was running easily beside him, breathing

no harder than Stile. Had the man been practicing, extending his endurance? How good was he, now?

Along the route were the refreshment stations, for liquid was vital for distance running. Sheen stood at the first, holding out a squeeze bottle to Stile, smiling. He was not yet thirsty, but accepted it, knowing that a hot human body could excrete water through the skin faster than the human digestive system could replace it. Running, for all its joy, was no casual exercise. Not at this velocity and this distance.

Hulk accepted his bottle from the standard station robot. No doubt it was a variant of the normal formula, containing some readily assimilable sugars in fermented form, restoring energy as well as fluid; why he had made a point of the distinction of his particular mix Stile wasn't sure. Maybe it was psychological for himself as well as his opponent—the notion that some trace element or herb lent extra strength.

With any modern formula, it was possible to reduce or even avoid the nefarious "wall" or point at which the body's reserves were exhausted. Ancient marathon runners had had to force their bodies to consume their own tissues to keep going, and this was unhealthy. Today's careful runners would make it without such debilitation —if they were in proper condition. But the psychology of it remained a major factor, and anything that psyched up a person to better performance was worth it—if it really worked. Yet Hulk was not a man to cater to any fakelore or superstition; he was supremely practical.

After they were clear of the station, and had disposed of their empty bottles in hoppers set for that purpose along the way, Hulk inquired: "She is yours?"

"Perhaps I am hers," Stile said. They were talking about Sheen, of course.

"Trade her to me; I will give you the Rung."

Stile laughed. Then it occurred to him that Hulk just might be serious. Could he have entered this no-win contest because he had seen Sheen with Stile, and coveted her, and hoped for an avenue to her acquaintance? Hulk was, like Stile, a bit diffident about the women he liked, in contrast to the ones that threw themselves upon him. He could not just walk up to Sheen and say, "Hello, I like your looks, I would like to take you away from Stile." He had to clear it with Stile first. This was another quality in him that Stile respected, and it interfered with his hate-his-opponent concentration. "I can not trade her. She is an independent sort. I must take the Rung to keep her."

"Then we had better race." This time Hulk stepped up the pace.

Now it occurred to Stile that Hulk did not actually covet Stile's girl; Hulk did have all the women any normal man would want, even if they tended to be the superficial muscle-gawking types. So his expressed interest was most likely a matter of courtesy. Either he was trying to make Stile feel at ease—which seemed a pointless strategy—or he was trying to deplete his urge to win. One thing Stile was sure of: however honest and polite Hulk might be, he wanted to win this race. Somehow.

Stile kept pace. He could not match Hulk's short-term velocity, while Hulk could not match Stile's endurance. The question was, at what point did the balance shift? No matter how he reasoned it, Stile could not see how the man could go the whole route, nearly fifty kilometers, at a sufficient rate to win. Right now Hulk was trying to push Stile beyond his natural pace, causing him to wear himself out prematurely. But this strategy could not succeed, for Stile would simply let the man go ahead, then pass him in the later stage. Hulk could not open up a two-kilometer lead against Stile; he would burst a blood vessel trying. No doubt Hulk had won other races against lesser competition that way, faking them out with his short-term power, making them lose heart and resign; but that was a vain hope here. The longer Stile kept Hulk's pace, the more futile that particular strategy became. Provided Stile did not overextend himself and pull a muscle.

On they ran, taking fluid at every station without pausing. Other runners kept pace with them on occasion, running in parallel tracks so as not to get in the way, but most of these were short-distance runners who had to desist after a kilometer or two. Stile and Hulk followed the track from dome to dome, staying on the marked route. It passed through a huge gym where young women were exercising, doing jumping jacks, laughing, their breasts bounding merrily. "Stop and get a workout, boys!" one called.

"Too rough," Hulk called back. "I'm getting out of here!"

They wound through the elaborate rock gardens of a sports-loving Citizen: the so-called outdoor sports of hunting, camping, canoeing, hiking, wildlife photography. There were no people participating; all was reserved for the lone delight of the owner. At one point the track passed between an artificial cliff and a waterfall: a nice effect. Farther along, a variable beam of light played across them, turning the region into a rainbow delight. Then down the main street of another Citizen's metropolis replica: skyscraper buildings on one-tenth scale, still almost too tall to fit within the dome.

At the next refreshment station a warner flared: FIELD DEFICIENCY, the sign advised. DETOUR AHEAD.

"They warned us," Stile said, taking a bottle from Sheen and flashing her a smile in passing. He remained in fine fettle, enjoying the run.

Hulk grabbed his own bottle, which seemed to be of a different type than before. He didn't use it immediately, but ran on for a short while in silence. When they were safely beyond the station, he exclaimed: "Detour, hell! This is a set route, not a garden path to be switched every time some Citizen has a party. This is a challenge leading to the Tourney. I mean to push on through."

Intriguing notion. If they ignored the detour, would they be able to defy the whim of some Citizen with impunity? Few serfs ever had the chance! "Could be trouble," Stile warned.

"I'll risk it." And Hulk passed the plainly marked detour and followed the original marathon track.

That forced Stile to stay on that track too, because a detour could add kilometers to the route, in effect putting him behind enough to disqualify him. Had that been Hulk's plan? To get ahead, take the main track, while Stile innocently took the detour and penalized himself? But that would mean that Hulk had known about this detour beforehand—and Stile had been the one to put the marathon on the grid.

A good competitor, though, kept abreast of all the options. Had Stile not been busy in Phaze, he would have known about the detour himself, and played accordingly. Well, he had kept pace with the giant, and foiled that particular ploy. But he did not much like this development. Detours, despite Hulk's complaint, were usually set for good reason.

Stile finished his drink and tossed the bottle in the bin. Hulk had hardly started his, and was carrying it along in his hand. Of course he could take as long as he wished; Stile preferred not to have any encumbrance longer than necessary.

They passed through a force-field wall, into an interdome tunnel. This was where the deficiency was. Stile felt it immediately; it was cold here, and some of the air had leaked out. His breathing became difficult; there was not enough oxygen to sustain him long at this level of exertion. He had become partially acclimatized to it in the course of his travels to and from Phaze, but that wasn't enough. Yet Hulk, perhaps drawing on reserves within his gross musculature, forged on.

If the field malfunction extended far, Stile would be in trouble. And Hulk knew it. Suddenly the race had changed complexion! Had Hulk anticipated this so far as to practice running in outerdome air? Was that why he had started with so much confidence? Stile's supposed strength had become his weakness, because of his opponent's superior research and preparation. If Hulk beat him, it would be because he had outplayed Stile in his area of strength: awareness of the hidden nuances of particular situations. He had turned the tables with extraordinary finesse, allowing Stile to lead himself into the trap.

Stile began to fall behind. He had to ease off, lest he faint; he had to reduce his oxygen consumption. He saw Hulk's back moving ever onward. Now Hulk was imbibing of his bottle, as if in no difficulty at all. What a show of strength! The lack of oxygen had to be hurting his lungs too, but he still could drink as he ran blithely on.

If the field malfunction extended for several kilometers, Hulk just might open up the necessary lead, and win by forfeit. Or, more likely, Hulk would win by forcing Stile to give up: endurance of another nature. Stile simply could not keep the pace.

He slowed to a walk, gasping. Hulk was now out of sight. Stile tramped on. There was another force-field intersection ahead. If that marked the end of the malfunction—

It did not. He entered a large tool shop. Robots worked in it, but human beings had been evacuated. The whole dome was low on oxygen.

Stile felt dizzy. He could not go on—yet he had to. The dome was whirling crazily about him as he ran. Ran? He should be walking! But Hulk was already through this dome, maybe back in oxygen-rich air, building up the critical lead while Stile staggered. . . .

A cleaning robot rolled up. "Refreshment—courtesy of Sheen," it said, extending a bottle.

Not having the present wit to question this oddity, Stile grabbed the bottle, put it to his mouth, squeezed.

Gas hissed into his mouth. Caught by surprise, he inhaled it, choking.

Air? *This was pure oxygen!*

Stile closed his lips about it, squeezed, inhaled. He had to guide his reflexes, reminding himself that this was not liquid. Oxygen—exactly what he needed! No law against this; he was entitled to any refreshment he wanted, liquid or solid—or gaseous. So long as it was not a proscribed drug.

"Thank you, Sheen!" he gasped, and ran on. He still felt dizzy, but now he knew he could make it.

Soon the oxygen gave out; there could not be much in a squeeze bottle. He wondered how that worked; perhaps the squeeze opened a pressure valve. He tossed

it in a disposal hopper and ran on. He had been recharged; he could make it to breathable territory now.

He did. The next field intersection marked the end of
the malfunction. Ah, glorious reprieve!

But he had been weakened by his deprivation of
oxygen, and had lost a lot of ground. Hulk must have
taken oxygen too—that was it! That strange bottle he
had nursed! Oxygen, hoarded for the rough run ahead!
Clever, clever man! Hulk had done nothing illegal or
even unethical; he had used his brains and done his
homework to outmaneuver Stile, and thereby had
nearly won his race right there. Now Stile would have
to catch up—and that would not be easy. Hulk was not
yet two kilometers ahead, for Stile had received no noti-
fication of forfeit; but he might be close to it. Hulk was
surely using up his last reserves of strength to get that
lead, in case Stile made it through the malfunction.

But if Hulk did not get the necessary lead, and Stile
gained on him, he still had to catch and pass him.
There were about thirty kilometers to go. Could he
endure? He had been seriously weakened.

He had to endure! He picked up speed, forcing his
body to perform. He had a headache, and his legs felt
heavy, and his chest hurt. But he was moving.

The track continued through the domes, scenic,
varied—but Stile had no energy now to spare for appreciation. His sodden brain had to concentrate on
forcing messages to his legs: lift-drop, lift-drop . . .
drop . . . drop. Every beat shook his body; the impacts
felt like sledgehammer blows along his spinal column.
Those beats threatened to overwhelm his consciousness.
They were booming through his entire being. He oriented on them, hearing a melody rising behind those
shocks. It was like the drumming of Neysa's hooves as
she trotted, and the music of her harmonica-horn came
up around the discomfort, faint and lovely. Excruciatingly lovely, to his present awareness. His pain became
a lonely kind of joy.

Beat—beat—beat. He found himself forming words
to that rhythm and tune. *Friend*ship, *friend*ship, *friend*-
ship, *friend*ship. *Friend*ship for *ever*, for *ever*, for *ever*,

for *ever. Friend*ship for *ever, u*niting, u*niting, u*niting. *Friend*ship forever uniting us *both, both, both.* Neysa was his friend. He started singing the improvised tune mostly in his head, for he was panting too hard to sing in reality. It was like a line of verse: anapestic tetrameter, or four metric feet, each foot consisting of three syllables, accented on the third. But not perfect, for the first foot was incomplete. But pattern scansion tended to be too artificial; then the pattern conflicted with what was natural. True poetry insisted on the natural. The best verse, to his way of thinking, was accent verse, whose only rhythmic requirement was an established number of accents to each line. Stile had, in his own poetic endeavors, dispensed with the artificiality of rhyme; meter and meaning were the crucial elements of his efforts. But in the fantasy frame of Phaze his magic was accomplished by rhyme. His friendship for the unicorn—

An abrupt wash of clarity passed through him as his brain resumed proper functioning. Neysa? What about Sheen? He was in Sheen's world now! Sheen had sent the oxygen!

Again he experienced his hopeless frustration. A tiny man had to take what he could get, even if that were only robots and animals. In lieu of true women.

And a surge of self-directed anger: what was wrong with robots and animals? Sheen and Neysa were the finest females he had known! Who cared about the ultimate nature of their flesh? He had made love to both, but that was not the appeal; they stood by him in his most desperate hours. He loved them both.

Yet he could not marry them both, or either one. Because he was a true man, and they were not true women. This was not a matter of law, but of his own private nature: he could be friends with anything, but he could marry only a completely human woman. And so he could not marry, because no woman worth having would have a dwarf.

And there was the ineradicable root again, as always: his size. No matter how hard he tried to prove his superiority, no matter how high on whatever ladder he rose, he remained what he was, inadequate. Because he was too small. To hell with logic and polite euphemisms; this was real.

Friendship forever, uniting us both. And never more than that. So stick with the nice robots and gentle animals; they offered all that he could ever have.

Sheen was there by the track, holding out a squeeze bottle. "He's tiring, Stile!" she called.

"So am I!" he gasped. "Your oxygen saved me, though."

"What oxygen?" she asked, running beside him.

"The robot—didn't you know there was a field deficiency along the route?"

"Didn't you take the detour?"

"We stuck to the original track. The air gave out. Hulk had oxygen, but I didn't. Until a robot—"

She shook her head. "It must have been my friend."

The self-willed machines—of course. They would have known what she did not. She had asked them to keep watch; they had done exactly that, acted on their own initiative when the need arose, and invoked Sheen's name to allay any possible suspicions. Yet they hadn't had to do this. Why were they so interested in his welfare? They had to want more from him than his silence about their nature; he had given his word on that, and they knew that word was inviolate. He would not break it merely because he washed out of the Tourney; in fact, they would be quite safe if his tenure ended early. Add this in to the small collection of incidental mysteries he was amassing; if he ever had time to do it, he would try to penetrate to the truth, here. "Anyway, thanks."

"I love you!" Sheen said, taking back the bottle.

Then she was gone, as he thudded on. *She* could love; why couldn't *he*? Did he need a damned program for it?

But strength was returning from somewhere, infusing itself into his legs, his laboring chest. His half-blurred vision clarified. Hulk was tiring at last, and Sheen loved him. What little meaning there was in his present life centered around these two things, it seemed. Was it necessary to make sense of it?

Stile picked up speed. Yes, he was stronger now; his world was solidifying around him. He could gain on Hulk. Whether he could gain enough, in the time/distance he had, remained to be seen, but at least he could make a fair try.

Why would a machine tell him she loved him?

Why would another machine help bail him out of a hole?

Stile mulled over these questions as he beat on with increasing power, and gradually the answers shaped themselves. Sheen had no purpose in existence except protecting him; how would she be able to distinguish that from love? And the self-willed machines could want him away from Proton—and the surest way to get him away was to make sure he entered the Tourney. Because if he failed to enter—which would happen if he lost this race—he would have three more years tenure, assuming he could land another employer. If he entered, he would last only as long as he continued winning. So of course they facilitated his entry. They were being positive, helping him . . . and their help would soon have him out of their cogs. Thus they harmed no Citizen and no man, while achieving their will.

Sheen was also a self-willed machine, subservient only to her program, her prime directive. Beyond that she had considerable latitude. She had entered him in the Tourney, in effect, by gaining him employment with a Citizen who was a major Game fan. Did *she*, Sheen, want his tenure to end? Yet she had no ulterior motive; his printout of her program had established that. His rape of her.

Rape—did she still resent that? No, he doubted it. She knew he had done what he had to, intending her no harm. He could not have known he was dealing with a self-willed machine, and he had apologized thereafter.

No, Sheen was doing what she felt was best for him. A jockey with bad knees and a Citizen enemy had poor prospects, so her options had been limited. She had done very well, considering that she had not even had assurance he would return to Proton, that first time he stepped through the curtain. She had done what an intelligent woman would do for the man she loved.

Onward. Yes, he was moving well, now—but how much ground did he have to make up? He had lost track of time and distance during his period of oxygen deprivation. Hulk might be just ahead—or still almost two kilometers distant. There was nothing for it except to run as fast as he could push it, hoping for the best.

Stile ran on. He went into a kind of trance, pushing his tired body on. For long stretches he ran with his eyes closed, trusting to the roughened edge of the track to inform him when he started to stray. It was a trick he had used before; he seemed to move better, blind.

He was making good time, he knew, almost certainly better than whatever Hulk was doing. But now his knees began to stiffen, then to hurt. He was putting more strain on them than he had since being lasered; ordinarily they bothered him only when deeply flexed.

He tried to change his stride, and that helped, but it also tired him more rapidly. He might save his knees—at the expense of his tenure. For if he won this race, and made it to the Tourney, then could not compete effectively because of immobile knees—

Would tenure loss be so bad? He would be forced to leave Proton, and cross the curtain to Phaze—permanently. That had its perverse appeal.

But two things interfered. First there was Sheen, who had really done her best for him, and should not be left stranded. Not without his best effort on her behalf. Second, he did not like the notion of losing this race to Hulk. Of allowing the big man to prove himself best. Not at all. Were these factors in conflict with each other? No, he was thinking that a loss in this marathon would wash out his tenure, and that was not quite so. Regardless, he had reason to try his hardest and to accept exile to Phaze only after his best effort here.

Stile bore down harder. To hell with his knees! He intended to win this Game. If that effort cost him his chance in the Tourney, so be it.

Suddenly, in a minute or an hour, he spied the giant, walking ahead of him. Hulk heard him, started, and took off. But the man's sprint soon became a lumber. Stile followed, losing ground, then holding even, then gaining again.

Hulk was panting. He staggered. There was drying froth on his cheek, extending from the corner of his mouth, and his hair was matted with sweat. He had carried a lot of mass a long way—a far greater burden than Stile's light weight. For weight lifting and wrestling, large muscles and substantial body mass were assets; for endurance running they were liabilities. Hulk was a superlative figure of a man, and clever too, and determined, and he had put his skills together to run one hell of a race—but he was overmatched here.

Stile drew abreast, running well now that his advantage was obvious. Hulk, in contrast, was struggling, his chest heaving like a great bellows, the air rasping in and out. He was at his wall; his resources were exhausted. Veins stood out on his neck. With each step, blood smeared from broken blisters on his feet. Yet still he pushed, lunging ahead, pulse pounding visibly at his chest and throat, eyes bloodshot, staggering so violently from side to side that he threatened momentarily to lurch entirely off the track.

Stile paced him, morbidly fascinated by the man's evident agony. What kept him going? Few people realized the nature of endurance running, the sheer effort of will required to push beyond normal human limits though the body be destroyed, the courage needed to continue when fatigue became pain. Hulk had carried triple Stile's mass to this point, using triple the energy; his demolition had not been evident before because Stile had been far back. Had Stile collapsed, or continued at a walking pace, Hulk could have won by default or by walking the remaining kilometers while conserving his dwindling resources. As it was, he was in danger of killing himself. He refused to yield, and his body was burning itself out.

Stile had felt the need to humble this man. He had done it, physically. He had failed, mentally. Hulk was literally bloody but unbowed. Stile was not proving his superiority, he was proving his brutality.

Stile was sorry for Hulk. The man had tried his best in an impossible situation. Now he was on the verge of heat prostration and perhaps shock—because he would not yield or plead for reprieve. Hulk had complete courage in adversity. He was in fact a kindred soul.

Stile now felt the same sympathy for Hulk he had felt for Sheen and for Neysa: those whose lot was worse than his own. Stile could not take his victory in such manner.

"Hulk!" he cried. "I proffer a draw."

The man barged on, not hearing.

"Draw! Draw!" Stile shouted. "We'll try another grid! Stop before you kill yourself!"

It got through. Hulk's body slowed to a stop. He stood there, swaying. His glazed eyes oriented on Stile. "No," he croaked. "You have beaten me. I yield."

Then Hulk crashed to the ground in a faint. Stile tried to catch him, to ease the shock of the fall, but was only borne to the track himself. Pinned beneath the body, he was suddenly overwhelmed by his own fatigue, that had been shoved into the background by his approach to victory. He passed out.

Stile survived. So did Hulk. It could have been a draw, since neither had completed the course, and they had fallen together. Hulk could have claimed that draw merely by remaining silent. But Hulk was an honest man. His first conscious act was to dictate his formal statement of concession.

Stile visited Hulk in the hospital, while Sheen stood nervous guard. She didn't like hospitals. Proton medicine could do wonders, but nature had to do some of it alone. It would be several days before Hulk was up and about.

"Several *hours*," Hulk said, divining his thought. "I bounce back fast."

"You did a generous thing," Stile said, proffering his hand.

Hulk took it, almost burying Stile's extremity in his huge paw. "I did what was right. I worked every angle I could, but you came through. You were the better man. You won."

Stile waved that aside. "I wanted to humble you, because you are so big. It was a bad motive. I'm sorry."

"Someday you should try being big," Hulk said. "To have people leery of you, staring at you, making mental pictures of gorillas as they look at you. Marveling at how stupid you must be, because everybody *knows* wit is in inverse proportion to mass. I wanted to prove I could match you in your specialty, pound for pound. I couldn't."

That did something further to Stile. The big man, seen as a freak. His life was no different from Stile's in that respect. He just happened to be at the other extreme of freakiness: the giant instead of the dwarf. Now Stile felt compelled to do something good for this man.

"Your tenure is short," he said. "You may not have time to reach the qualifying Rung. You will have to leave Proton soon. Are you interested in an alternative?"

"No. I do not care for the criminal life."

"No, no! A legitimate alternative, an honorable one. There is a world, a frame—an alternate place, like Proton, but with atmosphere, trees, water. No Citizens, no serfs, just people. Some can cross over, and remain there for life."

Hulk's eyes lighted. "A dream world! How does a man earn a living?"

"He can forage in the wilderness, eating fruits, hunting, gathering. It is not arduous, in that sense."

"Insufficient challenge. A man would grow soft."

"Men do use weapons there. Some animals are monsters. There are assorted threats. I think you would find it more of a challenge than the domes of Proton, and more compatible than most planets you might emigrate to, if you could cross the curtain. I don't know whether you can, but I think you might."

"This is not another world in space, but another

dimension? Why should I be able to cross, if others can't?"

"Because you came here as a serf. You weren't born here; you had no family here. So probably you don't exist in Phaze."

"I don't follow that."

"It is hard to follow, unless you see it directly. I will help you try to cross—if you want to."

Hulk's eyes narrowed. "You have more on your mind than just another place to live. Where's the catch?"

"There is magic there."

Hulk laughed. "You have suffered a delusion, little giant! I shall not go with you to that sort of realm."

Stile nodded sadly. He had expected this response, yet had been moved to try to make it up to the man he had humbled. "At least accompany me to the curtain where I cross, to see for yourself to what extent that world is real. Or talk to my girl Sheen. Perhaps you will change your mind."

Hulk shrugged. "I can not follow you today, but leave your girl with me. It will be a pleasure to talk with her, regardless."

"I will return to talk with you," Sheen told Hulk.

They shook hands again, and Stile left the room. Sheen accompanied him. "When I return to Phaze this time—" he began.

"I will tell Hulk what you know of that world," she finished. "Be assured he will pay attention."

"I will come back in another day to challenge for Rung Five. That will qualify me for the Tourney."

"But you are too tired to challenge again so soon!" she protested.

"I'm too tired to face the Yellow Adept too," he said. "But my friends must be freed. Meanwhile, we've already set the appointment for the Rung Five Game. I want to qualify rapidly, vindicating your judgment; nothing less will satisfy my new employer."

"Yes, of course," she agreed weakly. "It's logical."

She turned over the special materials he had ordered and took him to the proper section of the curtain. "My friends had an awful time gathering this stuff," she complained. "It really would have been easier if you had been a reasonable robot, instead of an unreasonable man."

"You have a reasonable robot in my image," he reminded her. "Be sure to reanimate him."

She made a mock-strike at him. "You know a robot can't compare to a real live man."

Stile kissed her and passed through.

CHAPTER 16

Blue

Stile emerged, as planned, just beyond the yellow fog that demarked the Yellow Demesnes. He could not, per his agreement and the curse Yellow had set against his return, enter that for himself—but he shouldn't need to. He set down the cage containing the owl and donned his clothing. In the pockets were a folded null-weight wetsuit and a metalsaw: the one to protect against thrown potions, the other to sever the cage bars. He hoped Kurrelgyre or Neysa would have the common sense to saw out a bar-section and use it as a lever to break the locks of the other cages. If they didn't, or if anything else went wrong—

Stile stifled that thought. He had to free his friends, one way or another. If he could not do it harmlessly, he would have to make arrangements to destroy the Yellow Adept—and he did not want to do that. She was not really a bad witch.

He stretched the pliant wetsuit into a cord and knotted it about the saw. He brought the owl out. "All right, owl. One service for me and you are free in this world, never again to serve man or to be caged." This was a modified owl, of high intelligence for its kind; it understood him. "Take this and drop it in the cauldron inside the yellow house." Stile presented the package of dry ice. "Take this and drop it in the unicorn's cage." He gave the bird the wetsuit-saw knot.

The owl blinked dubiously.

"Oh, you don't know what a unicorn is? Like a horse with a horn." The owl was reassured. "Then wing out of here—and out of there, quickly. You will be free. And if you should ever need me, let me know and I'll help you."

The owl took a package in each claw, spread its wings, and launched into the sky. "And don't let any liquid touch you, there!" Stile called after it.

He watched it go, hoping for the best. This was a jury-rigged effort, the best he could think of under the pressures of the moment. He wasn't sure what Proton artifacts would operate in Phaze, so was keeping it as simple as possible.

He was in luck. Soon he heard a scream from the witch. That would be the dry ice in the cauldron, making it bubble and steam through no agency of the Adept, interfering with the potion's effectiveness and releasing the owl from its spell, as well as distracting Yellow. Next could come the delivery of the suit and saw. After that, with luck, hell would break loose.

He waited nervously. So many things could go wrong! Then he heard the trumpeting of Darlin' Corey the pink elephant, and an increasing commotion among the captives. It grew into a considerable din, with bangings and crashes. Then at last shapes moved through the fog. A unicorn galloped toward Stile. It was Neysa —and she had a rider. Kurrelgyre, in man-form.

They arrived, and the werewolf dismounted. "My thanks to thee, fair mare. At such time as I may, I will return the favor." Then he handed the sword to Stile and changed back into wolf-form.

Stile stood for a moment, assimilating this. Why hadn't the werewolf simply run as a wolf, instead of performing the awkward, for him, feat of riding the unicorn? To carry the rapier, that he would otherwise have had to leave behind. His own clothing transformed with him, but the sword was foreign. He had wanted to return it to Stile. Why had Neysa tolerated this strange rider? Because she too had felt the need to return the sword. Yet it was no special weapon. It was the gift of her brother, belonging now to Stile—that was its only distinction. So they had both done it for him. Or so his present logic suggested. He was touched. "I thank you both. But I am chiefly glad you both are free without injury."

Kurrelgyre made a growl, and Neysa a note of assent. Neither was talking much, it seemed. Was this because they had not liked the necessity of working so closely together—or because they had liked it? That could be a serious complication for hereditary enemies.

"The Yellow Adept—was she hurt?"

Kurrelgyre changed back to man-form. "The witch brought me forth from my cage, fathoming my disguise," he said. "She claimed thou hadst sent her to me. And I, knowing not whether she spoke truth or lie, had to play along with her until I knew thy fate, intending to kill her if she had done thee harm. But she showed me thy prints going through the curtain, and told me how thou wouldst try to rescue us from afar, and said she would lay no traps against thee if I—"

"Yellowette is some fair witch," Stile said.

"I have been long absent from my were-bitch," Kurrelgyre agreed. "Yellow performs her business, as do we all. But ere she moved me, the potion wore off. . . ." He shrugged. "So I returned to my cage, to await thine effort. I could not flee in wolf-form because her summoning potion would have brought me back, and my man-form no longer wished to slay her."

"I believe she was willing to let thee go," Stile said. "But to save face, she could not do it until I launched mine effort. I suspect I owe her a favor."

"It seems some Adepts are people too," Kurrelgyre agreed grudgingly. "No animal harmed Yellow in the escape; they merely fled in different directions, and we too came here as soon as we winded thee." He returned to lupine form.

"Yellow told me who I am," Stile said.

The eyes of wolf and unicorn abruptly fixed on him.

"I am the Blue Adept." Stile paused, but neither gave any sign, positive or negative. "I know neither of you approve, but I am what I am. My alternate self was Blue. And I must know myself, as the Oracle said. I must go and set things straight at the Blue Demesnes."

Still they waited, not giving him any encouragement.

"I have freed you both from Yellow, as I had to," Stile continued. "I could not leave you in her clutches after both of you got there because of me. But now that

I know who I am, I can not ask either of you to help. I am the one that thou, Kurrelgyre, mayst not—"

The wolf shifted back into the man. "Too late, friend. I was lost when I met thee, knowing it not. The Oracle alone knew, when it told me to 'cultivate Blue.' I ask no favor of thee, but I will help thee investigate thine own situation. Perchance that which slew thine other self now lurks for thee at the Blue Demesnes, and a lupine nose will sniff it out in time."

"I thank thee, werewolf. Yet will I do no magic, so can not assist thee in thine own concern. It is a one-sided favor thou dost—" But Kurrelgyre had already reverted to wolf-form.

"And thee, Neysa," Stile continued. "I—"

The unicorn made a musical blast of negation. She gestured marginally with her nose, indicating that he should mount. Relieved, Stile did so. He remained tired from the marathon, and it was a great comfort to be on Neysa again. Now he could relax, for a little while, recovering from that grueling run. He needed about two days off his feet, to recuperate, but the time simply wasn't there. If he delayed his approach to the Blue Demesnes, Yellow might spread the word, and whatever lurked there would be thoroughly prepared for his arrival. He had to get there first.

Should he ask for another sniff of wolfsbane? No—that magic might not work for him as well a second time, and in any event he preferred to ride out his problems with his own strength, not leaning on magic too often.

Stile did not know where the Blue Demesnes were, but Kurrelgyre did. He led Neysa eastward at a fast clip. They moved back along the route they had come originally, through forest and field and badlands, hardly pausing for rest or food. Stile explained along the way about his need to report back to Proton on the morrow, so the two creatures were determined to get him where he was going before he had to return to Proton. Kurrelgyre did not pause to hunt, and Neysa never grazed despite Stile's urgings.

At length they passed the place where he had tamed

the unicorn: the start of that wild ride. So short and yet so long a time ago! They proceeded without pause to the castle Stile had first seen from his survey from the tall tree. Back virtually to his starting point—had he but known!

Dawn was breaking in its unmitigated splendor as they approached the castle. Stile, asleep on Neysa, had missed the pretty moonrisings and settings of the night. He squinted at the castle blearily. He had barely four hours left before his match for Rung Five in Proton—and he hadn't even settled the situation in Phaze yet. If only Blue hadn't been so far from Yellow—

Stile had slept, but it seemed the tensions of his mission had prevented him from unwinding properly. If the Blue Adept had really been murdered, who had done the deed? If Blue's magic had not saved him, how could Stile survive without the aid of magic? Yet this was the way it had to be. Even if magic had been permitted him, he would not be prepared with suitable verses.

Yet he still had to check this castle out. To know, finally, exactly what his situation was. Whatever it might be, whatever it might cost him. The Oracle had told him to know himself, and he believed it was good advice.

The environs of the Blue Demesnes were surprisingly pleasant. There was no black fog or yellow fog—not even any blue fog. Just the pure blue sky, and a lovely blue lake, and fields of bluebells and blue gentians and bluegrass. To Stile's eye this was the most pleasant of places—not at all like the lair of an Adept.

Still, he could not afford to be deceived by superficialities. "I think it would be best to enter in disguise, as before," Stile said. The animals agreed.

This time Stile donned Neysa's socks, while Kurrelgyre assumed man-form. Then the seeming man led the two seeming unicorns up to the castle gate.

The drawbridge was down across the small moat, and the gate stood open. An armed human guard strode forward, but his hand was not near his sword. He was, of course, garbed in blue. "What can we do for thee, man?" he inquired of Kurrelgyre.

"We come to see the Blue Adept," the werewolf said.
"Thine animals are ill?"

Surprised, Kurrelgyre improvised. "One has bad knees."

"We see not many unicorns here," the guard observed. "But surely the Lady Blue can handle it. Come into the courtyard."

Stile was startled. This was the first he had heard of a Lady Blue. How could she be the Adept, if the original had been a man, and was now dead? Unless she had been his wife. This complicated the picture considerably!

"But we wish to see the Adept himself," the werewolf protested.

"If thou'rt dying, thou seest the Adept," the guard said firmly. "If thine animal hath bad knees, thou seest the Lady."

Kurrelgyre yielded. He led his animals through the gate, along the broad front passage, and into the central court. This was similar to one of the courts of the palace of the Oracle, but smaller; it was dominated by a beautiful blue-blossomed jacaranda tree in the center. Beneath the tree was a deep blue pond fed by a rivulet from a fountain in the shape of a small blue whale that overhung one side. The Blue Adept evidently liked nature in all its forms, especially its blue forms. Stile found his taste similar.

There were several other animals in the yard: a lame jackrabbit, a snake with its tail squished, and a partly melted snow monster. Neysa eyed the last nervously, but the monster was not seeking any trouble with any other creature.

A maidservant entered the yard, wearing a blue print summer dress. "The Lady will be with thee soon," she said to Kurrelgyre. "Unless thou art in immediate pain?"

"No pressing pain," the werewolf said. He was evidently as perplexed by all this as Stile was. Where was the foul nature an Adept was supposed to have? If the Blue Adept were dead, where was the grief and ravage?

They might have had to fight their way into the castle; instead it was completely open and serene.

The girl picked up the snake carefully and carried it into the castle proper.

What was this, Stile wondered—an infirmary? Certainly it was a far cry from the Black or Yellow Demesnes, in more than physical distance. Where was the catch?

The girl came for the rabbit. The snake had not reappeared; was it healed—or dead? Why did the animals trust themselves to this castle? Considering the reputation of Adepts, these creatures should have stayed well clear.

Now another woman emerged. She wore a simple gown of blue, with blue slippers and a blue kerchief tying back her fair hair. She was well proportioned but not spectacular in face or figure. She went directly to the snow-monster. "For thee, a freeze-potion," she said. "A simple matter." She opened a vial and sprinkled its contents on the monster. Immediately the melt disappeared. "But get thee safely back to thy mountain fastness; the lowlands are not safe for the likes of thee," she admonished it with a smile that illuminated her face momentarily as if a cloud had passed from the face of the sun. "And seek thee no further quarrels with fire-breathing dragons!" The creature nodded and shuffled out.

Now the woman turned to Kurrelgyre. Stile was glad he was in disguise; that daylight smile had shaken him. The woman had seemed comely but ordinary until that smile. If there were evil in this creature, it was extraordinarily well hidden.

"We see not many unicorns here, sir," she said, echoing the sentiment of the guard at the gate. Stile was startled by the appellation, normally applied only to a Citizen of Proton. But this was not Proton. "Which one has the injured knees?"

The werewolf hesitated. Stile knew his problem, and stepped in. The unicorn costume was for sight only; any touch would betray the humanness of the actual body.

300

"I am the one with the knees," he said. "I am a man in unicorn disguise."

The Lady turned her gaze on him. Her eyes were blue, of course, and very fine, but her mouth turned grim. "We serve not men here, now. Why dost thou practice this deceit?"

"I must see the Blue Adept," Stile said. "Adepts have not been hospitable to me, ere now. I prefer to be anonymous."

"Thou soundest strangely familiar—" She halted. "Nay, that can not be. Come, I will examine thy knees, but I can promise nothing."

"I want only to see the Adept," Stile protested. But she was already kneeling before him, finding his legs through the unicorn illusion. He stood there helplessly, letting her slide her fingers over his boots and socks and up under his trouser legs, finding his calves and then at last his knees. Her touch was delicate and highly pleasant. The warmth of it infused his knees like the field of a microwave therapy machine. But this was no machine; it was wonderfully alive. He had never before experienced such a healing touch.

Stile looked down—and met the Lady's gaze. And something in him ignited, a flame kindled in dry tinder. *This was the woman his alternate self had married.*

"I feel the latent pain therein," the Lady Blue said. "But it is beyond my means to heal."

"The Adept can use magic," Stile said. Except that the Blue Adept was dead—wasn't he?

"The Adept is indisposed," she said firmly. She released his knees and stood with an easy motion. She was marvelously lithe, though there were worry-lines about her mouth and eyes. She was a lovely and talented woman, under great strain—how lovely and how talented and under how much strain he was now coming to appreciate by great jackrabbit bounds. Stile believed he knew what the nature of that strain might be.

Kurrelgyre and Neysa were standing by, awaiting Stile's decision. He made it: he bent carefully to draw

301

off the unicorn socks, revealing himself undisguised. "Woman, look at me," he said.

The Lady Blue looked. She paled, stepping back. "Why comest thou like this in costume, foul spirit?" she demanded. "Have I not covered assiduously for thee, who deservest it least?"

Stile was taken aback. He had anticipated gladness, disbelief or fear, depending on whether she took him for her husband, an illusion, or a ghost. But this—

"Though it be strange," the Lady murmured in an aside to herself. "Thy knees seemed flesh, not wood, and there was pain in them. Am I now being deluded by semblance spells?"

Stile looked at the werewolf. "Does this make sense to thee? Why should my knees not be flesh? Who would have wooden knees?"

"A golem!" Kurrelgyre exclaimed, catching on. "A wooden golem masquerading as the Adept! But why does she cover for the soulless one?"

The Lady whirled on the werewolf. "Why cover for thy henchman!" she exclaimed, her pale cheeks flushing now in anger. "Should I let the world know my love is dead, most foully murdered, and a monster put in his place—and let all the good works my lord achieved fall into ruin? Nay, I needs must salvage what I can, holding the vultures somewhat at bay, lest there be no longer any reprieve or hope for those in need. I needs must sustain at least the image of my beloved for these creatures, that they suffer not the horror I know."

She returned to bear on Stile, regal in her wrath. "But thou, thou fiend, thou creature of spite, thou damned thing! Play not these gruesome games with me, lest in mine agony I forget my nature and ideals and turn at last on thee and rend thee limb from limb and cut out from thy charred bosom the dead toad that is thy heart!" And she whirled and stalked into the building.

Stile stared after her, bathed in the heat of her fury. "There is a woman," he breathed raptly.

Neysa turned her head to look at him, but Stile was hardly aware of the import of her thought. The Lady

Blue—protecting her enemy from exposure, for the sake of the good work done by the former Blue Adept. Oh, what a wrong to be righted!

"I must slay that golem," Stile said.

Kurrelgyre nodded. "What must be, must be." He shifted to wolf-form and sniffed the air. Then he led the way into the castle.

Stile followed, but Neysa remained in the courtyard. She had run almost without surcease for a day and night, carrying him, and her body was so tired and hot she could scarce restrain the flames of her breath. Kurrelgyre, unfettered, had fared better; but Neysa needed time by herself to recover.

No one sought to stop them from entering the castle proper. The guard at the gate had been the only armed man they encountered, and he was back at his station. There were a few household servants, going innocently about their businesses. There was none of the grimness associated with the demesnes of the other Adepts he had encountered. This was an open castle.

The wolf followed his nose through clean halls and apertures until they arrived at a closed door. Kurrelgyre growled: the golem was here.

"Very well, werewolf," Stile said. "This needs must be my battle; go thou elsewhere." Kurrelgyre, understanding, disappeared.

Stile considered momentarily, then decided on the forthright approach. He knocked.

There was, as he expected, no answer. Stile did not know much about golems, but did not expect much from a construct of inanimate materials. Yet, he reminded himself, that was what the robot Sheen was. So he had to be careful not to underestimate this thing. He did not know the limits of magical animation. "Golem," he called. "Answer, or I come in regardless. Thine impersonation is at an end."

Then the door opened. A man stood there, garbed in a blue robe and blue boots. He was, Stile realized, the exact image of Stile himself. His clothing differed in detail, but a third party would not know the two of them apart.

"Begone, intruder, lest I enchant thee into a worm and crush thee underheel," the golem said.

So golems could talk. Good enough.

Stile drew his rapier. For this had werewolf and unicorn labored so diligently to return his weapon to him! "Perform thy magic quickly, then, impostor," he said, striding forward.

The golem was unarmed. Realizing this, Stile halted without attacking. "Take a weapon," he said. "I know thou canst not enchant me. Dost thou not recognize me, thou lifeless stick?"

The golem studied Stile. The creature was evidently not too bright—unsurprising if its brains were cellulose —but slowly Stile's aspect penetrated. "Thou'rt dead!" the golem exclaimed.

Stile menaced him with the sword. "*Thou* art dead, not I."

The golem kicked at him suddenly. Its move was almost untelegraphed, but Stile was not to be caught off guard in a situation like this. He swayed aside and clubbed the creature on the ear with his left fist.

Pain lanced through his hand. It was like striking a block of wood—as he should have known. This was a literal blockhead! While he paused, shaking his hand, the golem turned and butted him in the chest. Stile braced himself just in time, but he felt dull pain, as of a rib being bent or cartilage torn. The golem bulled on, shoving Stile against the wall, trying to grab him with hideously strong arms. Stile knew already that he could not match the thing's power.

Unarmed? The golem needed no overt weapon! Its body was wood. Stile got his sword oriented and stabbed the torso. Sure enough, the point lodged, not penetrating. This thing was not vulnerable to steel!

Now he knew what he was up against. Stile hauled up one of his feet and got his knee into the golem's body as it tried to butt again. His knee hurt as he bent it, but he shoved the creature away. The golem crashed against the far wall, its head striking with a sharp crack —but it was the wall that fractured, not the head.

Stile took a shallow breath, feeling his chest injury,

and looked around. Kurrelgyre was back, standing in the doorway, growling off other intruders. This would remain Stile's own personal fight, like a Game in the Proton-frame. All he had to do was destroy this undead wooden dummy. Before it battered him into the very state of demise he was supposedly already in.

He no longer had qualms about attacking an un-armed creature. He studied the golem. The creature might be made of wood, animated by magic, but it still had to obey certain basic laws of physics. It had to have joints in its limbs, and would be vulnerable in those joints, even as Stile was. It had to hear and see, so needed ears and eyes, though these would probably function only via magic. Whoever had made this golem must have a real knack for this kind of sorcery. An-other Adept, most likely, specializing in golems.

The golem came—and Stile plunged the point of his rapier like a hypodermic into the thing's right eye. The golem, evidently feeling no pain, continued forward, only twisting its head. The sword point, lodged in the wood, was wrenched about. It snapped off.

Stile had not been expert with this weapon, so this was less of a loss than it might have seemed. He aimed the broken end at the golem's other eye. But the crea-ture, aware of the danger, retreated. It turned and crashed through the window in the far wall.

Stile pursued it. He leaped through the broken window—and found himself back in the courtyard, where Neysa had been pacing restlessly, breathing out her heat. She paused, startled, at the appearance of the golem. Her eyes informed her it was Stile, with one eye destroyed, but her nose was more certain. She made an angry musical snort.

The golem cast about with its remaining eye. It spied the fountain-whale. It grabbed the statuary in both arms and ripped it from its mooring.

Neysa, alarmed, charged across the courtyard, her horn aimed at the golem. "Don't stab it!" Stile cried. "The thing is wood; it could break thy horn!"

As he spoke, the golem heaved the whale at him. The statue was solid; it flew like a boulder. Neysa leaped at

Stile, nosing him out of the way of it. The thing landed at her feet, fragmenting.

"Art thou all right, Neysa?" Stile cried, trying to get to his feet without bending his knees too far.

She gave a musical blast of alarm. Stile whirled. The golem was bearing down on him with a whale fragment, about to pulp his head.

Neysa lifted her head and snorted a jet of flame that would have done credit to a small dragon. It passed over Stile and scored on the golem.

Suddenly the golem was on fire. Its wood was dry, well-seasoned, and filled with pitch; it burned vigorously. The creature dropped the whale fragment and ran madly in a circle, trying to escape its torment. Blows and punctures might not bother it, but fire was the golem's ultimate nemesis.

Stile stared for a moment, amazed at this apparition: himself on fire! The golem's substance crackled. Smoke trailed from it, forming a torus as the creature continued around its awful circle.

And Stile, so recently out to destroy this thing, experienced sudden empathy with it. He could not let it be tortured in this fashion. He tried to quell his human softness, knowing the golem was a literally heartless, unliving thing, but he could not. The golem was now the underdog, worse off than Stile himself.

"The water!" Stile cried. "Jump in the pond! Douse the fire!"

The golem paused, flame jetting out of its punctured eye to form a momentary halo. Then it lurched for the pool, stumbled, and splashed in. There was a hiss and spurt of steam.

Stile saw Neysa and Kurrelgyre and the Lady Blue standing spaced about the courtyard, watching. He went to the pond and kneeled, carefully. The golem floated face down, its fire out. Probably it didn't need to breathe; still—

Stile reached out and caught a foot. He hauled it in, then wrestled the body out of the pond. But the golem was defunct, whether from the fire or the water Stile could not tell. It no longer resembled him, other than in outline. Its clothing was gone, its painted skin scorched, its head a bald mass of charcoal.

"I did not mean it to end quite this way," Stile said soberly. "I suppose thou wast only doing thy job, golem, what thou wert fashioned for, like a robot. I will bury thee."

The gate guard appeared. He looked at the scene, startled. "Who is master, now?"

Startled in turn, Stile realized that he should be the master, having deposed the impostor. But he knew things weren't settled yet. "Speak to the Lady," he said.

The guard turned to her. "A wolf comes, seeking one of its kind."

Kurrelgyre growled and stalked out to investigate.

"Speak naught of this outside," the Lady Blue directed the guard. Then she turned to Stile. "Thou'rt no golem. Comest thou now to destroy what remains of the Blue Demesnes?"

"I come to restore it," Stile said.

"And canst thou emulate my lord's power as thou dost impersonate his likeness?" she asked coldly.

Stile glanced at Neysa. "I can not, Lady, at this time. I have made an oath to do no magic—"

"How convenient," she said. "Then thou needst not prove thyself, having removed one impostor, and thou proposest to assume his place, contributing no more to these Demesnes than he did. And I must cover for thee, even as I did for the brute golem."

"Thou needst cover for nobody!" Stile cried in a flash of anger. "I came because the Oracle told me I was Blue! I shall do what Blue would have done!"

"Except his magic, that alone distinguished my lord from all others," she said.

Stile had no answer. She obviously did not believe him, but he would not break his oath to Neysa, though he wanted above all else to prove himself to the Lady Blue. She was such a stunning figure of a woman—his alternate self had had tastes identical to his own.

Kurrelgyre returned, assuming man-form. "A member of my pack brings bitter news to me," he said. "Friend, I must depart."

"Thou wert always free to do so," Stile said, turning to this distraction with a certain relief. "I thank thee for thy help. Without seeking to infringe upon thy prerogatives, if there is aught I can do in return—"

"My case is beyond help," the werewolf said. "The pack leader has slain mine oath-friend, and my sire is dying of distemper. I must go slay the pack leader—and be in turn torn apart by the pack."

Stile realized that werewolf politics were deadly serious matters. "Wait briefly, friend! I don't understand. What is an oath-friend, and why—?"

"I needs must pause to explain, since I shall not be able to do it hereafter," Kurrelgyre said. "Friendship such as exists between the two of us is casual; we met at random, part at random, and owe nothing to each other. Ours is an association of convenience and amicability. But I made an oath of friendship with Drowltoth, and when I was expelled from the pack he took my bitch—"

"He stole thy female?" Stile cried.

"Nay. What is a bitch, compared to oath-friendship? He took her as a service to me, that she be not shamed before the pack. Now, over a pointless bone, the leader has slain him, and I must avenge my friend. Since I am no longer of the pack, I may not do this legitimately; therefore must I do it by stealth, and pay the consequence, though my sire die of grief."

Oath-friendship. Stile had not heard of this before, but the concept was appealing. A liaison so strong it pre-empted male-female relations. That required absolute loyalty, and vengeance for a wrong against that friend, as for a wrong against oneself. Golden rule.

Yet something else nagged him. Stile pursued it through the tangled skein of his recent experience, integrating things he had learned, and caught it.

"There is another way," he said. "I did not grasp it before, because this frame evidently has a more violent manner of settling accounts than I am used to. Here, perhaps, it is proper to kill and be killed over minor points of honor—"

"Of course it is!" the werewolf agreed righteously.

"Just so. My apology if I misinterpret thine imperatives; I do not wish to give offense. But as I perceive it, thou couldst rejoin thy pack. Thou hast only to kill thy sire—"

"Kill my sire!" Kurrelgyre exclaimed. "I told thee—"

"Who is dying anyway," Stile continued inexorably. "Which death would he prefer—a lingering, painful, ignominious demise by disease, or an honorable, quick finish in the manner of his kind, as befits his former status, by the teeth of one he knows loves him?"

The werewolf stared at Stile, comprehending.

"And thus thou'rt restored to thy pack, having done thy duty, and can honorably avenge thine oath-friend, without penalty," Stile concluded. "And take back thy bitch, who otherwise would be shamed by the loss of both wolves she trusted."

"The Oracle spoke truly," Kurrelgyre murmured. "I did cultivate Blue, and Blue hath restored me to my heritage. I thought it was the anathema of Adept magic I was fated to receive, but it was the logic mine own canine brain was too confused to make."

"It was only an alternate perspective," Stile demurred. "I have yet to grasp the full import of mine own Oracular message."

"I will gnaw on that," the werewolf said. "Perhaps I shall come upon a similar insight. Farewell, meantime." And he shifted to wolf-form and moved out.

Stile looked at the sun. The day was three hours advanced. The challenge of Rung Five—in just one hour! He barely had time to get there. Fortunately, he knew exactly where the curtain was, and where his original aperture was. He had to move!

Yet he was hardly finished in this frame. He had slain the golem, with Neysa's help, but had little idea how to proceed here; he might do best to remove himself from this frame for a while, hoping for insights. Hoping to know himself better. What did he really want? That depended, in part, on how things fell out on Proton.

"I, too, have business elsewhere," Stile said. "I must

309

reach the curtain quickly, and get someone to spell me through."

Neysa brightened. She stepped up to him. She would handle it.

He mounted, and they galloped off. Neysa was still hot from her prior exertions, but knew Stile's deadline. In moments she had carried him into the pasture where they had first met.

"Neysa, I think it would be best if thou shouldst stay at the Blue Demesnes while I visit the other frame. I'd appreciate it if thou wouldst inform the Lady Blue about Proton, as thou hast heard it from the werewolf and from me; I don't think she knows." He felt a momentary *déjà vu*, and placed it: this was similar to the manner he was having Sheen tell Hulk about Phaze.

Neysa stiffened. "Is something wrong?" Stile asked.

She blew a note of negation, and relaxed. Stile, intent on the precise location of the curtain-site, did not pursue the matter. Such a short time to reach the Game-annex!

They reached the place in the forest where Stile had first entered this frame. The curtain was there, shimmering more strongly than before. Perhaps he had simply become better attuned to it. Stile divested himself of his clothes. "I will return to the Blue Demesnes within a day, I hope. If thou wilt spell me through now—"

She made a musical snort—and he was through the curtain, emerging in the service area behind the food machines. Only then did he wonder about the unicorn's reticence. Something was bothering Neysa—and now it was too late to ask her about it.

Well, he was sorry, but he was in a hurry. He had twenty minutes to reach the Game-annex, or forfeit.

CHAPTER 17

Tourney

He made it. The holder of Rung Five was Hair, who of course was almost bald. He was a well-balanced player, without many great strengths, but also without many weaknesses. That made him hard to handle on the grid. Hair would be playing to Stile's liabilities, not to his own strengths, and have a pretty good chance to land an advantageous game.

Hair studied Stile. "You look tired," he remarked.

"Apt observation," Stile agreed. Naturally his opponent knew all about yesterday's marathon run. Hair would capitalize on this, choosing the PHYSICAL column. Stile would negate this by going into MACHINE- or ANIMAL-assisted, so as not to have to depend on his own diminished strength. Of course Hair would anticipate that, and shift his column, perhaps into ART. He was good on the theremin. Stile was quite ready to challenge in the classification of music, but would prefer a normal, hand-powered instrument. So he would be better off in TOOL, where he could wind up with something like a trombone or a harmonica. In fact, the harmonica would be very nice right now, because he had been practicing it in the other frame.

But Hair had after all stuck with PHYSICAL, outmaneuvering him. 1B, tool-assisted physical games. The second grid appeared as the murmur of the audience rose.

Stile had the letter facet again. If he chose INDIVIDUAL, he could get caught in another endurance or strength exercise, and he was hardly up to it. If Hair selected BALL, it might work out to bowling, where Stile could win—or shot-put, where he could not. Hair was no Hulk, but he could heave an object a fair distance.

	1. BALL	2. VEHICLE	3. WEAPON	4. ATHLETIC	5. GENERAL
A. INDIVIDUAL					
B. INTERACTIVE					

Or he could go for VEHICLE, and they would be in a canoe race or bike race or skating race. Stile was fast on skates, but his legs were tired; this was not his day. WEAPONS was no better. He wasn't ready to bend a powerful bow to shoot at a target 300 meters distant. His aim would surely suffer. His separated cartilage in the rib cage gave a twinge; no, he could not draw a bow! But throwing the javelin or hammer was no better. Nor was pole-vaulting—God, no!—in the next box, or skiing, or even sledding. He pictured himself whomping belly first on a small sled and shooting the ice rapids, and his rib cage gave a worse twinge. Only in GENERAL did he have a fair chance, with things like hopscotch, horseshoes, or jacks. Or tiddlywinks—major Games had been won and lost in that game, with the audience as avidly breathless as it would have been for a saber match. Stile was expert in tiddlywinks—but knew he would not get to play them this time.

So it had to be INTERACTIVE. That had its pitfalls too, but in general skill was more important than power.

It came up 1B. Interactive ball games. Good—Stile was skilled in most of these, and should be able to take Hair—so long as Hair did not catch on to his special liabilities, like the ribs or the bruised left hand. Oh, that wooden head of the golem, that he had so blithely punched!

They set up the nine-box subgrid, filling in with marbles, *jeu de boules*, croquet, billiards, tennis, table-soccer, Ping-Pong, soccer and Earthball. The last would be a disaster; Stile played to avoid it, and the result was Ping-Pong.

Well, not good, but not bad. Stile was excellent at this sport, and his right hand remained good, but he would be off his game today. Hair was good enough to take advantage of Stile's present weaknesses—if he caught on to them in time.

They adjourned to the table-games gym. A number of games were in progress—pool, table-soccer, and of course Ping-Pong—but these were quickly wrapped up when the players saw who was coming. Stile's move up the ladder was already big news. They took a table, picked up the paddles, and volleyed. Several minutes were permitted for limbering prior to the game.

"Time," the machine scorekeeper announced. "Select service."

They did it in the archaic, time-honored fashion, similar to that for the game of Go. Hair took the ball, put it under the table in one hand, and spread his arms apart. Stile chose the right—and got it. He had the first serve.

It was a good break for him, for Stile was an offensive player whose serve was integral to his strategy. He needed to take and keep the initiative, to make up for his lack of reach. He would not be able to win points directly from his serve, against a player of Hair's caliber, but he could certainly put the man safely on the defensive. That was the way Stile liked it. It gave him necessary options. Of course the serve would change every five points—but once he had the lead, he could ride through to victory without pushing himself. Considering his present liabilities, that was important.

Stile served, a cross-court top-spin ball, fast and low over the net, striking neatly two centimeters from the back edge of the table. Hair returned it cautiously with an undercut to the center of Stile's court. The game was on.

Stile backhanded the ball with a flick of the wrist, to Hair's forehand court. Move it about, keep the other player reaching! Never let the opponent get set for his own strategy. Hair returned it to Stile's forehand, somewhat high and shaky, with almost no spin. Good—he was nervous! That diminished Stile's own tension. This was going his way. Stile made a forehand slam and took the point.

Stile served again the moment he had the ball, backhand crosscourt with an undercut. Hair flubbed it again. The score was 2–0. Hair was more visibly nervous now. Excellent. The psychology of nervousness was important in any competition.

But Hair's next return, played too low, nevertheless dribbled over the net, unreturnable. 2–1. These lucky shots occurred; it was usually of no significance. Only when the luck played obvious favorites, as sometimes happened despite the assurances of the experts on probability, was it a critical factor. Stile fired in a sidespin, and Hair sent it wide of the table. 3–1.

The next volley went longer, but Stile finally put it away with a good cross-court slam. 4–1. This game was not going to be a problem.

Now it was Hair's serve. He uncorked a weak dropshot that barely cleared the end of the table; Stile, expecting a harder shot, almost muffed it. But his return was a setup, and Hair put it away for the point. 2–4. In Ping-Pong the server's score was always listed first.

There was something funny about Hair's style, and in moments he took two more points. Stile bore down, overreached himself, and lost another. Now he was behind. Carelessness!

But the run continued. Stile suddenly seemed unable to do right. In moments he was behind 4–10, having lost nine points in a row, his own serve no longer helping him.

What was wrong? He had started well, then lost it. Had fatigue undercut him more than he realized, interfering with his precision? Stile didn't think so. He was playing well enough to win—except that he was losing. Why?

He served a dropshot that barely cleared the table. Hair returned it too softly; it was a setup shot that Stile swiftly put away. 5–10. Strange that the return had been so soft; Hair knew better.

Then Stile caught on. Hair was using a random-variable surface paddle! This was legal, as standards for table-tennis bats had never been instituted; but also tricky, for precision placement was difficult. The variations of bounce were not great, which was why it had not been obvious, but Stile should have noticed it before. *That* was how his fatigue let him down; he had not been alert to the unexpected.

In an instant Stile knew what he had to do. The variable-surface returns forced Hair to play conservatively, keeping his shots well within the margin of safety, though that sometimes set shots up for Stile. But Hair was aware of that. Stile, unaware, had been playing aggressively—and so those slightly changed returns had fouled him up more than his opponent. The more points he lost, the more aggressively he had played, aggravating the situation. A difference in ball velocity and travel so small as to be imperceptible to an onlooker could play havoc with a style like Stile's.

He couldn't handle it. Hair was good enough so that the paddle gave him the edge. Had Stile caught on early he could have played more conservatively himself, holding his lead, forcing Hair to make more aggressive shots that were increasingly risky. But with a 5–10 deficit that strategy wouldn't work; Stile was the one who had to get aggressive. And lose.

He had been suckered, just as he had in the marathon detour. His opponent had outplayed him, off the grid. Stile was in deep trouble again.

So—he had to change his game. He had to go all the way defensive. He needed to allow time and distance to analyze each return individually. This wasn't his normal game, but he had no choice now.

He tried. He had not played a lot of Ping-Pong recently—how could he, with all that had been going on in two worlds!—and had kept in shape only in his natural game. Offense. Spins, placements, slams, changes-of-pace—all fouled up by the marginal uncertainty of the variable-surface paddle. Now, thrown back on a long-neglected resource, he seemed to be in worse trouble yet. He lost a point, and another. 12–5. Soon the gap would be too large to close; sheer chance would give a few points to Hair in the end.

But Stile worked at it, making his shots high and

central and safe. This set him up neatly for Hair, who quickly adapted to the situation and started getting more aggressive. Hair had more leeway now; he could afford to indulge a normally weak offense. Stile was only digging himself in deeper.

Yet he had to do it. He extended himself, despite twinges from his rib cage, adapting to this mode. He could judge the shots better now, for he was playing far back, and he was getting the feel of it. He did know how to do it; he had only to remember, to dredge up long-unused reflexes. He fought the next point, covering all Hair's maneuvers, and won it. And lost the next. He still had not quite worked it out—and he needed to, because the point of no return was coming close.

The audience was hushed by this remarkable turn of the game. Now an announcer could be heard from the supposedly soundproofed telebooth. ". . . strangest Ping-Pong game of the season . . . Stile, the favorite, far behind and playing as if he wants to lose it worse yet . . . will be an inquest to determine whether someone has been paid off . . ."

As if he didn't have enough of a problem already! They thought he was throwing this game! That some other Citizen had proffered him lucrative employment if he missed the Tourney this year. Fortunately the computer analysis of the recording would refute that; all Stile's lost points were honest ones. But if he lost, what difference would it make whether it were honest or dishonest? He would still be finished. In this world, anyway.

But that was not the way he wanted to depart Proton. He had to recover this game!

Stile played the next serve carefully, extending the volley. He needed practice at this defensive game, and the longer the volleys continued the more practice he would get. He won the point, bringing up the change of service at 13–7.

His turn to serve—but if he used it to take the offense, he would lose. He had to give up his normal advantage, for the sake of his strategy, not breaking his continuity.

He served gently—and heard the response of the audience. Most of the watchers did not know why he had been missing points, and thought he was being driven to defense by the strength of Hair's offense. They thought he was foolish to throw away his principal weapon. The serve had always been his tool for the initiative. Some spectators were already leaving, satisfied that Stile had lost.

Hair was glad to continue the offense. He had nothing to gain by indulging in prolonged volleys. Now that Stile had neutralized the paddle-weapon, longer volleys would only give Hair more chances to make mistakes. He needed to put away his points quickly, before Stile got his defensive game in full shape, even if he lost two points for one.

But already Stile was strengthening. The volleys stretched out. Hair lost one, won two—but now he was sweating. Hair was not accustomed to continuous offensive, and as Stile's resistance stiffened—technically, became more fluid—Hair began to make errors of his own. The scales were balancing.

Still, Stile's knees limited him, and his ribs. His reach was minimal in the best of circumstances, and was even more restricted now. He had not quite closed the gap in skills, in this inverted mode, and the game was running out.

They exchanged more points, bringing the score to 17–10 during Hair's service. A seven-point deficit, with only four points to go for Hair. This was bad; if Stile did not rally now, strongly, he was done for.

Hair served. Stile returned it high and center, well toward the back edge so that Hair's shot would have plenty of distance to travel. A setup for a slam, but not for a trick shot. Hair had to hit it hard and long. He did, placing it to Stile's backhand, and Stile returned it with a smooth undercut. His ball arced over, slowing as it dropped, forcing Hair to strike with another undercut lest he lose control. An undercut, backspinning ball in Ping-Pong was a strange shot with special properties; it reacted in the air, on the table, and against the paddle, requiring careful handling.

In the ancient days of cork-, sandpaper- or rubber-surfaced paddles this was not too tricky; but as these gave way to foam rubber and specialized semi-adhesive synthetics the spin-imparting capacities of paddles had become devastating. It was possible to make a ball loop in air, or execute an almost right-angle turn as it bounced. However, such trick shots required skill and energy, and were obvious to a good player, who could then handle them with efficient counterspins. The spin on the incoming ball could be as devastating as the spin going out, making these surfaces a liability to the user, if he were not experienced. The key was to slip in spins that the opponent was not aware of—until too late, when he missed the shot.

Stile, playing back and often below the level of the table, had greater leeway in this respect, now, than Hair did. Hair knew it and was nervous—and doubly care-ful. He could not uncork full slams lest the hidden spin of the ball send them wide. Stile's proficiency in the mode was increasing, and the advantage was coming to him, at last. But that seven-point deficit—

Stile delivered a swooping undercut sidespin ball that struck the table and took off at an impressive angle. But Hair was ready for it. He countered the spin in the course of a soft-shot. The ball barely cleared the net, and would have dribbled three times on Stile's side be-fore it cleared the table—had not Stile dived to inter-cept it in time. As it was, he got it back—but only in the form of a high spinless setup.

Hair pounced on his opportunity. He slammed the ball off the backhand corner. Stile leaped back to inter-cept it, getting it safely over the net—but as another setup. Hair slammed again, this time to Stile's forehand corner, forcing him to dive for it. Stile felt a pain in his rib cage; he got the ball back, but at the expense of aggravating his recent injury. He was in extra trouble now! But he would not give up the point; he had worked too hard for it already.

Hair slammed again, driving him back. Had Hair been a natural offense player, Stile would have been finished; but these slams lacked the authority they needed. Stile managed to return it, again without adequate spin. Hair slammed yet again, harder. Stile retreated far to the rear, getting on top of it, and sent it back. But he had misjudged; the ball cleared the net, but landed too near it and bounced too high. Hair had a put-away setup. Stile braced desperately for the bullet to come—

And Hair made a dropshot. The ball slid off his paddle, bounced over the right edge of Stile's court, and headed for the floor. A sucker shot. Stile had fallen for it.

Stile, nonsensically, went for it. He launched himself forward, paddle hand outstretched. His feet left the floor as he did a racing bellyflop toward that descending ball. He landed and slid, his ribs parting further— but got his paddle under the ball three centimeters above the floor and flicked it up, violently.

From the floor Stile watched that ball sail high, spinning. Up, up, toward the ceiling, then down. Would it land on the proper side of the net? If it did, Hair would put it away, for Stile could never scramble back in time. Yet he had aimed it to—

The ball dropped beyond his line of sight. Hair hovered near, hardly believing his shot had been returned, primed for the finishing slam when the ball rebounded high. It was clearing the net, then!

Stile heard the strike of the ball on the table. Then hell broke loose. There was a gasp from the audience as Hair dived around the table, reaching for an impossible shot, as Stile had done. But Hair could not make it; he fell as his hand smacked into the net support. Then Hair's shoulder took out the center leg of the table, and the table sagged.

Underneath that impromptu tent, Hair's gaze met Stile's as the robot scorekeeper announced: "Point to Stile. Score 17–11."

"Your backspin carried the ball into the net before I could get to it," Hair explained. "Unless I could fetch it from the side as it dribbled down—"

"You didn't need to try for that one," Stile pointed out. "I made a desperation move because I'm up

319

against my point of no return, but you still have a six-point margin."

"Now he tells me," Hair muttered ruefully. "I don't think of that sort of thing when I'm going for a point."

"Your hand," Stile said. "It's bleeding."

Hair hauled his paddle hand around. "Bleeding? No wonder! I just broke two fingers—going for a point I didn't need."

It was no joke. A robot medic examined the hand as they climbed from the wreckage of the table, and sprayed an anesthetic on it. Shock had prevented Hair from feeling the pain initially, but it was coming now. Little scalpels flashed as the robot went to work, opening the skin, injecting bone restorative, resetting the breaks, binding the fingers in transparent splint-plastic.

"I don't think I'll be able to finish the game," Hair said. "I'm not much for left-handed play."

"Stile—by TKO!" someone in the audience exclaimed. Then there was foolish applause.

Rung Five was his. Stile had qualified for the Tourney. But he did not feel elated. He had wanted to win it honestly, not by a fluke. Now no one would believe that he could have done it on his own.

Hulk intercepted them as they left the Game premises. He looked a little wobbly, but was definitely on the mend. He had a rugged constitution. "Stile, about that offer—"

"Still open," Stile said with sudden gladness.

"Your girl was persuasive."

"Sheen has a logical mind," Stile agreed.

"I have nothing to lose," Hulk said. "I don't believe in magic, but if there's a primitive world there, where a man can prosper by the muscle of his arm and never have to say 'sir' to a Citizen—"

"See for yourself. I'm going there now."

"Stile, wait," Sheen protested. "You have injuries! You're worn out. You need rest, attention—"

Stile squeezed her hand. "There is none better than what you provide, Sheen. But across the curtain is a

320

Lady and a unicorn, and I fear they may be jealous of each other. I must hurry."

"I know about Neysa," she said. "She's no more human than I am, and why she puts up with you is beyond my circuitry. But now you have a lady too? A real live girl? What about *my* jealousy?"

"Maybe I broke in at the wrong time," Hulk said.

"Do not be concerned," Sheen told him sweetly. "I'm only a machine."

Stile knew he was in trouble again.

"You are a robot?" Hulk asked, perplexed. "You made a reference, but I thought it wasn't serious."

"All metal and plastics and foam rubber," Sheen assured him. "Therefore I have no feelings."

Hulk was in difficulty. His eyes flicked to the lusher portions of her anatomy that jiggled in most humanly provocative fashion as she walked, then guiltily away. "I thought—you certainly fooled me!" He bit his lip. "About the feelings, I mean, as well as—"

"She has feelings," Stile said. "She's as volatile as any living creature."

"You don't have to lie for me, Stile," Sheen said, with just that stiffness of body and voice that put him in his place. She had become expert at the human manner!

"Lie?" Hulk shook his head. "There's one thing you should know about Stile. He never—"

"She knows it," Stile said tiredly. "She's punishing me for my indiscretion in finding a living woman." .

"Sorry I mixed in," Hulk muttered.

Stile turned to Sheen. "I did not know I would encounter the Lady in the Blue Demesnes. I did not realize at first what she was. I destroyed the golem that had impersonated me, but did not realize the complications until later."

"And now that you do realize, you are eager to return to those complications," Sheen said coldly. "I understand that is man's nature. She must be very pretty."

"You want me to look out for Neysa's interest, don't you?" Stile said desperately, though he had the sensation of quicksand about his feet. "She's there in the Blue Castle, alone—"

"The Lady," Sheen interrupted with new insight. "The Lady Blue? The one your alternate self married?"

"Oh-oh," Hulk murmured.

Stile spread his hands. "What can I do?"

"Why couldn't I have been programmed to love a male robot!" Sheen exclaimed rhetorically. "You fleshmen are all alike! The moment you find a flesh-woman—"

"It's not like that," Stile protested. "She is devoted to the memory of her husband—"

"Who resembled you exactly—"

"She told me off when—"

"When you tried what?" she demanded.

Now Stile raised his hands in surrender. "If I stay here four hours longer—?"

"Eight hours," she said firmly.

"Six."

"Six. And you promise to return for the Tourney, after—"

"Yes."

"That will give me time to put my own affairs in order," Hulk said.

Sheen laughed. Oh, yes, she had her reactions down almost perfect now.

CHAPTER 18

Oath

They tried it and it worked: Hulk passed through the curtain. He stood amazed and gratified, looking around at the forest. It was dawn; Sheen had managed to hold Stile for more like eighteen hours, the last half of which was sleeping. Well, he had been in dire need of the rest, and she had treated him with assorted minor medical aids including a restorative heat lamp, so that he really felt much better now.

"I never saw anything so beautiful," Hulk said, gazing at the brightening world.

"Yes, it is that," Stile agreed. He had tended to forget the sheer loveliness of this land, when involved in other things. If all else were equal, he would prefer Phaze to Proton, for its natural beauty.

Hulk had brought along a costume, per Stile's advice. Now he watched Stile getting into his own. "Are you sure—?"

"That ordinary people wear clothes here? I'm sure. Another thing: the language differs slightly. You have to—"

He was interrupted by a sudden loud hissing. A smoke-exhaling serpent rose up, flapping its wings menacingly. It was a small dragon.

Stile backed off warily, but the dragon followed, sensing compatible prey. One spell could have banished it, but its fiery breath made a sword uncertain. In any event, Stile no longer had his sword. He retreated farther.

"Let me try my beast-man ploy," Hulk said. He jumped forward, bellowed incoherently to get the dragon's attention, then raised both arms in a dramatic muscleman pose. It was extraordinarily impresssive. He had spent years perfecting a body that was a natural marvel. He danced about, beating his chest and growling. He looked altogether, foolishly menacing.

The dragon turned tail and flapped off, whimpering. Stile dissolved in laughter.

Hulk abated his antics, smiling. "That was fun. You often don't need to fight, if you just look as if you'd like to. Was that thing really what it looked like?"

"Yes. This really is a land of fantasy. When you struck that pose, you looked like an ogre."

"Literal ogres exist here?"

"I believe they do. I've never actually seen one, but I'm sure that's the correct analogy."

Hulk looked dubiously at his costume, then started putting it on. "I didn't really believe in the magic aspect. I thought it might be matter transmission and odd effects."

"I had the same problem, at first. But it is better to believe; magic can kill you, here."

"I'll take my chances. It's like another aspect of the Game, with its special subset of rules. But it puts me in doubt what to do here. I don't know the first thing about magic."

"Most people don't practice it," Stile said. "But you do have to be aware of it, and there are certain conventions. Maybe you'd better come with me, until you catch on. I'm going to the Blue Demesnes."

"What would I do in colorful demesnes? I know even less about courtly manners than I do about magic, and if Sheen's suspicions about your Lady are correct, I should not be a witness."

"You might serve as my bodyguard."

Hulk laughed. "Since when do you need a bodyguard? You can beat anyone in your weight class in general combat, regardless of age."

"Here opposition doesn't necessarily come in my weight class. It comes in yours. Someone is trying to kill me, sending things like demon monsters after me. I would feel easier if a good big man were keeping an eye out. You are conversant with hand weapons—"

"All part of the Game," Hulk agreed.

324

"You could play dumb, like a monster, until you picked up the ways of this world, then go out on your own. You can cross back to Proton any time, too, by making a spell to pass you through the curtain."

"You have some status in this world? So it wouldn't look strange to have a brute bodyguard?"

"It seems I do. Or will achieve it shortly. If I survive the efforts of my anonymous enemy. So I'd really appreciate it if you—"

"You are a generous man, Stile. You do me a favor in the guise of asking for one."

Stile shrugged. Hulk was no fool. "I'll tell people I removed a thorn from your paw. But don't consider it too much a favor. There is danger. You could get killed, associating with me."

"I could get killed just running the marathon! Let's go."

They went. Stile led the way north as the sun cleared the forest and angled its fresh bright shafts between the branches, seeking the ground. They trotted across the opening fields toward the Blue Demesnes. As the castle came into view, a sun ray reflected from its highest turret in brilliant blue. This too, Stile thought, had to be added to the class of most beautiful things.

Then he paused. "Do you hear it, Hulk?"

Hulk listened. "Ground shaking. Getting louder."

"I don't know whether dragons stampede or whether they have earthquakes here. We'd better hurry."

They hurried. As they crossed the plain around the castle they saw it: a herd of animals charging toward the same object.

"Look like wild horses," Hulk said.

"Unicorns. What are they doing here?"

"A whole herd? Could be coming to the aid of one of their number. Wild animals can be like that."

"Neysa!" Stile cried. "If something happened to her—"

"We had better get over there and see," Hulk said.

"I should never have let Sheen delay me!"

"I doubt you had much choice in the matter, and we both did need the rest. Is Sheen really a robot?"

"She really is. Not that it makes much difference."

"And Neysa really is a horse—a unicorn who turns into a woman?"

"That too. And a firefly. You will see it soon enough —if all is well." Stile was increasingly nervous about that.

They ran, moving into the marathon pace. Neither man was in condition for it, because this was too soon after the real one they had run. But this was not to be the full course. They approached the Blue Demesnes.

But the unicorns were moving faster. Now their music sounded across the field, like a percussion-and-wind orchestra. In the lead was a great stallion whose tone was that of a fine accordion; on the flanks were lesser males whose horns were muted or silent. Evidently unicorns were not gelded, they were muted in public. In the center ran the mass of mature mares, carrying the burden of the melody. The stallion would play the theme, and the mares would reiterate it in complex harmonies. It was an impressive charge, visually and sonically.

Now, from the west appeared another group, dark and low to the ground, moving faster than the unicorns. Stile struggled to make it out. Then he heard the baying of a canine-type, and understood. "Wolves! Probably werewolves!" he cried.

"I am ignorant of conventions here, apart from what Sheen told me of what you had told her," Hulk puffed. "But is such convergence of herd and pack usual?"

"Not that I know of," Stile admitted. "It could be Kurrelgyre, returning with friends—but I don't see why. Or it could be the pack leader Kurrelgyre went to kill; if he were victorious, and sought revenge on the person who helped Kurrelgyre—I don't know. They certainly look grim."

"Werewolves and unicorns are natural enemies?"

"Yes. And both are normally unfriendly to man. Kurrelgyre and Neysa learned to get along, but—"

"Now I'm no genius and this is not my business, but it strikes me that the arrival of these two forces at this time strains coincidence. Could this relate to you? If

326

there were some alert, some way they would be aware of the moment you re-entered this frame—"

"That's what I'm afraid of," Stile said. "You see, I'm a natural magician in this frame—a focus of much power. But I have sworn off magic."

"And your frame-wife would like you to break that oath," Hulk said. "So you can preserve the Blue Demesnes from further harm. And the animals would want you to keep your oath, so you will not become anathema to them. These two types of animals may just be united—against you. You were not joking about needing a bodyguard!"

"You catch on rapidly," Stile agreed.

The two of them picked up speed though both were tiring, in an effort to reach the castle before either herd or pack. But it soon became evident that they would not succeed. The unicorn herd would arrive first, then the wolves.

Now the wolf pack veered, orienting on Stile instead of the castle. There seemed to be ninety or a hundred of them, large dark animals with heavy fur and gleaming eyes and teeth that showed whitely with their panting. "I hope, despite my reasoning, that they're on our side," Hulk said, slowing to a walk.

The wolves ringed them. One came forward, and shifted into man-form. A fresh scar ran across one cheek, and his left ear was missing. But it was Stile's friend.

"Kurrelgyre!" Stile exclaimed. "Thou wast victorious!"

"That was not in question, once thou hadst shown me the way," the werewolf replied. He peered at Hulk. "This monster-man—friend or foe?"

"Friend," Stile said quickly.

"Then I sniff tails with thee, ogre," Kurrelgyre said, extending his hand to Hulk.

"Sure," Hulk agreed awkwardly, taking the hand. He seemed to be having some trouble believing the transformation he had just seen.

"Hulk is from the other frame," Stile said quickly. "My bodyguard. He doesn't talk much." And he flashed

Hulk a warning glance. "To what do I owe the pleasure of this visit?"

"I fear I wronged thee inadvertently," the werewolf said. "I returned to my pack, but could not kill my sire without first explaining why—"

"You killed your—" Hulk began, startled.

Kurrelgyre turned, half-shifting into wolf-form. "Thou addressest me in that derogatory mode and tone?" he growled.

"He knows not our ways!" Stile cried. "Even as I did not, at first, and thou didst have to set me straight. He meant thee no offense."

The werewolf returned all the way to man-form. "Of course. I apologize for mistaking thy intent," he said to Hulk. "It remains a sensitive matter, and in a certain respect thou resemblest the type of monster that—"

"He understands," Stile said. "We all make errors of assumption, at first. Why shouldst thou not explain to thy sire? It was the kindest thing thou couldst do for one already ill to death."

Hulk nodded, beginning to understand. A mercy killing. Close enough.

"I came to my sire's den," Kurrelgyre said grimly. "He met me in man-form, and said, 'Why comest thou here? This place is not safe for thee, my pup.' I replied, 'I come to slay thee, as befits the love I have for thee, my sire, and the honor of our line. Then will I avenge mine oath-friend Drowltoth, and restore my bitch to prominence in the pack.' Hardly did he betray his dignity, or yield to the ravage of distemper I perceived in him; in that moment he stood as proud as I remembered him of old. 'I knew thou wouldst thus return in honor,' he said. 'How didst thou come to accept what must be done?' I told him, 'A man persuaded me, even as the Oracle foretold.' And he asked, 'Who was this good man?' and I replied, 'The Blue Adept,' and he asked, 'How is it that an Adept did this thing for thee?' I said, 'He was dead, and his double comes from the other frame to restore his demesnes.' Then my sire looked beyond me in alarm, and I turned and discovered that others of the pack had come up silently during my distraction, and overheard. Thus the pack knew that the Blue Demesnes were in flux, and the word spread quickly. And my bitch spoke, and said, 'Of all the Adepts, Blue alone has been known to do good works among animals, and if that should change—' "

"But that will not change!" Stile protested.

"I tried to tell them that. But mine own kind doubted, and when the unicorns learned that Neysa was prisoner at the Blue Demesnes—"

"Prisoner! She's not—" But Stile had to stop. "*Is* she?"

"We know not. But the unicorn stallion is of imperious bent."

"Well, if she is a prisoner, that will cease the moment I get there. But thou hast not finished thy story."

"It is simple enough," Kurrelgyre said. "The pack leader came, and my sire said, 'It is time.' We changed to wolf-form, and quickly and cleanly I tore the throat out of my sire, and knew then that I had done right, and never did I see a wolf so glad to die. I then whirled and challenged the pack leader while yet my sire's corpse lay steaming, and my right could not be denied before the pack. The pack leader was not so eager to die. He fought, and perhaps he injured me." Kurrelgyre smiled briefly, touching the stump of his ear. "His throat I did not tear; that were too honorable a demise for such a cur. I hamstrung him, spiked both his eyes, tore out his tongue, and drove him with bitten tail into the wilderness to die lame and blind among the monsters. It was an excellent reckoning."

Stile concealed his reaction to this savage tale of vengeance. Perhaps he would have done something similar, in a similar circumstance. "And thy bitch is well?" he inquired, glancing at the female wolf who stood nearest.

"As well as one might be, following exile of her stud, slaughter of his oath-friend, and forced heat to the pack leader. But she will recover. I am now pack leader, and she remains my chosen; all other bitches whine before her."

"A fitting resolution," Stile said, hoping that Hulk

had now grasped enough of the situation to avoid any further errors of manner.

"Yet she is marked," Kurrelgyre continued. "She it was who made me see that the mare needed support."

"Neysa," Stile agreed. "But I assure thee—"

Now the bitch shifted to woman-form. She was pretty enough, with a wild orange flare of hair, but did look peaked. She must have had as hard a recent life as the Lady Blue, and survived it as toughly. "What mode of man art thou," she demanded of Stile, "to trust thy female friend to the power of thy wife?"

"The Lady Blue is not my wife," Stile protested.

"Perhaps not so long as the mare lives. I know somewhat of these things." Surely an understatement! "When the mare is dead, thou wilt be freed of thine oath, and practice magic—"

"No!" Stile cried.

"I tried to tell her thou wert true," Kurrelgyre said. "No way wouldst thou harm the mare—"

"And like my wolf, innocent of the ways of the bitch," the female werewolf finished. "The mare is of a species we honor not, as they attempt to rival us as rulers of the wilds, but she brought thee to my love, and thou hast sent him home to me and to the honor he was due. I owe the mare. I perceive the danger thou dost not. The Lady Blue knows no limits to her determination to maintain her lord's demesnes. If thou savest not the mare, I will avenge her in the manner of an oathfriend, though there be no oath between us."

Could she be right? Had Stile sent Neysa to her doom in the Blue Demesnes? What a colossal miscalculation! Yet Neysa could take care of herself, and the Lady was no Adept. "If she is not safe, I will avenge her myself," Stile said. But he could not make an oath of it. Suppose the Lady Blue had—

"Others know thee not as I do," Kurrelgyre said. "So I felt it best to be on the scene when the herd arrived, lest unwarranted blame fall on thee. Thou mayest need guidance."

"I may indeed," Stile agreed. What a complex situation had blown up in his brief absence!

They proceeded toward the castle. The unicorns had drawn up before its gate, their music fading out. They were waiting for Stile to arrive. There were about fifty of them, almost evenly divided between mares and lesser males, with the huge stallion in front. The stallion stood some eighteen hands high at the shoulder, more than thirty centimeters—about a foot—above Stile's head, and all his mass was functional. A truly impressive creature.

Hulk studied the stallion with open admiration. Indeed, the two were similar, in proportion to their species.

Stile halted, for the unicorns blocked the way. The werewolves ranged beside him, grim but neutral. They were here because their new pack leader had brought them at the behest of his bitch; they were not too keen on unicorns, but also not too keen on human beings. Hulk stood back, heeding Stile's admonishment to be silent. There was much here that was not yet properly understood.

"Dost thou seek to bar me from my heritage?" Stile asked the stallion.

The unicorn did not answer. His glance fell on Stile from an impressive elevation, bisected by the long and deadly spiraling horn. His head was golden, his mane silver, and his body a nacreous gray deepening into black fetlocks and hooves. His tail matched his mane, beautifully flowing, reflecting the light of the sun almost blindingly. No horse ever had this coloration or this rugged splendor.

After a moment the stallion snorted: a brief accordion treble punctuated by two bass notes. One of the lesser males stepped forward, shifting shape. It was Clip, Neysa's brother. "I helped thee at my sister's behest," he said. "What hast thou to say for thyself now?"

"I mean to enter that castle and see how Neysa is doing," Stile said. But Kurrelgyre's remarks, and the apprehension of the bitch with regard to the conflict between the unicorn mare and the Lady Blue made him queasy. Had he really betrayed his steed and friend into doom? Had Neysa suspected it when she left him?

What kind of a woman was the Lady Blue, really, and what would she do with the associate of the man who had destroyed the golem impostor? Stile had thought she would be grateful, but she certainly had not greeted him with open arms.

Yet how could he believe that his alternate self, his likeness in every respect except environment, had married a woman who would callously murder any creature who stood in her way? Had the Lady Blue shown anything other than a sincere and praiseworthy dedication to her late husband's cause and memory? Yet again, if she knew that Stile alone could restore the greatness of the Blue Demesnes, hindered only by a foolish oath—

"And if she lives, what then?" Clip demanded. "The Herd Stallion demands to know."

"What does the Herd Stallion care about Neysa?" Stile retorted, knowing that in this respect he was voicing the sentiment Clip could not voice. "She was excluded from the herd for no valid reason. She's as pretty and fine a mare as any in the herd, I'll warrant. She should have been bred long ago."

Clip hesitated, understandably. He was at the moment the mouthpiece for his superior, yet his sister's welfare was dearest to his heart and he was loath to refute Stile's statement. "Thou hast not answered the Stallion's question. What will ye with Neysa—if she survives the treachery of Blue?"

"Treachery of Blue!" Stile cried in sudden fury. "*I* am Blue!" But he felt Hulk's hand on his shoulder, warning him to restraint. Without his magic, he could not really be the Blue Adept.

The unicorn herd faced him silently, and so did Kurrelgyre's bitch. Stile realized it was a fair question, and a hard one. No one had actually accused the Lady of murder; the question was about Stile's own loyalties. He was, potentially, the most powerful person here. If the Lady were exonerated, what would he do then?

"If you take Neysa into the herd, and breed her and treat her as befits a mare of quality, I welcome it. Otherwise she is welcome to stay with me, and be my honored steed, as long as she wishes."

"And what of thine oath to her?"

"What of it?" Stile snapped.

"What of Neysa, when thou breakest that oath?"

Stile suffered another abrupt siege of wrath. "Who claims I am a breaker of oaths?"

"The Stallion claims," Clip said with a certain satisfaction.

For a moment Stile's anger choked off his speech. His hand went for his sword, but slapped only cloth; he had no sword now. Only Hulk's firm, understanding hand held him back from a physical and foolish assault on the huge unicorn.

Kurrelgyre stepped forward and spoke instead. "I was with this man when the Black Adept imprisoned him, but he did no magic, though he was dying of thirst and knew that the simplest spell, such as even any one of us might do, would bring him water and freedom. He freed us from the clutch of the Yellow Adept without magic. He slew the golem of the Blue Demesnes by hand, without magic. He showed me how to regain my status in the pack, using no magic. Now he comes again to this frame—without magic. Never in my presence has he violated his oath. If the Stallion snorts otherwise, the Stallion offends me."

The Herd Stallion's horn flicked, glinting in the sun. He pawed the ground with one massive forehoof. The lesser males drew in to flank him, and the mares shifted position, every horn lowering to point forward. The unicorns were beautiful, garbed in their naturally bright reds, blues and greens, but they meant business.

The hairs on Kurrelgyre's neck lifted exactly like the hackles of a wolf, though he retained man-form. His pack closed in about him, wolves and bitches alike, with an almost subvocal snarling. They were quite ready to pick a quarrel with unicorns!

"Hark," Hulk said. He was the only one with the height and direction to see over the massed unicorns. "The Lady comes. And a small unicorn."

Stile felt abruptly weak with relief. The Herd Stallion turned, and snorted a triple-octave chord. The herd parted, forming a channel. Now everyone could see the

Lady Blue and Neysa walking from the castle gate, side by side, both healthy. There had, after all, been no trouble. No overt trouble.

The Lady was lovely. She wore a pale-blue gown, blue flower-petal slippers, and pointed blue headdress. Stile had admired her form before, but now she had flowered into matchless beauty. He had, in the past hectic hours, forgotten the impact the touch of her hands had had on him. Now, with his fear for Neysa's safety eased, his memory came back strongly, and his knees felt warm. What a woman she was!

And Neysa—what of her? She tripped daintily along beside the Lady, her black mane and tail in perfect order, her hooves and horn shining. She was beautiful too. Stile had never seen his relationship with her in terms of choice; he had tacitly assumed she would always be with him. But Neysa was more than a steed, and his association with her had been more than that of a man and animal. If he became the Blue Adept, not only would he practice the magic that she abhorred, he would take to himself the human woman. Stile and Neysa—they could not continue what had been. That disruption had been inevitable from the moment of the discovery that he could perform powerful magic. The wolves and other unicorns had understood this better than he had; they were more familiar with the imperatives of this world. Yet how could he betray Neysa?

They came to stand before Stile. Stile inclined his head, honoring formalities, though he had no notion what was about to happen. One issue had been defused; Neysa lived. The other issue remained to be settled. "Hello, Neysa. Hello, Lady Blue."

The two females made a slight nod, almost together, but did not speak. The Herd Stallion snorted another chord. "Choose," Clip said, translating.

"By what right dost thou make such demand of me?" Stile cried, reacting with half-guilty anger.

"The Stallion is responsible for the welfare of his herd," Clip replied. "He permitted thee to use a surplus mare, an she be not abused. But now she has yielded

334

her loyalty to thee, thou mayst not cast her aside with impunity."

"If I cast her aside, she returns to the herd," Stile replied, hating the words, but his caution was being overridden by his emotion. "Art thou trying to force me to do this—or *not* to do this?"

"An thou dost cast her aside, it is shame to the herd, and that shame must be abated in blood. Thou keepest her—or thou payest the consequence. The Stallion has so decreed."

"The Stallion is bloated with gas," Kurrelgyre growled. "Knows he not that he challenges the Blue Adept? With a single spell this man could banish this whole herd to the snows."

"Save that he made an oath of no magic to my sister," Clip retorted. "An he honors that oath, he has no need to banish any creature."

For the first time the Lady Blue spoke. "How convenient," she said dulcetly, as she had the first time Stile had met her.

Kurrelgyre turned on her. Stile remembered that the werewolf had left them just before this subject came up, yesterday. "What meanest thou, human bitch?"

If this were an insult—and Stile could not be sure of that—the Lady gave no sign. "Knowest thou not, wolf, that I have harbored an impostor these past ten days, lest news escape of the murder of my husband?" she demanded disdainfully. "Now another image comes, claiming to be Blue—but Blue is distinguished chiefly by his magic, the strongest in all the Land of Phaze— and this impostor performs none, as thou thyself hast testified so eloquently. Were he in sooth the alternate of my husband, he could indeed banish the herd from these demesnes; since he is not, he pleads an oath. I have no slightest doubt he has been true to his oath, and will remain true; he is in fact incapable of breaking it. He is not Blue."

Neysa's head swung angrily about, and she made a harmonica-snort that made the other mares' ears perk up in mute shock. The Lady's lips thinned. "The mare believes he is Adept. She is enamored of him. Has any other person or creature witnessed his alleged magic?"

Even Kurrelgyre had to admit he had not. "The oath was made before I met him. Yet I have no reason to doubt—"

"Without magic, thou hast no debate with the Stallion about the impostor's choice. He shall not be with me. Let him stay with the mare he has deluded."

Neysa's snort seemed to have the tinge of fire. So did the Stallion's. Stile suddenly appreciated how cleverly the Lady was maneuvering them all. Neither wolves nor unicorns really wanted Stile to show his magic, and Neysa was dead set against it—yet now all of them were on the defensive as long as he did not. And if he did perform magic—the Lady won. She needed that magic to maintain the Blue Demesnes, and she would, as Kurrelgyre's bitch had pointed out, do anything necessary to accomplish that purpose. Again he thought: what a woman she was!

"We have galloped here for the sake of a false Adept?" Clip demanded for the Stallion. "We have allowed the wish-fancy of a dwarf-mare to embarrass the herd?"

Once again Stile felt the heat rising. That word dwarf, now applied to Neysa . . .

Kurrelgyre looked at Stile, uncertain now. "Friend, I believe in thee, in thy honor and thy power. But I can not send my pack into battle on thy behalf without some token of thy status. Thou must be released from thine oath."

Stile looked helplessly at Neysa, who snorted emphatic negation. Stile could not blame her; his magic had accidentally sent her once to hell. Without magic he would not be able to assume the role of the Blue Adept, so would not be tempted to leave her. He knew this was not entirely selfish on her part; she feared he would be corrupted by magic. Stile was not sure her fear was unfounded; the other Adepts had certainly been corrupted to some degree, either by their magic or by the circumstance of being Adept. Yellow had to commit the atrocity of animal slavery in order to secure

336

her position with other Adepts; Black had to go to extraordinary extremes to isolate himself. If these people did not do such things, they could be killed by others who were less scrupulous. To be Adept was to be somewhat ruthless and somewhat paranoid. Could he, as Blue, withstand those pressures? The former Blue Adept seemed to have succeeded—and had been murdered. A lesson there?

"Without magic, there is no need for battle," Stile said. "Let the wolves and unicorns go home. Neysa and I will go our way." Yet he was not sure he could stay away from this castle or the Lady Blue. His destiny surely lay there, and until he understood the Blue Demesnes completely he had not really honored the Oracle's directive. To know himself, he had to know the Blue Adept.

Now the Stallion blew a medley of notes. "If thou art false, and caused this trouble for naught, needs must I slay thee," Clip translated. "If thou art true, thou wilst betray the mare who helped thee, and needs must I avenge her. Defend thyself in what manner thou canst; we shall have an end to this insult." And the huge unicorn stepped toward Stile.

Stile considered jumping onto the Stallion's back and riding him, as he had the first time with Neysa. But Stile was in worse shape than he had been then, and the Stallion was more than twice Neysa's mass. The chances of riding him were slim. But so were the chances of defeating him in honest combat—even had Stile had his rapier.

Kurrelgyre stepped between them. "What coward attacks the smallest of men, knowing that man to be unarmed and bound to use no magic?"

The Stallion's horn swung on the werewolf. The bitch shifted into wolf-form and came at the Stallion's off-side, snarling. But Kurrelgyre retained man-form. "Dost thou challenge the pair of us, unicorn? That were more of a fair match."

The lesser male unicorns stepped forward—but so did the other werewolves. Two for one. "Not so!" Stile

337

cried, perceiving needless mayhem in the making. "This is my quarrel, foolish as it may be, not thine."

"With bad knees, fatigue from a marathon run, separated ribs, and a bruised hand—against that monster?" Hulk inquired. "This is a job for your bodyguard. I daresay a karate chop at the base of that horn would set the animal back."

The Stallion paused. He glanced at Kurrelgyre and his bitch, then at Hulk. He snorted. "No one dares call the Herd Stallion coward," Clip said. "But his proper quarrel is not with thee, werewolf, nor with the ogre. It is with the impostor. Let Stile confess he is no Adept, and he will be spared, and the foolish mare chastened."

"Yes," the Lady Blue agreed. "It were indeed folly to fight because of an impostor."

Such an easy solution! All parties agreed on the compromise. Except for Neysa, who knew the truth, and Kurrelgyre, who believed it, and Stile himself. "I abhor the prospect of bloodshed here, but I will not confess to a lie," Stile said firmly.

"Then show thy magic!" Clip said.

"Thou knowest mine oath—"

The Stallion snorted. Neysa looked up, startled but adamant. "Release him of his vow," Clip translated for Stile's benefit.

"Now wait!" Stile cried. "I will not tolerate coercion! You have no right—"

Kurrelgyre raised a cautioning hand. "I hold no great affection for this horny brute," he said, indicating the Stallion. "But I must advise thee: he has the right, friend. He is the Herd Stallion. Even as my pack obeys me, so must his herd, and every member of it, obey him. So must it ever be, in this frame."

The Stallion snorted again, imperatively. Slowly Neysa bowed her horn. She played one forlorn note.

"Thou art released," the werewolf said. "Now the challenge is fair. I may no longer interfere. Use thy magic to defend thyself, Adept."

Stile looked again at Neysa. She averted her gaze. Obviously she had been overruled. She did not like it, but it was, as the werewolf had pointed out, legitimate.

By the custom of this frame, Stile had been released. He could use his magic—and would have to, for the Stallion was bringing his horn to bear, and there was no doubting his intent; and not one wolf would come to Stile's defense. To avoid magic now would be in effect to proclaim a lie, and that would not only cost Stile his life, it would shame those who had believed in him. He had to prove himself—for Kurrelgyre's sake and Neysa's sake as well as his own. Even though that would give the Lady the victory she had so cleverly schemed for.

But Stile was unprepared. He had not formulated any devastating rhymes, and in this sudden pressure could think of none. His magic was diffuse, uncollected without music. In addition, he didn't really want to hurt the Stallion, who seemed to be doing a competent job of managing his herd, with the exception of his treatment of Neysa. Why should anyone believe a man who claimed to be able to do magic, but never performed? Such a claimant should be put to the proof—and that was what the Stallion was doing.

Stile saw the Lady Blue watching him, a half-smile on her face. She had won; she had forced him to prove himself. He would either manifest as the Blue Adept—or die in the manner of an impostor on the horn of the Stallion. Vindication or destruction! Beside her, Neysa remained with gaze downcast, the loser either way.

"I am sorry, Neysa," Stile said.

Stile brought out his harmonica. Now it was a weapon. He played an improvised melody. Immediately the magic formed. The Stallion noted the aura and paused, uncertain what it was. The wolves and other unicorns looked too, as that intangible mass developed and loomed. Ears twitched nervously.

Good—this gave him a chance to figure out an applicable verse. What he needed was protection, like that of a wall. Wall—what rhymed with wall? Ball, fall, hall, tall. Unicorn, standing tall—

Abruptly the Stallion charged. Stile jumped aside. He stopped playing his harmonica and cried in a singsong:

"Unicorn Stallion, standing tall—form around this one a wall."

Immediately he knew he had not phrased it properly; he had technically asked the unicorn to form a wall around Stile, which was backward. But the image in his mind was a brick wall two meters high, encircling the Stallion—make that six feet high, to align the measurements with the standard of this frame—and that was what formed. His music was the power, his words the catalyst—but his mind did the fundamental shaping.

A shower of red bricks fell from nowhere, landing with uncanny precision in a circle around the Stallion, now forming row on row, building the wall before their eyes. The Stallion stood amazed, not daring to move lest he get struck by flying bricks, watching himself be penned. The pack and the herd watched with similar astonishment, frozen in place. Hulk's mouth hung open; he had not believed in magic, really, until this moment. Kurrelgyre was smiling in slow, grim satisfaction, his faith vindicated. And the Lady Blue's surprise was the greatest of all.

Only Neysa was not discomfited. She made an "I told thee so!" snort and turned her posterior on Stile, showing that she still did not approve. But Stile was sure she *did* approve, secretly. Whatever this might cost her.

After a moment, Kurrelgyre hitched himself up to sit on the just-completed wall. He tapped it with his fingers, verifying its solidity, as he spoke to the unicorn inside. "Thou desirest still to match thy prowess against the magic of the Blue Adept, here in the Blue Demesnes? Note that he spares thee, thou arrogant animal, only showing his power harmlessly. He could as easily have dropped these bricks on thy bone head. Is it not meet for thee to make apology for thy doubt?"

The Stallion glared at him in stony silence. He could readily have leaped out of the enclosure, but it was beneath his dignity to try. The issue was not his jumping ability, but Stile's magic—which had now been resolved.

"Not the Stallion's but mine is the apology," the

Lady Blue said. "I thought this man no Adept. Now I know he is. To a fine detail, this performance is like unto that of my love. Yet—"

All heads turned to her, as she hesitated. Slowly she worked it out. "My husband was murdered by an Adept. Now an Adept in the likeness of my love comes, yet I know my love is dead. This could therefore be an impostor, claiming to hail from another frame, but more likely an Adept from this frame, using his magic to change his aspect so that none will suspect his true identity. The Adept who murdered Blue."

Now all heads turned to Stile, the gazes of wolves and unicorns alike turning uncertain and hostile. Stile realized with a chill that he had misjudged the nature of his challenge. His real opposition was not the Stallion —it was the Lady Blue. She would not suffer even the suspicion of an impostor in these demesnes. Not any longer. Her first line of defense had been broken down; this was her second. The Lady was dangerous; he could die by the sole power of her voiced suspicions.

Neysa snorted indignantly. She was mad at Stile now, but she believed in him. Yet it was apparent that most of the others were in doubt again. The infernal logic of the Lady!

How could he refute this new challenge? There was one other person who knew his identity—but that was the Yellow Adept. Best not to bring her into this! He would simply have to present his case, and give them opportunity to verify it.

"I am not the Blue Adept. I am his alternate self, from the other frame. Anyone who is able and willing to pass through the curtain and make inquiries can ascertain my existence there. I am like Blue in all things, but lack his experience of this world. I am not an impostor, but neither am I this Lady's husband. Call me the brother of Blue. I apologize to those of you who may have had misconceptions; it was not my intent to mislead you." It still felt funny, using "you" in this frame, but it was the correct plural form. "Were I some other Adept, I would have little reason to masquerade as Blue; I could set up mine own Demesnes of whatever

341

color. My power of magic is real; why should I pretend to have another form than mine own?"

The others seemed mollified, but not the Lady Blue. "I would expect a murdering Adept to arrive prepared with a persuasive story. To come as a seeming savior, destroying the golem he himself had sent, to make himself appear legitimate. To emulate the form of magic that is Blue's. Why should he do this? I can think of two reasons, to begin. First, this would tend to conceal the murder he committed. Second, he might covet the things that are Blue's."

Kurrelgyre turned to her, his brow wrinkling. "An Adept of such power could create his own estate, as impressive as this, with less complication than this."

"Not quite," she said tightly.

"What has this estate, that a foreign Adept might covet and not be able to duplicate?"

The Lady hesitated, her color rising, but she had to answer. "It has me. It is said by some that I am fair—"

Telling point! "Fair indeed," Kurrelgyre agreed. "Motive enough. Yet if he honors the works of Blue and maintains the premises in good order—is this not what thou wishest?"

"To accept in these Demesnes the one who murdered my love?" she demanded, flashing. "I will not yield this proud heritage to that! The false Adept may destroy me with his magic, even as he destroyed my love, but never will he assume the mantle and privilege of Blue."

Kurrelgyre swiveled on the wall to face Stile. "I believe in thee, friend. But the Lady has a point. The magic of Adepts is beyond the fathoming of simple animals like ourselves. We can prove no necessary connection between Blue's alternate in Proton and thyself; that double could be dead also, and thou a construct adapted by magic, emulating the mode of Blue when in truth the real power lies in some other mode. We can all be deceived, and until we are assured of thy validity—"

Stile was baffled. "If neither my likeness nor my magic can convince her, and she will not take my word—"

"If I may ask two questions?" Hulk put in tentatively.

Stile laughed. "We already have more questions than answers! Go ahead and throw thine in the ring."

"For what was the Blue Adept noted, other than his appearance and his magic?"

"His integrity," the Lady said promptly. "Never did he tell a lie or otherwise practice deceit, ever in his whole life."

"Never has this one told a lie," Kurrelgyre said.

"That remains to be demonstrated," she retorted.

The werewolf shrugged. "Only time can demonstrate that quality. Was there nothing else, subject to more immediate trial?"

"His riding," the Lady said, brightening. "In all Phaze, only he could ride better than I. His love for animals was so great, especially horses—" She had to stop, for her emotion was choking her.

To have the love of such a woman! Stile thought. Her husband was dead, but she still defended him with all her power. She was right: another Adept might well covet her, and not merely for her beauty, and be willing to go to extraordinary lengths to win her.

Kurrelgyre turned to Stile. "How well dost thou ride?"

"I can answer that," Hulk said. "Stile is the finest rider on Proton. I doubt anyone in this frame either could match him on horseback."

The Lady looked startled. "This man can ride? Bareback on an untamed steed? I should be glad to put him to that test."

"No," Hulk said.

She glanced at him, frowning. "Thou guardest him, ogre, by preventing him from betraying incompetence on a steed?"

"I seek only to settle the issue properly," Hulk said. "We have seen that careless application settles nothing —such as Stile's demonstration of magic. For all the effect it had, he might as well not have bothered. To put him to a riding test now, when he has been weakened and injured—"

343

"There is that," Kurrelgyre agreed. "Yet the importance of this proof—"

"Which brings me to my second question," Hulk said. "Is the issue really between Stile and the Lady—or between the Lady and the mare?"

Lady and mare looked at each other, startled again. "He only *looks* like an ogre," Kurrelgyre murmured appreciatively. Then, to Stile: "He speaks sooth. Thy destiny must be settled by Lady and mare. They are the two with claims on thee. If thou provest thou art the Blue Adept, one of them must needs suffer. This is what brought both wolves and unicorns here."

Stile did not like this. "But—"

The Stallion honked from his enclave. "Only the finest of riders could break the least of unicorns," Clip translated. "This man conquered Neysa; we accept him as the Blue Adept."

Stile was astonished at this abrupt change on the part of the Stallion. "How couldst thou know I really—"

"We saw thee," Clip said. "We rooted for her to throw thee, but we can not claim she did. We recognize that whatever else thou art or art not, thou art indeed the finest rider of thy kind."

"But had she turned into a firefly—"

"She would then have admitted she could not conquer thee in her natural form," Clip said. "It matters not, now. No man ever rode like thee. The Stallion resented that, but now that he knows that was the mark of Blue—"

"I didn't really do it by myself," Stile said, remembering something. "I hummed, and that was magic, though I knew it not at the time. I used magic to stay on her."

"And unicorns are immune to magic," Clip said. "Except the magic of Adepts. Another Adept could have destroyed her, but never could he have ridden her. There is only one Adept we know of who can ride at all, and that is Blue. All this the Stallion considered before accepting thee."

"But I do not accept thee!" the Lady flared. "The unicorns could be in league with the false Adept, to foist an impostor on the Blue Demesnes. My love was a horseman, never partial to unicorns, nor they to him, though he would treat them on occasion if they deigned to come to him. The mare could have allowed this impostor to ride—"

Clip reacted angrily, but Kurrelgyre interposed. "Didst ever thou hear it mooted, Lady, that werewolves would collude with unicorns in aught?"

"Nay," she admitted. "The two are natural enemies."

"Then accept this word from this were: I have come to know this mare. She did not submit voluntarily, except in the sense that she refrained from using her own magic to destroy him. He conquered her physically— and then, when she saw what manner of man he was, the kind of man you describe as your lord, he conquered her emotionally. But first he did ride."

"Almost, I wish I could believe," the Lady murmured, and Stile saw the agony of her decision. She was not against him; she merely had to be sure of him, and dared not make an error.

Then she stiffened. "The mare could be easier to ride than other unicorns like to think," the Lady sniffed. "She is small, and not of true unicorn color; she could have other deficiencies."

Neysa stomped the ground with a forefoot, but did not otherwise protest this insult.

"She has no less spirit than any in this herd," Clip said evenly, speaking for himself now. "And even were she deficient, she remains a unicorn, a breed apart from common horses. No one but this man could have ridden her."

The Lady looked at him defiantly. "If he could ride an animal I could not, then would I believe."

"Therefore thou hast but to ride Neysa," Kurrelgyre pointed out to her. "Thou hast not the magic humming he had, but the mare remains tired from her long hard ride to reach this castle yestermorn. I ran with her all the way, unburdened, and I felt the strain of that travel —and I am a wolf. So I judge the challenge equivalent. In that manner thou canst prove Stile is no better rider than thee."

"She can't ride the unicorn!" Stile protested.

But the Lady was nodding, and so were the unicorns and werewolves. All were amenable to this trial, and thought it fair. Neysa, too, was glancing obliquely at the Lady, quite ready to try her strength.

"I maintain that anything thou canst ride in thy health, I can ride in mine," the Lady informed him. "There was no comparison between my lord and other men. He could have ridden a unicorn, had he so chosen."

The Stallion snorted angrily, and Stile needed no translation. The unicorns did not believe any normal human being could ride one of them, involuntarily. They had reason. Stile himself had not guessed what a challenge Neysa would be—until he was committed. "Lady," Stile said. "Do not put thyself to this ordeal. No one can ride Neysa!"

"No one but thee?" Her disdain was eloquent.

Stile realized that it had to be. The issue had to be settled, and this was, by general consensus, a valid test. Any choice he, Stile, made between Lady and mare would mean trouble, and it seemed he could not have both. If the Lady and the unicorn settled it themselves, he would become the prize of the winner.

Or would he? If the Lady won, the Blue Demesnes would fall, for there would be no accredited Adept to maintain them, and the news would be out. If Neysa won, there would be no Lady Blue, for she would be dead. As he would have been dead, had Neysa thrown him, that first challenge ride. It was the way of the unicorn, the way of life in Phaze, and all of them knew it, including the Lady. She was putting her life on the line. Either way, Stile lost.

With all his magic power restored to him, he was helpless to affect the outcome, or to determine his own destiny. Beautiful irony! "Know thyself," the Oracle had said, without informing him what the knowledge would cost.

"I know this be hard for thee," the werewolf said. "Even as it was for me to do what I had to do, when I

346

faced my sire. Yet thou must submit to the judgment of this lot. It is fair."

Fair! he thought incredulously. The outcome of this lot would be either death or a lie!

The lines of animals were expanding, forming a tremendous ring, bounded by the castle on one side and the magic wall on the other. The unicorns formed a half-circle, the werewolves another, complementing each other.

Neysa stood in the center of the new ring, the Lady beside her. Both were beautiful. Stile wished again that he could have both, and knew again that he could not. When he accepted the benefits of magic, he had also to accept its penalties. How blithely he had walked into this awful reckoning! If only he had not parked Neysa at the Blue Demesnes when he returned to Proton—yet perhaps this confrontation was inevitable.

The Lady made a dainty leap, despite her flowing gown, which was no riding habit. The moment she landed, Neysa took off. From a standing start to a full gallop in one bound, her four hooves flinging up circular divots—but the Lady hung on.

Neysa stopped, her feet churning up turf in parallel scrape-lines. The Lady stayed put. Neysa took off—sidewise. And backward. The Lady's skirt flared, but the Lady held on.

"She does know how to ride," Hulk remarked, impressed. "If I didn't know better, I'd swear that was you, Stile, in a dress. I've watched you win bronco-busting in the Game."

Stile was glumly silent. The Lady Blue could indeed ride, better than he had expected—but he knew she could not stay on the unicorn. When she fell, Neysa would kill her, if the fall itself did not. It was legitimate; it was expected. And what would he want with Neysa then?

The unicorn performed a backflip, then a four-spoked cartwheel, then a series of one-beat hops, followed by a bounce on her back. The Lady stayed on until the last moment, then jumped clear—and back on when Neysa scrambled to her feet.

Hulk was gaping. "What sort of animal is that? Those tricks are impossible!"

There was a chord-snort next to Stile. He glanced—and discovered the Herd Stallion beside him, front hooves comfortably crossed on the wall, eyes intent on the competition. "Not bad moves," Clip translated from the far side.

Neysa whirled and leaped, spinning about in air. The Lady's slippers flew off and her gown flung out so violently it rent; a fragment of blue gauze drifted to the ground. But her hands were locked in the unicorn's mane, and she was not dislodged.

Neysa did a sudden barrel-roll on the ground. Again the Lady jumped free—but a tattered hem of her garment was caught under the weight of the unicorn, trapping her. As the roll continued, the Lady was squeezed by the tightening cloth. She ripped her own gown asunder and danced free, abruptly nude.

"That is some figure of a woman!" Hulk breathed.

Neysa started to rise. The Lady grabbed her mane—and Neysa threw down her head on the ground, pinning the Lady's streaming golden hair beneath it. The Lady grabbed for the unicorn's ears, and Neysa lifted her head quickly; human hands could really hurt tender equine ears when they had to. Stile had not gone for the ears during his challenge ride; it was not his way. The Lady knew the tricks, all right! But Neysa had the end of the Lady's tresses clamped between her teeth, now. The unicorn knew the tricks too. Human intelligence in equine form—devastating! As the Lady tried to mount again, Neysa yanked her off balance by the hair.

"Beautiful!" Clip murmured.

But the Lady grasped her own hair with one hand and jammed her other fingers into Neysa's mouth where the bit would go on a horse. There was a separation there between the front teeth, used for ripping grass free of the ground, and the back teeth, used for chewing. Pressure in that gap could cause pain. Neysa's mouth opened under that expert inducement, and the Lady's hair was free. Then, as Neysa leaped away, the Lady sprang to her back again.

Neysa ran—but now the Lady was free of the liability of clothing, and had a more secure lodging than before. "She's winning!" Hulk said, obviously rooting for the Lady, forgetting in the excitement what this would mean to Stile.

Stile began to wonder. Was it possible that the Lady Blue could ride Neysa? She was, next to himself, the most expert rider he had seen.

The Stallion made an irate snort. "What's the matter with that mare?" Clip said. "She should have wiped out the rider by this time."

"She is torn by indecision," Kurrelgyre said. "If Neysa loses, she proves the Lady's belief that Stile is false. If Neysa wins, she vindicates him as the Blue Adept she wants him not to be. Would I could take from her that choice."

Stile kept his eyes forward, but felt a shiver. The werewolf had his bitch in the pack, even as Stile had Sheen in Proton. But Kurrelgyre obviously had developed a separate interest that cut across the lines of species—even as Stile had. Yet who could know Neysa and not like her and respect her?

"Yes," Stile agreed. He saw no acceptable outcome for this contest; whoever lost took away a major part of his own commitment. Neysa was his friend; the Lady represented his heritage. Which one was he to choose? Which one was fate about to choose for him? To choose—and eliminate, simultaneously?

"In the future, I will manage my destiny myself," Stile muttered. And heard, to his surprise, a snort of agreement from the Stallion.

Neysa galloped so fast that her mane and the Lady's hair flew out behind, the black and gold almost merging. Shadow and sunlight. She made turns that struck sparks from the rocks of the ground. She bucked and reared. But the Lady remained mounted.

Now the unicorn charged the castle. She hurdled the small moat with a magnificent leap, landed on her forefeet, and did her forward flip into the wall. There were growls of amazement from the wolves, and even

349

an appreciative snort from the Stallion. Neysa was really trying now—but the Lady had been smart enough to disengage in time. When the unicorn's hind feet returned to the ground, the Lady was on again.

They hurdled the moat, outward bound, and charged across the arena toward the magic brick wall. Now Stile saw the fire jetting from Neysa's nostrils and the bellows-heaving of her barrel as she put forth her critical effort. The Lady was almost hidden, as she rode low, her head down beside Neysa's neck.

Stile watched in growing disquiet as the unicorn's horn bore on the wall. Stile was directly in its path; he saw the horn endwise, as a compressed spiral on Neysa's forehead, coming at him like the point of a rotary drill. Her eyes were wide and turning bloodshot, and her flaring nostrils were rimmed with red. Neysa was near her limit—and still the Lady clung fast. Stile felt mixed relief for the Lady, sorrow for the unicorn, and apprehension for himself; he was at the focus of this agony.

Then Neysa swerved aside, kicking up her rear. Her flank smashed into the wall, knocking loose the top row of bricks and breaking the mortar-seal on several lower courses. She rebounded, getting her footing, breathing fire—and the Lady was clinging to her side, away from the wall. Otherwise the Lady's leg would have been crushed—and Stile himself might have been struck, as he had been too absorbed in the charge to move out of its way. Only the curvature of the wall and Neysa's swerve had spared him. Stile caught a glimpse of the Lady's neck, shoulder and breast behind one blood-streaked arm; then steed and rider were away, prancing to the center of the arena.

The Stallion shook a brick off his back. Neither he nor Kurrelgyre had flinched, either. All three of them were powdered with reddish brick dust. But some of that red was sticky: whose blood was it?

"They're playing for keeps," Hulk murmured, awed.

"It is the way, in Phaze," Kurrelgyre assured him.

But now Neysa was tiring. She had extended herself for a day and a night to bring Stile here, and the intervening day had not been enough to restore her to full vitality. Her maneuvers were becoming less extreme. Her brushoff pitch against the wall had been her last fling. The Lady's head lifted, her gaze triumphant—and at the same time her mouth was sad. Had she, in her secret heart, wanted Stile to be vindicated, though it cost her her life? What kind of existence did this indomitable woman face with her husband gone, and her vulnerability now known to the world? Had she lost, she would have been dead—but would have died with the knowledge that the Blue Demesnes would survive.

Then, desperately, without real hope, Neysa experimented with alternate gaits. The one-, two-, three-, and four-beat gaits gave the Lady no trouble—but evidently she had not before encountered the unicorn specialty of the five-beat. Immediately Neysa felt the uncertainty in her rider; she picked up the pace, exaggerating the peculiar step. Her strength returned, for this last fling.

"What is that?" Hulk asked, amazed.

The Stallion snorted with satisfaction. "That is the unicorn strut," Clip answered. "We use it mostly in special harmonies, for counterpoint cadence. We had no idea she could do it so well."

Suddenly the tables had been turned. The Lady clung to the mane, but her body bounced about with increasing roughness, unable to accommodate this unfamiliar motion. Stile knew exactly how it felt. Riding was not simply a matter of holding on; the rider had to make constant adjustments of balance and position, most of them automatic, based on ingrained experience. A completely unfamiliar gait made these automatic corrections only aggravate the problem. Stile himself had analyzed the gait in time, but the Lady—

One of the Lady Blue's hands tore away from the mane. Her body slid half off. One good lunge, now, and Neysa would dump her. "Kill her!" Clip breathed.

Abruptly Neysa halted. The Lady recovered her grip, hung on for a moment—then released the mane and slid to the ground. The ride was over.

"The little fool!" Clip exclaimed. "She had the win!

Why didn't she finish it?" And the Stallion snorted in deep disgust.

"She has forfeited her place in the herd," Kurrelgyre said sadly. "In thy parlance, she threw the game."

Stile jumped off the wall and walked toward the unicorn and Lady, who both stood as if frozen, facing away from each other. As he walked, understanding came to him. Stile played his harmonica as he worked it out, gathering the magic to him.

Neysa, after the specter of defeat, had had the victory in range. But Neysa wanted Stile's welfare more than she wanted her own. She had finally, unwillingly, recognized the fact that he could fulfill his destiny only as the Blue Adept, complete with magic. Once she had proven that he alone could ride the unicorn, what could she gain by killing or even humbling the Lady—who was his natural mate? Neysa had ceded him to the Lady, so that he could have it all, knowing himself and his Demesnes exactly as the Oracle had decreed. She had understood that he was already half-smitten with his alternate's wife, and understood further that the Lady Blue was indeed worthy of him.

Neysa had sacrificed her own love for Stile's. She had shown the one person she had to, the Lady Blue, that Stile was no impostor; wolves and unicorns could doubt it if they wished, but the Lady could not. For Stile had mastered the unicorn strut without being thrown; he really *was* the better rider. That was Neysa's gift to Stile. And he—had to accept it. Neysa was his ultimate steed, but the Lady was his ultimate woman. He hardly knew her yet, but he knew his other self would have chosen wisely, and everything he had observed so far confirmed this. He also knew his alternate self of Phaze would have wanted Stile to take over—for the Blue Adept was him, in other guise.

The Lady Blue, however, was not yet his woman. Stile had merely qualified for the Tourney, in this sense, and had won the right to court her. He would have to prove himself in other ways than magical and in riding ability, showing that he was worthy of her love. He would have to demonstrate convincingly to her that he was as good as her husband had been. Perhaps he would not succeed, for she was so steadfastly loyal to her first love that a second love might be impossible. But in the interim, he knew she would accept him as the master of the Blue Demesnes, and support him publicly as she had the golem—for the sake of the reputation and works of Blue. That was all he had a right to expect. It was, for the moment, more than enough.

It was Neysa he had to deal with. She who had made it all possible—and now would go, excluded from the herd, departing in shame to fling herself off the same cliff where they had first come to terms. She had lived always with the hope that eventually the Herd Stallion would relent and allow her full membership in the herd. He would have, had she destroyed the Lady in approved fashion. But for a creature who yielded a draw in a contest she could have won, shaming the vanity of the herd, there would be no forgiveness. The rigors of species pride were harsh.

Stile had, in the naïveté of his conscience, turned Neysa loose when he had conquered her, making a sacrifice no other man would have—and won a better friend than he had known. Now she had returned the favor.

Stile's head turned as he walked, his gaze passing over the unicorns and werewolves. All were somber, watching him, knowing what had to be, knowing this was his parting with his most loyal friend. They felt sympathy for him, and for the mare, and it was a minor tragedy, but this was the way of it—in Phaze.

Damn it! he thought. He was not truly of this world, and this proved it. He had been raised to a different order of integrity, where blood sacrifices were not required. How could he tolerate this senseless loss? Yet he knew it was not senseless, here. The laws of this society were harsh but valid.

The magic gathered close as he played. The strange cloud of it spread about him—and, as he approached, about the Lady and the unicorn. But what good was magic, in an ethical dilemma? What spell could he make, to eliminate the need for what he knew had to be?

Stile came to stand before Neysa, playing the music that had been inspired by the sound of her horn. Her body was heaving with the recent extremity of her effort. Her mane was disheveled, with dry leaves in it and several strands hanging over the left side. There were flecks of blood on her back; she must have scratched herself when she did the back-smash against the castle wall. He wished he could make a little spell to heal it for her, but knew this was not proper now. Her gaze met his, dully; she was waiting only for him to bid her farewell.

Fare*well*? What irony! It was death he would bid her.

This reminded Stile obscurely of his race in the marathon, in the other frame. He had been almost dead on his feet, as Neysa was now, but he had won—as she had—and then tried to give it back to an opponent he respected. Again, he had made a friend. Surely he could salvage his relationship with Neysa, if only he had the wit to find the way!

What had the werewolf said about oaths? They superseded all relationships, conflicting with none, not even the male-female ones. Kurrelgyre's oath-friend could do no wrong by Kurrelgyre's bitch; the oath made that irrelevant.

The marathon. The oath. What had passed through his mind, when . . . ?

And he had it.

Stile set the harmonica aside. With the magic intense about him, he sang with impromptu melody: "My name is Stile, called the Blue Adept; Standing before thee I proffer mine oath: To the unicorn Neysa, companion and steed—Friendship forever, uniting us both."

For an instant it was as if a dense cloud had darkened the sun. A sudden, odd, insweeping breeze rustled the distant trees and fluttered the blue pennants on the castle and stirred the manes and hackles of the animals. Neysa's eyes widened. Her ears switched back and

354

forth as comprehension came. She phased into girl-
form, equine-form, firefly-form and back to unicorn,
entirely nonplused.

The ripple of enchantment imploded about the two
of them in soft heat, then rebounded outward in a circle. The turf changed color, passing through the hues of
the rainbow and back to normal in a swiftly expanding
ring. The ripple intersected the naked Lady, whose tangled hair scintillated momentarily, and went on, leaving
that hair smoothly brushed.

The Lady turned. "Only perfect truth makes such
splash," she murmured. "Only my lord had such power
of magic."

Stile spread his arms. Neysa, overwhelmed, stepped
forward, her horn lifted clear. Stile reached around her
neck and chest and hugged her. "Never leave me, oath-
friend," he murmured. He heard her low whinny of
assent, and felt her velvet nuzzle at his shoulder. Then
he disengaged and stepped back.

The Lady Blue came forward. She put her arms
about Neysa. "Never again be there strife between us,"
she said, tears in her eyes. Neysa made a tiny snort of
acceptance.

Now the wolves and unicorns came in, forming a
ragged line, heedless of the mixing of species. In turn,
each wolf sniffed noses with Neysa and each unicorn
crossed horns, and went on. All of them were joining
in the Oath of Friendship. Even her brother Clip came,
and Kurrelgyre, and Hulk. Neysa accepted them all.

It was, Stile knew, the power of his spell. When he
had phrased his oath in verse and music, he had performed magic—and wrought a greater enchantment
than he had anticipated. The spell he had envisioned,
though not completed in words, had flung outward to
embrace the entire circle of creatures, compelling them
all to share Stile's feeling. Neysa would not now be
banned from the herd—or from the pack. She was
friend to all. But she would remain with Stile, having
accepted his power with his oath.

Only the Herd Stallion stood apart. He alone had
resisted the compulsion of the enchantment. He did not

interfere; he waited within his enclosure until the ceremony was over. Then he blew a great summoning blast of music and leaped over the wall. It had never truly restrained him; it had merely been the proof of the power of the Blue Adept, which power could as readily have been turned to a more destructive manifestation. Once the Herd Stallion had seen Stile was no impostor, his objection had ended. Now the unicorns rallied to him, galloping to form their formation. Playing as a mighty orchestra, they marched away.

Kurrelgyre shifted to wolf-form and bayed his own summons. His faith had also been vindicated, and his bitch had been satisfied. The wolves closed in about him, and the pack loped away in the opposite direction. In a moment only Stile, Neysa, the Lady Blue and Hulk remained by the Blue Demesnes.

Stile turned to the woman he would now be dealing with. Nothing was settled, either with her or with his anonymous murderer, or in the other frame. But it was a beginning. "Lady, wilt thou ride my steed?" he asked. There was no need to ask Neysa; as a friend she would do anything for him, and he for her. By the phrasing of his invitation, he was acknowledging that he had as yet only a partial claim on the Lady, and could not take her for granted. She was a challenge, not a friend.

The Lady Blue inclined her head, as regal in her nakedness as she had been in the gown. Lightly she mounted Neysa. Stile walked on one side, Hulk on the other. Together they approached the open castle.

ABOUT THE AUTHOR

It was not necessary, in England in 1934, to name a baby instantly; there was a grace period of a number of days. As the deadline loomed, the poor woman simply gave all the names she could think of: Piers Anthony Dillingham Jacob. The child moved to America, where it took three years and five schools to graduate him from first grade, because he couldn't learn to read. It was thus fated that he become a proofreader, an English teacher, or a writer. He tried them all, along with a dozen other employments—and liked only the least successful one. So he lopped off half his name, sent his wife out to earn their living, and concentrated on writing. That was the key to success; publishers would print material by an author whose name was short enough.

He sold his first story in 1962 and had his first novel, *Chthon*, published in 1967. His first fantasy in *The Magic of Xanth* Trilogy, *A Spell for Chameleon*, won the August Derleth Fantasy Award as the best novel in 1977. He has written approximately forty novels in the genres of science fiction, fantasy and martial arts.

He was married in 1956, right after graduating from college, to Carol Ann Marble. Their daughter Penny was born eleven years later, and their final daughter Cheryl in 1970. That was the beginning of a whole new existence, because little girls like animals. In 1978 they bought nice horses, and that experience, coupled with knee injuries in judo class, became *Split Infinity*. Piers Anthony is not the protagonist—he says he lacks the style—but Penny's horse Blue *is* the mundane model for the unicorn Neysa.